HER HEART BEATING WILDLY, SHE TOOK ANOTHER STEP FORWARD. . . .

Yuri raised his hand to stop her and shut his eyes. "Tanya!" His voice was husky. "Don't come any closer. I can't vouch for myself."

"Yuri, don't you see? I'm here because I love you. I want to marry you before you go away. Please, look at me!"

Slowly he lifted his head. "God, how beautiful you are! And how I want you!"

One instant she touched him; the next, she was in his arms, crushed against him. Thrust against his tensed body, her senses reeling, she leaned backward in a near faint.

"Yuri . . . Yuri . . . I love you!"

East Lies the Sun

ALLA CRONE

A DELL BOOK

Best wishes!

Alla Crone

15 March 1982

Published by
Dell Publishing Co., Inc.
1 Dag Hammarskjold Plaza
New York, New York 10017

Dell ® TM 681510, Dell Publishing Co., Inc.

ISBN: 0-440-12229-5

Printed in the United States of America

First printing—March 1982

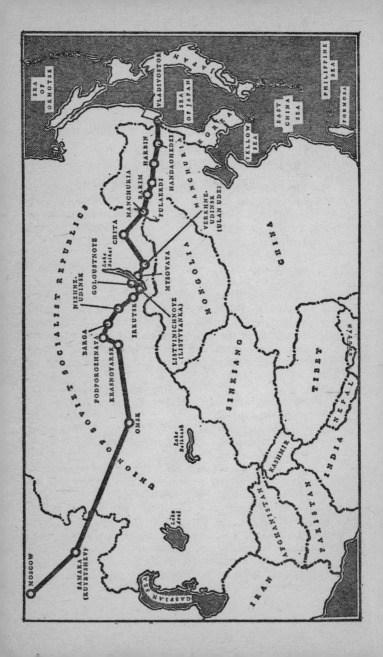

AUTHOR'S NOTE

Six hundred miles northwest of Russia's Pacific port of Vladivostok, in the geographical center of Manchuria, is the city of Harbin. Founded and built by Russian engineers in 1898 to be the capital of the far eastern Russian colony, a kind of Moscow of Asia, the city eventually became known as "the Paris of the Orient."

In connecting the Trans-Siberian Railroad with Vladivostok, Russia had a choice of building along the northern side of the Amur River or going through Chinese territory in northern Manchuria, thus shortening the line by some three hundred miles. In September 1896, after lengthy negotiations between the two countries, the Chinese government signed a contract with the newly established Russo-Chinese Bank for the construction and management of the Chinese Eastern Railroad.

The railway company soon built Russian colonial settlements in Manchuria, administering the large right-of-way area. During the Boxer Rebellion, when two thirds of the railway was destroyed, the company created its own police force, which later continued to guard the railroad from the raids of Chinese *hunhuzi* bandits.

At the turn of the century, Harbin, designed by Moscow engineers, emerged as a peculiarly Russian city, as if located somewhere along the Volga. Broad streets, graceful official buildings, railway clubs, hotels, and schools rapidly overflowed the original city limits, necessitating the construction of several suburbs. Millions were spent on government offices, hospitals, and sumptuous residences for high officials. Russian engineers, hired by the railway company, brought their families to Harbin, settling in company-provided housing or buying their own homes.

The railroad opened for commercial traffic in 1903; and by 1905, with the influx of the Tsar's armies during the Russo-Japanese war, Harbin's Russian civilian population burgeoned to fifteen thousand. Gambling and drinking flourished, with great profits to breweries and vodka distilleries; commercial ventures prospered; adventurous women flocked to the city, bringing with them the elegance and the atmosphere of Paris; theaters and nightclubs multiplied.

By 1917 the population increased to over eighty thousand, making Harbin an important cultural and political center in the Far East. Thus, it seemed, Russia had succeeded in creating its Asiatic metropolis.

CHAPTER 1

The predawn light of the full moon washed over Harbin, muting the contours, erasing the dry dirt, silvering the river. The city was bathed in blue and white, the colors soft and ethereal.

In spite of the early hour this June day, 1917, much activity was evident near the city shore of the Sungari River. Several rowboats, slow to dock, floated on the rippling surface of the water. Ordinarily, these flat-bottomed rowboats, used by their Chinese owners to taxi passengers across the river by day, were moored at the shore by night. Tonight, however, was a special event in the lives of the Russian youths, who had come to the river for a traditional ride; and the Chinese boatmen, always on the lookout for an extra *cumshaw*, were eager for business. Sitting in the center of their boats with oars poised in the air, they looked like sculptured shadows against the shimmering water. At the stern, young couples nestled on carpeted benches, arms around each other—young men in dark suits and patent-leather shoes, the girls in white ball gowns, their long batiste and silk skirts dotting the river like floating water lilies. Spread over the Sungari, the boats nosed their way toward the shore, narrowing the spaces among them as they closed in on the bank.

Thousands of miles away, the couples' countrymen were locked in the mortal combat of fratricide, fanning the Russian Revolution, fighting tyranny with tyranny. But the rumblings of their country's upheaval seemed far away to these young men and women, who were raised on Chinese soil and felt safe in remote Manchuria. The idea that their own lives might become deeply involved in the revolution was far from their minds on this sparkling, festive night.

A few boats docked. The girls disembarked, climbing the several dozen steps up the embankment with studious care, holding their skirts above their ankles, the large buckles of their high-heeled shoes glittering in the moonlight.

Tatiana Levitina stepped carefully onto the boat seat and grasped her escort's hand. Of medium height and willowy, she was fully aware of her dark beauty, of her lithe figure cinched into a laced corset. The boat wobbled, and Tanya, rocking to and fro, tried to regain her balance. Unaccustomed to high heels, her foot slipped, and she landed in Oleg Korchagov's arms. For a brief moment, encircled in his embrace, she wanted to lean against his chest to recapture the magic of the night. But one second was all that propriety allowed—after all, several pairs of eyes were watching her—and she quickly wriggled out of Oleg's arms.

"I had no idea it would be unsteady at the dock—the Sungari seems so calm tonight," Tanya gasped.

Oleg pointed to a dark spot shaded by the boat. "See that circle of water down there? Those whirlpools are hard to see, but they're much stronger underneath the surface."

Tanya peered across the river. "The other side is safer. I can hardly see the shore now. Have you ever gone swimming there?"

"Yes, in the Private Lagoon behind the Sunshine Island—but it's a dangerous river no matter where you swim. It seems to me the only safe place is inside the floating bathhouses you ladies use." Oleg looked at Tanya with a mischievous smile, but she made no reply: She detested those floating prisons with the sky for a ceiling and a boardwalk and benches and four ugly wooden walls sealing the nude women from the outside world. How could she tell him that although the women could bathe in privacy they were nevertheless exposed to one another's spiteful scrutiny?

She didn't have to be ashamed of her own figure, thank God, with its tiny waist, firm, high breasts, and well-rounded hips, of which her mother, Countess Tamara Sergeyevna, soundly approved. "Flat figures are not feminine," she said with authority; and when the countess spoke, everyone listened. Nevertheless, Tanya felt self-conscious when naked before a crowd of women. She had lost count of how many times her godmother, Galina Fedorovna, shook her head over a friend's layers of bouncing flesh, or clucked her tongue in pity over another's flat breasts.

Tonight, however, she didn't want to dwell on embarrassing thoughts. Picking up her skirts, she quickly climbed the long steps of the embankment; then, whirling around to let the folds swoosh about her ankles, she looked back at the river below.

Several boats were still gliding with the current, placid, forgetful of time. None ventured too close to the iron-trussed railroad bridge spanning the river to her right, where the heavy piers caused powerful whirlpools to swirl around them. A twinge of longing stirred within her, and she wished her parents were not so strict. Tonight, for the first time, she had not been given a deadline for coming home, but she didn't want to abuse this new privilege.

It had been a beautiful night. When she danced at her White Ball earlier that evening, she had wished it would go on forever, for she had been looking forward to it for many months, planning and dreaming about it. Held in the auditorium of the Oksakovskaya School for Girls at the corner of Bulvarny and Voksalny avenues, it was the big festive event of the year and required the graduating students to wear white ball gowns. The rules were strict. Each of the hundred and eleven girls graduating this year could bring only one guest. Even then, with the chaperoning faculty present, the ballroom was crowded. Tanya had asked Oleg, Lydia Korchagova's brother, to be her escort, because Lydia was her best friend, and because she was a little in love with him. In doing this she had defied her parents' wishes, and for once she had won the argument.

They had wanted her to ask Kurt Hochmeyer, but she couldn't bear the thought of spending the entire night in the company of the Swiss businessman, whose eyes, she knew, would follow her around the room with persistence. She was always aware of the look in his eyes—inscrutable, watching, as if a secret lay hidden in their depth; and all the while, his neck immobilized by a high starched collar, the fixed tilt of his angular head never wavered or relaxed.

He seldom spoke to her when he came to visit her parents, and she doubted he could even dance, since all he seemed to think about was the management of his clothing manufacturing firm. By his own admission, he rarely ventured out into society, preferring to indulge his one great passion—hunting. He probably could tell her a lot about the boar, the deer, and the pheasant he shot; but she was not at all interested in his hunting adventures, and on his frequent visits to her home, she always managed to avoid being left alone with him. Besides, he was almost twice her age . . . and dull, dull, dull!

Oleg was far more fun to be with; and tonight, at the ball, waltzing with half-closed eyes to the strains of the popular song "On the Hills of Manchuria," caught up in its rhythm, Tanya had whirled, relaxed against Oleg's encircling arm. Suddenly she spotted Kurt standing at the edge of the ballroom, watching her dance. She stiffened with annoyance. The sight of one of the teachers talking to Kurt with an air of familiarity and deference irritated her. How had he managed to get invited to the ball?

As soon as the waltz ended, Tanya slipped out of the ballroom and headed for the powder room.

Oleg's sister was inside, fixing her blond hair in front of the mirror. At the sight of Tanya, she raised her eyebrows. "You look angry, Tanya. Did my brother get fresh with you?"

"Lida, my night is ruined! Absolutely ruined! Kurt is here!"

"But we're allowed only one guest. How did he get in here?"

"I don't know. Maybe Maman had arranged it. I can't imagine Papa being mixed up in this."

"Well, Tanya, everyone knows the countess has her way around here. Her title is a powerful weapon. We mortals can't compete with her."

Tanya flushed at the reference to her mother, who had retained her title and maiden name after she married a commoner; but she elected to ignore the remark.

"I can't understand why Maman is so fond of Kurt. I would think she'd be bored to death with him; the man is a wooden mannequin. Why, I've never even heard him laugh!"

"Don't underestimate him, Tanya. Maybe he has nothing to laugh about. Do you know what I overheard this afternoon?" Lydia listened at the door to make sure no one was near, then confided: "Madame Popova told my mother she had learned from a reliable source that Kurt Hochmeyer has a disreputable past and fears someone will discover what it is and ruin his position in the community!"

Lydia dropped her voice to a whisper. "She said he's being blackmailed by someone who knew him in his home town of Smolensk."

Tanya raised her chin, quickly deciding to defend her parents' friend. "The reason I don't care for Kurt's company has nothing to do with his integrity. He may be a bore, but he's honorable and gentlemanly. I think people like Madame Popova indulge in malicious gossip because they're jealous of his success and wealth."

With a smile, Lydia shrugged her shoulders. "Suit yourself. But you needn't be so huffy about it. I thought maybe you could use this information to get your parents to give up on him." She straightened the bodice of her silk dress and gave Tanya a sidelong glance. "I feel uncomfortable in a new dress until I get used to it, don't you?" she added, a little too sweetly.

Instinctively, Tanya smoothed the batiste folds of her gown. It was a family heirloom that had belonged to her grandmother. The old dowager Countess Paulina Arkadyevna Merkulina lived in Moscow, and although Tanya had never met her, she had heard countless times of her wealth and position at court as the former lady-in-waiting to the dowager Empress Marie Fedorovna. Still, Tanya considered the dress a hand-me-down and would have preferred to have a new moire or a silk one like Lydia's, especially since she thought it would have looked better on her than on Lydia's bosomy figure. But her mother had insisted she wear her grandmother's dress, and, of course, the countess always got her own way.

Although she had not dared to argue against sentiment, Tanya suspected the real reason lay in the straitened cir-

cumstances in which her parents had found themselves recently. With the Tsar's abdication last March and the revolution now threatening the Russian Provisional Government, the old countess was unable to send Tanya's mother
handsome bank drafts, as had been her custom. She was
well aware of her daughter's extravagances, which went far
beyond the limits of her husband's salary. Ever since Tamara Sergeyevna had married the young engineer in 1898
and followed him to Manchuria, where he'd been sent to
help build the Chinese Eastern railway, the bank drafts
had arrived every month. When the money stopped, however, Tanya's father, though comfortably well off, couldn't
afford such luxuries as imported fabric for his daughter's
ball gown.

Was this the real reason behind the countess's courtesy
to Kurt, Tanya wondered uneasily, or was there another
reason she knew nothing about? Was she somehow being
manipulated by her mother? How could she convince her
that she was no longer a child, that she had a mind of her
own?

Whatever it was, she mustn't allow these thoughts to
spoil her evening. Opening the beaded and tasseled reticule
her mother had given her for her graduation, Tanya pulled
out her compact and lightly powdered the rounded tip of
her nose. "I'd better hurry, Lida. Oleg is waiting to take me
for a boat ride on the river. I want to slip out before Kurt
asks me to dance."

Her friend winked at her. "Enjoy yourself, Tanya. We
have to keep the tradition going, don't we? The White Ball
wouldn't be any fun without the moonlight ride on the Sungari! Maybe I'll see you there."

But as Tanya returned to the ballroom looking for Oleg,
Kurt intercepted her. "Good evening, Tanya!"

Easily thwarted in her attempt to avoid him, Tanya
struggled to hide her irritation beneath a polite smile.
"Good evening, Kurt!"

Somber in a brown suit, he stood a good head above her,
and his flat and narrow frame made him seem even taller.
His dark, usually enigmatic eyes looked at her with frank
admiration and unexpected warmth. "I've never seen you

look so beautiful, Tanya, nor so grown-up and sophisticated! May I have this one dance?"

Tanya was immediately disarmed. His last words betrayed a hidden sensitivity and the first compliment he'd ever paid her hinted at the existence of sentiment beneath all that boring aloofness he always seemed to display. Besides, Lydia's slanderous remarks had aroused her natural sense of loyalty. After all, wasn't he a good friend of her family, whom her parents trusted and liked? Even though her mother often had hinted that he would be a most desirable suitor for Tanya, she wanted to believe that Kurt felt nothing more than friendly affection for her, and she surely could not insult him now by refusing him.

Obediently, she let him guide her onto the dance floor, expecting to be bored by a clumsy partner. But he whirled her around faster and faster, gliding over the floor with a sure step, and Tanya, suddenly conscious of the natural rhythm in his body, found herself enjoying the dance. He was a marvelous dancer, and when his firm hand pressed against her back, guiding her into each new step, she felt a strange comfort in the security of his embrace. She was surprised and a little ashamed of the titillating feeling of pride at the sudden realization that she was the only one on the dance floor in the arms of a mature man who was paying her court. Unexpectedly, the duty dance turned into a pleasure.

"Thank you, Tanya," he said at the end of the dance. "Perhaps we shall do this again sometime soon." He smiled and bowed. "I'll release you to your escort. I know I've deprived him of your company, and I mustn't keep him waiting any longer."

"I've enjoyed dancing with you, Kurt," Tanya heard herself say, aware of a warm flush rising to her neck.

In the end she was pleased with herself for having been courteous to a family friend and for having shown Lydia Korchagova that she didn't believe one word of her gossip. Yet a nagging suspicion remained. Kurt's appearance at the ball—his first overt gesture of attention without her parents' presence—carried overtones of an arrangement she did not want to think about. And she was confused by the conflicting feelings of annoyance and loyalty she felt toward him. Anger at her own ambiguity flared within her, threatening to spoil the rest of the night. But in the euphoric hours that followed on the river, she had almost forgotten the episode, and when the boat ride was over and she stood on the shore waiting for Oleg to get a droshky, she wanted to remember every detail of the evening.

Oleg hailed a coachman who was sleeping upright in his droshky with his nose nearly touching his beard. Jumping off his high seat behind the horse, the Russian brushed the dust off the passenger seat before waving them in. Loath to leave the river, Tanya climbed in slowly, turning to take a last look at the boats.

The carriage rolled up Kitaiskaya Street, back into the world of stone, brick, and dust. The droshky moved past the familiar fronts of the Siemens-Schukert, Churin, the Japanese Matzuura stores. The clip-clop cadence of the horse's hoofs on the cobblestones had an exaggerated sound in the deserted streets, shrouding the memory of the moonlit river as the carriage rolled uptown toward Novy Gorod, crossing the viaduct above the railroad tracks and leaving the downtown area called Pristan behind.

A light breeze stirred, tickling Tanya's face and cooling her neck behind the high lace collar of her dress. She leaned against Oleg's shoulder in the circle of his arm, and heard herself agreeing to a stroll through the arboretum before going home.

It wasn't until later that she remembered her promise to be home at a reasonable hour.

CHAPTER 2

Dawn was breaking when Tanya returned home. In the vestibule she paused for a moment and closed her eyes, inhaling the scent of violets and lily of the valley that still permeated her clothes and hair. Her lips throbbed from Oleg's ardent kisses, and at first her mind refused to register the countess's sharp voice calling her from the living room.

She frowned at her mother's insistent voice. Had the countess guessed where she had been, and was she now in for a scolding? But then, what was wrong with a few kisses? Her face must be flushed, but her conscience was clear. Surely her mother must know that she wouldn't dream of allowing Oleg other liberties with her!

Nervously twisting a string of pearls around her wrist, Tanya lingered in the entry hall. She could hear her father's muffled voice and wondered why her parents were still up at this hour. The countess required many hours of sleep, and for her to stay awake so late was unusual. It *was* late, but after all, Tanya reminded herself, she had been given no time limit for coming home tonight. Something special must have happened. Something important enough for them to wait up so late for her.

Tanya removed her silk tasseled shawl and hung it in the hall wardrobe, dreading the coming interview with her parents.

The light from the parlor shone into the hall from beneath the closed door. Since her parents used the parlor only on special occasions, Tanya was surer than ever that something out of the ordinary was afoot. The parlor was usually reserved for formal callers and for the soirées that the countess held on Thursdays—a carryover from her days in Russia. .

At the door of the parlor, Tanya stood indecisively for a moment before walking in. The countess sat in an over-stuffed chair, her statuesque body wrapped in a salmon silk-and-lace peignoir, her luxurious chestnut hair piled loosely on top of her head. Andrei Victorovich Levitin sat at a distance from his wife, nervously drumming his fingers on the end table. Tall and distinguished, with a silver-streaked Vandyke, he looked more the aristocrat than his wife, even though it was she who presided over Harbin's society, setting the rules of etiquette and treating her husband as though she had done him a favor by marrying him. Tanya chafed at her mother's patronizing manner, but her father never raised his voice to his wife and usually listened to her demands with unfailing equanimity. He rarely reprimanded Tanya, and when he did, he always spoke kindly to her, so in contrast to her mother's peremptory scoldings.

"Good evening, Maman." Tanya curtsied and brushed a feathery kiss on her mother's powdered forehead before she went to hug her father and kiss his cheek.

"Rather, it's good *morning*, child," her mother said. "Sit down, Tanya. We have something to tell you."

To Tanya's surprise, the countess was smiling as she waved to an armchair opposite her. Andrei Victorovich remained silent. Tanya sank into a low-back chair, wondering why her mother exuded such obvious bonhomie at so late an hour.

The countess joined her hands on her lap in a gesture Tanya had learned to recognize as a prelude to a lecture, except that this time her face glowed with unconcealed satisfaction.

Tanya waited stiffly. The stays of her corset were cutting into her flesh, and, in the epilogue of the night, physical weariness crawled between her shoulders. She yearned for the cool sheets of her bed, the cozy warmth of the eiderdown comforter, the privacy of her dreams.

"Tanya, did you speak to Kurt at the ball?"

"Yes, Maman. I had one dance with him before Oleg and I left." Tanya looked at her mother curiously. So Lydia was right: Her mother had a hand in it. What was all this about?

"You should have talked to him before leaving the ball, Tanya," the countess said. "That was discourteous of you. I'm surprised. Truly a *mauvais ton*."

The words didn't match the countess's benevolent air. Tanya tensed. The reference to Kurt without his patronymic hadn't escaped her, and this unaccustomed familiarity by the usually formal countess made her shift in her chair uncomfortably.

"But today, *mon enfant*," the countess went on, "you're forgiven. Kurt has asked us for your hand in marriage." The triumph in her voice resounded in the quiet of the room. "We have given our consent, of course, and Kurt said he will come tomorrow evening to propose to you himself. Your father and I stayed up to give you this wonderful news."

Aghast, Tanya grabbed the arms of the chair, squeezing the plush velvet until it prickled the palms of her hands. She couldn't have heard it right. Kurt? Marry Kurt? She looked at her father. "Papa, you can't mean it! He's an old man!"

Andrei Victorovich cleared his throat. "Well, kitten, it's a desirable match, and we're honored by his proposal."

Desirable match . . . honored . . . Hot tears stung her eyes. Her father's words rang false in her ears. They sounded strained and rehearsed. Was it really her father speaking? Her gentle, kind Papa—was he now siding with her mother against her?

Tanya flashed back at her mother, "Maman, why didn't Kurt propose to me before speaking to you?"

The countess raised her eyebrows and lifted her chin. "Because, *mon enfant*, Kurt is a man of distinguished background and a gentleman of the old school who asks the parents' permission first."

"He may be a gentleman of the old school," Tanya retorted heatedly, "but had he talked to me first, he would have saved himself a lot of embarrassment. I'm sorry, Maman, to put you through this, but I'm not in love with him, and I'm not going to marry a man I don't love."

The countess looked at her daughter with shrewd appraisal. "Do you respect him?"

"Of course I do! I don't love him, that's all."

"Love will come with time, Tanya. You're too young to know these things. You'll learn to love him, and in the end that's all that matters."

Tanya's chin and lower lip began to tremble. Her voice shook when she repeated, "I'm not going to marry a man I don't love."

Levitin rose from his chair. "I'll leave you two ladies to discuss your differences in privacy. I think it's best done tête-à-tête. Good night, *ma chère*." He kissed his wife's hand and turned to Tanya. "Good night, kitten." He rumpled her hair, which was already windblown by the night's breeze. The large moire bow at the nape of her neck now slipped down her back. She was so weary she let it drop. When her father bent down to kiss her, she searched his face for encouragement, as she had done so often as a child when she pleaded with him to intercede for her with the countess. This time, however, she glimpsed only embarrassment and pain in his eyes. When he averted his gaze, she had a sinking feeling that this time she was going to have to stand up to both her parents.

Left alone to face her mother, she concentrated on keeping her hands from trembling. She mustn't show how hurt she was, how frightened by the thought of what her parents were expecting of her. The calmer she remained, she knew, the better chance she would have of convincing her mother.

The countess studied her with the air of assurance that Tanya always found disconcerting. Perhaps her mother considered this conversation a waste of time, a great ennui which she had to endure to make her daughter get over her childish rebellion. Tanya felt her resentment grow as she waited for her mother to speak.

"We live in troubled times, Tanya," the countess began, "and we can hardly afford the luxury of falling in love, much less permit ourselves to marry for love."

"What do you mean, Maman? Papa has a good position with the railway company. There's no reason to worry, is there?"

"Not for the moment, Tanya. No."

"Then surely we're not going to starve in the near future. So why do I have to sell myself to a man I don't love simply because he is rich?"

The countess winced. "Don't be crass, Tanya—it doesn't become you. No one is trying to sell you. Hear me out. The fact that Kurt is wealthy is convenient but incidental. There is something far more important than that. You're now eighteen years old—a young woman."

"But I do want to take accounting, Maman. You know how good I am in mathematics."

"Don't interrupt, Tanya. I'm not through yet. What I was trying to say to you has nothing to do with your choosing a career. You must be practical. You know that our country is in grave trouble. You may not realize it, but it's no small matter that our saintly Tsar Nicholas has abdicated. Someone has forced him to do it, for he would never have initiated such a step by himself. It is a great sorrow that his grandfather's assassination didn't convince him that our country isn't ready for democracy. In the fifty-six years since Alexander the Second liberated the peasants from serfdom, his liberal moves resulted only in encouraging freethinkers to foment unrest. Our Tsar should have been firm in these troubled times, but, instead, his abdication has started the revolution." The countess sighed and shook her head.

"You must understand what a worthless parliament that Duma is!" she said. "They can't agree on major issues and are totally ineffective in governing. That adventurer Kerensky and his Provisional Government have thrown our country into great turmoil. The ministers are appointed one day and resign the next, and no one seems to know who holds the authority. In the meantime, the Bolsheviks are propagating communism, and should they succeed, the intelligentsia will be the first to suffer. It will be exactly as it was in France in the eighteenth century."

Tanya winced. She had read enough about the horrors perpetrated against the nobility in France during the French Revolution. But, she thought in some confusion, what have the Tsar and democracy to do with my marrying Kurt? I wish Maman would get to the point.

"We don't know what the outcome will be," the countess went on, "and we have to think of the future. I don't want to go back to Russia and subject myself to the whims of a revolutionary tribunal. Yet if we stay here we'll become refugees, and subject to all sorts of humiliation without our government's protection."

"That will never happen!" Tanya interrupted.

The countess sighed. "What I'm trying to say, Tanya—and you make it very difficult—is that marrying a Russian now is a risky business. You'll be far safer married to Kurt, a Swiss subject. To have a foreign passport and a country to protect you is far more advantageous than all his wealth."

Tanya's throat began to tighten. Ever since she could remember, it cramped under stress and she lost her voice.

"Please, Maman," she managed to whisper, "let's not talk about it tonight. Let me visit Grandmaman. You promised I could go to Moscow after I finished school. It will give me time to think things over."

"Your stubborness is a sign of immaturity," her mother impatiently pointed out. "But I know you're not stupid. If you think things through, you'll come to the inevitable conclusion it would be foolish to refuse Kurt's proposal. As for visiting your grandmother, it is out of the question. I just finished telling you how unsettled things are in the motherland. For you to go back to Russia now would be taunting fate. I'm worried enough about my mother getting trapped in the revolution without having you endanger your life."

"If things are so threatening in Russia, why hasn't Grandmaman come here?"

"Because your grandmother is living in the past. She is the Countess Paulina Arkadyevna Merkulina and she refuses to believe the day may come when her title will no longer bring the deference and respect to which she has been accustomed all her life."

The countess turned in her chair and reached toward the heavy rolltop escritoire, from which she removed a letter.

"This letter from your grandmother arrived yesterday," she said, waving the folded paper in the air. "Let me read you a passage from it and perhaps you'll see what I mean.

" '. . . Last night's soirée was particularly stimulating.

Count Verantzev and Prince Golubin were both here—you
know how I still enjoy the gallantry of handsome young
men—and they entertained us with a debate on the literary
styles of Molière, Diderot, and Voltaire. . . .

" 'You are aware that I don't like Princess Volinskaya
for her tart tongue, but I had invited her this time because
she has become a controversial figure in our circles with
her involvement in politics and pursuit of women's rights.
Poor thing! I think it's gauche for a woman to meddle in
politics. . . .

" 'I have to say it was an exciting evening and I forbade
any gossip about political rumors that are rampant in the
city. They mention Bolsheviks. *Quel ennui!* They'll catch
the culprits soon enough and pack them off to Siberia
where they belong, as they had done with the Decembrists
in their time. We shouldn't honor these renegades by discussing them in our drawing rooms. Heavens, it'd be shocking! They'll be crawling on their hands and knees begging
our beloved Tsar to take his rightful place on the throne
again. I only hope they'll put that noisy Lenin in a cage
and bring him to Moscow for all to see, just like Catherine
the Great did with Pugachev.' "

The countess folded the letter, put it back in the envelope, and looked at her daughter.

"All this while we hear rumors that Lenin is gaining
power and the Tsar and his family are held prisoners in the
Palace at Tsarskoye Selo. Yet your grandmother refuses to
face reality."

The countess rose and paced the floor, fanning herself
with a lace handkerchief, her voluminous bosom heaving
with excitement.

Tanya found her voice. "But, Maman, the Provisional
Government is still in control, and I'm sure they'll find a
way to deal with Lenin. Could it be that because we're so
far away here in Manchuria, the rumors are blown all out
of proportion? You remember how Grandmaman worried
about us and asked you if we were ever threatened by *hunhuzi*? She thought they prowled the streets of Harbin!"

"Yes, I remember. But after I explained that those
Chinese bandits have a vigorous feudal code of honor and
stay in the areas which they inhabit, she never once men-

tioned the subject again. I suspect she hadn't thought much about it anyway. But now we're talking about the Bolsheviks and the passions of a revolution, not about the *hunhuzi!*"

"Surely Grandmaman has friends who would persuade her to leave if they thought she was in danger."

The countess sighed and dabbed at her eyes. "You don't know your grandmother." Suddenly, the countess wheeled to face Tanya. Her voice shook with suppressed hysteria. "Don't you see, Tanya, why I'm so happy about Kurt's proposal? Can you possibly understand a mother's concern? I couldn't bear to have you far away and in danger."

Tanya had never seen her mother with anything less than perfect composure. To see her stripped of her calm, to realize that beneath her façade of equanimity stormy emotions smoldered, shocked Tanya and filled her with sympathy. Yet she stood her ground.

"Please, Maman, I don't want to cause you added concern. Give me a little time to think. May I see you tomorrow afternoon before Kurt comes over?"

Her mother shook her head. "There's nothing to think over. Your godmother has invited your father and me to visit her dacha, and we're taking the rowboat to the Private Lagoon in the morning. I doubt we shall return before supper time. By then I fully expect you to come to your senses and to throw all this nonsense about love out of your head."

In control of herself again, the countess dismissed Tanya with a nod.

When, moments before, Tanya had wanted to pacify her mother, now she was filled with resentment at the countess's obvious conviction that her daughter would ultimately obey her.

Not trusting her voice, she curtsied silently and ran out of the parlor.

CHAPTER 3

In her bedroom, Tanya stepped out of her dress and hurriedly unlaced her corset. Her rib cage, imprisoned in the stays for so many hours, heaved in unrestrained freedom, and with it, unbidden, came angry tears.

Why did this have to happen to her? For weeks she had been looking forward to her graduation day, only to have it end like this!

She sobbed until she was exhausted and then, pulling down the lace coverlet on her bed, slipped under the blanket. Shivering from nervousness, she stared at the two windows framed in the anemic dawn light like a couple of mindless eyes. Outside, the thorns of the espaliered rose beneath her window scratched the windowsill. The sound needled her brain. Snug in the warmth under her eiderdown comforter, its feathery touch caressing her skin, she wondered about her future. Conflicting thoughts crowded upon her. She tried to shut them out, but in the solitude of her room reality refused to be dismissed, and she forced herself to think about Kurt.

Did he really bore her as much as she repeatedly told her mother, or had she only resented his quiet persistence? She had never considered him seriously as a future husband because she was not in love with him. It wasn't that she disliked him, she told herself. In fact, having him around had become a rather nice habit. He had been coming to their house for a long time, and she had become accustomed to seeing him in the family corner of their dining room, talking quietly to her father or listening attentively to her mother.

The countess first met him when she went to his office

to ask if he could order some imported fabric for her from Paris. Kurt was courteous and obliging, and the countess, impressed by his efficiency and deference to her, invited him to their house. She said he was dependable. That was it—dependable! He could be depended upon to be punctual, enchanting her parents by his impeccable manners and his measured, laconic sentences.

Now, pondering, she realized she'd always thought of him more as a member of the family than as a possible suitor. For a long time the real purpose of his visits had been obscure to her. Because he was sixteen years her senior, she took it for granted he was her father's friend. After all, he had never asked her out, or courted her, except for an occasional bouquet of flowers, which she accepted as a token of courtesy from a family friend. And when her mother had begun to drop hints of what a good match Kurt would make, Tanya had said he bored her.

Yet she knew him to be forthright and loyal; and, despite the gossip that Lydia had repeated to her earlier that evening, it was inconceivable to her there could be anything less than honorable in his background. But marriage? What would it be like married to Kurt? How would it feel, surrendering to him, enduring his caresses without the soaring of emotion, the thrilling heights of ecstasy described so aptly in the romantic novels she read? With Kurt, it wouldn't be love and passion, but an annoying duty, nothing more.

Why didn't he stir her romantically? She had to admit he was good-looking, in an academic, quiet way. She could not fault him for any ugliness of manner or appearance. But he did lack a certain quality—the debonair sex appeal and joie de vivre she found so appealing in Oleg.

Could she resign herself to a marriage of convenience, start a lifelong partnership without love, the most important element of a successful union? The countess had promised her she would grow fond of Kurt in time. But affection was a shabby substitute for love.

She thrashed and turned under her covers. No! Never! Why should I accept this fate? Just because Maman has exaggerated fears of a future that may never come to pass?

And in the meantime I would have to sacrifice myself? No.
I want love, romance!

Tanya felt her body swell with the yearning of youth, a
vague longing for love. She clenched her fists. Once, when
she confessed her dreams to her mother during one of
those rare talks when they exchanged confidences, the
countess told her that girls of proper breeding didn't indulge in such thoughts. But how could she prevent these
undefined yearnings from coming unbidden in the privacy
of the night, when no one was there to scold her? And why
was it wrong to succumb to delicious fantasies when solitude was her only partner?

But this morning she could not afford the luxury of
dreams that made her body restless. She mustn't let these
feelings interfere with her thoughts and plans for tomorrow. She had to think of what she would say to her father
later in the day. She would beg, she would cajole, she
would appeal to him to influence the countess to let her
visit her grandmother in Moscow. Perhaps in time her
mother would realize that her fears were unfounded and
allow Tanya to marry the man of her own choice.

If she could not persuade her father to convince the
countess to give her time, she resolved, she would stand up
to them on her own. . . .

When she awoke late in the morning, heavy rain
drummed on the windowpane, and the wind howled plaintively under the eaves. Whispering, whining sounds crept
along the walls, and as the storm raged outside, Tanya realized that her parents would not risk crossing the river in a
gale: Sungari's murky waters and whirlpools were noto-
riously hazardous in a storm. They would return home
early.

Oh, God—she was not ready to confront them! The arguments, the carefully chosen words she had prepared last
night had all vanished in broad daylight. Panic seized her.
What words could she use to sway her father?

She got out of bed and paced the floor, barefoot and
shivering, clutching her arms and rehearsing the elusive,
jumping phrases. None of them seemed to make sense, or
to be strong enough to convey her feelings.

Her vigil dragged interminably as she waited and dreaded their return. Then, as the morning slipped into the afternoon, Tanya's anxiety shifted focus.

Where were her parents?

Years later, she tried to remember her thoughts during those tense hours, but her memory had been mercifully blocked.

Her parents did not come home.

The storm had caught them in mid-river, and they were drowned when their boat was blown into a whirlpool and overturned. The Chinese boatman swam for his life, but the countess, who had never learned to swim, panicked, and Levitin drowned trying to save her.

In shock, Tanya lost her voice. In the evening, when Kurt came to propose, he found himself in the role of self-appointed guardian instead. With intuitive kindness he took charge of the arrangements, remaining silent and deferential to her grief. When it was necessary to speak, he did so with a minimum of words, as if sensing that it was beyond her endurance both to talk and to listen.

A sense of relief and freedom mingled with her grief. She sat without moving, allowing Kurt to manage things for her, as if it were in the nature of things for him to take over. She let him do everything that needed to be done, while she, immobilized, could not function, her thoughts oblique, circumventing the tragedy, rejecting the very emotions that filled her with guilt.

People came and went, murmuring words of sympathy that she did not acknowledge. Someone passed her a cup of water with valerian drops, which she drank without a word, and when Oleg's parents, the Korchagovs, said they were taking her to their house, she went with them meekly.

After the funeral, Tanya stayed on with the Korchagovs while she waited to hear from her grandmother in Moscow. Still in shock, she was unable to shed a tear, unable to speak more than short disjointed phrases. Over the next few days Oleg and Lydia tried to draw her out, but after a few unsuccessful attempts they left her alone. Then, one day, gently, Madame Korchagova showed her some snapshots of her parents and asked if she would like to have them. Slowly, painfully, the wave rose and spilled over. That night, Tanya cried herself to sleep.

Grieving, lonely, she had no qualms about her decision to visit Countess Merkulina now, and on that she was firm. She forestalled Kurt's proposal by telling him she was going to Russia because Harbin now held tragic memories for her. The Korchagovs tried to dissuade her from making the break final, and Kurt advised her not to sell the house, pointing out that if she rented it, she would have an income and a measure of financial independence.

"Tanya," he said firmly, "I'll be glad to rent the house for you. I'll do my best to get a satisfactory sum."

Tanya shook her head uncertainly. "I don't want to impose upon you further. You've already been too kind. Besides, I don't know when I'll come back."

A fleeting shadow crossed Kurt's face. Then, looking at her, he suddenly smiled, and she was aware of a warmth in his eyes that belied his aloofness.

"I won't hear any more about it!" he said, covering her hand with his. "I'd consider it a favor if you'd entrust the handling of this matter to me. It would give me an opportunity to repay, in however small a measure, all the kindnesses I enjoyed from your family."

He was careful to avoid any reference to his proposal, and his intuition surprised Tanya. Had she underestimated him? Maybe he was more sensitive than she had once believed, after all. Oh, why doesn't he unbend a little, she thought, exasperated by Kurt's ramrod posture, his rigid head. He's so stiff! If he were less formal, I'd like him a lot more. Aloud, she said, "Since you put it this way, I'd be deeply grateful for your help."

Impulsively, he took her hand again and, after a moment's hesitation, kissed it. "I'm so glad, Tanya! I want you to know that if the communication becomes unreliable, I'll keep the rent money for you in the bank."

Did she catch a slight break in his voice, or did she imagine it? Yet, when she looked at him, his face remained inscrutable.

As the day of her departure neared, she came to rely on him more and more for advice and friendship. It never occurred to her until she was boarding the train bound for

Moscow that he might be struggling with his own emotions and concealing them from her in time of her sorrow.

In the final good-byes, promises to write, and embraces and blessings from all the Korchagovs, she shook hands with Kurt, formally and awkwardly, avoiding the sight of his tear-filled eyes. As the train gathered speed out of Harbin station, however, she pressed her forehead against the dirty windowpane, looking in momentary panic at the motionless figure standing on the platform, and it wasn't until she lost sight of him that she remembered his parting words: "The door to the past will always be open, Tanya. I shall never forget you!"

CHAPTER 4

Ferries busily carried passengers across the Volga, and in the brisk September wind people huddled in the folds of their coats, their hands deep in their pockets. The crisp Samara day was charged with tension from rumors rife with embellishments and distortions about the approaching Bolsheviks, whose Red Army was engaged in fighting the Imperial White Army.

Samara, this granary of Russia and trade center on the Volga, was a city of several hundred thousand people which lay some four hundred miles southeast of Moscow. The Social Revolutionaries, or the SR's as they were called, a faction opposed to the Bolsheviks, were entrenched in the city since the previous June, when the Czechs, sent to Russia with the Allied Forces, liberated Samara from the Reds. But the SR's, known for their violent measures, inspired no confidence in the populace, and the peasantry refused to till the fertile black soil of the surrounding steppes.

The Bolsheviks were gaining strength in the north, while the SR's, feeling the short-lived power slipping from their grasp, intensified their campaign of hatred against the Reds. An air of confusion and indecision hung over the city, but Tanya, oblivious to the explosive atmosphere around her, walked along the bank toward a garden square for her rendezvous with Captain Yuri Bolganov.

Dressed in a broadcloth coat and fur-trimmed boots her grandmother had bought her before they left Moscow a year earlier, Tanya smiled at the thought of the countess's pampering concern. "You must not catch cold, *ma petite*. We're going to a new area where good doctors may be hard to find," she said.

In the advent of the advancing Bolsheviks, Countess

Merkulina had fled from her home in Moscow the previous October, but she seemed more concerned over Tanya's welfare than over the loss of her vast estate. A reality too enormous for her to acknowledge, she blocked out the Red threat even when she arrived in Samara and found the city already in Bolshevik hands. The new regime, however, struggling to establish itself and retain its power, had not disturbed the countess's household, and soon the Reds were routed out of the city by the Czechs.

Tanya had adored her grandmother from the moment she met her upon her arrival in Moscow. Countess Merkulina had wept when she enfolded Tanya in her arms for the first time, grieving over the loss of her daughter and son-in-law, whose tragic deaths she could not accept. She held Tanya's face between her hands and studied it hungrily, as if imagining in the daughter of her only child an image of herself.

At sixty-four, a faded beauty with a cameo face and large blue eyes, Countess Merkulina seemed to look onto the world with quiet resolve. She never mentioned the tragic accident again, only lavished gifts and affection on her grandchild, introducing her to Moscow society and allowing her to be the center of attention at her Thursday soirées.

It was at one of these literary evenings that Tanya had met Yuri Bolganov. The son of friends of the countess, he had been taken under her wing when Yuri was orphaned early in life; she had supervised his education and showered him with maternal affection. Now, a captain in the Imperial Army on leave from the German front, impeccable in his uniform and gleaming boots, he presented a glamorous figure.

"Tanya, I want you to meet my Yuri," the countess said, introducing them. "You are my two favorite people and I want you to be friends." The mischievous twinkle in her grandmother's eyes had not escaped Tanya, and she hoped that Yuri had not noticed it. His ready smile, his open admiration of her, attracted Tanya at once.

"I hope we shall become good friends," he said, gently squeezing her hand. "The countess is very close to me, and her granddaughter shall be my special charge."

He bowed to her gallantly, and Tanya blushed profusely. The aura of a dashing war hero left without a rudder in the advent of his army's destruction proved irresistible, and she fell in love with the darkly handsome officer with all the ardor of youth.

It was a new experience for her, not at all like the familiar comfort she had felt in Kurt's presence. She lived for her grandmother's Thursday soirées, when they could spend the evening oblivious of the other guests, sitting in the drawing room of the countess's elegant white-pillared mansion, and talk for hours. Yuri had a way of accompanying his sentences with a teasing look in his eyes that made her blush, and when he covered her hand with his in a protective gesture, his touch seemed to ignite a spark within her that took her breath away.

In the daytime they roamed the streets of Moscow, where Yuri delighted in showing Tanya the ancient capital. The mansion was in a quiet side street, a twenty-minute walk across the Moskva River from the Kremlin, whose gilded domes glittered in the sun, and Tanya listened to the Sunday church bells, awed by their resounding echo in this city of forty times forty churches.

They spent hours at the nearby Tretyakov Art Gallery, where Tanya stood before Shishkin originals; as a child she had admired reproductions of his forest scenes. She clapped her hands in childlike delight before her favorite, *Morning in the Pine Forest*. Quite forgetting herself, she tugged excitedly at Yuri's sleeve.

"Yuri, look! There is the bear and the three cubs! And the sunshine—look at the sunshine streaming above them! Oh, I love it!"

Yuri smiled indulgently and took advantage of her gesture to hold her hand on his arm. "I love your enthusiasm, Tanya—and I agree, the painting is beautiful and depicts our Russia at its best. But there is also another side to our history. Let's go to St. Basil's Cathedral on the Red Square. Do you know the legend attached to it?"

Tanya became aware of her entrapped hand, the warmth of his touch, and did not want to break the spell. "No, I don't know the details. All I know is that Ivan the Terrible wanted the church to be unique and ordered that no two cupola designs would be alike. Frankly, I think it is rather barbaric, with all that gingerbread coloring."

"Well, then, let me take you to the Sparrow Hills, from where you can get the panorama of the city, and then I'll tell you the legend."

Reluctant to break away from the fantasy world of the art gallery, where Yuri's nearness created an illusion of intimacy, she followed him outside with regret.

Once they reached the Sparrow Hills, however, Yuri captivated her when he pointed in the direction of the cathedral.

"The legend has it, Tanya," he said, "that when the two architects, Barma and Posnik Yakovlev, were commissioned by Ivan the Terrible in 1555 to build the cathedral, the Tsar rewarded the men's unique creation by plucking their eyes out to keep them from reproducing their own work."

Tanya gasped. "How awful! The poor men!"

Yuri moved closer and put his arm around her shoulders. "Our country is still at war," he said softly, "and with the internal unrest brewing, I'm afraid we have a lot to face yet in the future."

Without thinking, Tanya snuggled against Yuri's shoulder, and the two of them stood silently, looking at this ancient city that was seasoned and weighted by the bloody history of the Russ princes, and now spread beneath them like a weary pawn in a new fraternal dispute.

In the days that followed, Tanya discovered that Yuri shared her love of poetry, so dear to a Russian soul, and, like herself, preferred Lermontov to Pushkin. One day he recited the Demon's oath to Tamara, his voice ringing with such passion that Tanya knew he was speaking directly to her. She listened intently to the impassioned words, titillated by the subtlety of his approach, filled with excitement, for in Yuri's voice the words took on a new meaning.

So absorbed were they in each other, so immersed in burgeoning love, that they chose to ignore the darkening storm clouds of the revolution. When Countess Merkulina finally left Moscow and took Tanya to her smaller estate in Samara, Yuri followed, staying with them at the mansion. Since the move, they had seen each other every day, spend-

ing long hours together, for Yuri avoided venturing outside,
where the unruly Bolshevik crowds roamed the streets with
random debauchery. Chafing from the humiliation of having to act as a fugitive in his own country, he had to shed
his White Army uniform in favor of the more unobtrusive
civilian clothes that he wore until the SR's entered the city.

Through it all, their love grew, the unspoken commit-
ment understood and accepted. And now, as Tanya walked
on the narrow path along the river to keep her rendezvous
with Yuri, she was filled with such happiness that even the
sight of the fretful crowd she had left behind on Dvoryan-
skaya Street did not alarm her.

She shrugged, thinking of the furtive people she had
passed. What typical Russian fatalists they were! The Russian soul thrived on tragedy and doom. Even in Harbin her
parents had talked about enjoying the melancholy tunes of
the Gypsy violins in their favorite nightclub as though the
ultimate in pleasure had to be washed with tears. Tanya
could not understand this searching out the gloom, Her joy
was so complete these days, she resented each passerby
whose face showed anxiety.

As she neared the square with its wooden gazebo and
benches, someone grabbed her arm from behind. Startled,
she turned around. A youth, almost as tall as herself, stood
before her. He had a runny nose and sallow skin, and his
tattered clothes were grimy.

Suddenly, Tanya felt self-conscious in her warm coat
and lined boots. Then, angered by the audacity of the
stranger and offended by the sour odor of his clothes, she
wrenched free.

"What do you want?"

The youth sniffed and, wiping his nose with the back of
his hand, stroked the thick cloth of her sleeve with his chil-
blained fingers. Tanya recoiled.

"How dare you! Keep your hands off me!"

"You're warm, citizen, I wager, in that fancy coat of
yours," the youth said. "I thought you might spare a kopek
for a less fortunate comrade."

Irritated by the communist jargon, Tanya started forward, but the youth blocked her way. "I haven't eaten in a
couple of days, citizen. Won't you help me?"

Tanya looked at him. There were no earflaps on his cap and his ears were red. A fine tremor shook his body as he stood waiting.

"I'm not your comrade. Don't you dare call me 'citizen'! If you want to get a kopek out of me, your Bolshevik jargon isn't going to do it."

"I'm sorry if I used the wrong words, *barishnya*, but I'm hungry and have no money."

"Then what are you doing in Samara? Why don't you join the Bolsheviks up north and ask *them* to feed you?"

His eyes watering, the youth shook his head. "The Bolsheviks don't have much themselves. I came to Samara because my father was dying. Then I got caught by the SR's, and they beat me before letting me go yesterday."

Tanya frowned. "You're lying. I don't believe the Social Revolutionaries would abuse you that way."

Without a word, the youth pulled back his sleeve and showed her his wrist, where ugly purple welts crisscrossed his forearm. Tanya shuddered. "I still don't believe the SR's would do this to you," she said uncertainly, looking at the shivering youth. He was bold and impertinent, but he was also cold and hungry.

"Very well," she relented, her sympathies tapped, "I'll give you a few kopeks so you can get something to eat."

She opened her muff and pulled out a small suede money purse. Unsnapping it, she fumbled with her gloved hand for some change. At the sound of loose coins, a feverish glint appeared in the youth's watering eyes. He watched greedily as she took out a ten-kopek piece and placed it on his outstretched palm. Snapping the porte-monnaie shut, she started putting it back in her muff.

With lightning speed, the youth snatched it out of her hand.

Stunned but unafraid, Tanya grabbed his wrist. "You should be ashamed of yourself. Give it back to me at once!"

The youth shoved her aside and ran down the path toward town. Frantically, Tanya glanced toward the square, but Yuri was nowhere in sight. She stood motionless for a few moments, trying to regain her composure.

For the first time she realized she was quite alone on the bank of the river. All the pedestrians crowded near the ferry several hundred yards away, and no one strolled on the path, willing to brave the raw cold of late September. A shiver shook her. Lifting the collar of her coat, she walked briskly to the square.

It wasn't until she sat down on the bench that reaction set in and she began to shake. Remembering the youth's unsavory appearance, she pursed her lips. That's the kind of element the Bolsheviks attract, she thought. Criminals, paupers. They always want something for nothing at the expense of someone else.

"Why so pensive?"

At the sound of Yuri's voice, Tanya jumped. Yuri laughed. "So deep in thought you didn't hear me come up!"

One look at Tanya's face and he grew serious. "You're upset." He sat down, pulling her next to him. "What happened?"

When she told him, he shook his head and patted her hand. "I'm sorry, Tanya. Nothing so impertinent could have taken place before, but this is all part of the contrary times we live in. Communist propaganda about equality breeds this sort of insolence." He paused, his face grave. "The news I bring is bad, Tanya. The Bolsheviks are firmly entrenched in Moscow. It's been ten months now, and it's only a matter of time before they catch up with us here. The SR's aren't strong enough to confront them. I heard a Colonel Kappel is organizing a volunteer army here so he can reinforce Admiral Kolchak's forces in Siberia. I've decided to join this Colonel Kappel. I understand he is young—only thirty-seven years old—and fearless. We need more men like him if we're to liberate our country from the Red menace."

Yuri looked deeply into Tanya's eyes. "But before I do that, I want to tell you something." He took both her hands in his. "Tanya, darling, I'm sure you know what I'm about to say. I love you! And I feel you love me. I've been in love with you ever since I first set my eyes on you—a wide-eyed, bewildered girl from Manchuria trying desperately to appear worldly."

He smiled and pressed her hand to his cheek. "Tanya, I'd give anything to be able to ask you to marry me, but I can't. Not now, when times are so unsettled."

"Why not, Yuri? I'd follow you anywhere!"

"That wouldn't be fair to you, darling. I love you too much to subject you, a new wife, to the privations of a military campaign."

"What difference does it make as long as we're together?"

"That's just it—I can't guarantee we'll always be together, and . . ." He hesitated and looked away. " . . . I wouldn't want to make you suffer widowhood."

"No! Don't ever say that!" Tanya got up and started pacing the gravel path in front of the bench. Yuri rose and stood watching her, his face pained. "I've already lost my parents," Tanya spoke quietly. "I can't believe God would take *you* away from me too. You alone are denying me my happiness."

"Darling, please, try to understand. Don't make it any more difficult for me. I yearn to hold you, to call you my own, but if I'm killed, it will be easier for you not to have the memories of our marriage."

Tanya shook her head. "You're wrong! If such a terrible thing should happen, I'd rather have those memories to sustain me than be deprived of them altogether."

In broad daylight, in the square, conventions ignored, Yuri took Tanya in his arms and held her close.

"Darling, I want only the best for my wife. What can I offer you now? Possible loneliness and some rented flats along the way? Never! Not for my wife!"

"Does it matter where you live if you're in love?"

Yuri's face darkened. "Yes, to me it does. I'm a military man and trained for hardships, but my wife has to be protected, cherished!"

"Life is so short, Yuri—why shouldn't we take our happiness while we can?"

Yuri shook his head. "Not under these circumstances. You'll eventually agree that I am right."

Tanya rubbed her face against the rough fabric of his greatcoat. "I'll make you change your mind. You'll see!"

The ferry's horn sounded in the distance. An occasional

pedestrian hurried by, coat collar up, intent on private thoughts. The wind picked up from the river, blowing dried leaves along the path, scraping the gravel, wailing. Darkened clouds crept across the pale sky, spreading shadows beneath the sun. But the two lovers stood still, oblivious to nature, fused to one another in a desperate embrace, suspended in time.

CHAPTER 5

For the next few days Yuri studiously avoided being left alone with Tanya. They met at meals, talked in generalities, allowing the countess to lead the conversation; and as soon as good manners permitted, Yuri retreated to his rooms at the west wing of the mansion.

No matter how altruistic his reasons, Tanya agonized over being rejected. Yuri avoided looking at her, and all her attempts to talk to him privately failed. It was humiliating. Earlier in the week, she had hoped to change his mind with further arguments, but he had managed to deprive her of any opportunity to confront him.

There was only one other way. She could go to his room at night, where he would not be able to resist her. It would involve courage, a break with conventions, and a certain element of risk that could end in her dishonor. The thought of what she was contemplating sent ripples of excitement through her. But before she took this step, bold and irrevocable, she hoped to have one more chance to talk to Yuri and break down his resolve not to marry her.

She could hear her mother's prim words: "You sully your reputation if you sleep with a man before marriage." But was she really scheming to sleep with a man before marriage, or was she planning to ensure that the marriage took place? Would Yuri think her promiscuous? What if he lost respect for her and refused to marry her afterward? The thought was intolerable.

Yes, the risk was there; but the more she thought about it, the clearer became the alternative. If she didn't do something soon, she would lose Yuri forever. Russia was vast, and with the civil war raging, there was danger of losing each other to history. Her hesitation disintegrated in the face of a single threat—the ultimate and irrevocable loss of Yuri. Whenever, for a fleeting moment, her scruples surfaced, this one thought, this obsessive fear, was enough to strengthen her decision to go ahead with her daring plan.

Her fears were magnified one night at the supper table by Yuri's glowing report on the new volunteer army he was eager to join. The countess's questions only fanned his enthusiasm. "Who is this Colonel Kappel? I've never heard of him. Tell me about him, Yuri."

"He has the reputation of being a man of uncommon courage and integrity. They say his loyalty to the White Army is above reproach. So far, he has only about three hundred and fifty men in his volunteer force, and already his victories have been heroic. He seems to project some kind of magnetism over his men and inspire them with conviction of his own invincibility. I've never heard of anything like it!"

Yuri got up from the table and, caught up in his own excitement, began to pace the room. But the countess scoffed: "A few skirmishes, perhaps—but what can he do with three hundred and fifty men on a larger scale?"

"Other men like myself will be joining him, and his volunteer army will grow enough to be powerful. Mark my words!"

"That's all in the future. In the meantime, it behooves us to place our hopes in the Allies, who promise to help."

Yuri threw his arms up in desperation. "Bah! The only foreigners in the vicinity are the Czechs, and their behavior is not exactly exemplary. They've whipped some peasants near here, in Maryevka, simply because half of them refused to fight the Bolsheviks. And they whipped the wrong half, at that!"

The countess shrugged her shoulders. "Don't forget, the Czechs were the ones who liberated Samara from the Bolsheviks last June."

Yuri pursed his lips. "I remember. But then what happened? The Social Revolutionaries took it over immediately, and you'll be interested to hear that Colonel Kappel won't let them near his men!"

He shook a finger in the air. "What's more, I predict

that when the Bolsheviks return, they'll have no trouble in
repossessing Samara. The SR's will run for their lives."

The countess changed the subject. "What does your
Colonel Kappel look like?" she asked.

Yuri smiled and bending over, kissed her hand. "You're
still the same femme fatale, and I love you for being forever young! For your information, Colonel Kappel is safely
married with two children, and his gray-blue eyes are supposed to be cold and forbidding. Or so they say. You see, I
haven't met him yet—but I intend to, and very soon!"

Tanya listened, her heart drumming alarm, Yuri's last
words forging into her brain like hot irons. Very soon. *Very
soon.*

She didn't have any more time to procrastinate over her
plan. If she were to hold Yuri, she had to act without delay.
In these troubled times, no engagement time would be necessary. They could be married at once in the neighborhood
church. She wouldn't take time to get a wedding dress or
plan a traditional ceremony. Besides, she would rather not
have the choir welcome her entrance into the church with
the customary hymn, "Come forth, pure dove," for if her
plan worked, she would no longer be what the words implied. She felt a blush spread over her face.

"Tanya—come here, child!"

The countess's gentle voice startled Tanya out of her reverie. Her blush intensified, as if the countess had caught
her red-handed at some forbidden activity.

They were still in the dining room, the supper dishes
cleared away by the servants, Yuri already gone to his
room. Obediently, she walked over to where the countess
was sitting on a large settee, embroidering a tablecloth, and
sat down stiffly on the edge beside her. The scene reminded her of their dining room in Harbin, where her
mother continued the custom of having a cozy sitting area
near the dining table for after-supper conversation. For a
few seconds memories of her parents threatened to over-
whelm her. With an effort she forced herself to look at her
grandmother.

The countess's wispy curls hung over her face, concealing her clear eyes. Without looking up, she chuckled. "Relax, darling—I'm not going to scold you for anything."

It was uncanny. Lighthearted and gay, the old countess surprised Tanya time and again by her perceptiveness and keen observation at the very time when her mind seemed to be miles away, absorbed in the activity of the moment. Tanya found it disconcerting, and squirmed under her grandmother's gaze, fearful that the countess had indeed read her shameful thoughts.

"Tell me," the older woman said, still bent over her work, "did a cat run between you and Yuri? You seem to be strained with each other."

Tanya winced at her grandmother's habit of speaking in proverbs. "No, Grandmaman," she answered carefully, "we had no argument."

"I've known Yuri since the day he was born, and I love him as much as I would my own grandchild. I watched your courtship with the secret hope you'd get married—the two people I love more than life itself."

The countess paused, lowered the cloth, the needle with the red thread still in her fingers, and looked up. "Tanya, I have a right to know what happened between you two. Maybe I can help. Don't insult my intelligence by denying there is anything wrong."

Tanya bit her lower lip to keep it from trembling. Not trusting her voice, she remained silent.

The countess put her embroidery to the side and, moving closer, took Tanya in her arms. Suddenly, the years rolled back and Tanya was a little girl again, cradled in her father's arms, hurt and crying.

"That bad?" said the countess, stroking Tanya's hair. "It'll be easier if you get it off your chest, my child—and who knows? Together we might find the answer to your problem."

Weeping, Tanya poured her story out to her grandmother. All but her last plan. The old countess listened without interrupting until Tanya's longing, frustration, and fears were voiced. Then she sighed.

"Men and their chivalry! They think they're heroes when they make a sacrifice. What misplaced heroism! They forget we women are resilient, that while we harbor resentments, we exist on good memories. We husband our strength more wisely and survive when they perish. What right do they have to deny us the knowledge of love, especially at a time like this, when the future can test us with adversity? Oh, Tanya, Tanya—these men! Our fortress, our refuge, and our Achilles heel! We seek their strength, but in the end we coddle them with our love. When they lose their heads we yield to them, and then they feel honor bound to marry the girl they deflower. Lord only knows how many marriages would not have taken place otherwise!"

The countess glanced up quickly, and then, looking behind her, picked up her embroidery. "As a matter of fact," she continued, her fingers busy again with the needle, "your mother was born nine months after your grandfather and I were married, and at the time there were whispers and gossip that angered my parents. But I was too proud to admit or deny the rumors. It didn't bother me in the least. On the contrary, I felt like a woman of mystery and enjoyed the controversy around me."

With a quick laugh, the countess put the tablecloth down and poured herself a cup of tea from a steaming brass samovar left on the table by her faithful cook, Oksana.

"Would you like another cup, dear?" asked the countess. Tanya shook her head. "No, thank you, Grandmaman."

The countess reached for a tiny dish of black currant jam as Tanya looked at her grandmother's shapely figure and marveled at her willpower in eating everything in such small amounts. Her own mother had been less conservative.

"Well, Tanya," the countess said, stirring a teaspoonful of the jam into her tea, "all this talk doesn't solve your dilemma right now, does it? The most obvious thing to do is for me to have a little chat with Yuri. Fortunately, he still respects my opinion. However, I'd like to give you young people a couple of days more to see if you can work something out between you."

The corners of her mouth twitched slightly as she looked at Tanya with her large, clear eyes. "Lovers do manage to solve their private problems themselves. Especially when the interfering grandmothers stay out of it." Her eyes twinkled mischievously. "I don't think Yuri will be able to resist you for very long!"

* * *

In her bedroom, undressing with the help of the old nanny, Praskovya, Tanya pondered her grandmother's words. Her last sentence kept ringing in her ears. She wasn't going to wait. She would go to Yuri this very night. Praskovya's movements seemed interminably slow. Every muscle taut, afraid to betray her anxiety and prompt the old woman's solicitous questions, Tanya sat on the edge of her bed, waiting. Praskovya crossed herself and bowed before the icon hanging in the corner of the room, then took down the vigil light suspended from the ceiling by a triple chain, and checked its wick and oil. Satisfied, she turned to Tanya.

"Why are you sitting on the bed with your bare feet on the floor?" she asked sternly. "Get in bed! Get in before you catch cold!"

Without a word, Tanya slipped under the down coverlet. All nannies are the same, thought Tanya tenderly, watching Praskovya's labored movements. They are our surrogate mothers and they chide and scold out of love. The old nanny smoothed the folds of the blanket more from habit than from necessity and made a sign of the cross over Tanya. "Good night, *kasatka*. Sleep well."

When the old woman's sighs and shuffling died down in the corridor, Tanya jumped out of bed, put on her satin slippers and her peignoir, listened at the doorway, and slipped out of her room without putting on the light. Afraid to stumble in the dark, she felt her way along the wall of the hallway. She turned the corner into Yuri's wing of the house, her heart pounding loudly in her ears.

At the door to Yuri's bedroom, she began to lose courage. What am I doing? I can't go through with this. What if . . . ? Stubbornly, she refused to finish the thought. No; she had no alternative. No sacrifice was too great to win Yuri. Besides, the clandestine nature of her visit— even though she was ashamed of the feeling—only added to the rising pitch of her excitement. Timidly, she knocked. A few seconds later, she heard Yuri's muffled tenor.

"*Entrez!*"

Tanya closed her eyes and took a deep breath. Don't lose your nerve now, she encouraged herself, opening the door.

Yuri stood near his canopied bed, holding a book in his hand. Dressed in a dark-green brocade lounging coat with quilted lapels and a satin sash, he was evidently preparing to read in bed, where the eiderdown quilt was neatly folded back for him. When he saw Tanya in her silk negligée, his eyes widened and his lips parted in astonishment. He watched without moving as she walked in and closed the door behind her. Then he put his book down.

"Tanya, darling, what is it?"

Tanya felt faint. Oh, God, she thought, do I have to tell you? She looked at him pleadingly. "Yuri, this is the only way I could find to talk to you alone. You've been avoiding me this entire week. I'm hurt!"

"Oh, Tanya, Tanya—I tried so hard!" He shook his head.

"Yuri, I love you! I . . . came to you!"

She moved toward him, and, slowly, the satin belt that held her peignoir loosened and slipped to the floor, revealing the clinging silk nightgown underneath.

With a quick intake of breath, Yuri grasped the bedpost, staring at her hungrily. A delicious longing began to spread through her body as his stare lingered on her erect nipples straining against the smooth fabric, then moved down the narrow waist to the curve of her hips and, finally, to the small hillock between her thighs.

She felt naked standing there before him, for the opaque fabric of her gown proved woefully inadequate under the eyes of the man whose impassioned glance was roaming over her body as if the gown weren't there.

Her heart beating wildly, she took another step forward. Yuri raised his hand to stop her and shut his eyes. "Tanya!" His voice was husky. "Don't come any closer. I can't vouch for myself."

"Yuri, don't you see? I'm here because I love you. I want to marry you before you go away. Please, look at me!"

Slowly, he lifted his head. "God, how beautiful you are! And how I want you!"

Forgetting everything but the nearness of him, she reached out to this man, her Yuri, of whom she dreamed,

for whom she yearned, whom she loved above all else she'd
ever known. As their hands touched, she gasped, surprised
at the reaction in her body, and, inhaling deeply, felt the
button on her bodice tear.

The dam broke. One instant she touched him; the next,
she was in his arms, crushed against him, his mouth on
hers, his hands pulling her gown up the small of her back,
sending a sensuous ripple down her legs.

Thrust against his tensed body, her senses reeling, she
leaned backward in a near faint. "Yuri . . . Yuri . . . I
love you!"

She felt herself lifted in his arms and carried to the bed.
In one impatient movement, he threw her peignoir to the
floor and turned the lights out. His kisses rained upon her
face, her neck, sliding down to her shoulders and the silken
breasts, whose rigid points he teased between his lips. She
felt his hands brush over her skin with a feathery caress,
lingering, searching, as if no part of her could he refrain
from touching.

Her nerves taut, she was lifted on a swelling tidal wave,
waiting for the crest to sweep her wildly into the mystery
of virgin union. She held him close, and with a single bolt
of light that seared her brain, she was his and he belonged
to her, this strong, passionate man, rendered helpless in her
arms, joined in a fugue of flesh and skin and eager limbs.

Surely this couldn't be wrong, the wonderment of it, the
magic of their love's expression; and now she knew her
arguments with conscience were valid, her sin absolved.
What did all her fear and shame have to do with this sublime experience? Was this not better than defiling the
sanctity of such a love by a loveless union? She was a
woman now, contented, loved, belonging.

Jealous of the stolen hours, she did not sleep, and lay
beside him quietly, enjoying his closeness. He put his arm
around her. "I lost my head, Tanyusha. Did I hurt you?"

"No," she answered. "I love you, Yuri. You know that
now, don't you?"

"I want to see it in your eyes." He raised himself on one
elbow and, leaning over her, reached for the lamp on the
night table. A soft golden hue suffused the room, and in
the light Tanya's bliss vanished. Abruptly, she pulled the

blanket over her breasts and turned her face away. He chuckled and cupped her chin in his hand, forcing her head toward him.

"You vixen! From the moment you stepped through that door, I knew I was lost. Look at me, you seductress!"

But Tanya kept her eyes shut. Yuri grew serious. "Oh, darling, look at me! Don't deprive me of the look of love in your eyes."

Slowly, Tanya opened her eyes and looked at Yuri. His face blurred, and two tears slipped out of the corners of her eyes, tickling her ears. Yuri bent over her. "Darling, what is it?"

Tanya's lips quivered. "I'm so ashamed."

Yuri turned the light out and scooped her into his arms again. "Ashamed of what, Tanya? Of loving me enough to offer me your most precious possession—yourself? Love beautifies the soul, ennobles that which is profane. I shall love and cherish you always."

He pulled down the covers, exposing her to the waist. In the dark, she didn't protest. He stroked her gently. "I'm glad you came to me tonight. In my misguided resolve we would have cheated ourselves of this prelude to what is yet to come. Thank you, darling, for being the wiser of us two." He kissed her on the nose, the forehead, the eyes. "We'll be married immediately. Unless, of course, the countess wants a large wedding—which I doubt in these troubled days."

Tanya suddenly clutched him to her fiercely and whispered, "Oh, Yuri, what a terrible time to be young! What's going to happen to us?"

For a while Yuri didn't answer. Then he said slowly, "I don't know, Tanya. I don't know! Of one thing I'm certain. I'm going to fight the Bolsheviks for as long as I live. Colonel Kappel will accept me, I'm sure, and then we'll follow him."

She put her arms around his neck. "Promise me we'll never be separated!"

"Don't talk of it now, darling. Don't fret over what is to come on a night like this!" His hand, resting on her waist, slipped upward. She tensed under his touch, her nerves tingling.

"You're irresistible, beloved—do you know that?" he whispered, caressing her ear with his lips. "This night is ours, and dawn is far away." He pressed her to him. "I love you, Tanya."

They would be married, he said. The future was uncertain; but what did it matter if they had each other?

Happy, she clung to him.

CHAPTER 6

They were married in the little church nearby, where Father Nikanor performed the ceremony. "What is the world coming to?" he grumbled, shaking his head, when the countess informed him there would be no guests and no wedding attendants. "Who's going to hold the crowns over the young couple's heads during the ceremony? And no choir?" The priest threw up his arms in desperation. "My dear countess," he lamented, "who's going to bring the bride in? Why such a hurry?" And when the countess explained that the groom was about to leave for the front and there was no time for lavish festivities, the old priest only shook his head and mumbled under his breath.

Aware of the Russian custom of parents absenting themselves from the church during the wedding, Tanya begged her grandmother not to abide by the ancient rule. The countess chuckled. "I have no intention, my dear child, to miss out on the joy of seeing my two children united in marriage. Besides"—she winked mischievously—"I want to be the one to place the white satin cloth at your feet before you step toward the altar. This is one of the old wives' tales I do believe in: Step on it first and you will be the dominant partner in marriage!"

Tanya was deeply grateful to her grandmother, who not only hadn't asked any questions, but had looked at her granddaughter in a straightforward manner, without the searching glances Tanya dreaded. When told of their intention to marry immediately, the countess clasped them both in a warm embrace and showed no resistance to their wish for a private ceremony.

The day before the wedding, she called them into her boudoir and ordered them both to kneel before her. Two matching icons of Christ and the Virgin Mary, encased in hammered gold leaf with blue enameled halos, stood on the small table by her chaise longue. With tears in her eyes, the countess blessed Tanya with the icon of the Virgin Mary and Yuri with Our Lord's.

"Keep these icons always with you, children, and treasure them. My dearest wish of seeing you love each other has come true." The countess smiled and wiped away a tear. "You made me very happy."

Tanya received the icons into her arms reverently, almost afraid to show her joy in the midst of general fear and uncertainty. "What a terrible time to be young," she had said to him that night. But as long as they *were* young, why shouldn't they enjoy the happiness given them? They'd be fools to reject it. They hadn't selected this time to be young; and the joy of this moment, she believed—this wonderful moment—could never be duplicated.

Happy to have a small wedding with no strangers around to watch and gossip, Tanya chose a simple ankle-length gown of blue velvet, her luxurious hair swept up in a thick chignon on top of her head. A few old women in the dark alcoves of the church knelt before the candle-lit icons, crossing themselves in wide sweeping movements and touching their foreheads to the floor. Incense permeated the air, allowing only a hint of human odors to filter through. A church attendant shuffled from one candle stand to another, removing the burnt-out stubs—a silent shadow creeping along the wall. The only indication that anything special was taking place in the church were dozens of flickering candles illuminating the mosaic icons in the gold-encrusted iconostasis.

Listening to Father Nikanor's chanting, she was acutely aware of Yuri's nearness, and wondered whether the warmth that encircled her came from the flame of the candle she was holding or from the presence of the man whose love had enveloped her totally.

They had not been together again since that one night— Tanya timid, Yuri attentive and warm, but studiously avoiding the silent language of passion. He must have guessed her wish to forget what she had done and to pretend that today was not only her wedding day but the true moment when she was to become a woman. In the days preceding the ceremony he was correct in his behavior, and only once, as he said good night to her on the eve of their wedding, did he let slip his impatience.

Kissing her hands tenderly, he looked into her eyes and whispered, "I won't see you until the ceremony tomorrow, but the next time we're alone again I won't be so disciplined!"

Tanya flushed, yielding to the rushing memory of his lovemaking. Yuri smiled, his index finger lifting her chin. "It'll be better next time, my darling, I promise you!"

Now, standing beside him, absorbed in her dreams, she hadn't even noticed who had stepped on the satin cloth first.

Then the wedding was over, and a plain gold band circled the ring finger of her right hand. The countess and the few witnesses crowded around, wishing her and Yuri lasting happiness. She listened to the words and read a special meaning into them. What greater fulfillment could she experience than the union with the man whom her soul and her heart and her body had chosen?

Glowing with happiness, she was looking around the little church when her glance fell on an old woman. Tanya stared at the woman's waxy skin, her beak nose, hypnotized by a message of unease in the woman's faded eyes. As Yuri led her past the crone, the woman's gaze shifted to him, boring into him, seeming to scream in a silent cry of pain. The dark eyes filled with tears and glistened in the candlelight. Yuri's forearm tightened, squeezing Tanya's hand against him, and she knew that he, too, had reacted to the look in the old woman's eyes. Oh, how she wished at that moment that Russians didn't have so many superstitions, for then she wouldn't have found a sadness in the old woman's tears!

With quickened steps they left the church, and by the time they reached the house she had pushed the incident to the back of her mind.

Servants were waiting for the newlyweds at the mansion. Oksana and Yuri's faithful old Matvei stood on the doorstep in their Sunday finery. Matvei wore a white shirt with a rounded collar embroidered with cross-stitched bright colors and buttoned down the side of his chest. Bloused to the hips, it was nipped at the waist with a tasseled blue cord. His usually unruly brown hair was parted near the middle and pomaded sleekly to the sides.

In spite of the biting autumn air, Oksana wore a matching embroidered blouse under her red *sarafan*, the bodice falling loosely over her bountiful bosom. A white runner, festively embroidered, hung over her outstretched arms, and on it rested a round loaf of bread with a silver salt cellar perched on top in the traditional custom of welcoming newlyweds home with bread and salt. Behind her, Praskovya, rotund and beaming, whispered loudly, "Lord, grant them happiness!"

Inside, Oksana had prepared a feast worthy of the occasion. The table was laden with delicacies: smoked domestic goose, whole suckling pig, ham, cold lamb, pickled mushrooms, beluga and salmon caviar, and sliced smoked sturgeon. Several raised dough pirogi with meat, cabbage, and fish stood on a separate table, ready to be served.

The only guests were Yuri's two army friends, Lieutenants Penkov and Virsky. Of the two, Virsky was older, heavier, his attention riveted to the food before him, a benevolent smile creasing his face. Gleb Penkov was a redheaded youth with light gray eyes who seemed to worship Yuri and hang on to each word he uttered. Yuri, mature for his twenty-six years, acted like an older brother to the young lieutenant, who had just turned twenty-two. Earlier, Yuri had told Tanya that Gleb Penkov had decided to join him and follow Colonel Kappel, and now Tanya already looked upon him as an old friend, although she had met him only once before. There was a certain ingenuous warmth in the young man, and Tanya felt that if she had had a brother, she would have liked him to be like Gleb.

At the mansion, Gleb lifted his glass of champagne and, grinning at the newlyweds, cried, "*Gorko, gorko!*" Tanya flushed and lifted her mouth to Yuri to be kissed, as the custom dictated, in response to the wedding toast. Then it was Lieutenant Virsky's turn to toast the couple in his deep bass with the repeated toasts of "*gorko, gorko.*"

Everywhere Tanya looked, she was surrounded by smiling, friendly faces. Gleb Penkov and Virsky kissed her hand repeatedly; her grandmother glowed with the kind of total happiness Tanya had not seen on her face before; the priest's approving eyes twinkled; and the servants lingered in the room, eager to please.

For a few hours all thought of the revolution and its menace was shut out completely. Tanya and Yuri had each other, and the outside world would not dare to intrude.

In the whirl of toasts and kisses the rest of the day became a blur. Then it was night, and she was being led by her young husband to their room. Opening the door to the bedroom, Yuri smiled and bowed ceremoniously: *"Après vous*, Madame Bolganova!"

As she took a step forward, thrilled by the sound of her new name, Yuri suddenly lifted her in his arms and carried her inside.

It was better this time. She had a right to be there: a right to his bed, a right to submit to his loving, to yield, to dissolve in his arms, to banish shame, and to learn what he taught her.

With care and endearments, gentle, unhurried, he guided her hands to himself, encouraged her curiosity, introduced her to the thrill of giving. A new dimension was added to her love, a wonderful sense of an as yet untapped source of power over this strong man seeking, waiting for her touch. And she responded to him with unrestrained passion, caught in the intensity of their love.

CHAPTER 7

Yuri was bending over the map spread on the dining room table and tracing the movements of the Red Army when Gleb walked in. After greeting Tanya and her grandmother, the young lieutenant turned to Yuri.

"I've just come from Colonel Kappel's office," he said, running his hand through his curly red hair with splayed fingers—a gesture Tanya had come to recognize in their young friend in the last few weeks as one of uncertainty and tension.

"He's ordering us to join him," Gleb went on, "and head for Admiral Kolchak's headquarters in Omsk."

Yuri, his hand poised over the map, raised his head and looked at Gleb for a few silent moments. Then, using a pencil, he drew a line from Samara to Omsk, well east into Siberia.

"It's over a thousand versts from here," he said, straightening and tapping his index finger on the map. "Considering the overloaded trains, it will take us quite a few days to reach Omsk."

Tanya walked over to where the countess was sitting in the corner of the settee, absorbed in her crocheting. I must sit down to keep my legs from trembling, Tanya thought, lowering herself carefully on the settee. Let the men talk, let them discuss the situation thoroughly, and maybe the problem will go away. She looked at her grandmother. The countess seemed oblivious of the conversation, but Tanya knew better, for she had come to know her grandmother well. Intelligent, gentle, tactful, she often listened to the young people's debates without interfering, yet giving her opinion when asked, and frequently throwing out an idea

that solved a current dispute with simple logic. Tanya had
learned that her mother had been wrong to think that the
old countess did not consider the current political dilemma.
She was very aware of the constant military threat. Tanya
had watched her and marveled, feeling a closer kinship with
her grandmother than she had ever felt with her own
mother.

The weeks since her marriage would have been the
happiest in her life were it not for the rumors of the burgeoning Bolshevik power and the growing unrest in Samara.

With a thoughtful grandmother and doting servants,
Tanya had no domestic cares, and, pampered by an adoring husband, she would have devoted her entire time to
enjoying the novelty of being a young matron, but the wors-
ening political turmoil created an uneasy atmosphere in the
household. Ideological conflicts among revolutionary factions struggling to overthrow the current government con-
tributed to the general confusion. The White Army had no
trust in the Social Revolutionaries, and in return the SR's
undermined the White Imperial Army by accusing them of
being monarchists and counterrevolutionaries and refusing
to join forces against their common enemy, the Bolsheviks.

The large, bustling city took on a depressing look. The
wide boulevards teamed with people who seemed to move
about aimlessly, hushed by fear. The absence of the usual
urban pulse underscored the air of menace that settled over
the town, and more and more Tanya found excuses to remain within the walls of the house she had come to love
and associate with her happiness.

As she listened now to Gleb Penkov and watched the
excitement in the two men's faces, she knew the moment
she dreaded had come.

"There's no longer any doubt as to what we must do,"
Yuri said, folding the map. His voice was unsteady. "We've
been living like ostriches, refusing to see what is going on
around us. I walked on Shikhobalovksaya Street yesterday,
and it was an eerie experience. You know how crowded the
streets usually are. Well, they were crowded again—I
would say mobbed—but what really bothered me was the

almost total absence of noise. The crowds moved quietly, listlessly. It's as if they are now resigned to their fate and are waiting for the axe to fall."

Yuri hit the table with his fist, rattling his cup and saucer. He turned to the countess. "We can't wait any longer, Paulina Arkadyevna. When the Bolsheviks come, Samara will show no resistance. I can feel it in the air. Gleb and I have to follow our orders, and you and Tanya must come with us."

Tanya's heart leaped. Whatever the future held in store for them, she and Yuri were not going to be separated. She sensed the urgency in Yuri's voice and looked at her grandmother. "Grandmaman, I'll be glad to help you supervise the packing."

The countess did not answer; she turned to Yuri instead. "Is there any chance Kerensky and his Provisional Government will return?"

Yuri stared at her for a few seconds in amazement. "You know Kerensky was pushed north and fled through Murmansk months ago! No one has heard a word from him since. Besides, his leadership was shaky at best."

The countess shrugged. "Various parts of the country are occupied by different factions—Bolsheviks, White Army, Social Revolutionaries. There may be others we don't even know about. Cities have changed hands several times in the last few months, and—who knows?—Kerensky may come back and take over again."

"Paulina Arkadyevna, this is hardly the time for conjecture. If Kerensky does attempt a return—which I strongly doubt after all these months—we have no clue as to when it might happen. In the meantime, we're faced with the immediate danger of Samara falling into Bolshevik hands. We have to face facts, unpleasant as they are! In any case"—Yuri waved his hand, dismissing the whole subject—"whatever our hopes or convictions may be, we have to obey orders, and right now they are for us to go to Omsk."

Gleb cleared his throat. "We'll have to leave soon. I hear the trains are so full, no advance reservations are possible. If we wait much longer, seats will be taken at gunpoint."

Yuri put his hand on the young man's narrow shoulder.
"Gleb, my friend, you'll have to leave immediately and
find a place for us to live in Omsk, while I wait and escort
the ladies." Then, moving toward the countess, he asked,
"How long will it take you to get ready to leave? You
know, of course, there isn't time to make proper disposition
of your property and belongings. You'll have to take what
you can carry with you in a suitcase, and entrust the rest of
the packing and shipping to one of your servants."

The countess put down her crocheting, rose slowly, and,
without answering Yuri, walked over to the window. It
looked over a stretch of the garden, sparse in autumn na-
kedness, its trees bare, unadorned. Beyond the iron fence,
the street teamed with people who seemed to be moving in
slow motion.

When the countess turned around and looked at the
three young people, tears glistened in her eyes. The setting
sun filtered through the wisps of her hair, gifting her with
a golden halo. Regal, poised, she studied their faces.

"I'm not leaving Samara, children," she said quietly.
"My place is here, in my house. I have already deserted
my home in Moscow. Once is enough. I'm not going to
abandon this one."

"Paulina Arkadyevna! Do you know what you are saying? Aren't you aware of the danger?"

Yuri's voice shook, and it made the countess pull herself
up to her full five-foot-four height. "Don't be an alarmist,
Yuri. Providence has always been good to me, and this
storm will pass me by."

Yuri pushed the chair behind him so hard it fell over. "I
can't let you stay behind," he said, striding over to the
countess and grasping her hands. "I insist you come with
us!"

A whimsical smile crossed the countess's lips. "I love
your passion and determination, Yuri, and I'll miss them. I
had almost forgotten over the years how good it is to be
surrounded by youth; but now you must go fight for victory, and I must stay here. I don't want to make new ad-
justments. As it is, I miss Moscow and my friends." She
patted him on the cheek. "Yuri, don't look so crestfallen.

It's going to be only for a short while, and then you'll join me again."

Yuri threw his hands up. "Paulina Arkadyevna, I want to spare your sensibilities, but I can tell you what the Bolsheviks will do if they find you here when they take Samara this time."

Undaunted, the countess shook her head. "They won't bother an old woman, dear. Stop worrying!"

"Grandmaman, please listen to us!" Tanya pleaded as she put her arm around her grandmother's shoulders. "The Bolsheviks showed no mercy when they killed the Tsar and his whole family. It's been only three months since the massacre. What makes you think they would spare you? The White Army didn't get to Ekaterinburg in time to save the imperial family. Once we're gone, we may not get back to help you."

"Why should they bother with me? I've never meddled in politics thank God, and I pose no threat to them."

"Paulina Arkadyevna!" Yuri's voice sounded exasperated. "Your judgment is based on principles of civilized behavior. You give the Reds too much credit. They may have killed the Tsar for a purpose, but they massacre the gentry less for individual transgressions than for the idea that we represent as a whole—the ruling class, against which their hatred is now unleashed. Believe me—the whim of the roaming Bolshevik bands is unpredictable. Without discipline, there is going to be anarchy."

"Yuri dear, youth in its enthusiasm tends to exaggerate the point of their argument. You forget, I have an obligation, a duty to my servants who depend upon me. They have been loyal and I can't abandon them."

Yuri looked at the countess closely. "How many rumors have we heard in the past year of the so-called loyal servants who had turned against their benefactors and even killed them at the slightest taste of power? These very servants for whom you are willing to risk your life may betray you at the time when you need their help the most."

"You're being melodramatic, Yuri. I have no reason to suspect that my good fortune should turn against me so late in my life." The countess turned and smiled at Tanya.

"We're going to be busy from now on, Tanyusha. I'm sure we can get you ready to leave within twenty-four hours."

The countess made a move to leave the room, but Yuri blocked her way. "And if we all refuse to leave without you?"

Paulina Arkadyevna looked firmly into Yuri's eyes and shook her head. "I don't want to call your bluff, Yuri dear. I'm too old to make another move, but you—young people—have to go, and you know it. Let's not waste any more time arguing."

Yuri sighed. "I beg you, then, for one last favor. Choose carefully one or two servants whom you can trust, and promise me you'll keep them near you at all times."

"I promise, if it will make you happy."

"It won't make me happy, Paulina Arkadyevna, but at least I'll know you won't be entirely alone here."

Tanya took the countess by her arms. "Grandmaman, won't you please reconsider? You say you have an obligation toward your servants. What about us? We're your family!" Tanya stumbled, in search of words. "It was hard enough to lose my parents, Grandmaman, and now you threaten me with a separation that may be forever!"

At the mention of her daughter's tragic death, the countess stiffened. "My obligation is to remain here. You can stand on your own feet—and, most important, you have each other. God will be with you, and I know it won't be long before we're reunited."

Firmly, the countess removed Tanya's hands from her arms and walked out of the room.

Yuri watched her in dismay. "I know her. Indomitable will. Her faith can never be shaken. We must pray, Tanya, that the Bolsheviks will leave her alone when they get here. In the meantime, we have no time to lose. Gleb is right. We must leave at once, while there is still room on the trains."

In the short days of packing, somewhere deep inside Tanya an undercurrent of anger fermented: anger against the revolution; anger against fate, for squandering her youth during this time of upheaval; anger against the Bolsheviks. Especially against the Bolsheviks. A mob of hood-lums, she thought, ruffians whose level of intelligence didn't rise above a satisfied belly and a greed for power they didn't even know how to exercise. Surely they couldn't triumph for long, and the Imperial Army would soon bring them to their knees.

Still, the thought of leaving her grandmother behind worried her, and she fretted. With the countess staying behind, Gleb refused to go ahead, and when the three of them left two days later, Tanya realized that she was saying good-bye to her last living relative.

For a long time afterward she couldn't erase the sight of her grandmother's erect figure standing at the door of the mansion, flanked by the faithful Oksana and Matvei, and smiling broadly as their carriage rolled away from the house. Tanya turned to look at her grandmother for one more time and watched the first snowflakes sift to the ground, powdering the countess's uncovered head and aging her with whiteness. Cradled in Yuri's arms, she cried all the way to the train.

CHAPTER 8

After the first day on the road, Tanya was convinced she would always associate a train ride with sorrow. On her journey from Harbin to Moscow the previous year, the loss of her parents was still a fresh wound, mitigated only by the hope of a happier life with her grandmother. On that trip she was reasonably comfortable, sharing her compartment with three older women, who watched over her and provided her with companionship and extra food.

How different was this train ride! Crowded beyond capacity with men, women, and children in the same compartment, there was no room to lie down, and whenever sleep overcame her, Tanya leaned on Yuri's shoulder. Sometimes, when the fitful dreams took the edge off her weariness, she would open her eyes to find Yuri's shoulder had been replaced by Gleb's, while Yuri slipped out to the railroad station during their frequent stops for refueling to bring back some hot cabbage-filled *piroshki* and, occasionally, a pickle.

The train corridors were packed with travelers who slept on their suitcases, hugging their bundles or screaming obscenities at strangers who trampled over them. At each stop, waiting crowds engulfed the train like an army of locusts: men shouting, women wailing, and all fighting the conductor, while the more agile ones scrambled aboard, pushing their way inside, eyes glazed with hysteria and fear. In spite of the officials' refusal to take on any more passengers, a few were sucked in by the puffing train as it labored along the tracks. The three friends sat together, with Tanya squeezed tightly in the middle, the warmth from their bodies comforting her and cushioning the jolts of the rough track beneath them. They didn't talk. What words were necessary were spoken with economy of thought, as if the mind, preoccupied with the magnitude of their upheaval, refused to touch on trivia.

The train rolled, its rhythmic knocking counting off the versts, their number multiplying, stretching out the distance from Samara. Dressed in a coating of ice, birches and evergreens sparkled in the sun. Forests, houses, people, flashed past Tanya's window as the engines pulled the train through the changing scenery of steppes and mountains, rushing on into space and uncertainty.

In the Omsk railroad station they were told the hotels were full, and as they stood wondering where to search for a place to stay, a harassed female vendor, in a moment of unexpected compassion, directed them to a friend's house on Tverskaya Street. Yuri crossed the street to hire the droshky to take them to town. The driver wanted ten rubles. Cut off from the source of her income, unsure of Yuri's next salary, Tanya insisted on taking the *vyetka*— the branch-line train—which was standing on the track ready to make the three-verst trip to the city for only thirty kopeks.

Once in town, they took a droshky for the short ride to Tverskaya Street. As their carriage raced through the broad streets, well-laid in square blocks, Tanya was fascinated by the sight of muscular, healthy-looking people. Heavily bundled women waddled slowly, like animated puppets; coatless workmen puttered about on high telegraph poles, fixing wires; and a newsboy selling papers on the street corner continually removed his mitt, in spite of the autumn chill, to dive into his pocket for change. A number of people were hauling carts filled with wood, and suddenly Tanya realized that it had been a long time since she had seen such industrious street activity. Reaching for Yuri, she slipped her arm through his and pressed her shoulder against him, encouraged to hope that their life here wouldn't be as grim as they had anticipated.

They found the address the vendor had given them and rented two rooms, with bathroom and kitchen privileges. As in most Siberian cities, there was no municipal water system in Omsk. The landlady informed them it cost twenty rubles a month to have a man bring the water in barrels once a week, and another twenty for each additional visit.

Gallantly, Gleb took the smaller of the two rooms, allowing Yuri and Tanya to have one with a glassed-in porch. There was a small potbellied stove in one corner and a tiny bin of wood for which they paid in advance. Two leather armchairs were grouped near a brass double bed, which drew Tanya like a magnet, beckoning to her in the twilight. After days of sitting in the train, the sensuousness of stretching her body between the sheets loomed tantalizingly within reach. She walked over to the bed and looked at Yuri. A languid smile touched her lips as she lowered herself onto the pillows. "Captain Bolganov, your wife is on strike and refuses to rise to her duties!"

Poised on the edge of consciousness, her mind quavered, then sank into limbo between sleep and awareness, her supple limbs cooperating as familiar hands undressed and caressed her, a warm body possessed her, fusing to her briefly, mixing sweetness and warmth and moisture, and lulling her into a dreamlike state of bliss, wrapped in the silken embrace of the man whom she loved and who adored her.

She must have slept late, for when she awoke, human noises were all around her, and Yuri was gone. He had pulled a chair from the table and placed it against the bed to serve as a nightstand, and on it he had left her a note.

"My angel," she read, "I'm off to report to the headquarters and to meet my new commander. It's too early for me to leave yet, so I'm writing this while watching you sleep. I hate to awaken you, for you look so pleased with your dreams: your arms flung in abandon, the chestnut fullness of your hair sprawled so thick it's sinful, your slightly opened mouth pink and soft and warm and oh, so invitingly unguarded! I mustn't yield to my temptation, for then I shall wake you for another reason!

"Rest well, my darling, while I'm gone. I'm anxious to learn what my assignment will be and what sort of a commander I shall get. Much of our future depends on that. I hope he's a strong and fair leader. I'll be back as soon as I can, and if I'm delayed, I'll telephone you."

Tanya kissed the bold writing and, folding the note carefully, put it in her purse. It was cold in the room, and she dressed hurriedly under the covers, where the warmth from her body still lingered. She realized helplessly that she couldn't start the stove: She didn't know how. Wrapping herself in the blanket, she drew her knees under her chin and, hugging her legs, surveyed the room. The night before, she was so happy to be off the train and to have a bed to sleep in, she had paid little attention to the room that was going to be her home. This morning, however, in the cold autumn light that shone into the room, its un-adorned bourgeois furnishings glared back at her like pee-vish gargoyles. In the center of the floor, a round, tapestry-covered table with four straight-back chairs around it dominated the room; a massive dark oak wardrobe and a matching dressing table stood against one wall; a worn Bukhara rug was spread underneath the dining table, and the rest of the room showed wide planks of painted wood. Shabby, it was in sharp contrast to the mansion she had left a few days ago; and although she tried to dwell on the idea that this was her first home with Yuri alone—that the old cliché about a hut becoming a palace when one is in love was true in her case—she couldn't keep a whimper from rising in her throat.

If only she knew how long they would have to stay in Omsk before returning to Samara, perhaps it would be eas-ier to become detached and look upon it as a transient ex-perience. But she couldn't even fantasize. How long would it be? A month? A year? Forever? No; not that. There was no point in speculating when all the guesses would remain just that—guesses. She would have to find something to do to fill her time and keep her mind from courting fear.

What could she do? What particular talents did she have? Her mother had never encouraged her to seek a pro-fession. Then it came to her. Of course! She had always wanted to study accounting. She would start with book-keeping, and be qualified to work at something that had always appealed to her—figures, arithmetic.

When Yuri returned a few hours later, he was exultant. Scooping Tanya into his arms, he whirled her around the room several times and then put her down gently.

"Tanya, I'm so thrilled! For the first time in many months I'm going to be busy. Really busy! I've been assigned to the headquarters here to help straighten out the communications involved in the maze of troop movements. It's temporary, mind you, for eventually I hope to go into the field. Every soldier wants that. But right now I'll be right here, in Omsk with you. Gleb is going to be helping me, so I'm glad for that, too, for I would have felt guilty if I were assigned in the rear and he were sent out to the front." He looked at Tanya sheepishly. "You know how protective I feel about him. He's all alone, and since I've taken him under my wing all these months, I'm glad he'll be with me for a while."

Tanya clapped her hands. "I'm so happy, Yuri. We'll be a little family away from home!"

"Yes, darling." Yuri took her into his arms again. "And I will introduce you to other families here."

"What about your new commander? Does he have a family?"

"No, he's not married, although they say he's thirty years old. His name is Prince Paul Veragin, and he reports directly to Colonel Kappel and even to Admiral Kolchak, and he is a colonel himself. He seems a decent enough fellow, although somewhat reserved. I'm sure we'll get along fine. Now we have to think of finding something to do for you."

"You needn't worry about me, darling. I've already thought of what I can do. I'm going to school here and learn bookkeeping. This will take up my time, and I won't feel the lonely hours without you during the day."

Yuri winced. "Bookkeeping? That's a job for the bourgeoisie. Who put that idea into your pretty head? You don't need to earn a living. I was talking about some volunteer work for you. Lord knows, the local hospitals must be crying for any kind of help you can give them."

Tanya shook her head. "No one put the idea into my head. I've always wanted to have a profession, and I've loved mathematics in school. As a matter of fact, I was going to take accounting in Harbin right after finishing school."

"Harbin is a long way from here, angel." Yuri threw his head back and laughed. "I can't imagine you in the role of a petty clerk bent over some company's ledgers! You belong in the salons of Petrograd or Moscow, my darling, not in some seedy office balancing sheets."

Tanya marveled how easily Yuri switched to calling St. Petersburg Petrograd after it was renamed during the war to its Russian version. But she didn't think his remark was funny. She saw nothing wrong in an honest profession. Without warning, she thought of Kurt. This was one time when they would have been in accord, for Kurt would have thoroughly approved and never have denigrated her choice. They had Harbin in common; and in Harbin, any honest profession, no matter how lowly, was approved and even encouraged. How could she explain this to Yuri? He was a product of a different society, and for the first time Tanya studied him soberly. It hadn't occurred to her that they might have a different set of values.

"I was brought up to believe that a woman who has the means to earn a living doesn't regret it, even if she never has to use her skills. In the meantime, we're a long way from the salons of the capital, Yuri—and there's a chance we may never see it again."

Yuri's dark eyes flashed. "Tanya, you surprise me. I wouldn't want Prince Veragin to hear your words. You sound as if you have already resigned yourself to something we don't permit to enter our minds!"

Tanya shrugged. The first spark of anger within her evaporated. She laughed softly to cover her discomfort. "I'm not a traitor to your cause, Yuri. You know that. I'm simply practical and realistic. Until we conquer the Bolsheviks, there is always that chance we won't get back to the capital. Besides, I hate to see blood and could never volunteer for hospital work."

Yuri sighed. "All right, darling . . . but I have to ask you one favor. Please don't tell anyone you're learning bookkeeping with the idea you may have to work. It's demeaning to me. I'd rather you said you enjoy working with figures and want to add this education for your personal use."

"If that will make you feel better, of course, Yuri."
Tanya paused, then added gently, "But I hope this civil
war will change your mind about the role we women must
play in society."

Yuri grabbed her by the hand and pulled her toward
him. "I know one role I thoroughly approve of," he said,
burying his face in her hair. "My desire for you seems to
be insatiable, darling."

She wriggled out of his arms. "Yuri, please, not now.
There are so many things that have to be attended to im-
mediately." She hesitated and looked around the room.
"For instance, I don't even know how to light the stove.
Will you show me?"

Yuri picked up some kindling and crisscrossed it on top
of several pieces of crumpled newspaper that were already
on the bottom of the stove. Then he placed some logs on
top and lit a match to the newspaper. He closed the tiny
door, leaving a minuscule vent open, and in a few minutes
the warm air brushed Tanya's face and limbered up her
chilled fingers. She smiled and kissed Yuri lightly on the
nose, determined to ignore their difference of a short while
ago.

"Now I can attend to my wifely chores and unpack our
belongings."

CHAPTER 9

Tanya started the bookkeeping courses at a local school that offered a business curriculum and enjoyed the discipline of studying again. Although Yuri had introduced her to several other military couples, she singled out only one woman, a petite blonde, Sophie Pavlova, who lived within three blocks of them. They became friends. Her husband, Alexei, was fighting under the direct command of Colonel Kappel, and Sophie spent much time nursing at the hospital. Frequently, after Tanya finished her classes, she stopped at Sophie's hospital to see if she was ready to go home with her, a brisk twenty-minute walk through the streets of a shivering city.

The winter had settled over Omsk in earnest. Temperatures ranged between twenty and twenty-five below, although up till then not much snow had fallen. Christmas was around the corner, and Tanya had difficulty thinking of it according to the newly adopted Gregorian calendar, which pushed everything two weeks ahead. The clergy called it the "Bolshevik" calendar and refused to give up the Julian style of the Orthodox Church, thus forcing the faithful to celebrate Christmas on the seventh of January.

One afternoon close to New Year's, she skipped going to the hospital to pick up Sophie and went shopping instead.

It was a particularly cold day, and by the time she reached the long business blocks, it had begun to snow, and the wind had started swirling the powder along the road. She went from shop to shop and found nothing to buy. The bookstore was empty, and in the stationery store there were no calendars or paper of any kind and no pens or pencils available at all. She could find no dishes or silverware and finally in desperation bought a tablespoon for fifty rubles. It wasn't even silver.

She felt unreasonably extravagant, but it was to be her present to Yuri, who had been using a wooden spoon to eat his favorite *rassolnik*. She cooked it for him with bits of dill pickle, kidney, and vegetables to make the soup taste both sour and rich, and decided that he should have a decent spoon to eat it with.

Suddenly, she understood why she had frequently seen little children fight over a broken toy; she had thought them poorly disciplined. There were no toy stores anywhere in town. Until today she had been unaware that the private stores were mostly out of consumer goods.

Depressed, she hugged the tiny package to her chest and, passing a cooperative shop offering meat, butter, and cheese, went inside. Here the atmosphere was entirely different. Cheerful peasants were doing lively business next to their offices, where several dozen typewriters clicked busily away.

She had almost exhausted her budget on the spoon, but Tanya bought half a pound of butter for one and a half rubles, which with careful rationing should last them for several days, and walked out of the cooperative store.

Out again on the sidewalk, she was shocked to find the earlier snowfall had become a blizzard. The streets were practically deserted, and those pedestrians who were caught in the storm were plastered against houses and railings like cardboard dolls. She tried walking against the wind, but the snow lashing her face was unbearable; and like the others, she hugged the walls, inching her way forward. A loud clanking noise rent the air above her. Huge store signs, which hung above the doors supported by iron hooks, swung freely in the wind, slamming against the stone walls.

Frightened, Tanya realized that if one of these huge signs fell, it could kill her, and moved out into the street. Her face started to frost, and after trying to wipe her nose and cheeks a few times, she discovered it was warmer to let the ice stay on. When it thickened and blocked her vision, she punched holes to see where she was going. It took her an hour to do an ordinarily twenty-minute walk, and when she finally entered the house, she carefully removed her ice mask and showed it to Yuri.

He examined it, shaking his head, and then threw it in a pan of water by the stove. "I'm glad you're home before your pretty nose got frostbitten. It wouldn't do to go without it to a party."

He kissed her lightly on the tip of her nose and told her that his commanding officer, Prince Veragin, had invited them to a party at the Red Cross Hospital.

"May I have this dance?" Yuri clicked his heels in mock bow and whirled Tanya, her packages and all, around the room.

"Stop, silly. I'll drop the butter and crush it!" she said, laughing, her face on fire from the heat in the room. "We'll have nothing left for dinner."

"To the devil with dinner!"

Yuri's eyes roamed over Tanya's face, as if he wanted to memorize its every line . . . her dewy skin . . . the fan of her thick lashes, which she now lowered under his gaze . . . the muted outline of her soft, unrouged mouth. He pressed her against him, taking the pins out of her hair and entwining his fingers in a cascade of her dark curls. She felt immobilized, helpless, felt her head pulled back, and with a gasp parted her lips. He came down on them hard, crushing her against his body. She circled his neck with her arms, felt herself lifted, carried across the room, enfolded in the outpouring of their youthful love; and, yielding to it, she blocked out the world around them, packages forgotten, the blizzard outside raging and whining in impotent fury.

The Red Cross Hospital was fifteen versts away, and Yuri had to pay fifty rubles for the sleigh ride. It was worth it to Tanya, in spite of her frugal nature which bristled at the price. She had not attended a party in ages, and she prepared for it with care. Dressing for it earlier in her room, she surveyed herself in the wardrobe mirror with satisfaction. The simple lines of the green velvet dress, which she'd brought with her from Samara, fell to her ankles, relieved only by a cream-colored edging of lace at the high neck and cuffs. A wide, matching satin belt circled her slender waist; and her wavy hair, parted in the middle and pulled severely into a knot in the back, framed her face, accentuating her dark eyes and generous mouth.

At the party, while Yuri went in search of Prince Veragin, Tanya was drawn like a magnet to the table with cakes, cookies, and candies laden in such profusion that her mouth watered. It had been a long time since she was afforded a choice of pastries, and she began to sample an assortment of sweets with relish.

It wasn't until she heard her name called that she was able to tear herself away from the food. Turning around to the sound of Yuri's voice, she saw him standing with an erect, powerfully built officer.

"Your Excellency, may I present my wife, Tatiana Andreyevna."

The officer clicked his heels and bent over Tanya's hand.

"Veragin *à votre service,* madame."

So this is Yuri's commander, thought Tanya, studying him curiously. He was very tall and muscular; and, as he straightened to look at her, she thought for a ridiculous moment that the ghost of Alexander the First had reincarnated a hundred years later, for not only did Paul Veragin bear an uncanny resemblance to the Tsar who conquered Napoleon, but he also seemed to possess the same legendary magnetism. His dark blond hair framed a high forehead, accentuating large, piercing eyes. She had never seen eyes so blue or so deep. They seemed to bore through her, and she was shaken by their power. Never before had she reacted like this to a man, and the feeling was not entirely pleasant, for it left her confused and surprised at her emotional response to a total stranger.

She wondered if she was overreacting because this man's order could send Yuri away to the front and shatter her life. It was this fear that made her uncomfortable in his presence, she decided.

"*Enchantée,*" she murmured, moving over to Yuri, and, nodding toward the table, she forced a smile at the prince. "I hope my husband isn't keeping you from all these delicacies, *mon prince,*" she said, glad for the hours she had spent practicing her French with her mother in Harbin.

Prince Veragin laughed. It was a spontaneous laugh, unrestrained and warm, and it transformed his face wondrously. Watching him, she thought that perhaps at some future time she might learn to be at ease with him.

"*Madame est charmante*," he said. "How did you guess I have a weakness for sweets?"

Tanya covered her embarrassment by laughing in return, and was chagrined to see that Yuri hadn't found the exchange between them amusing.

"It was a lucky guess, *mon prince*. For men who work as long hours as you do, a repast is always helpful."

The prince shot a quick glance in Yuri's direction and then bowed slightly to Tanya.

"The subtlety of your rebuke enchants me, Tatiana Andreyevna. Will you join me?"

He offered his arm, and Tanya, a little frightened by her own audacity, only nodded in reply and slipped her arm through his.

They nibbled on cookies and chocolates while Yuri moved away to talk to other officers.

"Are you comfortably situated in Omsk?" asked Prince Veragin. Tanya thought of the rented room she and Yuri shared, of the tiny stove she had to learn to heat, but aloud she said:

"Considering the war, Prince, I guess you'd say we're comfortable."

Prince Paul looked at her with a smile and bowed slightly. "Well said, Tatiana Andreyevna. With so many complaints I hear daily, the country would do well with more women like you."

Embarrassed by the unexpected compliment, Tanya demurred. "When I think of what the wives of the Decembrists had to put up with a hundred years ago, I could hardly complain. I'm lucky to be with my husband."

"It is your husband who's lucky," replied the prince gallantly, and without giving her a chance to respond he smoothly changed the subject.

He passed a tray of pastries to her. "I understand you've lived in Moscow only a short time. Where is your home, then?"

"I'm from Harbin, Prince," Tanya replied. If he was surprised, he showed no sign of it. Putting down the tray, Prince Paul turned to her. Their eyes met, and a spark of amusement twinkled in his.

"Aha! Paris of the Orient! Your flawless French proves it. I would never have guessed you were not a product of our capital."

Unaccountably, Tanya felt irritated. Was he mocking her, or was he sincere? It was difficult to tell what lay hidden behind that clear, noncommittal look, and to her horror she heard herself say: "My mother, Countess Merkulina, was raised in Petrograd, and she believed in passing on the tradition of speaking French at home."

The moment it was out she regretted it. Why should she be explaining herself to this self-assured man, who seemed to intimidate her solely by virtue of his position as Yuri's superior?

When Yuri came back, he gave her a searching look and then stayed with her for the rest of the evening. Rescued from her increasing discomfort, Tanya realized that Prince Veragin had revealed nothing about himself. He had behaved in a courtly manner, with the ease of a born aristocrat, and with enough sincerity to be convincing, but she had not glimpsed anything of the real man beneath that polished exterior.

With the party over, they found themselves together outside, looking for a sleigh to take them all back to town. Most of the drivers wanted an exorbitant eighty rubles for the ride. Then an old peasant staggered toward them and, reeking of vodka, offered to drive them back for fifty. Yuri reeled from the onslaught of the liquor fumes, but Veragin shrugged and chuckled. "Why not, Bolganov? He'll be facing the other way, and the horse will get us home."

This unexpected side to the prince in the face of necessity appealed to Tanya. He's practical, she thought, amused by Yuri's reluctant acquiescence.

Yuri helped her up onto the sleigh; he and Veragin followed her. It soon became apparent that the old peasant was so drunk he could hardly keep his balance behind the horse. Other coachmen, who had cursed him at first for underbidding them, now watched with glee as he swung from side to side on his seat.

"Hey, *ded*—grandpa—you belong on top of the stove in your izba! Where are you taking the noble folk to? The devil himself won't manage you!"

A roar of laughter accompanied the joshing as they started on their way. Everything went fine until they reached the railroad tracks, where the snow had been scraped away from the rails. As the sleigh rung hit the bare rails, it bounced hard, breaking one of the runner supports and holding down the sleigh tightly.

They all got out to inspect the damage and lighten the sleigh. The men pushed it off the tracks, and with this momentum the horse lurched forward and took off riderless down the road, the drunken peasant staring after it in a stupor.

Tanya, overcome by giggles, hid her face in her muff and watched as Yuri, who for some reason had been sulking all evening, grabbed the driver by the collar and shook him vigorously. Prince Paul, however, reacted differently. In a few running strides, he caught up with the sleigh, jumped on it in one leap, and, grabbing the reins, brought the horse under control.

The old drunk whined and shook his head. "I'm too old for this business, *barin*!"

"Not too old, but too drunk!" snapped Yuri.

The peasant sighed and sniffled loudly. "I can take you as far as the last *vyetka* of the train, and then you can get to town yourselves." A slow grin spread blissfully across his face. "You must forgive an old man. A glass of vodka makes my life a shallow sea—no deeper than my knee." He bent down to demonstrate and lurched forward, nearly falling in the process.

Prince Paul smiled good-humoredly and slapped the drunk on the back. "Come on, *ded*, let's get going before we all freeze to death."

It seemed to Tanya that the sleigh cavorted all over the field before it delivered them at the *vyetka*. Yuri was silent, and she sensed that he held his temper under control only because of his commander's presence.

They returned home without incident, and Tanya went to bed exhilarated by the evening, ignoring Yuri's strange silence.

Although she didn't stop to question herself why, all the next day the picture of Prince Paul's splendid figure leaping onto the sleigh kept floating before her mind's eye.

In the evening, when Yuri came home, she started to talk about the party and the sleigh ride adventure, only to check herself at the sight of Yuri's sullen face.

"What is the matter, Yuri? You were angry during the whole party last night and you've been so ever since. Have I done something wrong?"

"You shouldn't have hinted at my long hours, Tanya. Prince Paul is no fool. How else would you know except through my own long days that he works late?"

"He didn't seem to mind. Surely he understood it as a joke."

"Nevertheless, it was presumptuous of you to hint that he was keeping me late. Besides, you spent entirely too long talking to him alone."

Tanya looked at him in surprise. "Why, Yuri, you're jealous of him!"

"I am not!" Yuri flared. "And you needn't be insulting. I admire him tremendously. He's a brilliant strategist and he doesn't spare himself. He's tough but fair, and I'd hate for him to think that . . . that . . ."

"What, Yuri? That you have a nagging wife and that you're under her heel?"

"This is becoming ridiculous, Tanya. I don't see why you have to be so touchy when I correct you."

"You're the one who is making an elephant out of a fly. The prince thought my remark was clever. I think you're unreasonable."

Yuri looked at her with suspicion. "Why are you so defensive? You've only met the man briefly. Does he attract you?"

Tanya, who was stooping to pick up a basket of eggs from the floor, slowly straightened. "That remark was uncalled for. I had no idea you're so jealous. What has happened to you? He's your commanding officer and naturally I'm interested in him. You're not the only one who's under pressure. While you are fighting the civil war, I am not exactly idle either. I had to miss class today in order to wait five hours in line for this loaf of bread." She shook rye bread in the air. "I felt like a criminal who's identified by a number."

Yuri frowned. "What do you mean?"

Tanya sighed, remembering the long hours she had stood in line to get a loaf of bread. In the penetrating cold she had stomped her boots on one spot to keep the circulation going as an official advanced slowly, tracing huge numbers with white chalk on the backs of those waiting in line. When her turn came, she automatically turned her back to the man and felt her coat marred by the harried official. Like a prisoner, she thought at the time. Is it our fault there is no bread and we have to wait in line?

Now she picked up her coat to show the number to Yuri. She knew without looking that it was still there: 179. Yuri paled and, grabbing a moist rag, rubbed it off.

"You see, darling, the official drew numbers on our backs so that there wouldn't be any cheating and fights over getting bread out of turn." She shrugged and added casually, "I suppose I should be thankful I stood only five hours. A woman in line said that at the other end of town people spent the whole night waiting."

Feeling chastised by her patience and ashamed of his jealousy, Yuri kept shaking his head, and Tanya smiled and wondered what Prince Veragin would have said if he knew about the lovers' quarrel he unwittingly had caused.

CHAPTER 10

By September 1919 the situation in Omsk had deteriorated. The British troops, positioned in the city with the Allies, had begun their withdrawal deeper into Siberia. The city had become the refuge of the demoralized soldiers falling back from the onslaught of the Red Army.

Fighting was fierce from village to village. Rebellious peasants who coveted the estates of the gentry and who at first had joined the mutinous Red soldiers, students, and workers, had soon become disillusioned. They flocked to towns with bundles of clothing on their backs, sleeping in the railroad stations, waiting for the trains to take them farther into the interior of the country, away from the growing power of the Bolsheviks. The Soviet regime in Moscow, facing economic chaos, began to requisition food and, with calculated terrorism, recruited poorer peasants to suppress all resistance to the Bolsheviks. As a result, the broken ranks of the retreating White Army were joined by civilian populace of all classes, fleeing from the vengeance of the Red Terror.

What the Bolsheviks hadn't destroyed along their way was ravaged by typhus and hunger. In Omsk, there were shortages of food and fuel, and Tanya began to harbor all the scraps of wood she could find, locking the door to their room whenever she left.

On the streets, people were trading their valuables for food. A silver samovar for a few eggs; an ornate epergne for half a loaf of bread. Whenever Tanya walked along the boardwalks, she looked straight ahead to avoid the temptation to buy something with the food she couldn't afford to spare.

More and more often Yuri came home dispirited, bringing tales of fear, treachery, and confusion.

"Tanyusha," he said one day, "our Supreme Ruler, Admiral Kolchak, can no longer arouse patriotism or even loyalty among his troops. Our headquarters is flooded with alarming intelligence reports. The truth is, Kolchak's front line is disintegrating. Troops, officers, and even some of the generals are defecting to the Reds."

A strange apathy festered in the surrounding country, a reluctance to fight that Yuri could not understand. Tanya listened, refusing to believe the rumors he recounted. The small towns and villages around them had been occupied several times by the Reds and the Whites, and each had pillaged and ravaged the population. There was scarcely a family left where at least one member had not been killed or maimed.

Tanya was incensed by the talk. She couldn't allow her idealistic image of the White Army to be tainted, and blamed the Reds for spreading rumors about the Whites' atrocities in order to justify their own lawlessness.

Yuri tried to reason with her. "Darling, we can't always control our own troops when they unleash their vengeance. If war is bestial, then civil war can bring about an apocalypse."

Slowly her anger disappeared, and she was frightened. "Oh, Yuri, Yuri, what are we going to do? Omsk is doomed, isn't it?" She searched his face for any encouragement, but Yuri avoided her eyes. He freed himself gently from her clinging arms.

"I wish I could tell you what you want to hear, but I can't. Yes, Omsk will fall. It is obvious to everyone except to Admiral Kolchak."

"Then why doesn't someone convince him and let us evacuate before it's too late?"

"Because our Supreme Ruler is a fanatic who refuses to admit defeat. He cannot rally his troops, and with the Allies already gone we don't stand a chance of defending Omsk successfully." Yuri turned to look at Tanya, and for the first time she saw tears in his eyes.

"Everything is lost, Tanyusha. I feel such impotence

when I watch Admiral Kolchak's delusion of eventual victory, and the generals, seeing his paranoia, resort to flattery and lies and find excuses to retreat further east ahead of him. General Kappel is the only one who has the courage to tell him the truth, and although he's now a general, he is falling into disfavor for appealing to the admiral's reason."

"Why is he so blind to the situation? Doesn't he realize he's endangering not only his staff, but their families as well?"

"He's not really blind to the situation on the front, angel. The appalling truth is that he believes his troops possess a miraculous kind of superpower that could be unleashed under the command of a fiery leader, and he feels his generals have turned cowards and betrayed him. He is a dedicated and honorable man who imagines he cannot fail in his preordained destiny to liberate the country from the Red Terror. Therein lies Kolchak's greatest tragedy."

"And we're supposed to perish with him? Oh, Yuri, why don't we flee? We can go to Krasnoyarsk or Irkutsk and wait for Kolchak there—if he ever gets out of here alive. Why should we all be victimized?"

Yuri held her close. "You know we can't do that, darling. It would be desertion, dishonor. No. We have to remain here and obey orders."

"I would rather you be called a deserter than become a dead hero. Besides, if they kill you, what do you think the Bolsheviks will do to me, a White officer's widow?"

Yuri blanched. "Oh, Tanyusha, don't say things like that. There's a solution, and that's for you to leave without me and go as far as possible. To Irkutsk, or even to Vladivostok, where you'll be safe."

"You know I'll never leave you. Whatever fate has in store for us, we'll weather it together. But I do believe in lending a hand to fate. You know the proverb—'Water won't run beneath an immobile stone.' "

"Exactly, darling—and that's why you should leave. You don't want to be trapped like Grandmaman, do you?"

Tanya paled. Ever since a letter came two weeks earlier, smuggled to her through the Bolshevik lines by a refugee, she had trouble sleeping nights. In tight but deceptively cheerful words, the countess wrote them that she was still living in her mansion, occupying the dining room with only the loyal Oksana left to attend her, while the rest of the house was requisitioned by the proletariat officials for offices for the local soviet. At first Tanya cried; but, as Yuri pointed out, at least the countess was alive and not molested, and when the civil war was over, God willing, they could establish communications with her.

The countess went on to say that Praskovya had died shortly after they left, but omitted the cause of her death, which made Tanya wonder if she had been killed defending the countess. Matvei was now an important official with the local soviet, and for that, the countess said, she was grateful.

"This explains her relative safety," Yuri said. "Matvei must have remained loyal and is protecting her."

Now, listening to Yuri's pleas for her to leave, Tanya knew how her grandmother must have felt when she refused to leave with them. She shook her head firmly. "No, Yuri. Don't waste words trying to convince me I should go, because I agree with you. My common sense tells me I wouldn't be as lucky as Grandmaman, for we have no Matvei around here. But my heart is stronger than my head." Her voice broke, but she smiled and added, "You see, darling, what a stubborn girl you've married?"

In the following weeks they didn't talk about it anymore. Tanya's days were full. She stood in food lines, which were growing longer and longer, and walked to the edge of town where she collected wood to heat their room. Although their house was on the outskirts of town, it was still twelve blocks from the open field, and without a wheelbarrow Tanya could bring home only what she could carry in her arms. It was tedious work, and progressively more difficult as other scavengers discovered the same area. She was glad her bookkeeping classes were over and she could now devote all her time to the needs for their survival.

On one of her trips for wood, she ran into a peasant woman pulling a small cart behind her. With a weather-beaten face and a shawl wrapped around her head, she could have passed for an old woman were it not for her eyes. Dark and slightly tilted, they sparkled with energy and frank curiosity. Reluctant to engage in a conversation, Tanya bent over to pick up a few pieces of kindling that someone had dropped, and as she did so, the woman stopped and watched her for a few moments without saying a word. Tanya straightened and stared back, taking in her husky, well-fed body and peasant clothing. Then she saw that the woman's cart was full of beautiful large logs. She closed her eyes, too proud to show the envy she couldn't hide, and when she looked again, the woman was nodding her head in tiny, rapid movements, as if she knew exactly what was going through Tanya's mind. Looking down the road, she jerked the cart, the wheels grinding the dry earth, and moved on.

As the cart went past her, Tanya, on an impulse she couldn't explain later, moved out of the woman's range of vision and, grabbing the top log, walked rapidly in the opposite direction. But not fast enough. The woman saw her and yelled, "Hey, *bourzhuika*, common labor's too hard for you, but stealing isn't below the likes of you? Put it back this minute!"

Mortified, Tanya couldn't bring herself to face her and started running. The woman was agile, however, and in a few strides caught up with Tanya. Wheeling her roughly by the arm, she wrestled the log from Tanya and slapped her hard on the face. Reeling from the impact of the slap, Tanya lost her balance and fell on the hard earth along the road, instinctively cradling her cheek.

"That'll teach you to respect God's people!" the woman shouted. "*Byeloruchka*! White hands! I bet you have no calluses on your hands like all the rest of us labor-loving peasants!"

The woman spat on the ground and stomped back to her load.

In spite of the cold, Tanya's face was on fire. She looked around furtively, hoping no one had seen her degradation. Satisfied that she was alone, she buried her face in her hands. What had possessed her to steal? A distant memory of her indignation at the youth who stole her purse in Samara suddenly rose to accuse her. Now it was she who had crossed the barriers, and, driven by deprivation, she had debased herself before a peasant.

All at once she felt dizzy and faint. Filled with humiliation, she looked about her. The milky sky was speckled with rooks. They soared toward the clouds, vanishing into the mist, only to reappear and chase one another back to earth. The wind hissed, boxing her ears and whispering obscenities she could not even understand. The wind and the birds were the only witnesses to her disgrace. They patrolled the steppes watching her with suspicion.

No one must know, no one must ever find out, she thought fiercely. Not Yuri, not Sophie, not Prince Veragin . . . especially not Paul Veragin! She blushed hotly. That man! She had seen him several times in the last few months, and each time she was disturbed by the encounter. The prince seemed to inspire her with awe and a discomfort she couldn't identify. Was it a coincidence that every time she looked at him she seemed to catch his gaze upon her? It flattered her, and she was ashamed of the thought that in her imagination she fantasized the prince's interest in her where none probably existed.

What would Prince Paul say if he knew of today's incident? Most probably he would give her a withering look of contempt. And Yuri? How would he react to her petty thievery? He loved her, of course, and he would forgive, but she knew she would never tell him.

And what would her friend Sophie say? As another woman, she would probably understand, but Tanya couldn't see herself telling her. Sophie was expecting a baby in February, and whenever Tanya felt sorry for herself, she thought of Sophie and how much greater was her predicament with the added burden of pregnancy.

Tanya began to gather the bits of wood scraps that had scattered around her when she fell. Brushing off her coat, she walked back to town slowly, hoping to regain her composure while she went through the streets of Omsk. Bulging with refugees, it was an overgrown village, windblown from the surrounding steppes, the air dampened by the bordering Irtysh River. The houses where she walked were widely separated. Each had a chicken coop, a stable, and a cow shed in its courtyard—all were empty now, no doubt plundered by marauding bands of deserters. Even Samara, provincial as it seemed after Moscow, looked more like a city than this gloomy, hateful place.

When she came home, Yuri was already waiting for her, and she immediately forgot the humiliating incident as she listened with mounting apprehension to what he had to tell her.

CHAPTER 11

Yuri was pacing the floor, his hands clasped behind him. "As you know, we've been waiting for the river to freeze. This morning we learned that the Irtysh has finally frozen enough for us to cross it. But it's the tenth of November already, so you see, Tanyusha, I have to leave immediately. General Kappel issued orders for us to mass on the banks of the Irtysh with his Second Army. We'll be screening Admiral Kolchak's evacuation, and then I have additional orders from Prince Veragin to move out into the fields and engage the advancing Reds with delaying tactics."

Each word rent the silence in the room. Yuri stopped and looked directly at Tanya. "We can't stop the onslaught of the Reds. We can only delay them."

"But that's suicide!" Tanya cried, her body shaking violently. "Why you? You can't leave me!"

"Why jump to conclusions? Those are my orders, darling. I have to obey them. After that, I'll follow you. Right now you have to leave the city. It's only a matter of days or even hours before they take Omsk. General Janin has already gone ahead to pave the way to Irkutsk for Admiral Kolchak."

"That pompous Frenchman I saw at the parade recently?" Tanya asked, remembering the French commander of the Czech forces. He had stood at attention next to Kolchak as the soldiers trooped by. Tall and handsome, with a neatly trimmed moustache, his military hat heavily encrusted with gold leaf embroidery, he had towered over the slightly built Kolchak.

Whether pompous or merely self-assured, Tanya knew General Maurice Janin was someone to be reckoned with.

He had been chosen by the Czech National Council in Paris to command the Czech troops with the Allies in Russia, in addition to heading his own French military mission. Still, there was something about him she disliked. Could it be that she resented his detached air of authority because he didn't carry the burden of his country's involvement in the deadly combat her countrymen were engaged in?

Yuri's reproving voice aborted her thoughts. "Tanyusha, General Janin is now one of the Allied commanders in Siberia and, as such, is our ally too." After a moment's pause he continued: "You must leave immediately. Take only the bundle you have ready and go with Gleb to the railroad station. Wait there for the train to Krasnoyarsk and from there to Irkutsk. Thank God for Gleb! I'm so thankful he wasn't ordered to the front with me. He'll watch over you."

So this is it, thought Tanya. She had wondered how it would feel when the time came. She had prayed so hard that she and Yuri would never be separated, even though he had often warned her it could happen. But she hadn't expected it to happen so soon.

"Yuri, I'm afraid." She squeezed her hands tightly between her thighs. "I'm so afraid! How are we going to find each other again?"

"I'll be only a few days behind you, darling, and I know you'll be with my regiment. It won't be hard to trace its movements and find out where you are."

Tanya stared at Yuri, his face swimming before her through a flood of tears. "Kolchak! It's all Kolchak's fault. Why did he wait this long? We could have all evacuated together long before this. Now we have to be separated, and you have to face danger. I can't bear the thought of it!"

"Tanya, Omsk is Kolchak's seat of government. He had to wait till the last possible moment before he could agree to give it up."

"What about his generals, who were supposed to command the defense of Omsk? Didn't they advise him to leave long before now?"

"Yes, Tanyusha, they did. General Dietrichs dared to tell the Supreme Ruler that the defense of Omsk was impossible, and what happened? He was promptly replaced by General Sakharov." Yuri shook his head sadly. "It took General Sakharov only a couple of days to realize there'd be no support from the civilian population here. He in turn told the admiral that the defense of Omsk is out of the question. I was in the room when General Sakharov recommended evacuating Omsk and regrouping in Irkutsk."

Yuri laughed a mirthless, dry laugh. "Do you know what Admiral Kolchak answered? I couldn't believe my ears. The Supreme Ruler is out of touch with reality. He said he wanted to control Moscow, not Irkutsk!"

"Is it possible we could lose, Yuri?"

Yuri shook his head and waved his arm. "We'll destroy the Bolsheviks yet, Tanyusha, I promise you that—but not under commanders like Kolchak. Never Kolchak! We need realists, strategists with psychological acumen—someone like Kappel—to lead us to victory." Suddenly he smiled. "Ah, darling! I'd follow General Kappel to the end of the earth!"

Tanya stiffened. He's actually looking forward to this expedition, she thought. He is really thrilled to be going into battle! We're playing games with each other, she realized, as Yuri crossed the room to join her. We both know we may be parting forever, and yet we're pretending it's a short separation, for a few days.

But to say it, to voice it, was a bad omen. She had to pretend she believed Yuri, and maybe, if she wished hard enough, she would be able to cheat fate.

"Yuri, when do you have to go? Tonight? Tomorrow?"

Yuri took her in his arms. "I mean right now, this minute, darling. And you have to leave, too. I can't even stay to see you to the station, but Gleb is due here any moment and he'll help you after I leave."

"There is something else." He held Tanya at arm's length and said quietly, "Tanyusha, on your way to the station go to Sophie Pavlova. Alexei was killed this morning while out on patrol. That's where Gleb is now. You and Gleb are to pick her up after you leave here."

Tanya gasped and clamped her hand over her mouth. Oh, God! Sophie—soft, rounded, delicate Sophie, six months pregnant, now bereaved and in flight like herself.

For a brief moment Tanya clung to Yuri, afraid to linger and prolong the frightful pain of their parting. But in the face of Sophie's sorrow, how could she complain? At least Yuri was still alive, and there was no unborn child to worry about. But Yuri found her lips, and she drank of his mouth with the insatiable hunger of a suckling infant drinking its mother's milk for sustenance. This final kiss, this last physical union in which she tried to cheat the ticking clock, would have to last her through the next few days without him. It *would* be only a few days.

An urgent knock on the door brought Gleb into the room. Tanya smiled at him through her tears. Gentle, sweet Gleb. How glad she was to have him there! She listened to his unhurried, soft-spoken voice telling them that Sophie, although in shock, was packing her things and waiting for them.

Dazed, Tanya moved mechanically, reaching for the neat bundle she had prepared long ago for this emergency; and when she heard the sound of the opening door, the thought that Yuri was leaving refused to register. Instinctively, she moved to follow him, but Gleb put his arm around her waist and held her back. She was grateful to him later when she realized that she couldn't have touched Yuri again without breaking down completely.

Then Yuri was gone, and Gleb released her. "Are there any other things you want to take with you, Tanya?" he asked. "Think quickly, for the sooner we get to the station, the better our chances of getting on the train."

Tanya tried to go to the window to catch a final glimpse of Yuri, but Gleb caught her by the wrist. He held on to her hand, talking rapidly about bundles and coats and felt boots, so that even the sound of the horse's hoofs on the road was muffled by his words. With Gleb urging her to hurry, it was impossible to dwell on the enormity of the moment, and for that too she was later thankful.

"I'll wait while you change your clothes, and then we'll go," said Gleb, turning his back to the glassed-in porch.

It had been decided long before that when the time came to leave, all the officers' wives would give up their batistes, their velvets, and their laces for the coarse clothes they acquired from the local peasants, in order to blend with the rest of the proletariat in the event they ran into Soviet partisans or Red regulars along the way.

Tanya dressed quickly, squirming from the unaccustomed rough fabric against her skin, and pinned to her chemise a carefully sewn pouch with all her jewelry and gold rubles. "Money is not a permanent security, for if the ruble is devalued it can become worthless," her grandmother had said in Samara. "It's your jewelry and gold that will keep you from starving." And so Tanya had weighted herself down with jewelry and coins and extra layers of clothing to keep warm. Under her long black skirt she pulled on *valenki*—high felt boots—and over her sweater she put on the coarse *tulup*—a sheepskin jacket. She then wrapped herself in a huge angora shawl, the way old Praskovya had taught her: First she put it over her head, then she crisscrossed it over her chest, bringing it around the back and knotting the ends in front. When she reentered the room, her girth was several inches broader, and Gleb stared at her open-mouthed. "Tanya," he whispered in awe, "your disguise is superb!"

"This tulup doesn't smell very good. I'll have to get used to it." Tanya wrinkled her nose, and her glance fell on a bottle of French perfume standing by her bed. She had husbanded this luxury—a fragile link with her past—ever since she brought it with her all the way from Samara. Automatically, she reached for it now, but before she could open the crystal top Gleb took it out of her hands and put it back on the table.

"Your disguise would be useless at the first whiff of French perfume."

"I guess I not only have to look like a peasant but also smell like one."

She untied her bundle and checked its contents. One change of clothing with extra woolens, a small bag of salt, a bottle of iodine, a roll of bandages, a few medicines, a pair of shoes, and a bar of carbolic soap. A toothbrush, a comb, a sewing kit, and a few utensils completed the bundle. Tucked between the soft folds of an extra shawl was a small icon of St. Nicholas the Miracle Worker. Unconsciously she touched the baptismal cross that hung on a

gold chain around her neck. Although it was hidden under
her clothing, its hard edges were comforting against her
breast. She crossed herself and sat down on a chair, holding
the bundle on her lap.

Gleb shook his head. "Tanya! We must go!"

"I know. But it's been a custom in our family to sit
down for a moment of silent prayer before a journey. Sit
down, Gleb!"

Gleb obeyed, and for a few seconds of quiet pause the
room crowded upon them, as if the walls, the heavy furniture, the stuffy air itself, urged them not to linger. Then
Tanya rose and crossed herself once more. "Let's go, Gleb.
Now that Yuri is gone, I can't wait to leave this place."

But at the door she turned to look for the last time at the
room that was her home for many months. Yuri's slippers
peeked from under the fringe of the bed cover; a book he
had left unfinished lay on the chair; and high in the corner
the two wedding icons glittered in the shadow. Tanya remembered her grandmother's words: "Keep these icons
with you always." But the icons were too large to carry in
a bundle, and, looking at them now, Tanya was gripped
with foreboding. She sank to her knees and beat the down
comforter with her fists, tears wetting her cheeks as she
rubbed her face against the soft fabric of the cover.

She felt Gleb's gentle hand on her shoulder. "Tanya! My
dear, dear Tanya! How I wish I could let you cry your
anguish out! But we *must* go to Sophie. She's all alone with
her grief. She needs us."

Tanya raised her head and looked at Gleb. Hot shame
flushed her face: Sophie, grieving and alone . . . Waiting
for them. Picking up her bundle, Tanya opened the door.
"Let's go!"

At the foot of the stairs the landlady, buxom and greasy,
stood with her arms propped up at her sides. As Tanya
tried to slip past her, she clucked her tongue. "So! I never
thought I'd see the day when a *bourzhuika* would hide under a peasant's skirt." Her voice oozed sarcasm. "You better get across Siberia while the winter is still here so you
can keep your mittens on. You can't rub calluses on your
palms overnight!"

Tanya stiffened. "We wouldn't have to hide," she snapped back, "if your kind weren't such beasts."

Gleb's protective arm around her shoulders prodded her outside before the woman had time to recover from her surprise. Tanya was mortified; she leaned on Gleb's arm, suddenly ashamed of her cruel statement. But to her the landlady's insolent, shiny face with its rancid odor seemed to embody all the evil of the Bolshevik cause.

Gleb's long, thin face was pale and his voice quiet as he said, "It's as if we have been isolated from life itself; we've never associated before with this kind of people. We're not used to them and don't understand them. And," he added pensively, "I'm afraid it's only the beginning. We'll have to go through a toughening-up process, and I don't mean only physically, but emotionally, too. One thing we must not forget is that their insults are directed against all of the gentry and not at us as individuals."

Tanya moved awkwardly along the street. The valenki, cumbersome on her feet, hampered her normal gait, and although she had put on several pairs of socks, she had the sensation of waddling like a duck.

The streets were mobbed. Two-storey stone buildings and wooden log houses vibrated with life. Their dark entrances and courtyard archways vomited people in rivers of panicked humanity who ran tripping and falling to the frozen ground and scampering out of the way of an occasional droshky.

Holding on to their bundles, Gleb and Tanya zigzagged their way through the running crowds and covered the three blocks to Sophie's rooming house in a few minutes.

When they entered her room, a neighbor was putting a rope around a bundle. The room was a shambles. The bed was unmade and the drawers were pulled open with clothing hanging over the edges. Her eyes red and swollen, Sophie sat at the table, watching dully. Tanya threw her arms around Sophie, and the two young women, dressed in the same peasant clothing, hugged each other for a long moment. Both had been stripped of their identities, deprived of their husbands; and although Yuri was still alive, Tanya grieved with Sophie.

"I can't leave without burying him," Sophie said quietly. "I can't abandon him without a Christian funeral. No grave, no resting place. To know that he is out there in the field being trampled on, pushed and shoved and left for the wolves to feast on—" Her voice rose hysterically. "I can't stand it! I can't stand it!"

She pounded her fists on the table and began to cry. The stern neighbor, a local seamstress who had mended some of Tanya's clothes in the past, threw the bundle onto the chair and ambled toward the door. With her hand on the handle, she hesitated, then turned to look at Sophie. "There is no such thing as *can't* in our language, only *won't*. He's not alone out there in the field. Other wives have lost their husbands, too. Better pray for his soul, and the body will be taken care of."

Sophie looked bewildered. "I don't know how to live alone. What can I do? Where shall I go?"

Tanya hugged her again. "You are not alone, Sophie. You have me and Gleb—and later, Yuri. Come on now— we must go."

Sophie pushed Tanya away. "Don't touch me! I'm going to be sick." She bent her head, holding her stomach. The seamstress opened the door. "Wait a minute! I'll bring her some camomile tea to settle her stomach."

Tanya looked at her gratefully and stroked Sophie's head. As Gleb picked up Sophie's bundle, the seamstress returned with a steaming glass of yellow tea. Sophie took a few sips, then rose from her chair and, steadying herself, started for the door. With a last glance at the room, she looked at the seamstress, who remained standing by the table, her hands folded on her stomach, and said: "Thank you, Anisya!" Sophie's voice shook. "I know you mean well, but for me it would be best to die."

"Don't anger God!" Anisya shook her finger at Sophie and pointed to her swollen abdomen. "What about the child you're carrying inside your belly? Or have you forgotten that?"

Sophie started to say something, then shook her head and walked out.

* * *

At the station, the chaos was worse than they had anticipated. Women, children, the aged, and the wounded filled
every nook of the waiting room. They lounged and slept in
awkward positions, heads propped up by their bundles,
women screaming and fighting over each minuscule space
on the floor. Nerves raw; tempers flared from the slightest
spark; and wherever they moved, the three friends had to
elbow their way through the mass of unyielding flesh.

Working his way through the crowds to check on the
next available train, Gleb managed to buy food from the
vendors outside and bring it to the jealously guarded corner
where Tanya and Sophie spread their belongings to husband an extra few inches for him.

They waited for four days, and on the fourteenth of
November they learned that the next available train was
due to leave in a few hours. They fought their way onto the
platform, hoping to get as close to the tracks as possible.
After being immobilized inside the unventilated station,
where human breath and body odors befouled her lungs,
Tanya drank deeply of the frosty November air, and suddenly vertigo spun the platform around her. She grabbed at
a nearby post to steady herself and leaned against a billboard. In a few moments she straightened, and the board
came into focus. It was covered with pinned, handwritten
scraps of paper. Thinking that there might be a train movement announcement, she started to read: ". . . Misha,
we're leaving on train No. 411, November 4. I'll wait in
Krasnoyarsk. L . . ." "Vanya, I'm taking the children on
train No. 513 to our village. Will wait for you there. O . . ."

There were dozens of them. All told the same story of
separation, flight, hope. Impulsively, Tanya tore off a
scrap from one of the larger notes. Then she hesitated.
What could she say? She didn't know the number of the
train they would get on, or its final destination. But she
could tell Yuri the day she was leaving, and perhaps later,
if she had the chance to learn about the train's route, she
could return to add additional information.

She had heard rumors that all the leaders were already
gone. Kolchak had left that morning, and with him went
his cabinet in seven trains, one of which carried gold bullion, the total reserve of the White government treasury.

No doubt Prince Paul had left, too, she thought bitterly. With the government evacuating, there was no reason for his headquarters to remain behind. The leaders had managed to escape in comfort, while the rest of them had to struggle and fend for themselves.

She scribbled a few words to Yuri. Then, as she reached up to pin the note to the board, a man's gloved hand pulled the note away. Startled, Tanya turned to look at the intruder and found herself staring into the pale, set face of Prince Paul.

CHAPTER 12

Although he had been conditioned to the cold, Yuri's lungs were burning with each intake of air as he crouched behind the gun emplacements. This is how it must feel when the bayonets cut your flesh, he thought, looking around at the other men. Numb from the freezing cold, exhausted, their faces grim and eyes glazed with despair, they waited. Yuri shuddered. The certainty of defeat, and the possibility of annihilation, crawled like vermin through his flesh.

He clenched his fists. What had happened to his enthusiasm, his drive for victory, the challenge of an expedition he had dreamed about, yearned for? Maybe he had waited too long, hungered too long. He felt cheated. He knew that now even the legendary aura of General Kappel's leadership couldn't arouse his meager troops. Inert and limp, they had already surrendered in spirit and would only fire their guns like robots.

Hazed by low fog, the sun, like a shiny steel plate, hung low over the earth. Earlier, when they had crossed the frozen river, it had glinted in the setting sun in macabre glee over delivering the men into the open gates of death. The hush persisted, and only an occasional slapping of arms to shake out the cold bruised the fragile calm of the fields. Too weary to move, the men had no stomach for banter.

The waiting was the worst of all. Like the fine tuning of a string instrument, Yuri's nerves grew taut, his muscles tightened, and impatience swelled to bursting.

Where were the Reds? Yuri strained, listening.

Nothing.

Now the twilight around him had deepened to dusk, blurring the terrain's outlines with its hillocks and gullies, shrouding the men in a protective cocoon. Small puffs of snow began to cling to Yuri's face; and, as he brushed off the icy flakes, a distant rumbling infringed upon the silence.

Even before he saw the rolling numbers of the Reds, he knew that to open fire, to fight the sweeping armies of the Bolsheviks, was suicidal. But orders were explicit: Engage the enemy, delay the advance. Somewhere behind him Tanya waited for the train. Every passing hour, every snuffed-out life around him, would widen the distance between her and danger.

So he gave the order to fire, and there was no turning back. The enemy was yet far away, but the frosted, windless air became rent by sparks and skeins of blue-white light arching into the black void. High-pitched whining sounds whistled past Yuri's ear, and soon all around him the cacophony of machine-gun fire and explosions was punctuated by shrieks of pain from the wounded and the dying.

"Help! Help! *Bratiki*, help me!"

Yuri turned in the direction of the cry and was hit in the face by a large flying object which dropped to his feet. As he stepped over it, he saw a booted leg roll down the slope. A soldier moaned nearby and Yuri knelt beside him. He was hardly old enough to be in uniform, or to fight another Russian for a cause he possibly didn't even understand. The boy's abdomen was torn open. Crazed by the sight, the boy shrieked, "I don't want to die! Don't let me die!"

Gently, Yuri lifted the boy's shoulders and cradled his head in his arm. Eyes stinging with tears, he prayed for the boy to die. Through all his time at the German front, he had never become used to the horror of mutilations, could never watch the agony of painful death without feeling guilty for being whole himself. But now this was the worst of all. The dying soldier shuddered, his eyes glazed, and with a thin wail of "Ma-a-ama!" his rigid body went limp in Yuri's arms.

Unashamedly, Yuri wept: for the boy he didn't know; for the enemy who had killed him and who spoke the same language and who was possibly from the same village; for a world turned upside down.

He lowered the dead boy's head carefully to the slope, where the ground shook and spewed geysers of dirt and rock in the air. Seeking cover, he turned toward the gully.

He didn't feel the impact that knocked him to the ground. He tried to rise, but his knees refused to lift him. As he clawed at the stubby, crusty earth beneath him, a shaft of searing fire shot through his hip. He screamed in agony and dropped back to the ground. He raised his head and saw a blinding yellow ball explode above his head with a deafening eruption. In its center Tanya's weeping face flashed at him, and he opened his mouth to scream her name.

There was no time.

He was flung into this brilliance and torn apart in mid-air, raining down with the shrapnel, mud, and bits of iron, back to the crusty earth waiting to receive him.

In his office at Omsk headquarters, Prince Paul Veragin waited. After Admiral Kolchak and his cabinet had left, he lingered behind for further scraps of news from General Kappel's forces screening the retreat on the west side of the Irtysh River.

Although he was entitled to join Admiral Kolchak's train, he had chosen to remain. Paul looked out the window. A bleak vista of slate gray sky and somber buildings stared back at him, as if the naked, gloomy landscape were nagging at his conscience.

Unbidden came thoughts of Tatiana Andreyevna, Yuri's wife. "Tanya," he whispered, and jumped at the rustling sound of his own voice. He had never known a woman like her, and he couldn't even say she was the most beautiful woman he had ever met. She was refreshingly different from other wives in his regiment, who complained about their living conditions and whined over the loss of their comforts. Tanya was spirited, honest, adaptable.

He knew he had no desire for a light flirtation with her, yet all these months he hadn't been able to get her out of his mind. He'd fought the feeling within him, but like a flowering plant it had blossomed. A year ago he would have laughed if anyone had told him he would become emotionally involved with a married woman. He'd been sure he was too intelligent to let this happen. But it had happened. How and when he couldn't tell, or even what it was that he felt for her. Whatever his feelings, they were strong enough to rob him of trust in his own judgment; to fill him with doubt and confusion.

The evacuation well underway, Paul was alone now. Even his faithful orderly, Ilya, who had been with him on all the campaigns, had fled that morning after Paul had called him into his office and had given him the choice of remaining by his side or leaving with the echelon. Avoiding Paul's direct gaze, Ilya shifted from one foot to the other and remained silent. Paul walked over to a little side table and poured two glasses of vodka from a crystal carafe. Turning, he handed one to the soldier.

"Let's drink together for old times' sake, Ilya."

Shaken by the unaccustomed familiarity from his superior, the orderly took the glass into his trembling hand and bowed deeply to the prince. Then, holding the glass in his left hand, he crossed himself broadly and downed the vodka in one gulp. Smacking his lips, he wiped them with his sleeve and put down the glass.

"Thank you, Your Excellency. God bless you! I'd like to stay by your side, but pity my six children if they become orphans. Who'll feed them, Excellency? The wife is illiterate—so what can she do? I beg your forgiveness."

Ilya bowed deeply again.

"There's nothing to forgive, Ilya. I understand. You have served me well and faithfully, and I don't blame you for wanting to evacuate. Go with God!"

Paul opened his arms and the two men embraced, kissing each other three times on both cheeks.

A tear trickled down Ilya's cheek and vanished into his thick beard as he backed toward the door. "Excellency, trust in God, but do not dally yourself. Allow me to speak boldly. It isn't the first time you've sent the troops out to fight. Your presence here isn't going to help them. Why aren't you evacuating?" His eyes slid sideways; without waiting for a reply, he shuffled out of the room.

Uneasy, Paul downed another glass of vodka. What had Ilya meant? "Why aren't you evacuating?" he had asked.

Why, indeed! Paul wished he knew the answer. He thought of the men he had sent to battle with the Reds. Did Yuri have something to do with his unease? He hadn't been able to get Bolganov out of his mind since he'd sent him out into the field. Yuri would have been the natural choice even if Paul hadn't known him personally. Besides his excellent record, he was one of the most experienced officers on his staff. Yes, Yuri had been the obvious one to go. Then why the doubt? Why was he waiting and hoping to hear that they had engaged the enemy with minimal losses and were making an orderly retreat after four days of fighting? Paul swore to himself, knowing his hope was unrealistic and that by lingering behind he was jeopardizing his own life.

Had he sent Yuri away in the secret hope he wouldn't return? Of course not! How could he think for one moment that he was capable of such betrayal? His mind was overwrought, playing tricks with his imagination. Even the suspicion was unworthy of his character. His upbringing in a military cadet school since early adolescence was based on honor and duty to his country, and his personal life was subjugated to these high ideals.

His childhood family life, such as it was—he sighed at the thought—had revolved around a daily routine with tutors, and his contact with his parents had been limited to short, awkward visits.

His mother had died when he was eight. He remembered her as a sickly, coughing woman who reclined on a chaise longue in her boudoir, holding a lace handkerchief at her mouth, caressing Paul from a distance with her limpid eyes. He was never allowed to kiss her and was shooed rapidly out of her room and into his father's presence. With his hands behind his back, the older Prince Veragin questioned Paul about his lessons and then dismissed him hurriedly into the care of his tutors, precluding any nurturing of sentiment or affection. When he died of a heart attack, leaving Paul at the age of twenty an heir to a vast estate, his death evoked no deep regrets in his son. As the last living Prince Veragin, he felt only a greater sense of responsibility to his country for the noble name he carried.

And now he was doubting his own motives. He hit the desk with his fist. He had made the right choice. He would have been derelict in his duties had he allowed personal feelings to enter into his decisions. Yuri will come back alive, and if he doesn't, I can't go through life blaming myself for his death. He sat down at his desk, burying his head in his hands. This was ridiculous. Men were dying out there in the field, and here he was, caught in a personal conflict.

He looked up, realizing suddenly how long he'd been sitting there. It was time to leave. He crossed the room to call for his aide and nearly collided with him at the door. Without a word, the aide handed him the dispatch, then stood waiting, nervously clenching his hands.

Paul scanned the paper. The message was brief. General Kappel had succeeded in his evasive action and was now retreating east after delaying the enemy on the banks of the Irtysh. So far only a few of the dead had been identified.

Yuri Bolganov's name headed the list.

Paul crumpled the paper in his fist, the letters dancing before his eyes. His jaw tightened, and he felt a vein throb in his temple. The Reds must be entering the city by now. There was no time to lose, no time for self-recrimination. If Tanya was still waiting at the railroad station, he must help her get aboard. This much at least he could do for her.

Grabbing his hat and coat, Paul rushed out of the office, and, jumping on his horse, spurred it forward. Sleds and horses blocked the roads, and there were people everywhere—on the streets, on the boardwalks, running out of gates, climbing over fences. Priests in their billowing robes, long-bearded Jews in tattered black coats, Tatars in their pantaloons and sashes, deserters in sundry uniforms, women and children—all zigzagged and stumbled over frozen and stripped bodies of old people and starved children lying on the sidewalks.

A disheveled woman in a long mud-caked skirt ran alongside Paul's horse shouting, "Colonel, help me, do something! They took my last horse!" She was shoved aside by the frantic crowd before Paul could answer. A well-dressed man with a karakul hat and collar sneered at Paul: "Still playing soldier, eh, Colonel?" and a wiry teen-ager whistled derisively from behind a large bush. Only the drunk and belligerent Bolshevik sympathizers stayed in the taverns, flaunting their debauchery, in grotesque contrast to the panic around them. At the sound of rapid shooting, Paul reined in his horse long enough to see a soldier inside the tavern, its door torn off and hanging lopsided on one hinge, shoot at the portrait of the Tsar on the wall.

Along the street every fence seemed to have a large placard proclaiming that General Sakharov had made Omsk an impregnable fortress that could never fall. There was something incongruous in those bold words screaming their message at everyone and no one stopping to read it. But Paul noticed. And having noticed, he seethed, because General Sakharov himself was already gone, and so was his successor, General Kappel.

When, half an hour later, Paul reached the station, he had to fight his way through the thick crowd to get to the door of the waiting room. He was about to go in when he turned to look at the train slowing to a stop. Familiar features swam into his range of vision, and, although her disguise was good, Paul recognized Tanya at once. He saw the note she was pinning to the billboard, and a deep ache spread through his chest. He had sent Yuri to his death, and now he had to face Bolganov's widow and say the words that would destroy her world. Painfully, he knew he couldn't let her pin that note addressed to a dead man. In a few steps he was beside her, taking the paper from her hand.

For a long moment she stared at the note, and when he took her hand in both of his, she stiffened. Slowly she raised her head to look at him, and their eyes met. Her face turned ashen, and Paul knew he wouldn't have to voice the dreaded words after all.

Anger flared in her eyes for a second, and then the light went out of them. In a flat, listless voice she said, "You sent him out there. It's all over, isn't it?"

The words hurt, but not as much as the hopelessness in her voice. He wanted desperately to be alone with her, to explain, justify himself to her, and he cursed the revolution, the hate and madness that had turned them into fugitives, their lives forever scarred by fratricide.

CHAPTER 13

Tanya had no time to grieve, for the freight train pulled into the station and the shouting, swearing crowd converged on the cars in chaos. Thrust into the sea of hostile strangers, all driven by a primeval instinct for survival, Tanya found herself separated from Gleb and Veragin and carried away on a human wave. She fought her way toward a boxcar, using her elbows to protect Sophie and to keep from being crushed in the melee. Then, out of this bedlam of fighting bodies, Prince Paul's face floated into focus and she stretched her arm toward him, but before she could reach him a heavy boot came down on her valenki, crushing her toes. Blindly, she drove her knee in the direction of the weight and swung her bundle high above her head. An arm reached out and tugged at it. Slipping easily out of her mittened hand, the bundle fell into the arms of a round-faced peasant woman. Enraged, Tanya pulled the mitten off her right hand and, stretching her arm until she thought her shoulder would tear from its socket, reached for the woman's face, digging into its leathery skin with her nails. The woman screeched and swung at Tanya with the bundle, hitting her in the face. Stunned by the blow, Tanya nevertheless grabbed at the bundle and held on to it with both arms.

"You scratching bitch!" yelled the woman, as the momentum of shoving bodies carried her away.

Prince Paul reappeared near her, and she heard herself scream, "Paul! Paul! Help me!"

She felt herself lifted and carried by the crushing bodies to one of the boxcars. Veragin pushed her inside, then lifted Sophie after her, and it was he who slid the door

shut. Only later did she realize that she had called him by
his first name, omitting his title and patronymic, establish-
ing a familiarity with the man she had blamed for sending
her husband into battle.

The first jolt of the moving train threw her against the
siding, and she slid to the floor. With nowhere else to run,
the pursuit no longer imminent, she slumped and gave in to
a flow of tears.

The train rolled out of the station, picking up speed,
heading east through the vast expanse of the Siberian
steppe which lay on either side, farther and farther from
Omsk. Ticking off the time: minutes . . . hours . . .
How many? Tanya couldn't tell. She sat on the floor
against the wall, huddled beneath her shawl. Although she
still sighed spasmodically, the rhythmic clacking of the
train had a hypnotic effect, and tears no longer ran down
her cheeks.

Through the crack in the door she looked at the blinding
whiteness sparkling in the sun like a myriad of diamond
chips. Every once in a while, charred villages rose out of it
like spectral sentinels guarding the dead. Beyond them the
virgin snow stretched, meeting the sky at all points of her
vision. Tanya wanted to stop the clock and live this moment without remembering the past or fearing the future,
to pretend she was a mindless fleck softly burying itself
into the white oblivion.

She looked around as someone groaned behind her. For
a moment she had almost forgotten that she was not alone,
that Yuri's fellow officers, their wives and new widows
like herself, were in the car with her. Even Sophie's presence didn't make it any easier. Everyone was nursing his
own tragedy, and she was left alone with her grief.

Most of the women sat huddled together on a piece of
torn canvas in the far corner of the car. Some of the men
were asleep; others stared into space without moving. Any
moment she expected to see Yuri among them. She felt
numb; even now it was impossible to accept his death.

She shifted her position, her back stiff and sore from
leaning against the hard siding. In spite of the shawl and
the tulup's padding, her slim shoulder, meager of flesh,

took the brunt of her weight, and she winced in pain. Someone moved near her and sighed deeply, exuding the fetid breath of an empty stomach. Her own churned from hunger. How she yearned to sleep without dreams, without nightmares—to sink into a slumber where grief and torment could not reach her!

Her gaze wandered over the other women. Sophie was nearby. With her arms clasped over her rounded abdomen, the corners of her mouth turned down in the fixed position of an abused child, she looked bewildered and tense. Tanya reached over and touched her shoulder. "Are you comfortable this way, Sophie?"

"No," whispered Sophie with an effort. "My legs are hurting."

"Move closer to me and put your feet on my legs. Then they won't fill so much with fluid."

Sophie moved, and Tanya put her arm around her. How alike they all looked in their tulups! All distinction disappeared behind the wool kerchiefs tied under their chins, the drab jackets, the felt valenki on their feet, and the shawls that some of them wore around their shoulders. She wondered if hostile peasants would spot their smooth skin and make them turn their hands palms up—a trick the Red Army soldiers used to expose disguised women of gentry. If their hands had no calluses, they'd be taken to the local commissar. She winced, remembering the stories she'd heard of what happened to the women when their disguises were discovered.

To relieve the stiffness in her legs, she changed position again and brushed against a leather boot. She looked up. Prince Paul stood above her. His eyes, tired and hooded, stared into space; his usually neat appearance was untidy, the tunic of his uniform torn and muddy, and Tanya guessed that it must have been difficult for this man, who had never permitted his subordinates to see him less than perfectly groomed, to scramble aboard the boxcar along with the other frantic members of his command.

Yet she wasn't sorry for him. He had sent her husband to his death. Not deliberately; she knew that. Prince Paul couldn't have wished for Yuri's death. But indirectly he was responsible for it. The thought obsessed her, for memories were not so easily dismissed; they forced themselves upon her, half dreams, half reality. Was God punishing her for her childish, unfounded fantasies about Prince Paul? Surely she had never encouraged him, nor ever once had given him reason to believe there was anything but respect on her part. Unexpectedly, she felt a stab of self-reproach. It had been Paul Veragin, after all, who had helped her get aboard the train. Prince Paul who had pushed his way to her; Prince Paul who had protected her and Sophie from the blows of others; Paul who had helped them inside the boxcar. To her horror she fought a sudden impulse to cling to him, to feel his strong arms encircle her. She needed comfort, for Yuri was dead. *Dead!* The word had no meaning to her, no depth.

Who was she now? Where was she going? And who was there left in her world? Grandmaman far behind, maybe lost to her forever; and ahead, far away—loneliness, strangers, unfriendly land. Beyond that, over the border, were a few familiar names and a home that was hers. "The door to the past will always be open, Tanya," Kurt had said. But that was beyond her reach now. In the end she was alone in the world, and alone in the train boxcar.

For hours the train rolled on, with only a few brief stops for water and fuel. Thank God there were no children in the car with them. Most of the women were young like herself, and only Sophie was pregnant. She wondered if Gleb was able to get on the same train, and she was glad Sophie was with her—it took the edge off her loneliness. She worried about Sophie going into premature labor on the train and prayed her friend would not lose the baby.

We're all animals huddled here together, she thought, looking at the tattered cloth partition hanging at one end of the boxcar. It had been hung over a rope to give some semblance of privacy to the men and women when they had to use the corner as a privy. One of the officers had torn out a plank in the floor to improve the sanitation problem. Still, the women agonized the first few hours when they had to use the primitive facility. By the second day, however, modesty was gone.

Screeching brakes jolted Tanya, tensing her body. The train was coming to a stop. Through the crack in the sliding door she could see the name of the village: Udachnoye. "The lucky one," the name meant, and she wondered what luck it might bring them. The platform was strangely quiet, without the usual hustle and bustle of most railroad stations. The deserted tracks were caked with ice, and no one was waiting to board the train.

Suddenly she stiffened as a group of silent peasants, standing at one end of the station, came within the periphery of her narrow vision. They were watching a detachment of Red Army soldiers lead three White Army officers toward the end of the platform.

"Everyone be quiet," Paul whispered. "We mustn't be discovered, or this will turn into a massacre."

Tanya looked at him, aware of his nearness. In spite of her fear, she couldn't help wondering what kind of a man he would turn out to be if he were to trade places with those officers on the platform.

The train began to move out of the station, sluggishly picking up speed. The timing had saved them, for the soldiers were busy with their three prisoners and paid no attention to the freight train passing by. For the moment they were safe. But how many more close calls would they encounter before reaching true safety? Where was it? How far would they have to go before they were safe? Better not think about it. Only the present, this moment, was important, this enormous, almost physical relief from danger.

Keeping her face pressed against the crack in the door, Tanya watched as the train slid past the station's building and the rest of the deserted platform. Several rusted sidings unraveled like a ribbon alongside their boxcar, an empty train with a few open platform cars parked on one of them. Several of the flatcars were piled high with cordwood neatly roped and covered with a thick layer of snow. Chilled inside the inadequately heated boxcar, Tanya looked as the logs, exposed to the elements, neared her. Her nose, flattened against the door, was numb from the wind, but she couldn't turn away and motioned for Sophie to look. "See that wood?" Tanya whispered. "Wish we had it here!"

Some of the snow slipped from the roped stacks, and suddenly the words stuck in Tanya's throat as the logs she coveted turned out to be frozen corpses. Sickened, she stared and stared at the expanding steppe and its protective winter clothing, which hid the scars of war and man's atrocities to man.

Hours, days, rolled into one another, nights replacing days and dawn washing the darkness out again. She had lost count of time since they had left Omsk, for their train was delayed more and more frequently along the over-loaded single down-line track east. The overworked rail-road men labored long hours fighting the Siberian winter. They used pitch fires to thaw locked switches, and each time the train started from the station, the sandbox inside the locomotive scattered sand under the wheels. The engine fireboxes had to be kept burning to prevent the pipes from freezing.

Sometimes they had to wait a long time for fuel, and these delays were terrifying. The up line was reserved for priority traffic and had been seized by the Czechs, who refused passage to refugee echelons. The threat of the Bol-sheviks catching up with them was real, for they listened with mounting apprehension to accounts of the Reds cap-turing stalled trains and either slaughtering the refugees or throwing them out to freeze in the snow. Waiting at the railroad stations, sleeping on the floor, accepting the food that Paul always managed to get for them, had become a way of survival.

They were on the road for six weeks when Gleb ap-peared in the crowd and fought his way over to them, cheering Tanya by his presence. Now they were together again, and he even managed to make the women laugh. At one of the stops he bought a small can of kerosene from a brakeman and insisted that Tanya and Sophie smear their necks, wrists, and ankles with it for protection against lice. When they were through, in spite of a strong smell and burning skin, Tanya felt good. She was cared for, thought of, by a friend who had also been Yuri's friend. There was a little kerosene left in the tin, and, impulsively, she of-fered it to Paul. After all, he looked after her, too, even though he kept himself at a distance and hardly ever spoke to her or Sophie. Tanya wondered if the real man beneath that strong exterior was afraid to remove his mask of authority and risk exposure.

Through a fog of weariness, she heard him tell someone that their only safety lay beyond Lake Baikal. Baikal! She stirred. Beautiful Lake Baikal, eulogized as a mystical sea in song and ballad, would soon stretch before them.

Fatigue gone, she listened intently to every word Paul said as he discussed various possibilities ahead. Krasnoyarsk was next on the line. There they would join General Kappel's forces and go on, first to Nizhne-Udinsk five hundred versts to the southeast, and then an equal distance farther to Irkutsk. After that, unless they could circle Lake Baikal on its south side through the forty railway tunnels, it would stand in their way as a formidable obstacle, for with the Reds to the north they would be forced to cross the frozen lake on foot.

Weary again, Tanya shook her head. That was in the future, and she mustn't think beyond today. They had already gone thirteen hundred versts from Omsk, and with Irkutsk another thousand versts from Krasnoyarsk, it meant they had traveled more than halfway.

Resting against the sliding door, she drifted into sleep, blissfully unaware that the commander at Krasnoyarsk, General Zinevich, had gone over to the Reds and the town was already in Bolshevik hands.

CHAPTER 14

A jolt brought Tanya upright, instantly awake. Her heart pounded. Why had they stopped this time? She peered through the gathering darkness, barely able to discern the moving shapes of her fellow passengers.

Somewhere a voice whispered, "Where are we?"

The door slid open, a gray square with Paul silhouetted against it. "We're near Krasnoyarsk."

Stiff, crouching shapes gave no immediate response, until a stranger's harsh voice shouted from outside:

"Get out! The train has reached its final stop. Hurry!"

Tanya climbed down behind the others and clutched her bundle to her chest. They stood close together, a small island of frightened men and women in a sea of moving humanity. Soldiers and civilians laden with bundles tumbled out of other boxcars, running in all directions. A small boy stood crying, looking up at the strange faces that pushed past him. A peasant woman, her scarf askew over one eye, nearly knocked Tanya to the ground as she dashed past her toward the child, crying above the rumble of the crowd: "Mishka, Mishka, here I am!"

The air, frosty and sharp, scraped Tanya's lungs like a prong of a pitchfork. Paul fought his way to the station office while Tanya, Sophie, and the others waited outside. In a few minutes he returned, his face somber.

"The Bolsheviks have taken Krasnoyarsk. Remnants of General Kappel's army are assembling from all sides." His voice was tense. "There seems to be no leadership, no organized regiment, not even a small company left to fight. Everyone is on his own."

An officer shouldered his way to Paul through the crowd. "How did they take Krasnoyarsk so fast?"

Paul looked away. "They didn't have to. They were welcomed in. General Zinevich went over to the Reds."

The enormity of the news hung in the air like the sword
of Damocles. No one spoke. Tanya and Sophie stood hugging each other, both frightened and shivering.

"The stationmaster told me," Paul went on, "of some
peasants on the outskirts of the village here who might be
willing to give us space for the night in their izbas, but we
must hurry before others get there first." He waved his
arm. "Follow me!"

Tanya looked around for Gleb, but in the darkness and
confusion he was nowhere to be seen. She pulled Sophie by
the arm. "Come on, Sophie, let's go! We can't wait for
Gleb. He'll find us tomorrow in the daylight."

In spite of her fear, Tanya felt excitement rising within
her. She was strangely happy, if only to be out of the boxcar, which had been both her haven and her prison these
past weeks. She remembered that as a child she had often
gone with her nanny into a peasant home when they visited
Russian villages along the western branch of the railroad in
Manchuria. Inside, there was always a wooden table in the
center of the room, and benches used as beds along the
walls, but what had dominated the izba was a huge ma-
sonry stove that looked more like a fireplace than a stove,
its oven at eye level and a ledge on the top wide enough to
be used as a bed. Because of its warmth and comfort, it
was always reserved for the senior member of the family.

Now, half running to keep up with Paul, she smiled. Although it was possible that she was going to sleep in an
izba, the stove, she was sure, would be reserved for someone else.

In the village the beamed izbas, built of century-old cedar logs, lined the dirty, snow-packed roads. Although
there were fewer fences here, this village, thousands of
miles from her home, wasn't much different from the Russian villages she'd visited in Manchuria. There were people
everywhere—soldiers, officers on horseback, peasants pulling loaded carts, sleighs being readied for the journey
ahead.

From the naked branches of a nearby oak, rooks fluffed
their feathers in the dropping temperature of the dusk and

surveyed the human travail with detachment. The falling
snow clung to the fur-lined caps of men and the woolen
shawls of scurrying women; it frosted the manes of snorting horses, hid the dirt, clouded the outlines of man and
beast.

At the edge of the village, Paul stopped and turned to
face the small group behind him. Deep lines of strain
edged the corners of his mouth and weariness dulled his
eyes as his glance wandered over Tanya and Sophie. For
the first time Tanya became concerned for him. She
shouldn't be blaming him for her tragedy, shouldn't think
him responsible for Yuri's death. He was doing his best for
them now, and she had no right to resent him.

"I must tell you that there are no more trains between
here and Nizhne-Udinsk." Paul's voice was hoarse. "We
have to make it the rest of the way by sleigh and on horseback. If you can't bribe the villagers along the way into
giving you what you need, then use other means of getting
it."

Why, Tanya thought in astonishment, he's telling us to
steal! This was incredible. Her life as the wife of an officer
in a gallant world, impeccable in its honesty, idealistic in
its principles, was now far away. Thievery, once practiced
by the underprivileged, now belonged to the gentry. The
old standards no longer applied. When life itself was at
stake, and stealing made a difference between survival and
death, the crime was justified.

Tanya thought of the log she had tried to steal from the
peasant woman in Omsk. Was that so different? A shiver
rippled down her back. She would have to learn to dispense
with the old principles. At least she and Sophie had no
need to steal extra clothing. Their valenki were relatively
new, and their tulups, though stained, kept them warm.
She had plenty of underclothes, and in her bundle she carried Yuri's fur-lined cap with ear flaps. Although she
hadn't worn it yet, because she was afraid she would break
down, she knew that eventually she would need the cap.

Paul touched her arm and, slipping his other hand under
Sophie's elbow, led them toward the nearest izba. For the
first time since Yuri's death she didn't mind this contact.

Exhausted, cold, she leaned against his arm, grateful for his warmth.

As if he had risen from the ground below, Gleb appeared before them. Tanya rushed at him and threw her arms around his neck. "Oh, Gleb, I'm so glad to see you!"

She stepped back, her eyes widening at the sight of a black eye. "What happened, Gleb?"

His face colored. "Someone tried to steal my bundle while I was asleep and I had to fight to get it back." He took her hand and raised it automatically to his lips. Tanya smiled. Disguised as they all were, the parlor gallantry among the gentry remained intact.

Turning to Paul, Gleb saluted. "Your Excellency, Lieutenant Penkov at your service. What are your orders?"

Paul looked him over, his eyes cool and thoughtful. "The best assistance you can give me, Lieutenant, is to spend the night in another izba. Who knows how many Bolsheviks and Red sympathizers there are among the peasants. If you hear anything I should know, inform me at once. Take Madame Pavlova with you. We'll have a better chance of getting a place in an izba in smaller groups." Then, as he turned to Sophie, his voice softened. "Sophie, Lieutenant Penkov will look after you."

Gleb glanced at Tanya and started to say something, but Paul interrupted. "You're dismissed, Lieutenant."

Clicking his heels, Gleb saluted and gave Tanya a brief bow before leading Sophie away.

Tanya was choking with anger. "Paul, why couldn't Gleb and Sophie stay with us in the same izba? I'm sure we could have found room for them. I wanted so much to have a friend with me."

She had blurted out the words without thinking. A half-smile touched Paul's lips. "I'm trying to be your friend, Tanya. Lieutenant Penkov will prove to be of much more use to us if he overhears important information in another izba than by keeping you company here. Besides, I'm convinced we're much more likely to get a place inside an already crowded izba if there are only two of us."

She knew her petulance was childish. He was right. He was always right, damn him! But he admitted to wanting to be her friend, and a glimmer of emotion had broken through his aristocratic aloofness, had cracked the reserve he had maintained since Yuri's death, and it brought out a restiveness within her she did not welcome.

Inside the izba, Paul went over to talk to the owner. The air was stifling. The windows were sealed for the winter, and the moisture, the odor of sweat, human breath, the sour smell of melted frost dripping from the dirty tulups, had nowhere to escape. Soldiers, officers, and peasants crowded the room. Some were asleep on the benches along the walls; others sat on the floor leaning against one another and dozed.

Two soldiers sat cross-legged on the floor, carefully dividing a pinch of loose shag. After rolling it into bits of paper, one of them lit a match to it and with half-closed eyes inhaled the smoke slowly. The other soldier pulled off his muddy valenki and wiggled his feet. Strips of foot cloth, wrapped up to his knees and secured with a long string, were stained with mud, and small patches of blood had seeped through the heels.

"Hey, Pyetka," the first soldier said, "the heels are worn out, eh?"

The other soldier shrugged wearily. "On the march they get numb in the cold. They'll heal with time."

Tanya winced and glanced toward the top of the stove. There, on the warm ledge, lay an ancient crone, like Baba Yaga—the witch of the Russian fairy tales—covered by a tattered shawl.

Tanya leaned against the frame of the door, feeling dizzy and ill at the thought of spending the night in the room packed with strangers, being squeezed once more among bodies whose clothes, she was sure, were infested with lice. She had become used to the smell of kerosene on her body and hoped it would keep the vermin away, for the spotted fever, typhus—the scourge that followed war like a shadow—was never far away.

A young woman, the front of her tulup unbuttoned, nursed a red-faced toddler at her uncovered breast. Tanya averted her eyes and looked closer at the sleeping people. One soldier's head lolled on his shoulder, and with each snoring breath a thin trickle of saliva glistened on his beard. A fat woman slept curled up on the floor, her head tilted impossibly at right angles against the buttocks of a man who squatted with his head low between his knees. Tanya sighed. There was something indecent in the postures of sleep stripped of privacy, awkward and vulnerable.

She glanced at the old woman high on the stove just as the *babushka* slowly raised her head. Peering at Tanya, she smacked her lips and cackled with a toothless mouth. Then her stretched lips disappeared below a hooked nose. She shook a knotted finger at Tanya.

"So, my *byeloruchka*, you'd like to trade places with me, wouldn't you? Times have changed, *barinka*. At last I've lived long enough to have you envy *me* for a change. Heh, heh!"

The old woman's face crinkled like cracked parchment. Under her scrutiny, Tanya felt naked. If an old Baba Yaga had seen through her disguise so easily, then she could only hope never to come face to face with the Reds.

At a square wooden table in the middle of the room, two peasant women shared *ukha*, spooning the fish soup noisily from a large bowl. Tanya's mouth watered. Her only food in the last two days had been dry pancakes made of flour and water. The younger of the two women rose, poured a small bowl full of hot soup, broke off a chunk of black bread, and, sprinkling it with salt, offered the food to Tanya.

Their eyes met and held for a moment before Tanya's vision blurred. "Thank you," she whispered, taking the *ukha* and the bread. As she swallowed a spoonful of the soup, it came to her that her favorite beluga caviar had never tasted as good as this simple peasant food.

Paul beckoned to her. He had spread his greatcoat on the floor and made a place for her near the wall. The space was small, and she squeezed herself tightly between him and the peasant woman with the child. Tanya shared her food with Paul, who took it without protest. Watching him eat, she couldn't help wondering if Gleb and Sophie were as lucky in the next izba. After finishing the *ukha*, Paul leaned against the wall. Neither of them spoke. If he was aware of the closeness of their bodies, he gave no sign of it. In the crowded room there were no familiar faces, and Tanya suspected that Paul had to bribe the izba's

owner into letting them spend the night in the already
packed room.

She felt safe in his presence, yet she couldn't bring herself to thank him; and as weariness overcame her, she
struggled against the pull to lean her head against his
shoulder.

A large candle dripped wax onto the table, its flame
throwing an elongated shadow on the wall—darting, jumping, like an angered goblin flushed out of his warren. High
in one corner a vigil light in a red glass container illuminated the icon, bathing the dark wall with its reddish glow.
The woman next to her began to nurse her child again.
Tanya watched, her thoughts turning to her nanny, long
dead in Harbin, and then to her grandmother. Where was
she now? Was she still alive, and how was she going to find
out? And when? She bit her lip, damming the tears, as
voices, real and imaginary, whispered in her ear, taunting,
mocking, threatening.

Uncomfortable in her cramped space on the floor, she
couldn't squelch a sudden fear that grew inside her. The
worst was yet to come. The crossing of the frozen Lake
Baikal loomed ahead, and there was no turning back. They
had no choice. If they stayed behind, an ugly death at the
hands of the Bolsheviks was a certainty. With youth,
health, and faith, with men like General Kappel—and
Paul—to lead them, surely they would survive the crossing.
So why wouldn't the nagging doubt go away?

What sort of a man was General Kappel? His troops
adored him, although he was reputed to be a tough commander. He was known to drive himself beyond the limits
of normal endurance. Was he an understanding human
being as well as a courageous officer? Would he make al-
lowances for the difference in stamina between a seasoned
soldier and an untrained civilian?

Tanya slipped deeper into the folds of her tulup to hide
her tremor and glanced up at Paul. Slowly, he raised his
arm and circled her shoulders. She looked into his eyes,
their clear blue now slightly darkened, and read something
in them that hadn't been there before: a message so elusive
she couldn't put it into words. Then he was smiling, his
eyes twinkling at her.

"I don't bite, Tanya. We both need rest, and this way we can economize on space and help each other be more comfortable."

She leaned her head against his chest. *I should be grateful. Why do I fear him? He's treated me well, like a friend. So why do I keep feeling uncomfortable with him? Do I still blame him for Yuri's death?*

Now the tears began to flow, and she did not hide them. Although she sniffled like a child, no one paid any attention to her, as if it were the most natural thing in the world for a grown woman to sit on the floor and weep.

She felt Paul's hand on her head. He stroked her hair gently and let her cry. It was the first time since Yuri's death that she had been physically comforted and cradled by a man. When his lips softly touched her damp forehead, she didn't move away, and she fought the urge to lift her face to him as well.

Glancing at the icon in the right corner of the room, she made the sign of the cross and snuggled closer to Paul.

Dawn would come with greater hope.

CHAPTER 15

At the junction of the mighty Yenisei River and its tributary, Kan, some fifty miles northeast of Krasnoyarsk, nestled the remote village of Podporozhnaya. The name meant "beneath the rapids," and its inhabitants had learned a long time ago to have a healthy respect for the treacherous currents of the Kan.

Nevertheless, after learning of General Zinevich's betrayal, General Kappel decided to skirt Krasnoyarsk and go north to Podporozhnaya, from where he could pick up the trail southeast along the River Kan. He told his troops they were free to leave his army if they wished and go over to General Zinevich in Krasnoyarsk. His own chief of staff, General Bogoslovsky, chose to surrender and was subsequently shot by the Reds.

The remaining troops followed Kappel blindly, obeyed his orders implicitly, believed in him with a faith bordering on adulation. It seemed that his was the power to inspire and hold them together, and they sensed it instinctively, believing their lives to be otherwise forfeit.

Paul felt no such adulation for Kappel. He was a regular army officer, not a member of Kappel's volunteer army, and his loyalty was more to the cause than to the man. He was aware of General Kappel's aura of authority, which was sustained less by conviction in the ultimate victory than by his fanatical sense of loyalty to his troops and implacable determination to take them to safety and remain with them to the end.

The general's pale gray eyes reflected a quality of power that Paul had never encountered before, and in spite of his cool appraisal of the man, he found it difficult not to fall under his spell.

In Podporozhnaya, Kappel gathered the tattered remnants of his forces, and the civilians who had chosen to
place their trust in him, to begin the march toward Nizhne-
Udinsk.

On the eighth of January, 1920, the village was the
scene of total confusion. An atmosphere of urgency pulsated in the air, an apprehension that time was running
out, that each delay could prove disastrous. The refugees,
driven by the threat of a Bolshevik ambush, fought viciously over coveted spaces on the sleighs, leaving scores of
injured or dead. Paul and Gleb used their fists to keep
intruders away from Tanya and Sophie's sled.

After a restless night in the crowded izba near Krasnoyarsk, they had reached Podporozhnaya that day and joined
General Kappel's regrouped echelons. Anxious to ride at
the head of the column with General Kappel and his deputy, Colonel Vyrypaev, Paul turned to Gleb: "Lieutenant!
Ride alongside Tatiana Andreyevna's sled." Gleb gave him
a measured look, as if wondering what his interest was in
Tanya. Paul, his temper already testy, gave Gleb another
curt and unnecessary command to take his position and
then, annoyed with himself, spurred his horse forward.

A blurred image of the warm izba passed through his
mind; he could have sworn he smelled the polyglot odors of
the stuffy room with its sour sweat, the boiled fish, the
smoking embers in the stove, and felt Tanya snuggling in
his arms, her moist, smooth forehead under his lips. He
had heard of soldiers hallucinating on a long march, but
this was a real scene from the immediate past, and he
ached when he remembered the feel of her soft body pushing against his chest in search of solace.

As he followed General Kappel, his horse started a steep
descent, cautiously picking its way to the river. Paul
tensed. He had been warned by the villagers in Podporozhnaya about the mortal danger of the Riven Kan. Somewhere near the shore's precipices, hot springs defied the
winter and, hidden beneath the shroud of snow, rushed
their waters over the frozen river. Woe to the traveler un-
lucky enough to step into such a place, for he would sink
through the soft layer into the invisible water below, and a
few steps later his soaked feet would become encased in

blocks of ice. Horses would tear their hoofs, sleighs would be soldered to the surface, and nature would claim yet another victim.

Jagged cliffs hung on either side of the Kan, looming above them as they came down on the river and started toward the next village of Barga, fifty miles from Podporozhnaya. Chilled by the hostile scene, the brooding menace surrounding him, Paul crossed himself and turned around. Tanya's sleigh was close behind. He felt a sudden resentment toward her. Why was she so much in his thoughts when he should be concentrating on doing his military duty? But, for whatever reason, Tanya had become an embodiment of his sense of duty. Even his country's glory and the hope of restoring its noble past had dimmed before his obsession to see Tanya through this ordeal.

"Prince Veragin!"

General Kappel's ringing voice startled Paul. He spurred his horse and came abreast of the general. It was a wondrous metamorphosis to see the steely eyes sparkle with humor and warmth as Kappel smiled at Paul and patted his shoulder.

"Keep us company, Prince. We all look like grouchy bears dragged out of their lairs. I wish we could strike up a marching song, but I'm afraid we'd be swallowing icicles instead."

General Kappel brushed the frost off his eyebrows and looked at his deputy. "What do you say, Vyrypaev—should we dismount and give our horses a break for a while?"

Colonel Vyrypaev nodded. "As you say, Your Excellency."

The three men dismounted and started pulling their horses by their bridles. Kappel looked back at the black ribbon of shuffling people.

"Come on, *rebyata*! Why hang your noses?" he cried, using the homey colloquialism. "We can't give up now! The going isn't too bad. Sorry I can't provide sleigh bells for you, but we have a surplus of snowballs. I'll sell you some for cheap!"

A few cautious ripples of laughter greeted his words. Paul marveled. No wonder the soldiers idolized him. They had even christened themselves *Kappelevtsi*—belonging to him. In the foggy, forty-below-zero temperature they marched, mixing day and night, bribing hunger with a handful of flour or a piece of frozen raw meat. With their frostbitten, blackened faces, worn valenki, and mismatched coats, they truly looked like sluggish bears aroused out of hibernation.

Paul walked abreast of the general and Colonel Vyrypaev. Around them towered walls of snow-covered cliffs, dwarfing and squeezing them into an icy embrace. They plodded on, unaware of the hours they put behind them, conscious only of the gloom and the foreboding that hung in the air.

"How far do you think we've gone?" Paul finally asked, feeling the cold air pour down his throat like liquid ice. Even his stomach seemed lined with frost.

Vyrypaev shook his head. "I'm not sure, but I think about twenty versts. That leaves seventy more to Barga."

"If all goes well, we should be there in a couple of days, an—" General Kappel didn't finish his sentence, and when Paul turned to look at him he was no longer there. For an infinitesimal fraction of a second Paul found himself looking at Vyrypaev instead, before both men saw the general waist deep in the snow.

When they had pulled him out, he said apologetically, as if an explanation were imperative: "My *burki* seem to have become heavy."

Vyrypaev urged him to remove his *burki* and ride a sleigh, but General Kappel refused adamantly. Their eyes met. After a second General Kappel shrugged. "I'm neither the first nor the last. It is too bad, but I'll manage. *Aidà!* Forward!"

Before long, his gait grew stiff and unnatural, and he moved his legs as if he were walking on stilts. Soon he handed the bridle to the soldier behind him and concentrated on forcing his legs forward, one after the other . . . one after the other.

Paul's heart sank. Unobtrusively he glanced at the general's leather-trimmed felt boots. They were frosted; his feet were literally entombed in ice. Paul was watching a man in agony, yet he was powerless to help him, for he knew that astride a horse Kappel's legs would be without any circulation at all. General Kappel stared ahead, no longer talking, his eyes glazed, indifferent to what went on around him, intent on one superhuman effort—how to move the frozen stumps that once had been his feet.

Time had lost all meaning to Paul as he waited for General Kappel to collapse. He looked at Colonel Vyrypaev, and the two men's eyes locked. There was denial and anger in the colonel's glance, and as they stared at each other, their valiant leader fell forward, unconscious. Simultaneously, they reached for him, but before they could lift him, General Kappel came around. "Get me my horse, Vyrypaev," he whispered, leaning on the colonel's arm.

The three of them mounted, and Paul watched as the general's iron will began to bend under the physical weight of pain. When at last he slumped forward over the horse's mane, several men rushed forward and helped Paul and Vyrypaev take him off the horse and place him in a sleigh.

Fate, however, had ruled otherwise. At the next brief stop, the sleigh, too, sank through to the water below and froze instantly. Strong arms lifted the unconscious general back onto the horse, and a burly giant of a soldier rode by his side, supporting him around the waist.

As if there wasn't enough of it already, fresh snow fell heavily upon them, and every soldier falling from exhaustion soon became yet another mound neatly blended into the landscape.

Shortly before reaching Barga, they left the riverbed and stopped to place General Kappel in another sleigh. As Paul dismounted, he saw Tanya struggling to get out of her sleigh. His nerves on edge from exhaustion, he shouted: "Tanya, stay in your sleigh!" and watched her face, pained and obedient, crumple beneath her shawl.

Foolish girl—if she had left the sleigh, she would never have regained her place, and there were still several versts to Barga. Out of the corner of his eye he watched Gleb lean over and say something to her. Good. Maybe she will listen to *him*. Did she take to Gleb simply because he was Yuri's friend, or was there something more? Well, he would see her through to safety and then rid himself of this malady, this feverish attachment to the woman whom, in his fantasy, he had wronged. His mind must be wandering.

He grasped the bridle tightly, peering ahead. Thank God, the outlines of Barga loomed in the distance.

They carried the general into a warm, spacious izba, wiping their feet on the folded burlap sack at the door, shuffling, stumbling, handling their unconscious leader with a tenderness remarkable in the toughened, gruff soldiers. Safe from the lethal frost, Paul and Vyrypaev cut his frozen boots with a butcher knife, cracking the shell of ice cautiously to avoid injuring his legs, then pulled the boots off his feet. From the knees down his legs were white and wooden. Several eager hands helped to rub them with snow, and soon the calves began to regain color. The feet, however, stayed rigid.

No one spoke in the face of the ominous sight; everyone waited for orders.

"Go find a doctor!"

Colonel Vyrypaev's voice rang with urgency. Several men rushed out.

They found a doctor among the troops and brought him into the izba. He examined the general's feet and shook his head. "The heels and some of the toes should be amputated immediately."

Colonel Vyrypaev stepped forward. "Is there an alternative?"

"No. Either an amputation or gangrene."

Vyrypaev paled, hesitated a moment, then nodded. "Go ahead, doctor."

The surgeon spread his hands. "All my instruments have been lost along the way. What am I going to use?"

He looked around the room and spotted the butcher knife on the table. Picking it up, he looked at it for a few moments indecisively. "I'll do what I can," he muttered, then began issuing orders.

"Get me alcohol, hot water, and a couple of assistants. Open the stove!"

He placed the knife into the fire. Alcohol appeared on the table, and the wife of the izba's owner rolled up her sleeves.

"What else do you need?" she asked briskly. The doctor

picked up the bottle of alcohol and poured some of it over the knife.

"We have the bandages, but we'll need some clean towels. And I need another assistant." He looked around the crowded room, and his glance fell on Tanya's pale face near the door. "You! Come here and help!"

Before Tanya could make a step, Gleb's arm blocked her way. "Doctor, you'll have to find someone else. This woman is exhausted and may faint on you."

Gleb's words irritated Paul. Tanya needed toughening, not overprotection from the violence of life. Besides, she was under *his* protection, and he resented Gleb's interference.

"Tatiana Andreyevna!" Paul's voice rang with authority in the quiet izba. "Please do as you're told. You are needed, and I know you'll do your part in helping the doctor." He turned to Gleb. The young man was ashen. "We're all exhausted, Lieutenant, but in an emergency we can always call upon our reserves." His words were measured and deliberate. Gleb started to say something, but Paul's icy gaze silenced him.

He looked at Tanya. She was already on her knees, her tulup thrown on the floor, sleeves up to her elbows, arranging comfort for the unconscious general with the practiced assistance of the peasant woman. Paul pursed his lips and told himself he was right. His instinct hadn't failed him when he judged Tanya to be made of tougher stuff than appeared on the surface of that delicate cameo face. He smiled faintly. He had a hunch she would come through this all right.

She must be seething at him right now, but he couldn't help that. He had to do what needed to be done, and if his actions increased her resentment, he had to ignore it. It was important that she take responsibility for herself as soon as possible. That's why he'd kept Gleb away from her in the last izba, left her alone in the sleigh today, making sure she had not been aware that he was always within earshot, ready to step in if she needed him. He had ordered her to stay in her sleigh when she obviously wanted to help, and now, when Gleb would have spared her from an experience that would be rough even on stronger stomachs, he had interfered, knowing that the more she was exposed to life in the raw, the greater her chances of survival.

His face tightened as he looked at the three people working over the general. Thank God he's unconscious, he thought. There probably wasn't enough vodka in the neighborhood to numb General Kappel's senses enough for him to endure the agony of amputation.

Someone removed the folded greatcoat from under Kappel's shoulders and laid him flat on the bed. The doctor shouted: "Put it back, damn it! And add another coat for good measure! The less circulation he gets to his head, the better off he'll be. We don't want him coming around now."

Tension hung in the room like an axe. Seasoned soldiers, their faces wet with tears, stood at a respectful distance and watched as the surgeon amputated the general's toes and heels. Tanya, who held the bucket underneath the general's feet, blanched, but continued to hold it steadily as the doctor dabbed the wounds with alcohol and then bandaged the feet.

None of the women in the izba fainted or became hysterical. In the face of the real threat of death hovering over everyone, what's a few frozen toes? Paul thought grimly. He had been holding the doorknob in his hand, refusing entrance to anyone; and as he surveyed the room, his glance fell on Sophie, pale and catatonic, reclining on the bench along the wall. He walked over and took her hand. It was clammy and limp.

"Courage, Sophie!"

He wanted to add more, but words would have sounded hollow to this young woman who not only was recently widowed but was also carrying her dead husband's child. What could he say to her? How was she going to endure the rest of the way to Irkutsk?

Sophie looked at him with her large, round eyes, and there was such dullness, such emptiness in them that he was overcome with pity. He raised her hand to his lips and kissed it gently. "Sophie, can I do anything for you?"

She didn't answer. Her breathing was labored and noisy,

and Paul, concerned, bent over her. "Do you need anything?"

He barely heard her whisper, "Sleep. . . ."

Folding his greatcoat, he lifted her feet and helped her to lie down. Then he turned to look at Tanya. She was bending over the general, wiping his sweaty face with a towel, pushing his damp hair off his forehead, tucking the blanket in around him. Paul leaned against the door and watched her through half-closed eyes. He was right about her. She was resilient, strong. There was nothing timid in her movements as she went about her nursing chores, dictated by instinct rather than training.

They stayed in Barga the next day, and when General Kappel regained consciousness, he recognized the surgeon. "Doctor, why the hellish pain in my feet?" he asked. He absorbed the reply calmly, and in a few minutes he dismissed the news with a shrug. Paul walked over.

"Your Excellency, is there anything I can do to make you more comfortable?"

General Kappel studied him for a while and then, ignoring the question, began issuing orders for his staff. When a large, comfortable sleigh was procured for him from a wealthy Barga fur dealer, he refused to use it and ordered a horse instead. With his legs wrapped in blankets, they lifted him into his saddle. Gritting his teeth in pain, he saluted his troops, his hand steady at the edge of his tall

Between Barga and Nizhne-Udinsk, they moved along

papakha, the Caucasian sheepskin hat he favored.

the highway; and the relief of having left the River Kan was so great that Paul felt safe not to check on Tanya and Sophie for hours at a time. They rested along the way in villages, carrying General Kappel in and out of izbas, for he no longer was able to walk. The doctor was concerned over his feet, unaware of the feverish delirium that periodically assailed the general. Paul listened with alarm to the paroxysmal attacks of coughing that left the general weak and trembling, though still able to direct the troop movements.

Shortly before they reached Nizhne-Udinsk, Paul said to Vyrypaev: "Colonel, this can't go on. The General is killing himself. We must do something to persuade him to give up command."

Vyrypaev only looked at Paul dejectedly and nodded. "Easier said than done, Prince. We'll do our best, but our general has a mind of his own!"

Finally, after they had reached Nizhne-Udinsk, the general recognized his ebbing strength and appointed General Voitzekhovsky to replace him.

Temporarily relieved from the Bolshevik pursuit, the army rested. The remainder of the way to Irkutsk and Admiral Kolchak's headquarters would be along the railroad tracks occupied by the Allies, mostly Czech and Romanian forces. They would be friendly—or so Paul thought.

CHAPTER 16

For the first time since leaving Omsk, Paul was able to go to the barber and get a good shave and a haircut. Although it cost him five hundred and fifty rubles, he was so delighted that the Omsk currency he was carrying still circulated, he didn't mind the outrageous price.

Refreshed, he returned to the railroad station, where several Czech trains were parked. The platform was mobbed by refugees, who eyed the cars with envy. The Czechs stood guard, their guns at the ready to discourage anyone who might try to board the trains without authorization. Each side watched the other with suspicion and antagonism. Paul's regiment was housed nearby; he headed in that direction when he saw Tanya walking arm in arm with Gleb. The sight of the two friends together suddenly irritated Paul. There was no mistaking the warmth with which Tanya spoke to Gleb. Why should it bother me? Paul thought. Surely I'm not trying to compete with the young lieutenant. It's ridiculous and undignified. All I'm trying to do is to protect her, and that's something I'm in a better position to do than he is.

He watched covertly as Tanya, her cheeks scarlet from the nippy air, her eyes dark and wide, listened intently to Gleb. Could it be that the sight of the Czech echelons created a false atmosphere of safety for her and revived her natural optimism? Or was there something else? He would have given much to see that animation directed at him.

He looked at the train, and as he looked, an idea began to germinate in his mind. Was it possible that he could arrange for Tanya and Sophie to go on the Czech train? Would it be safe—two women alone with the troops? Of course, they wouldn't be unprotected. There were officers aboard, officers of the Allies. They wouldn't dare permit debauchery, especially if he convinced them that Tanya was someone important.

He had reached her now. He returned Gleb's salute and looked at Tanya. "There's going to be another tough march between here and Irkutsk." He paused and glanced briefly at Gleb. "And then there's Baikal. We don't know what's waiting for us there."

He squinted and nodded toward a Czech officer who was leaning against the train door, smoking a cigarette.

"Come with me, Tanya. I'm going to try to get you and Sophie aboard that Czech echelon."

Tanya hesitated. "It may prove impossible for both of us to be taken aboard. Sophie is pregnant. If they will take only one of us, she should be the one. It'll be easier to get her aboard when the Czechs see that she's expecting."

Paul shrugged. "The war hardens people, Tanya. It'll take more than Sophie's condition to soften the Czechs and make an exception to their rule. You know they have strict orders not to take any refugees aboard. But maybe—" Paul broke off and looked at Gleb. "Lieutenant Penkov, bring Madame Pavlova here." Gleb saluted and walked off to carry out his order.

As they walked toward the Czech officer, Paul lowered his voice. "Tanya, show no surprise at anything I say. Agree with everything."

Tanya nodded, glancing at him curiously. Paul saluted the officer. "Prince Veragin, with General Kappel's army."

Lazily, the Czech officer returned the salute. "Captain Marcek of the Czech forces under General Janin. How is General Kappel?"

"No improvement. He's feverish and can no longer walk. General Voitzekhovsky has taken over his command."

The Czech shook his head. "We've offered repeatedly to take him aboard, even extended our invitation to his aides, but he refuses to leave his army. Too bad. We have great admiration for the general and would have liked to be of assistance to him."

"He wants to remain with his troops and share their fate."

Captain Marcek shrugged his shoulders. "He's not much good to his soldiers if he's too ill to lead them. A dead hero is less effective than a live one, even if he's removed from direct contact with his army."

Irked by the remark, Paul clenched his fists. Impudent son of a bitch. What could a well-fed foreigner riding in a warm passenger car possibly know about the hardships they had just endured? How could this Czech understand that the only cohesive force that held the White Russian troops together was their beloved leader's physical presence among them? Controlling his anger with an effort, Paul changed the subject.

"Captain, this is my sister, Princess Veragina. She has just recovered from pneumonia, and I'd be much obliged if you made an exception and allowed her and her companion a passage on your train."

"I'm sorry, Prince. My orders are strict. If we make one exception, we'll have a riot on our hands. We'll be stampeded." The captain bowed stiffly to Tanya, his eyes cold and disinterested. "I'm sorry, Princess. Perhaps the Prince, your brother, could purchase a separate sleigh in town. I understand there are some still available at a price."

Paul stiffened. This was the first time in his life he had asked a favor from a lower-ranking officer and been refused. In Tanya's presence the humiliation was especially rankling.

"This is most unfortunate, Captain," Paul bluffed. "When General Janin last dined in my parents' home, he repeated his offer to be of any assistance to my family. It is regrettable that I'll have to report to him when I see him that the first time I attempted to avail myself of his generous offer, I was turned down by one of his officers."

At the mention of General Janin's name, the Czech flushed and came to attention. For a few seconds he studied Paul's face, and Paul, aided by his anger, stared back boldly. The Czech's glance wavered. "This changes everything, Prince. General Janin's wishes, of course, would supersede any other orders." He turned to Tanya and clicked his heels stiffly. "Allow me to help you aboard, Princess."

Sophie and Gleb approached. Turning to her friend,

Tanya took Sophie by her arm and smiled at Captain Marcek beguilingly. As Paul watched in fascination, she fell easily into her role and spoke as one used to command.

"*Merci,* Captain . . . and of course my friend and companion, Madame Pavlova, will come with me."

Captain Marcek hesitated only a moment, then bowed and motioned the women to the train. At the top of the steps, Tanya paused and looked back. Paul nodded encouragingly.

"I'll see you in Irkutsk!" she called uncertainly.

The two men saluted. The relief was so enormous that for the first time in many weeks Paul felt like laughing. "Penkov, I'd love to see Captain Marcek's face if he ever discovers that I duped him. I wonder when the train will leave? The sooner the better."

Gleb peered toward the locomotive. "It looks as if they're preparing to leave right now."

"Let's get out of the captain's sight before he changes his mind and tells us to take the ladies off the train."

They turned and hurried toward the end of the platform, rounding the storage barracks and heading for the street. Large burlap sacks filled with goods and tied securely with heavy ropes lay on the frozen ground against the wall of the storehouse. Paul stopped. "Penkov, since these are left outside unguarded, they're fair game for us. We can't be too scrupulous when our soldiers are starving. Let's take a look inside these sacks, and be careful how you untie them. If it's flour, we don't want to lose one precious spoonful."

Paul pulled out a knife from his belt holster and cut the rope, while Gleb knelt and held the ends of the sack to prevent anything from spilling out. Replacing his knife, Paul stooped and, grabbing the other edge of the sack, pulled it open. A silky strand of what looked like blond flax fell out. Disappointed, Paul frowned. "Why would they store corn? There's such a shortage of flour and sugar and salt!"

The younger man's face turned ashen. "This is not flax, sir. It's a woman's hair."

Gleb rose from his knee and turned away, holding his stomach. Paul knelt and peered into the sack. "The bastards!" he swore. "She was alive when stuffed into that sack. I wonder who she is?"

He glanced at the other sacks and suddenly felt sickened. "God!"

"Better don't look. It's not a pretty sight."

The voice came from behind them, and Paul wheeled around. The bearded, tousled stationmaster stood before them. Teeth clenched, Paul asked, "Who did it?"

The stationmaster wiped an icicle from the tip of his nose with his sleeve.

"The Czechoslovaki," he said, enunciating every syllable.

Paul was shocked. "The Czechs? Are you sure?"

"I know what I'm talking about. I saw them."

"Saw whom?"

"I saw the Czechs throw the sacks out."

"Then why didn't you pull the women out? They were still alive when they were stuffed in these sacks!"

The stationmaster shook his head. "No. By the time I saw them, they were all frozen. When the Czechs were piling them up here I thought it was grain. I looked inside after they had left. The women were all dead."

"Who are these women?"

The stationmaster spat into the snow. "They deserved to die."

"Nobody deserves to die like this. Who were they?"

"They were all holders of the yellow card. Women of easy virtue always look for a quick escape and they sold themselves to the Czechs."

"Then why did the Czechs kill them?"

The stationmaster shrugged. "Who knows? Maybe they were bored with them or got tired of feeding them. Or maybe—" A long train whistle drowned the man's last words. Startled, Paul looked toward the platform. The train was pulling out of the station, its wheels grating, whining with each sluggish turn.

Paul and Gleb looked at each other, and for a brief moment their eyes locked. Tanya and Sophie were on that train alone with the Czechs. Pregnant Sophie and beautiful, desirable Tanya.

"Penkov! Return to your regiment!"

Barking his order at Gleb, Paul shoved the stationmaster aside and sprinted forward, oblivious to his bundle which he had left behind, swallowing gulps of dagger-sharp air, intent only on reaching the train.

It was gathering speed. The last car, with its rusted railing chugging along the platform, wobbled a few yards away.

As he pounded down the track, the irony was almost unbearable. He had wanted comfort for Tanya, protection from the elements of nature, but he'd forgotten the treachery of man. Danger lurked inside that train, and he had led her into it. If anything happened to her it would be his fault, a direct result of his actions. Oh, God, he couldn't live with that.

He *had* to catch that train.

CHAPTER 17

It wasn't until the train started moving that Tanya, sitting with Sophie in a red plush upholstered compartment, realized what had happened to her. On one hand, it was a miracle to be surrounded by such luxury as an entire seat to herself, its comfortable soft cushions coddling her with their warmth. On the other, she and Sophie were completely alone, severed from their group, isolated in an alien environment. Everything had happened so fast, she'd had no time to think about it. Besides, she had become accustomed to obeying Paul's orders without question. Now she was alarmed because there was no one to turn to for advice. What if they were never to see Paul or Gleb again?

She thought about them standing on the platform as the train moved out of the station. Though she would miss Gleb, Paul was the one she needed more, and in admitting this she knew how dependent on him she had become. It was Paul who had watched over them, Paul who had come to her rescue and had made decisions for her without giving her time to ponder them. He made the hardships somehow more bearable when he had shown his faith in her and she found she had more strength than she had ever suspected. During all the terrible events of the past few days, she had been sustained by her determination not to disappoint Paul, to live up to what he expected of her.

Now, deprived of his support, she was alone with strangers for the first time. Worse, she had Sophie with her as an added concern. She would have to fall back on her own resources, think and act on her own initiative, and the prospect worried her. Could she handle her new responsibility and make the right decisions? Did she have the will to carry off the role imposed upon her? What if the Czechs proved unfriendly or tried to take advantage of two defenseless women?

When the train began to pull out of the station, she had to fight the urge to run out on the platform and shout to Paul that she didn't want to leave, that she wanted to stay with him and take her chances with the others on the march to Irkutsk. But Sophie was having trouble breathing after climbing onto the train; her ankles were swollen; and Tanya knew that for her friend's sake alone, if for nothing else, she must ride the train for as long as the Czechs would let them. She felt more lonely and desolate than she had been since they left Omsk, and in an effort to control rising panic, she turned to Sophie.

Her friend moaned and slowly lifted her legs onto the seat. "God, I've forgotten what it's like to have such comforts," she said, leaning back on the padded cushion behind her. "Tanya, I don't know how to thank Prince Paul for his concern over me. Every minute I'm awake has become such a living nightmare, all I can think of is how to get through one day at a time."

She looked down at her legs and shook her head. "They're so swollen and throbbing. Do you know something? I resent the child I'm carrying. It may cost me my life without ever being born. This impossible march! I'll never make it if the baby doesn't come soon." She put the palm of her hand on her belly. "No father, no material comforts, and after it is born how can it possibly survive the rest of the journey? And if by some miracle it should, how shall I provide for it? It's better off dead."

"Don't grumble against fate, Sophie," Tanya said gently. "God gave you a child, and that baby will be the extension of Alexei. Just think how wonderful it will be for you to know that through the birth of his baby, Alexei lives on. You're lucky. I wish I could have had Yuri's child."

"Don't wish it, Tanya. I envy *you*. You have nobody to worry about but yourself. You're the lucky one."

Tanya leaned over and squeezed Sophie's hand. "I'd like to make you more comfortable. I wonder if we could get some tea? I'll go find out."

Pulling off her shawl, Tanya opened the compartment

door, but before she could step out into the corridor Captain Marcek blocked her way.

"Princess Veragina, I'm afraid I'll have to restrict you and your companion to the compartment for your own safety."

Only briefly did Tanya blink her eyelids at the sound of the strange name bestowed upon her. Something in the Czech's attitude put her on guard. Trying not to show her nervousness, she took a step backward and sat down. The captain followed her into the compartment. There was a touch of insolence in his smile as he sat down uninvited.

"It's for your own good, Princess. I can't follow you all over the train. In times of war, principles of morality are different. An unexplained presence of a beautiful woman on a military train could easily be misinterpreted, don't you think?"

He gave her a significant smile. Tanya flushed.

"In other words, a woman isn't safe with your men?"

"Not necessarily. We've had ladies aboard who were quite willing to entertain us." He paused, letting his words sink in. "So you see, Princess, I don't want my troops to misunderstand the reason for your presence."

Anger and fear alternately played hopscotch with Tanya's stomach. She glanced at Sophie. The train's rhythmic clatter was drowning out the sound of their voices, and Sophie dozed in the opposite corner of the compartment.

Captain Marcek's glance traveled down Tanya's body and paused on her hands. She looked down and suddenly felt exposed, for the wedding band on her right hand, which she had forgotten to remove, was in plain sight. Their eyes met, and Captain Marcek's took on a mocking glint.

"Where is your husband, Princess?"

"My husband is . . . I'm a widow."

The Czech's face became a mask. "Why didn't your brother tell me your real name?"

God, thought Tanya, what am I going to tell him? Paul would know what to say.

"Why did your brother call you by your maiden name? Who was your husband?" the Czech persisted.

The words *maiden name* triggered a memory. Countess

Merkulina. Her mother had retained her maiden name while married to her father. Boldly, she looked at Captain Marcek.

"I'm proud of my family name, Captain. I was married for only a short time, and after my husband was killed I resumed my maiden name and title."

He studied her speculatively. "I hope for your sake, Princess, that you're telling me the truth. We Czechs don't like to be fooled. For the time being you're safe. I can't disturb General Janin with a dispatch of such trivia, but rest assured, when we reach our destination I'll check on you. If I find that you're not the real Princess Veragina, well . . ." The captain smiled slowly and spread his hands. ". . . I won't be obliged to offer my protection to you any longer. You understand?"

He nodded, clicked his heels, and started toward the door.

Tanya understood only too well. He's playing cat and mouse with me, she thought. He'd never have dared to talk to me like this if he hadn't been quite sure of himself. She and Sophie were safe only as long as the train was moving—but when it reached Irkutsk, what would she do then? If only Paul were there, he would have known how to handle this. Her throat felt constricted. What was she going to do?

Suddenly Tanya knew she must bluff the captain by showing him she was not afraid.

"Captain Marcek!" she called after him, forcing her voice to ring with assurance.

The captain turned around. "Yes, Princess?"

"We're thirsty. Since you've confined us to the compartment, please be good enough to send us some hot tea."

Captain Marcek raised his eyebrows and looked at her with mild surprise. Tanya stared back without blinking. I'm going to outstare you, Captain, she thought, and you'll never know how scared I am.

The Czech nodded, amusement twinkling in his eyes. "Of course, Princess. I'll send someone to fetch it immediately." Then, as an afterthought, he added, "Have a pleasant journey."

He bowed slightly and left.

Perspiration moistened the nape of Tanya's neck and tickled the spot between her shoulder blades. Limp with relief, she sank on to the seat, wanting but not daring to cry, when Sophie's labored breathing drew her attention.

"I hope he doesn't check on us before we get to our last stop," whispered Sophie. "I'm not sure I can take any more of his snooping. I have trouble breathing as it is."

"You'll have to take yourself in hand, Sophie dear. In your condition, you couldn't withstand the journey outside the train for any length of time—and it's not over yet. So why don't you try to rest and take advantage of the train ride."

Sophie sighed and didn't answer. Tanya closed her eyes. There was no point in agonizing and trying to guess the immediate future. They were trapped on this train no matter what awaited them, and she might as well appreciate the ride and trust her ingenuity to bail them out of the next confrontation.

The more she thought about Captain Marcek, the angrier she became. The moment he suspected they were vulnerable, he started to scheme how he could take advantage of two helpless women. Well, she'd show him she wasn't helpless. She'd think of something.

The soft cushion at the back of her head absorbed the rocking of the train and lulled her anxiety. She must have dozed off, for she dreamed about Paul and heard his voice gently calling her name. Somewhere in a sun-splashed room she saw him smiling at her with outstretched arms, but as he moved toward her, his voice grew louder and more insistent, and soon she realized that someone was tugging at her sleeve. Though she was reluctant to let go of the dream, she opened her eyes, and then the dream was no longer a dream, and she was looking straight into Paul's anxious face.

She didn't take time to think or question. Impulsively, she threw her arms around his neck and rubbed her face against the side of his cheek, scraping her hand on his shoulder boards, her thoughts and her words all smothered in one all-embracing relief: Paul was there.

With her arms roped around him, she held him fiercely, forgetting to check whether he was a willing captive to her embrace.

"Prince Veragin!" Captain Marcek's sarcastic voice sounded behind them. "I wasn't aware that you, too, had requested a ride."

Paul disentangled himself from Tanya's clutching arms. "You're right, Captain, I didn't request a passage for myself—but at the last minute I realized that since Princess Veragina is still not strong after her illness and Madame Pavlova may have her *accouchement* anytime now, I may be needed to assist the ladies."

The excuse sounded flimsy even to Tanya's unpracticed ear. Anxiously, she looked at Captain Marcek. He was studying Paul indecisively, but Paul pursued the matter. "Captain, may I remind you that General Janin will be pleased with your courtesy to his friends. Besides, my presence on this train will neither discommode you nor add to your burden. It can only ease it should one of the ladies become ill."

"I suppose so, Prince." The captain's voice sounded vague.

"Strange rumors about what goes on aboard your trains are circulating among our troops, Captain." Paul busied himself with his greatcoat and avoided looking at the Czech. "I took them for what they are—slander out of envy—and that's why I entrusted my own sister into your care. I'm glad I came aboard, though, for I'll be able personally to dispel any rumors that might reach General Janin."

The threat was subtle but clear, even though Tanya didn't know to what he was alluding. Captain Marcek clicked his heels and disappeared.

Tanya raised her eyebrows. Before she could ask Paul what all this meant, he put his finger to his lips in warning. After checking the corridor, he sat down next to her. "Don't ask, Tanya," he said quietly. "Something has happened that made me feel you'd be safer with me aboard. Did the captain say anything while you were alone?"

"He suspects I'm not your sister," Tanya said, then told

him about her conversation with the Czech. "I had the feeling," she concluded, "that if he discovered the truth, worse things could have happened to us."

Paul clenched his hands and winced.

"What's the matter, Paul? Are you hurt? Let me see!" She took his hand and looked at it. His palm was scuffed and pink with smeared blood. "What happened?"

Paul shrugged. "I didn't catch the train railing on the first two tries. When I did, it was slippery and seared my hand."

Looking for iodine, Tanya busied herself with her bundle, uncomfortably aware that the sight of his injury was upsetting her more than General Kappel's frozen feet. As she dressed his hand, she thought of her embrace, and her face grew hot with shame as she realized that he had not responded to her outburst of joy.

The train moved slowly, making frequent stops along the line with long waits for refueling. Once in a while they saw Admiral Kolchak's green and white pennant flutter in the wind and knew they were getting close to their destination.

Whenever they stopped, Tanya and Sophie watched horror-stricken through the window as desperate women with faces blackened from cold, their infants in their arms, clawed at the train and fought for a foothold on the landing. Under orders to protect the train from the refugees, the Czech guards beat them off with rifle butts, leaving them stranded in the freezing cold.

Tanya's flesh crawled. The winter mowed down all life—man, woman, child. It was impartial.

Along the way, Captain Marcek, who had remained courteous, supplied his passengers with a piece of grim news. General Kappel had died on January 26 from double pneumonia, in spite of the Romanian doctor's efforts to save him after he had been finally taken unconscious aboard their train. His body, placed in a wooden coffin, was accompanying the marching army, which kept almost abreast of the slow-moving train. The general's troops refused to abandon their dead leader, and a rumor sprang up that he was not dead at all, but leading them at the head of the column.

Tanya burst into tears when she heard the news. She wept for the dead man, for his army, for all of them caught in this war.

At Innokentyevskaya station a few miles north of Irkutsk, Captain Marcek entered their compartment again. The embarrassment which colored his face was so out of character for this man whom Tanya had come to judge as an opportunist, that her heart turned over in a premonition.

"Your army is here, Prince Veragin," the captain said, "and I strongly recommend you and the ladies rejoin them before we go any farther. The Reds are now in Irkutsk, and I regret to inform you that your Supreme Ruler, Admiral Kolchak, was executed yesterday by a firing squad."

Paul gasped. "My God, we're only twenty versts from Irkutsk! How could this have happened? General Janin was personally responsible for Admiral Kolchak's safety!"

Captain Marcek avoided looking into Paul's eyes. "I have no idea of what has happened, Prince Veragin. I don't make policies. I only obey orders. General Janin is no longer in Irkutsk. He's gone to the Trans-Baikal area. I must insist you leave this train at once."

"Yes, of course, Captain," Paul replied, his face pale. "We'll leave immediately. I suppose I ought to thank you for not turning us over to the Reds, but you must forgive me if I dispense with amenities now. The news you've just brought us is difficult to absorb."

So Admiral Kolchak is dead, Tanya thought with sadness. Kappel had overestimated his body's endurance, and Kolchak had failed to recognize that he was expendable to the Allies. Even General Janin must have found it expedient to abandon him. The Allies looked out for themselves.

She looked at Captain Marcek with disdain. The Czech, obviously ill at ease, cleared his throat. "I think you should also know that General Voitzekhovsky decided against taking Irkutsk. He's planning to skirt the city and go to Listvinichnoye for the crossing of Lake Baikal."

Tanya hugged her bundle. They were too late. There would be no train now to take them around the southern shore, and they would have to face the awesome lake in a combat of man against nature never before attempted.

Turning to Sophie, she clasped her in her arms.

CHAPTER 18

After the luxury of a warm passenger train, Tanya felt the chill of the winter cold creeping through her bones. Shivering, aching, she struggled to hold back the tears. Ashamed of her weakness, she thought of how much more difficult it must be for Sophie. The train ride had only intensified the hardships they had endured. It was as if Tanya's body, once numbed to the cold and then allowed to thaw and rest, were suddenly plunged into the frost again to suffer anew a period of adjustment.

Her resentment against the Czechs mounted. What were the Allies doing there anyway? They weren't helping either side, and she couldn't understand their presence. She felt ashamed to be a refugee in her own country, fleeing from her own people under the eyes of the foreigners who watched their indignities with impartial detachment. She hated the Reds, and her hatred grew with each passing day.

The whole of Siberia had gone insane with terror because of them. Hitherto untrampled vast deserts of snow lay ravaged by war. Nature, as if avenging her molested territory, struck back, and the wrath of the Siberian winter fell upon them. Weakened by skirmishes with the pursuing Red Army, harassed by partisans who lurked in the impasable taiga, the retreating White troops pushed on, their wills undermined by the uncertainty of what awaited them ahead.

Even Tanya's reunion with Gleb, who had found the three of them waiting for their regiment at the edge of Innokentyevskaya, had not cheered her. He looked gaunt, his eyes sunken, his body trembling so uncontrollably that she wanted to hold his face close to hers and warm it with her breath. Other men's faces, equally dehumanized, floated past her, and it was then that the full impact of what lay ahead hit her. Was it the fear of death or a grim determination against impossible odds that she saw in their eyes?

As they joined the echelon marching toward the River Angara, her legs began to tremble and her stomach churned. Someone tugged at her sleeve, and she looked up into Gleb's face.

"Can you manage, Tanya?" he asked, his voice hoarse and rasping.

She nodded. "Yes, thank you, Gleb."

He looked hesitantly at Paul. "Then I'll fall back to the rear."

Paul dismissed him with a nod. Tiny icicles glistened on Paul's eyelashes as his eyes watered in the wind. He had found a horse somewhere and was pulling it behind him. Wearing a fur cap tied snugly under his chin, he looked shorter and less formal. His thoughtfulness during the entire flight had endeared him to her. Occasionally, however, she wondered whether his concern for her was motivated by the guilt he felt or by a wish to win her affection.

As a sleigh drew alongside, he pushed her and Sophie toward it. Several women from their regiment huddled inside.

"Get in," he urged, half lifting them onto the sleigh. Tanya leaned on Paul's muscular arm and fought the desire to press her face against him, to feel his arms encircle her, and to hide, if only for a moment—a single blessed moment—from all the horror of their plight.

A few women held out their hands to help Sophie up, and as they squeezed themselves into the small space, she looked back at Paul. He smiled at her briefly and mounted his horse.

A wind whipped up a flurry as they left the sanctuary of the village, and Tanya was grateful for the surrounding bodies shielding her from its razor-sharp blasts.

Their objective for the first day was the village of Taltsi on the River Angara and, if their progress were good, then on to Listvinichnoye on Lake Baikal. The going was tortuous. The snow was deep, the road narrow, and when the sleighs skidded into a drift, the echelon had to stop to re-group. To free each sleigh that became stuck would have taken too much energy and time, neither of which the men could afford.

After a few hours, Tanya's sleigh skidded into a road bank. Chunks of snow crumbled over the rungs and packed, instantly frozen. Several men unharnessed the horse. Paul, never too far from Tanya and Sophie, dis-mounted and helped them climb into the following sleigh. Although already crowded, the women pushed against one another wearily, watching Sophie's laborious movements. It was impossible to sit down, and Tanya stood facing the wind, her shawl over her nose and mouth, eyelids heavy with icicles. Just a little more and we'll be in Taltsi. Grimly, she kept turning the words over and over in her mind, forcing her brain to reject the intrusion of sleep.

As if he had read her thoughts, Paul reined in his horse and waited till her sleigh came alongside him. "Hold on, Tanya, we're about fifteen versts from the village."

The wind rushed at them from the cliff-bordered gorges with whistles and howls, blanketing the moving life with sifted snow.

In Taltsi they stopped. The villagers greeted them warmly and warned them not to push on to Listvinichnoye the same day, but to conserve their energies for the cross-ing of Baikal. They stayed overnight in Taltsi, running to invade the izbas like an army of ants, fighting their way in, oblivious of everything except the all-consuming desire for warmth and sleep.

In the morning the sun was up, but its pale light, filter-ing through the haze, brought no warmth to the shivering echelon as they approached Listvinichnoye over the frozen Angara. At the river's source, the powerful current too fast for the ice to bind it, rushed the transparent waters from Lake Baikal.

Taken by surprise, the rider ahead of the column failed to stop his horse in time and fell into the water. He scram-bled on the hard, icy surface and, grabbing the bridle of the sinking horse, shouted, "Come on, *bratsi*, give a hand!"

Numbed bodies moved sluggishly, but Tanya, herself stiff from standing in the sleigh, pushed her way out of the encircling women without stopping to consider what she could do. She ran toward the rider, feeling the blood coursing through her veins, glad to be moving. The rider threw her one end of the bridle, and, as she grabbed it, several hands reached to help her, and together they pulled, bracing themselves against the clumps of frozen debris at their feet.

Grating rasps and snorts came from the animal as it struggled for breath. Horrified by the sight, Tanya released her end of the bridle, which was wound around the horse's neck.

The bridle slackened momentarily before the other men regained their footing, but it was enough to unleash the rider's temper against Tanya. He shoved her out of his way with such force that she slid several yards, coming to rest against the rungs of a sleigh.

Her elbow hit the metal, but she felt no pain; her attention was riveted to the animal's agony. As the horse gulped air, its body half rose above the water. Several hands grabbed the beast from all sides, and the slipping, snorting horse was hoisted onto solid ice. Tanya looked at the huge, terrified eyes of the animal as it stood shivering, docile, while the soldiers wiped the freezing water off its body and mane, and suddenly she felt more pity for this hapless horse than for all the human beings who had fallen by the road and frozen to death.

Sitting on ice against a snowdrift, cushioned by snow, she hadn't been this comfortable for a long time, and her adrenaline had now turned in upon itself, withdrawing the energy from her extremities and replacing the void with a numbing weight she had no desire to lift. Fear, hunger, exhaustion, departed; she felt a sedentary calm so pleasant she closed her eyes to savor it fully.

She heard the sleigh rungs squeal past her, and then the thumping of marching feet. The arrhythmic multitude of sounds drugged her mind, lulling her will. Into this blissful serenity came Paul's insistent voice.

"Tanya, get up! Get up immediately!"

Opening her eyes, Tanya looked into Paul's face above

her. He was angry, angrier than she had ever seen him. He was pulling her up roughly by the arm. "Your sleigh is coming up. Run to it and stay in it from now on! As long as you stay in that sleigh, you have a chance."

He jerked his horse by the bridle and turned to look at her again. "And something else. Stop playing the heroine. It would have been stupid to lose your life on account of a horse!"

Tanya revived. The image of Paul's infuriated face was the most welcome sight since Omsk. He cared. It was important that he cared, but she had no time to ponder why. The sleigh was within reach, and, jumping on it, she dared not look back.

At last they entered Listvinichnoye and faced the lake, too numb to thrill to the sight of it. So this is Baikal, thought Tanya without emotion, remembering that Baikal meant "great sacred sea" in the Buryat language of the region. The vast expanse stretched before her, and, unbidden, the words of the familiar folk song ran through her mind: "Glorious sea, sacred Baikal. . . ."

It was indeed like a sea. The largest body of fresh water in the world, it was three hundred and sixty miles long and fifty-three miles across at its widest point. A mile deep, it froze in the winter; and now, poised on the western edge of the lake, she thought that nothing in her studies about it had prepared her for its vastness, for the man-sized hosts of white mounds that covered the surface, looming in front of her like an army of watchful guards. Sadness gripped her. She felt unwelcome, an intruder upon the majesty of the frozen lake, imagining that this dormant giant was eyeing her warily.

Uneasy, Tanya turned to look behind her. Listvinichnoye nestled on a narrow strip of land at the foot of steep, cedar-covered hills that rose high above the lake. At their base a cluster of izbas huddled together like a group of gossiping women. Puffs of snow cascaded down from the rooftops, sliding noiselessly over the icicles and showering the passing men. A single road ran through the center of the village, ending abruptly at the base of a cliff.

As if drawn by an invisible force, Tanya felt compelled to look at Baikal again. A low fog rolled and churned over the lake, concealing the structure of the frozen surface, as if something were unwilling to reveal its secrets all at once. In several places the sun cut hazy shafts through the fog, allowing a glimpse of the glistening ice hammocks crowding into infinity. The quiet of the morning pervaded the air.

Tanya remained by her sleigh, transfixed by the sight, oblivious of the growing activity around her, until Paul came to stand beside her.

"I talked to the villagers," he said in a drawn voice. "We have to go to Goloustnoye. It's forty-five versts north of here. From there it's the shortest way across the lake to Mysovaya—another forty-five versts. They say there's a railroad station at Mysovaya."

Paul pulled the strings of his cap tighter around his chin. "The first echelon has already started out toward Goloustnoye. There's no road, so they've gone down on the lake along the shore." As he paused, squinting and looking toward the lake, Tanya noticed that his eyes were bloodshot and weary.

"Nobody knows who's on the other side," he continued. "Some say Japanese Expeditionary Forces sent by the Allies are waiting to help us, and others spread the rumor that the Reds are there already. Soldiers talk about machine-gun fire they have heard, but the villagers say it's only Baikal being restless."

Tanya pressed her elbows tighter against her body to keep warmer, but said nothing.

"I also heard that the Allies have lifted their economic blockade of Russia," Paul went on. "If this is true, it means the Allied forces will be withdrawn from Siberia, and with them, our last hope of victory. A few people here, however, swear they've seen the slant-eyed Japanese in the vicinity. Let's pray they're right."

Before Tanya could fully comprehend what he had said, the morning calm was shattered by commotion and shouts from the lake. Men, horses, sleighs, appeared out of the fog, scrambling ashore in panic.

Paul grabbed a running soldier by the arm. "What happened?"

The man's eyes bulged out of their sockets and he trembled and jerked.

Paul shook him. "Speak up! What happened out there?"

The man gasped. "Holy Mother of God! The earth opened up to swallow us!"

The soldier tried to wrench free, but Paul held him tight. "What are you talking about, you fool? What earth? There's ice out there!"

The terrified man opened his mouth and stared at Paul. Then his face contorted and he sniffled, "Oh, Your Excellency, we heard this sound—a rumbling sound, far, far away, and then thunder came from the lake. I swear it, Excellency"—he nodded several times—"thunder underneath the lake. Such wonders!"

Paul slapped him across the face. "You babbling idiot! Make sense! Then what happened?"

Wiping the frozen droplets from under his nose with his sleeve, the soldier looked at Paul as if he were seeing him for the first time. "Ah, Excellency—we've never seen the likes of it before! The thunder stopped and all was quiet when suddenly—the devil take us"—the soldier opened his eyes wide and spread his arms—"suddenly, the ice parted. Right in front of us!"

Paul shrugged. "So what? Where do you come from, *durak*? Haven't you ever seen the ice crack in the cold?"

The man shook his head vigorously. "Not like this, Excellency. Not like this! This one didn't crack. It just moved apart and then closed again. Without any noise. Believe me, Excellency, as God is my witness, there wasn't a single sound of any kind. And that wasn't all! The terrible part came next. It didn't stay closed, Excellency. It separated again, and this time the pit got wider and wider—and all the time without a sound! A curse—a curse upon us all!"

Crossing himself, the soldier shuffled away, and Paul made no move to stop him.

"Damn!" he swore. "This will delay us. We'll probably have to spend the night in Goloustnoye."

Tanya climbed back into her sleigh. They would be next. They would have to go on the ice. There was no other way. And at any time that ice could part and swallow them without warning.

When they left Listvinichnoye, their echelon came across the crack in the ice. The gaping crevasse had already frozen over, but the men stopped. Someone shouted from the shore: "Everyone able to move, help with the straw!"

Tanya climbed down with the other women, leaving Sophie behind. Quickly a line formed, passing sheaves of straw from the village peasants to the front of the echelon. The straw was heavy, but no one complained. Several men spread it over the frozen crevasse, flooding it with water that was carried in buckets by the villagers to reinforce the freshly frozen crust. Layer upon layer the straw was placed down, until the villagers directing the work were satisfied.

Several young village girls waved from shore. A soldier waved back. "Come with me, wench," he called. "I'll make it worth your while!"

"Naaah! Not you!" retorted a young peasant girl. "The Bolsheviks will kill you and then where'll I be?"

A few chuckles came from the soldiers, but the girl's words hurt. The villagers hadn't reproached the retreating men for not staying behind and defending them against the Bolsheviks. They regarded the soldiers as already doomed to extinction and offered them pity instead. And to be pitied was the greatest hurt of all.

Skirting the reinforced crevasse, the horses pulled the sleighs with greater ease on ice than on shore. Knowing there was no solid ground under her feet, Tanya's alarm mounted. Somewhere underneath there was water—cold, merciless water. Always afraid of drowning, Tanya fought panic. To die in the icy depths of Baikal was terrifying. But the sleigh was gliding, the echelon moving on solid ice, and soon her panic was lulled by the cold and the fog and the whispering sounds of shuffling feet.

By the time the echelon reached Goloustnoye, it was dusk, and bonfires were burning in the village. It was a small hamlet, with a handful of log izbas that were already filled with those who had arrived there first. Turned away from the shelters, the latecomers settled for the night in their sleighs, huddling together to keep from freezing.

Tanya stayed in her sleigh and looked with longing at the izbas' lighted windows, remembering the welcome heat inside, the comfort of hot, pungent *ukha*. Since early childhood she had heard about the majesty and beauty of Baikal. Today she had seen that beauty, and conceded to the terror that she now knew it disguised. But now she thought of the legends surrounding it, concentrating on the delicacy of Baikal's omul—so much like salmon, yet different, the coveted prize of every visitor. Indeed, the abundance of fish, some of a species not found anywhere else in the world, lured the fishermen, many of whom perished in Baikal's turbulent waters. She dwelt on the omul, picturing the fish sauteed and hot, its imaginary fragrance intensifying her hunger pangs. All the trials she had suffered, the hardships meted out to her in such a short time, culminated into this final want, the most important, most cruel of all deprivations—hunger. Self-pity choked her, and she felt the elbow that had been scraped when she fell against the sleigh smart from the coarse fabric of her sleeve, which rubbed the raw place on her skin. She swallowed tears in rapid succession, determined to keep them from filling her eyes and freezing her eyelids together.

Sophie, exhausted, crouched in the corner of the sleigh in an uncomfortable sleep. Tanya envied her friend. She yearned to rest; but for her, sleep was impossible. She spent the night dozing to the sounds of shuffling boots and muted voices. Only half-conscious of the other women, she was painfully aware of the cold that crept inside her skin, sapped her energy, consumed her mind.

And tomorrow? Maybe death.

CHAPTER 19

The first stripes of light glowed across the horizon, cutting through the charcoal clouds and breaking the night into various shades of darkness. The snow took on a blue tinge, and soon the luminous shafts of early dawn were lost in the murky skies. A distant howl of wolves echoed and dissolved plaintively in the frostbitten air as the flickering lights appeared in the izbas. Soon coils of smoke began to rise from the chimneys, permeating the air with the odor of burning cedar.

The village was awake. Shapeless figures darted out of doors, crouching, with bundles in their arms. Quiet still prevailed, as though man and nature in wordless communion strove to forestall the birth of the day, to prolong that last moment of peace before the struggle with death began again.

When the east turned crimson with dawn, a sonorous voice broke the morning silence.

"Kuzma, Kuzma!" shouted a towering man in cossack uniform, peering from under a large karakul hat that nearly concealed his eyes, and checking two rows of cartridges neatly sewn into the cloth of his chest. "Has Prokhor gone to awaken the rest?"

Another cossack, loading bundles on a cart, turned. "Yes sir, Ataman, the cossacks are getting ready."

Along the road now, doors flew open, and crowds of men, women, and children began to file outside. They shuffled with a crunching sound under their feet—officers, soldiers, wives, nurses, all unrecognizable beneath the weight of their extra clothes. Children, bundled in thick coats, angora shawls, and felt boots, held on to their mothers' skirts and waddled along like bear cubs.

While she waited in the sleigh, Tanya munched on a piece of dried pancake that a passing peasant woman had shared with her. Although made only of flour and water without salt, she ate it hungrily, finishing not only her share but the piece that Sophie had refused to eat. As she chewed on the last bite, Paul appeared at the side of the sleigh, his clothes covered with frozen dirt.

"Where did you spend the night?" she asked without thinking, and was surprised by her own concern. If it pleased him, his face betrayed no emotion.

"There was no room anywhere in the village, so I spent the night with the soldiers at the cemetery." He brushed dirty snow off his sleeves and added, "We slept between the graves."

"At least you were able to find some rest."

Paul mounted his horse. "It's almost time to start, Tanya." Leaning toward her, he lowered his voice. "Try to push yourself and Sophie toward the center of the sleigh. That way you'll be better protected from the wind."

He touched the tip of his cap, bowed slightly, and spurred his horse forward. The women in Tanya's sleigh didn't talk. Besides a couple of wives from their regiment, the rest were peasant women. Sophie, slumped in the corner with her hands clasped around her abdomen, looked pale and listless. Tanya bent over.

"How are you doing, Sophie?"

"I've been having pains this morning. I hope we get across Baikal before I go into labor. They say it's going to be fifty below all day." Sophie's voice sounded hollow, and she stared ahead blankly. Tanya pulled the shawl over Sophie's forehead and cheeks, forming a triangle around her eyes. "Don't breathe through your mouth, Sophie."

Two large tears spilled over Sophie's lashes, dropping down onto her shawl. Tanya brushed the moisture off the angora wool. An older woman with high cheekbones and tilted eyes had been watching them. She moved aside to make room for Tanya and then said to Sophie: "Don't worry, *kasatka*, I'm a midwife. I'll take care of you if need be. Pray that we won't be hit by *booran*, the angry snowstorm, and all will be well."

Sophie shook her head. "I can't have my child in freezing weather."

The older woman looked at her for a while and then stated firmly: "You'll survive."

The sleigh began to move. Behind them, Tanya could see no end to the black, moving mass of people, horses, and sleighs. Ahead of them, the first group of people had stopped on the bank of the lake. A distant voice echoed: "With God, forward!"

A human ribbon started to funnel onto a narrow path stamped out by other echelons between the formations of frozen water. As they descended onto the bumpy surface, women shoved and pushed for a better look.

"Look at those *torosi*—Mother of God, there's a wonder for you!" wailed a woman in front of Tanya, swinging the upper portion of her body from side to side.

Tanya turned to the midwife. "What's a *torosi?*"

The midwife pointed to the giant fissures in the frozen lake and the hummocks around them. "We Siberians call those *torosi*," she said. "In severe cold the ice breaks, and when cracks appear, chunks of it pile up on each side. When the *bargoozin*—the northern wind—hits the water, it blows a spray up in the air, freezing it in flight." She pointed to a cluster of intricately patterned crystalline schists that reflected the light with a myriad of diamond-like sparkles, even through the mist of the morning.

Awed, Tanya studied them. Lacy, chrysanthemum-shaped, plumed, spiked, they crowded along the zigzagging crevasses, resembling giant building blocks, each different in shape and size. Above, the sky had turned a dull gray, its overall evenness a forerunner of a storm.

All around them the lines of demarcation disappeared, and only the toiling line of humanity kept the vastness of the lake in perspective, reassuring Tanya that she was still on earth and not suspended somewhere in limbo, among strange shapes of the shadow world.

She closed her eyes, struggling to blot out the present by evoking images of childhood, but all she could remember was Yuri. His laughter, his voice—she could hear them echo in her brain; and listening to the ebbing sounds, she knew, without anguish at last, that he now belonged to a treasured past.

Indignant voices drifted from the sleigh ahead. Soldiers who marched on foot were arguing with someone on the sleigh, tugging at a dangling leg.

"Let go, you Antichrist! Don't you see the soldier is wounded?" a woman shouted from the sleigh. Laughter erupted below. "Yeah, tell us more! He's already stiff from his wounds. A sly guy you've got with you, woman. Some fellows will stop at nothing to get a ride!"

The guffaws drowned the woman's reply, and over her screams, several hands grabbed the corpse and pulled the dead man off the sleigh. Deftly, they stripped him of tulup and valenki and, swinging him in the air to gather momentum, threw the body far into the *torosi*. The woman's screams changed to a thin wail. "Thieves! Atheists! *Besbozhniki*! Even took his valenki! Couldn't you have left those at least?"

The soldiers exploded into another round of mirth. "What for, woman? Is he going to dispatch himself to the other world on foot?"

Such irreverence toward a corpse no longer shocked Tanya. She sensed now that these men used humor as their only defense against insanity. Taking the dead man's valenki meant survival for the living, not disrespect for the dead.

The sleighs moved forward. Although there was no road on the lake, it wasn't difficult to follow in the path of the earlier echelon that had left its traces the day before. Wooden planks, straw, and ropes for constructing bridges across fissures lay strewn all around them, frozen into ice. The farther they moved, the more debris they encountered. Abandoned sleighs began to appear, then frozen horses, and, finally, frozen men. Covered with snow and ice, they sat and sprawled in grotesque positions, like frosted sculptures molded into twisted shapes and arranged in a macabre tableau.

She was not sure how many hours had passed, or even whether she had fallen asleep, for the wind had subsided, and the relative warmth from the surrounding bodies had shielded her from the frost. No one spoke. Apathy lurked in the eyes of the women around her, an apathy so deadly that some of them faced the storm with uncovered faces.

Worried about Sophie, Tanya looked behind her. Her friend was crouching on the floor of the sleigh, protected from the wind by surrounding bodies. She was restless and gasping. Tanya bent over her. "Sophie, are you hurting?"

Sophie opened her eyes. "My pains are becoming more regular now. Oh, Tanya, I'm so scared! Pray we get across before the baby comes!"

"Keep still, Sophie. With God's help, we'll make it!"

The shuffling of the felt boots, the clicking of spurs, and the rhythmic crunching of hoofs eventually dulled Tanya's senses. The wind began to whine and bite, anew, slapping her face viciously. She opened her eyes, dreading the sight she would see. Blowing around them, the powdered snow shrouded the people, transforming them into ghosts. The men's beards turned white, and their frosted brows and lashes blurred all features into one common face.

We're going to be buried alive, she thought without emotion. Death no longer terrified her. Freezing was easy—no pain, no torture, a simple surrender to sleep.

As their sleigh cleared the *torosi* and emerged onto smoother surface, the wind picked up fury, swirling the snow at their feet into constantly changing patterns. To keep from being blown out of the marching line, the men held on to one another. The horses that were not properly shod glided and slipped, recovering their footing with difficulty. A short distance ahead, one of them lost its balance and fell with its cadet rider. The young man screamed. His legs were pinned under the horse and he fought to free himself, but the animal stayed down, thrashing convulsively in a futile effort to get a foothold.

A few soldiers leaned over to grasp his hand, but they would not leave the moving line and couldn't reach him. One of the men bent toward him, lost his balance, and would have fallen if his comrades hadn't pulled him back.

"Hey!" someone shouted. "There's an old man over here with a cane. Quick, get it from him!"

Tanya watched without interest. It was difficult to hear through the howling storm. So many had fallen and per-

ished around her that the surrounding death no longer affected her. She could barely see the old man fighting the
two soldiers as they tried to wrench the cane from him, but
his voice carried feebly above the *booran*. "Bratsi! I can't
make it without my cane. I'll die—have pity!"

His words were cut off by a shrill scream as the horse,
struggling to raise itself, crushed the cadet's legs. The basso
of a tall soldier boomed above the screaming: "Give up the
cane, grandpa—your days are numbered anyway. What are
you good for, *stary khren*? All you do is pollute the air!"

After a brief scuffle, the cane appeared above their
heads, and its hooked end was handed to the now moaning
cadet, who grasped it with both hands. Three soldiers
pulled on the other end, but their mittens were slippery. A
strong gust of wind shoved the horse and the cadet away
from the path, and they skidded along the mirror surface
of the lake like a twirling hockey puck.

When the cadet's screams faded in a dying echo and the
mounting storm engulfed his struggling shape, Tanya's
stomach fluttered from nausea and emptiness. She watched
the echelon move on without pausing, without looking back.
The old man stumbled and sank to the ground. Moments
later he, too, was blown off the road and disappeared in
the quicksand of snow.

The midwife crossed herself, whispering, "Kingdom in
Heaven to him."

"He may still be alive," Tanya thought aloud. "Why
don't they go after him?"

The woman looked at her levelly. "To go after him is to
perish with him. You can't fight *booran*—he'll sweep you
away every time." She drew her shawl over her face, peering at Tanya with black eyes. "Better lose one life than
many."

She reached over and pulled Tanya's shawl low over her
forehead. "Keep your face down—the less the wind hits it
head-on, the less your chances of a frozen nose."

Curious about this woman, whose face was unrecognizable behind the frosted brows and lashes, Tanya asked,
"What's your name?"

"Marfa," answered the midwife and turned away.

Her blunt words had their effect on Tanya. Looking at the women's bowed heads and huddled shoulders, she felt a kinship toward her. Theirs was a common tragedy. It engulfed them all. She had been thinking of the revolution as a tragedy of the gentry, but all classes of society were fleeing the Bolsheviks, and they were enduring together, she realized now for the first time.

She envied Marfa's resignation to whatever fate meted out to her. It was not a weakness, but a fortitude born of centuries of serfdom and abuse, and a wisdom of silent acceptance of adversity when the odds were against one. The peasant accepted the hardships of his land with a simple philosophy: "What the Lord does is always for the best." Tanya pondered such simplicity and knew she could never resign herself to it.

She peered ahead, looking for Paul. He was near her sleigh, bending forward against the onslaught of the storm.

Seconds, minutes, hours . . . time and space blended into one white blur; and as the twilight descended upon them, it seemed to her that all the witches and demons from the fairy tales she had heard in childhood taunted her in the blizzard. She buried her head deeper into her arms and leaned on Marfa. Her face stung from the frost, and the shawl, usually so warm, now seemed to harbor the cold around her shoulders.

The silence—oh, the silence! No one spoke, not even a whisper, and the magnitude of this silence frightened her. She refused to consider that hundreds were perishing in this crossing, that the ranks of the echelon were thinning before her eyes.

The slippery surface had disappeared as abruptly as it had come upon them, and the way once again was bumpy and rough. Even seeing Paul a short distance in front of the sleigh was no longer a comfort. Nothing seemed to matter anymore. Her hands and feet were numb, her eyelids heavy with icicles that she was too lethargic to remove, and her mind wrestled with only one thought: how to stay awake until they reached Mysovaya, for the alternative was death.

She hadn't seen Gleb since the day before, and she wondered if he had joined another echelon. The wind played

tricks around them, cavorting and whistling between the
ice hummocks, thrusting new sounds upon the weary column. There were echoes of explosions and thunder and a
rumble of shearing ice. Sophie was moaning on the floor of
the sleigh, her pains more frequent now.

Tanya stood up, anxious now to reach Mysovaya, and
peered into the thickening dusk. A horse slipped on the
water that surfaced through a crack, throwing its rider
clear. She could see the officer's spurred boots but not his
face. He struggled to get up, his clothes instantly frozen.
Handicapped by stiffness, moving like a drowsy animal, he
tried over and over to sit up, and each time he fell back,
thrown off balance.

No one reached out to help him. He was too far from
the plodding echelon, and the stumbling soldiers didn't
even look in his direction. Although it was easier to ignore
the plight of a fellow human being by not watching his
struggle with death, Tanya couldn't take her eyes off the
fallen officer. There was something familiar in the turn of
his head and the angle of his shoulders. As the sleigh drew
near, a new gust of wind pinned him to the ice hummock,
and then, picking him up, hurled him into the air. His body
came down, slamming against the top of the mound with a
sickening snap of broken bones. His frozen clothes scraped
the ice as he slid over it, and his cap fell off his head to
reveal red hair turning crimson with blood.

"*Aaaah!*" Tanya howled, and the sound emerged from
the depth of her guts, held a second unchecked, then stran-
gled itself, choked off by the wind's ferocity.

She stared mouthing Gleb's name, racked by dry sobs
and whimpering, hiccuping, as the sleigh went by, but still
watching, watching as Gleb, limp, broken, crumbled and
skidded into darkness like a heap of waste.

Little pools of snow swished around with a hiss, covered
the bloodstains, erased them.

Deranged by grief and shock, she fought to get off the
sleigh and go after him, but strong arms restrained her and
held her in a viselike grip. Stunned, she could think of
nothing but Gleb's boots disappearing out of her sight, and
she dwelt on the thought that no one had tried to take
them. The importance of the boots preoccupied her mind,

filled it to the exclusion of everything else. It comforted
her. Although her teeth chattered uncontrollably, she
smiled with gladness, looked into Marfa's face without
seeing her, and said:

"His boots went with him. They didn't take his boots."

Marfa nodded, then cradled Tanya's head in her arms
and rocked her and rocked her without a word.

Thus they stood, moving into the night and total darkness. The echelon came to a stop. Voices, snatches of
phrases, floated through the air, their meaning too obscure
for her apathetic brain to understand. In the blackness, the
front convoy couldn't see its way, and men were crawling
on their hands and knees looking for any debris or foot-
prints to guide them.

Suddenly, a hysterical shriek echoed through the air.

"A light! A light! I see a light!"

Electrified, the echelon tensed, pushing, shoving, peering
ahead. Tanya rubbed the frost off her lashes with her mittens and blinked to clear her eyes. A flickering light
winked at her out of the night, like a beacon in a shoreless
sea. They pushed toward it, afraid to lose it, when another
appeared beside it, and soon dozens of them beckoned to
the weary column. They stumbled on, recharged by hope,
guided and drawn by the lights, cheered by the thought
that the nightmare was ending. They strained to hear a
break in the silence, perhaps an echo of human life from
the shore. And then it came: a faint barking of a dog.

After moving for hours without any outside living
sounds, a link with life was near—and with it a shore, an
izba, so coveted with its heat and body smells. She choked
her sobs, afraid their sound might silence the barking and
destroy the mirage, exposing a trick of a fevered imagination.

But the barking continued, and the lights loomed bright-
er and closer. It was real and it was getting bigger. Safety
was near. Safety! She remembered Paul's doubts. Who was
waiting for them on the shore? What if they had survived
all the superhuman trials only to walk into a trap set up for
them in Mysovaya?

Bending her head, she prayed.

CHAPTER 20

"Banzai! Banzai!"

The strange cry echoed in the night. Silhouetted against the lights of Mysovaya, a crowd of people stood waiting on the shore. Torches, their flames dancing in the wind, illuminated the alien sight of Oriental faces and strangely clad men in furry parkas. In reply, a less boisterous *"Urra! Urra!"* reverberated through the echelon as the first men stumbled up the bank.

The crossing of Baikal was accomplished and they were safe at last, welcomed by the friendly Japanese expeditionary forces. The nightmare was over, but at what cost? The number of the dead could never be counted. Gaunt phantoms staggered into Mysovaya, pulling the horses up the bank with the last strength of their half-frozen bodies. Villagers watched as the echelon from Goloustuoye scrambled ashore, their beards frozen in icicles, their eyes, bloodshot from the winds and lack of sleep, staring from under the white eyelashes like burning coals.

The engulfing silence broke all at once, with shouts and chatter and forgotten noises of sporadic laughter as the villagers and the Japanese mingled with the half-frozen men, patting and hugging some, supporting others as they limped toward the nearest izbas.

Surrounded by the warmth of human sounds, dizzy from hunger, Tanya felt a free-floating sensation in her head that numbed her movements. Even Gleb's death seemed predictably expected—its memory filed away in the subconscious, her grief pocketed. She stood immobilized, unaware that someone was pushing her off the sleigh.

"Come on, *barinya,* you must help me," the midwife was saying to her. "Your friend is in labor and I need your help." Marfa turned to Sophie. "Hold on, *golubka*," she said, half carrying, half dragging her off the sleigh.

Tanya slipped her arm around Sophie's waist, and her friend leaned on her shoulder, near collapse. Paul, already ashore, saw the three women struggle below him. He dismounted, posted his horse, and in a few strides was beside Sophie. The women stepped aside as he picked her up and started toward the corner izba.

"Aaah!" screamed Sophie, clutching Paul's neck, her face contorted, head far back. "Oh, God, I can't stand it! Aaah!"

"Sh-sh-sh!" Paul soothed her, and, kicking the door with his boot, carried her in. Tanya and Marfa followed.

Inside, a woman was lighting the stove. With one glance at Sophie, she pointed to the bed in the far corner of the room. "Undress her," she said simply. "I'll get the water boiling in a minute."

Carefully, gently, Paul lowered Sophie on the bed and knelt beside it. Several wet curls drooped over her eyes; he pushed them off her face with a stroking motion of his hand. Then he kissed her limp hand and slowly backed away.

Unexpectedly, Tanya felt a stab of jealousy. She had no inkling that Paul could be so tender, could act with such gentleness. She stood waiting for him to give her a word of encouragement for the help she was ready to offer Sophie—a word of support she had come to expect from him. But Paul walked past her and out of the izba without glancing in her direction. Her eyes filled with stinging tears, but she swallowed hard and forced them back. Paul's attention to Sophie shouldn't bother her. She needed him, yes, and had made a fool of herself—she could see it now—when she clung to him on the train, but at the time she was simply glad to see him and have his protection. That was all. . . . And the feathery kiss he had brushed on her forehead that night near Krasnoyarsk—God, it seemed so long ago!—that light kiss from him had been no more than a brotherly pat for a weeping child. A man of honor, he had seen to it that she survived. Still, a little more gentleness, a touch of warmth, would have been welcome. . . .

"Come on, *barinya*, move!"

At the sound of Marfa's exasperated voice, Tanya started and dropped to her knees to remove Sophie's valenki. She then removed her own outer clothing and placed the three pairs of valenki to dry by the stove. Following Marfa's example, she rolled up her sleeves and waited for the midwife's instructions.

The broken bag of water tinged with blood saturated Sophie's skirt and spilled over her thighs and legs. Tanya cleaned her with the moist, hot towel, careful not to look at the human estuary of emerging life.

Marfa, who had been massaging Sophie's abdomen rhythmically, now grabbed her thigh and pulled the leg aside. She examined her and nodded with satisfaction. "It's coming!" Then, turning to Tanya and ignoring Sophie's shrieks, she ordered crisply: "Keep her thighs apart. It won't be long now." To Sophie she said: "Bear down, *kasatka*—bear down harder." But Sophie only screamed in return, "I can't, I can't!"

Marfa straightened and looked at her sternly. "Do you want to lie here in pain or do you want to get it over with?"

Sophie gasped, "I can't stand it much longer."

"Then bear down hard!" ordered Marfa, and Sophie obeyed.

Mesmerized, shocked, Tanya held Sophie's thighs apart, forced to watch as the delicate opening stretched miraculously without tearing and filled with a moist globe streaked with a few wisps of wet black hair. Marfa's experienced hands continued to massage and push on the abdomen, and when the tiny head began to emerge, she manipulated the shoulders and pulled the infant out. Tanya's arms began to shake from strain, and she released the pressure on Sophie's thighs.

"Stay where you are," Marfa ordered. "We have to wait for the afterbirth." She cut the umbilical cord, and Tanya felt the weight of Sophie's legs on her arms as she went limp and fell back on the pillows.

Tanya watched curiously as Marfa picked up the infant by its feet and slapped it soundly several times. It was the ugliest thing Tanya had ever seen. Wet and blue, wrinkled and shriveled, it resembled a tadpole. Suspended from

Marfa's hand, the baby hung limply, without responding to her repeated slaps. She walked over to the table, placed the baby on the towel, and examined it with her back to Tanya. After a minute she handed the baby to the peasant woman and returned to Sophie's side.

"The baby is dead," she said calmly and looked at Sophie. "Good thing she fainted. No need to tell her right away." Then she added quietly, "It was a boy."

Marfa lowered herself wearily on a tabouret by the side of the bed. "I'll watch for the afterbirth now." Looking at Tanya, she added: "Go to the table and eat something before you swoon on me, too."

At first, Tanya didn't think her wobbly legs in stocking feet were going to support her, and she held on to the rough beams as she moved along the wall. The dead baby—how could she swallow anything after what she had just witnessed? But the sight and smell of the steaming bowl of soup and glistening crust of black bread drew her to the bench at the table, and she slid onto it with hunger-propelled agility.

She ate ravenously, annoyed by the tears that fell into the soup. After she ladled the last spoonful of the soup, scooping up the remaining puree of vegetables with the few kernels of buckwheat kasha on the bottom of the plate, a childhood rhyme floated through her mind: "Cabbage soup and kasha truly is our food."

Just being free from the threat of immediate death was a heady experience. Intoxicated by the warmth of the izba and the languor of appeased hunger, she dropped her head over her arms on the table and closed her eyes. All that was missing was a soft down comforter and the embrace of a loved human being. She would even settle for one tender look in Paul's blue eyes; but she mustn't dwell on these dangerous thoughts. She had been too long without a caress, without love or a loved one. She clung to Paul because he was the only remaining link with her past. She mustn't yearn for a touch, mustn't think of a man.

Sinking into a fretful sleep, she dreamt of a hot sun, a gliding rowboat on the Sungari, and of Harbin, and, strangely, of Kurt—his calm, reserved manner, his supportive words. But the hot sun on the Sungari returned, and the rowboat rocked, until she realized that someone was shaking the arm on which her head rested. Reluctantly, she raised her head to see Marfa's face so crisscrossed by a network of wrinkles that it was difficult to tell the extent of her exhaustion.

"*Barinya,* the young mother is now dozing. While she is asleep, we should dispose of the child."

Instinctively, Tanya looked toward a small altar in a corner of the room. The walls' wooden beams made the already dark izba look even darker, and the frosted windows allowed only a part of the torch lights to seep through. The flickering vigil light illuminated a triangular ledge covered with a piece of white linen cloth embroidered in colorful cross-stitch. On it stood a wooden triptych icon with images of Christ in the center and the archangels Michael and Gabriel on either side. An identical triptych hung in her bedroom in Harbin. She crossed herself and looked anxiously at Marfa.

"What do you want me to do?"

The midwife handed her the stillborn wrapped in a bloodied rag. Tanya recoiled. "Why me? I don't know what to do with it!"

Marfa's accusing eyes bored into Tanya. "You're her only friend here. No one else knows her. You're the one who must replace the mother to say a prayer at the burial. It is in the nature of things that it should be so." She nodded at izba's owner: "Pelagya will show you out and get some help."

Following several men to the back of the izba, Tanya watched as they went to work as a practiced team. With a pick and an axe, they chopped at the ground, spraying sharp, icy slivers around them. It was slow work in the darkness. The baby lay on the frozen ground while the men worked, and Tanya couldn't bring herself to touch it. She stood waiting for the ordeal to be over, the frost creeping under her skirt.

When the grave was large enough, they placed the infant into it, removed their caps in spite of the biting cold, and crossed themselves. Automatically, Tanya mouthed a re-

quiem prayer: "Eternal peace grant to him, O Lord. . . ."
The men refilled the hole, stacked their tools against the
side of the izba, and ambled away without once looking at
Tanya.

As she walked back to the izba, bonfires were crackling
along the road, and human shadows moved around them.
She didn't see Paul, and she wasn't sure she could have
said anything coherent to him at that moment.

How much more was there to endure? Sophie's agony
seemed to have been stretched out torturously long, and
with what result? A dead child, a mockery of her suffering, dispatched methodically as human waste. Five minutes
to dig a hole, thirty seconds to say a prayer, then back to
the chores of the living. She couldn't blame these moujiks
for their impersonal attitude. They acted properly, with rehearsed respect, and she could hardly expect any more
from the men, who must have been burying grown men
and women daily.

By the time she reached the izba door, she was shivering
from reaction and the cold. The moon had not come out,
and the wind bit into her face with renewed viciousness.
Once inside, she gulped a cup of scalding tea and watched
Sophie's rhythmic breathing. How was she going to react to
the news that her little son was dead? In spite of what she
had said about not wanting this child, Tanya suspected that
Sophie's maternal instinct would rebel. Tanya did not know
what words of comfort she could offer her friend.

Pelagya broke into her thoughts. "She can rest tomorrow," she said, nodding at Sophie, "but when my moujik
comes home at night, she'll have to give up the bed. If she
wants to stay here for another day, she can stretch her
tulup on the floor and sleep on it—the benches along the
wall are too narrow."

Tanya stared at the plump woman, who had propped her
thick waist with her fists and was looking at her calmly.

"I can't believe you would ask a sick woman to give up
the bed to a moujik!"

Pelagya raised her eyebrows. "Sick? The midwife says it
was a normal delivery."

Tanya glanced at Marfa, but the midwife's face was impassive.

"She was lucky to have a midwife at all," the woman went on. "Many of us drop our babies in the fields with no one to help us and bring them home in the folds of our skirts."

"How awful!"

Pelagya looked at her levelly. "Hold your tongue behind your teeth, *barinya*. These are unsettled times, and it is dangerous to be so high-minded. My moujik works hard on the railroad. Some nights like tonight, he doesn't come home at all—so when he does come back to the izba, he is entitled to his bed."

After toying with a wooden spoon for a while, Pelagya relented. "You can ask her when she wakes up if she can climb on top of the stove. She will be more comfortable up there."

Sophie slept deeply, however, and the three women decided not to disturb her. For the first time in her life, Tanya climbed on top of the stove, that coveted ledge in the household, and, feeling its heat seep into her body, folded her tulup under her head, afraid to trust her luck.

She looked down and watched Marfa and Pelagya arrange themselves on the floor. Suddenly she realized how deeply indebted she was to Marfa: for taking the responsibility for Sophie; for the comfort she had offered at the time of Gleb's death; for all the other mothering she had done in the last twelve hours.

"Thank you!" she whispered, but her words were drowned in a loud and insistent knocking on the door.

Pelagya was instantly on her feet. "Stay quiet, you two!" she ordered. "I'm not going to let anyone else in my izba. There's plenty of room in Mysovaya—let them double up somewhere else."

The knocking continued. Grumbling, she went to the door, but didn't open it. "Who's there?" she asked.

A muffled voice came through. "Prince Veragin."

In one movement Tanya jumped down from the stove. "Let him in!"

When the woman looked doubtful, she added irritably, "Open the door, I tell you! He's the one who brought my friend in."

Pelagya unbolted the door and opened it just wide

enough to let Paul in. His glance swept over the women and rested on the sleeping Sophie. In a moment, he looked at Tanya questioningly.

"She's fine, Paul, but the baby is dead."

Paul winced, then looked around the room. "Where's the baby?"

"It was awful, Paul," she began, but Marfa silenced her with one stern look.

"It's all taken care of, Your Excellency."

"So quickly?" questioned Paul, doubt in his voice. "It's only been two hours since we brought her in."

"It was an easy delivery, Excellency, and the mother is resting comfortably." Marfa nodded toward Sophie.

"What have you done with the infant?" demanded Paul, searching Marfa's face. "Even a stillborn deserves a Christian burial."

"The baby was properly buried, Excellency," replied Marfa, leveling her gaze on Tanya.

Not trusting her voice, Tanya nodded. Marfa was right. The baby was buried with prayers and respect. What purpose would it serve to create a scene now, to seem ungrateful for the best that could have been done?

Pelagya came to her rescue. Bowing low from the waist, she said: "Honor my poor izba, Prince, by breaking bread with us. There is plenty on the table."

She addressed him with a familiar *thou* and called him "Prince" instead of "Excellency" in the ancient custom of peasantry expressing affection and respect for nobility.

A sudden warmth illuminated Paul's features. "Thank you, good mistress, but I have already eaten. I came to tell my friends that there's going to be a *panikhida* for General Kappel tonight. Can you tell us where the church is?"

"There are two of them here. Try the one on the square."

"Where did they bury him?" Tanya asked.

"They didn't, Tanya. They can't bear to leave him behind, and talk about taking him along to their final destination—wherever that might be."

She stared at him. "He's been dead for over two weeks! How did they bring him across Baikal?" Her voice rose nervously; a picture of living, snow-covered phantoms carrying their dead leader across Baikal was too awful to imagine.

"We have to hurry. I'll tell you on the way."

Grabbing their tulups from the ledge of the stove, Tanya and Marfa followed Paul outside.

CHAPTER 21

Running to keep up with Paul's hurried stride, the two women panted beside him, clouds of vapor curling from their mouths.

"Even in death," Paul was saying, "General Kappel upheld the spirit of his army. Without his presence, I'm convinced, the morale would have broken down and the army surrendered. It was psychologically impossible for the Kappelevtsi to give up the body of their leader."

"God, it's horrible! How did they bring him across the lake?"

"They had the coffin on a sleigh, but the horse had been poorly shod and kept falling. At one point, it fell and refused to get up. Evidently someone suggested they lower the body under the ice and have a kind of burial at sea, but no one would hear of it. Then one of Kappel's volunteers dismounted and told them to harness his horse into the sleigh, and it came across without incident. Now the men believe it was the hand of Providence that aided them. They are determined to bury the general only when they themselves stop fleeing."

"How far are we going, Paul? When shall we stop running and be safe?"

Paul didn't answer at once. "I don't know, Tanya," he said pensively. "We can't decide now. The Japanese tell us the Bolsheviks control most of the country, and the only way left to us is to go farther—to Khabarovsk or Vladivostok—or even push our way across the border into Manchuria, where we'd be safe from the Bolsheviks once and for all."

Tanya's heart skipped a beat. Manchuria! That meant

Harbin. Why hadn't she thought of it before? Harbin was home. Familiar places, childhood memories. There were the Korchagovs—her school friend Lydia and her brother, Oleg . . . and the sweet memories of the graduation ball . . . and Kurt. Dependable, loyal Kurt. But for Paul and Sophie and Marfa . . . well, it could easily become their home, too. After all, it had been built by the Russians and looked just like a piece of Russia in a foreign land. With the future uncertain, the only place they could be safe would be out of Russia. They could all live there without terror, without thinking of fleeing to yet another place. Her family home was large, and with the accumulated rent money that Kurt was to have saved for her, she could afford to make her home available to her friends.

How wonderful it would be to be home in Harbin again! She grasped Paul by the arm.

"Paul, of course! Manchuria is the best, the safest place for all of us. That's where we must go."

Paul shook his head. "How can we judge what's best for us at this point, Tanya? I think we'll know more after we reach Chita and find out at Ataman Semenov's headquarters what the situation is for the Whites."

"Ataman Semenov commands the cossack division in the Trans-Baikal region, doesn't he?"

"I don't believe the rumor, but they say that since Admiral Kolchak's death he has proclaimed himself the Supreme Commander of the remaining White Forces."

"You don't like this Ataman Semenov, do you, Paul?"

"There has never been much trust between the White Army officers and the cossacks, Tanya, and while I've never met Ataman Semenov, I hear strange things about him. He is only twenty-eight years old and very ambitious. I have a feeling he's primarily for Ataman Semenov and secondly for his country's welfare. There are other rumors, too. . . ."

Paul's voice trailed off, but Tanya pressed. "What rumors, Paul?"

Paul shrugged. "This is only hearsay, Tanya. It's dangerous to lean heavily on rumors. Still, there's never smoke without fire. Semenov is feared in his Trans-Baikal area. It seems there's a touch of sadism in his character, and he spreads terror as he rides in style in his armored train, the *bronevik*. There's some mystery about those armored cars, but I haven't been able to find out what it is."

Tanya fell silent and, shivering, pulled at her tulup collar with both hands.

The road was filling with people as they neared the church. It was on the far side of the square, and the crowd was so dense it was impossible to get through. They stood surrounded by tightly packed soldiers, several of whom held torches, spotlighting expectant faces of the Kappelevtsi, the general's loyal men, who yearned to catch a glimpse of the open coffin and to recharge their ebbing spirit with a last look at their beloved leader. The warmth from the flames took the chill off Tanya's face, and she was glad to be next to Paul, protected from the abrasive wind.

The words of the requiem hymn floated past her on the wind's flight—"Eternal peace . . . with the saints . . ."— and echoed with the rising wail from the crowd. Tanya watched hardened men weep and listened to snatches of their whisperings: "Lord, who's going to lead us now? What's to become of us . . . ?"

Whom did they mourn, she wondered, their leader, or themselves—left debased, abandoned, and in ignorance? She pitied them, and with them she dreaded the future for herself.

Paul turned to her. "Do you want to push your way into the church?"

Tanya shook her head vigorously. "The last time I saw him he was alive. That's how I want to remember him."

Marfa looked at her. "I'll try to get inside, *barinya*. The Church is my solace and hope; without hope no man can exist—least of all me, a mother praying for her prodigal son."

She crossed herself and bowed from her waist to a corpulent priest who appeared on the steps of the church, swinging his censer in three directions and spreading a thin vapor of incense around him.

"A son? I didn't know you had a son!"

"How could you? I hadn't told you."

"Oh, Marfa! I hadn't thought . . . there wasn't . . . "
Tanya groped for words, and finding none, gave up. She
clasped Marfa in her arms, and the two women clung to
each other for a brief moment.

"You must tell me about him, Marfa," Tanya said, pushing her a little away and looking into her face. Marfa nodded. "I will. Tomorrow."

Paul hooked his arm under Tanya's. *"Panikhida* is over,
Tanya. We better get some rest. We need it."

The two of them walked back slowly, guided by the
moving torches, whose fire pranced ahead of them, playing
tricks on their weary minds. An izba loomed before them,
walls sliding, vanishing into the night; and human features,
sharply clear, flashed before them through the flames.

At their izba, Tanya moved toward the door, but Paul
put his hand on her arm and swung her around to face
him.

"Tanya, are you all right?"

There was tenderness in his voice, concern, and a shade
of something else . . . so fleeting, she didn't dare to speak
for fear of shattering the mood. She nodded.

"We're out of danger for the time being. At least we can
sleep peacefully, Tanya."

His voice was low, and it caressed her name. Her throat
tightened, choking her. She clung to him then and felt his
arms circle her in firm embrace. His breath tickled her
forehead, making her heart race foolishly. The cold melted
away, weariness receded, and the world righted itself as
she lifted her head and looked into his face, so close to
hers—so close, she hungered for his mouth, unwilling to
admit it, only longing to remain with him like this.

The torchlight shadows slid across his face, hiding the
message in his eyes and erasing the mood too fragile to
capture. Paul released her.

"Rest well, Tanyusha."

A gust of wind picked up the words, lifting the endear-
ment of her name with an echo: " . . . nyusha . . .
usha . . . "; and Tanya, burning inside, confused, bewildered, went into the izba.

* * *

Much of what followed was a blur in Tanya's memory.
They rested in Mysovaya for several days, watching other
echelons appear on the shores of Baikal; by the fourteenth
of February, all of the fleeing White armies and refugees
had crossed the lake. The final echelon counted some three
hundred fallen horses that were still alive and gave permission to the local peasants to rescue them and claim them
as their property.

Atamán Semenov sent a trainload of provisions and
grain from Chita, and for the first time in many weeks the
ever-present, gnawing hunger was satisfied. The produce
train was soon followed by a hospital train, which took
most of the sick and the wounded out of Mysovaya, before
the regular freight trains would pick up the rest of the refugees. It took a while to assign and quarter all the patients,
and after a couple of days of rest, Tanya and Marfa volunteered to help, working side by side along the sanitation
trains, aiding the wounded at the railroad station.

Sophie had recovered from childbirth, but after the initial hysterical outburst she withdrew into herself and spent
the days sitting in the izba where they were quartered, listless and gloomy. Only once, soon after the weeping subsided, did she confess to Tanya that she had secretly hung
on to the idea that the baby would be a living link with
Alexei. Now she felt there was no reason left for her to
live.

Tanya, concerned about her friend's depression, sought
Paul's advice. He was unloading boxes of medical supplies
from a freight car when Tanya found him. Clean-shaven
and rested, he looked again the commanding officer she
had met in Omsk; and, unaccountably, she felt a distance
widen between them. Shyly, she told him about Sophie.
Paul responded warmly.

"Give her time, Tanya. Sometimes the spirit doesn't heal
as fast as the body. If we don't push her, and treat her with
kindness and consideration, I'm sure she'll be herself again
soon enough. Be more patient with her."

He was tolerant of Sophie's depression, urging Tanya to
be kind and considerate, but he didn't seem interested in
her emotional state. He took it for granted she could fend
for herself. With the exception of the one instance on the

night of the *panikhida*, when he'd asked her if she was all right, he had remained aloof. Again she felt inexplicably hurt.

"What about yourself, Tanya? How are you doing?"

He lifted her chin with his thumb and forefinger and was looking at her with a smile. There was kindness and affection in his voice, but instead of being pleased, Tanya was angry. *He's treating me like a child, like a troublesome child placed in his care—sometimes to be petted, sometimes to be disciplined.*

"I'm fine, thank you," she answered stiffly. "And thanks for your advice about Sophie."

She turned abruptly on her heel, aware that she left Paul surprised, probably wondering what had caused her frosty response.

It was something she couldn't explain to herself. He had helped her survive a horrendous ordeal that would probably go down in the history of the war as the hardest in human endurance, and he had shown his concern for her on many occasions. What was it, then, that she wanted from him? Confused, she was annoyed with herself for her unreasonable anger against Paul. All the people who were once close to her were now gone: her parents, Yuri, Gleb, possibly Grandmaman. She needed a friend desperately, someone strong she could depend upon. What exactly *did* she feel for Paul? The answer would not come—or maybe it was one she didn't dare be honest about. And as she reached Marfa's side, a strange, unwelcome flush warmed her face.

In the ensuing days they continued to help where needed, waiting and hoping for the first available train to take them to Chita and the security of the White Army headquarters, pushing out of their minds the disturbing rumors they heard about Ataman Semenov.

At times Tanya thought about Marfa's son and wondered what had become of him, but when she questioned her, the older woman seemed reluctant to talk. It wasn't until a detachment of smartly uniformed cadets from Chita military academy arrived in Mysovaya to form the honor guard for their new commander, General Voitzekhovsky, and Marfa watched the young men march through the village, that her composure crumpled.

Weeping, she struggled to control herself while Tanya waited, patting her gently on the shoulder. After she calmed down a little, Marfa stumbled over several disjointed, incoherent phrases, then took a deep breath and began to talk, words tumbling out, as if the grief she'd been harboring so long demanded an outlet.

"I'm from Glaskov, Tatiana Andreyevna," she said, bridging the social gap between the two women by addressing Tanya directly by her name and patronymic instead of the more subservient *barinya.* "A suburb of Irkutsk it is, and now the Bolsheviks are there. We managed well, believe me, the three of us. We Buryats are strong and resourceful. We never starved. On Sundays we had pork and ground beef in our *pelmeni,* and fish and cabbage and potatoes during weekdays. Our izba was not large, but clean and hospitable.

"My moujik, Ivan, was a good man, sober most of the time, and hardworking. He loved me, for he beat me on occasion to show that he cared, and even then only when the village reeve gave him too much vodka on holidays.

"A big hunter he was. He'd go off into the taiga for the hunt and be gone a long time. When he came home, tired but happy, he'd bring the pelts with him for the fur trade.

"A good provider he was, and a strict father to our son, Tikhon. Then, one day a year ago, he went on his usual hunt and didn't come back. A she-bear got him when he accidentally disturbed her cubs. They brought back what was left of him wrapped in pelts on the sleigh. . . . God rest his soul."

"Tikhon and I were left alone, but he was twenty years old by then, and already a man—the apple of my eye!" Marfa pressed her mittened fingers over her trembling lips for a moment. "Yes, my Tikhon! A smart boy he is. He went to school, you know. He can read and write. I was so proud of him.

"And then, after Ivan was torn by the bear, Tikhon changed. It was as if the devil himself had entered his soul. He became restless, willful. I'd come home after midwifing and Tikhon would be gone, and when he returned late in the night, he'd brood in his corner and not tell me where he'd been except to say he had attended some meeting in Irkutsk.

"Then, one night, I found him drunk, and I'd never seen him drink as much as one glass of vodka before. He told me he was leaving Glaskov and going north of Baikal, deep into the dense taiga, where the Red partisans were hiding. He said he was going to join them. My Tikhon! My quiet, obedient Tikhon told me he was tired of hard labor without justice; said he hated the old regime with its cruelty toward the poor; and, finally, told me he believed in the Bolsheviks, who promised freedom and equal opportunities for all workers and peasants.

"I confess, I lost my temper and screamed at him that he was taking advantage of his old mother, and were his father alive, he'd take the besom to his ass and thrash all the nonsense out of his head. But Tikhon only said that his mind was made up and he'd send me money from time to time. He tied a small bundle to the end of a birch pole, threw it over his shoulder, took his father's rifle, and said he wanted to build a better order for his fellow men. Some better order! Murder, rape, brother killing brother."

Marfa began to wring her hands. "Where is my Tikhon now? Has he become a murderer, too? Is that the way to avenge injustice, a tooth for a tooth? Is he ashamed to face his mother? If only I knew where he is and if all is well with him! I haven't heard a word from him since he left six months ago."

Tanya sat stunned, unable to find the right words to console the older woman. The life she had described was an alien world to Tanya, where hardships and pain were endured without protest, where physical abuse from a spouse was deemed an expression of love, and where death regularly swept a wide path through the living. She had read of this in ancient ballads, but hadn't thought of the possibility that it still existed now, in the twentieth century.

For the first time, a seed of doubt crept into Tanya's neatly packaged worlds of "us" and "them." Was it possible they had reason to revolt? Perhaps they had. But the methods they employed could never be condoned. Looting, burning, wanton killings of women and children, a rampage of vengeance unleashed against innocent victims—all betrayed the savagery of an undisciplined mob. Such license was inadmissable among the Whites. No, she couldn't forgive the Bolsheviks, couldn't understand Marfa's son wanting to remain with the Reds.

"Marfa, don't grieve over Tikhon. He may be hiding from the partisans and afraid to appear in the open. Be patient. Wait. He'll survive, I'm sure, and you'll find each other when this nightmare is over."

The air was turning colder, and she took Marfa's hand. "Come, Marfa dear, let's go inside—it's cold, and we don't want to catch a fever. We have a long way to go yet before we reach Chita."

The next day the skies were clear for the first time since their arrival in Mysovaya, and the sun, unhampered by stray clouds, bathed the village in its shining light. The brilliance, reflected in the snow's crystalline sparkles, created an illusion of warmth and drew Tanya outdoors like a magnet. She urged Sophie to leave the dark, stuffy izba and venture out for a walk, but her friend, refusing to move, shook her head.

Outside, there was no *booran*—no breeze at all—and the air, the frosty air that pinched her cheeks playfully, sent blood coursing through her veins with a rediscovered joy of being young and living.

She walked aimlessly along the road, smiling at the remembered childhood pleasure of the crunching sound under her feet in the undisturbed serenity of a winter day. Above her, a clump of snow slid off a cedar branch, dusting her uplifted face with prickly flakes. There was no wasted movement on the street; bundled men and women scurried back and forth with a purpose. But Tanya felt no guilt for being idle on this perfect morning.

Another pair of crunching footsteps fell in beside her, and she looked up to see Paul's rested, smiling face. She was struck anew by his blond handsomeness, framed now by a new sable hat.

"Good morning, Tanya!"

"Good morning, Paul!"

They stopped, each looking at the other in mute surprise.

In spite of the heavy winter clothing, Tanya saw a younger Paul, the lines of stress smoothed over, the muscles around his mouth relaxed. Perhaps the sun, perhaps the softness of the morning scene, had caused the change; but the aloof commanding officer from Omsk had vanished, and she watched a warmer smile and possibly a teasing twinkle in his eye when he asked, "Why are you walking away from Baikal, Tanya? It is so beautiful today."

"I don't know, Paul. Come to think of it, ever since we've been here, I seem to head naturally in this direction whenever I leave the izba."

"Are you reluctant to see the lake again?"

"Perhaps that's the reason, now that you mention it."

"If you're afraid to relive the nightmare of our crossing, then there's no better time than right now to erase those impressions."

"Why now?"

"For two reasons. First, on such a clear day it's hard to think of past horrors, and Baikal is an enchanted world when frozen in the sun. Second, the local fishermen are catching omul, and it's a fascinating thing to watch."

"Fishing in winter?"

"Yes. Omul is a highly commercial product, and they need it for their livelihood. Let's go and watch, Tanya!"

He took her firmly under the arm. "They say the omul gives off a sharp cry when it's hauled out of the water," he said, steering her toward the lake.

"That must be old wives' tales, Paul. Fish die silently."

"They do, but omul is an exception. Haven't you heard the local expression yet, 'Stop yelping like an omul'?"

Tanya laughed. "I can hardly believe it's true."

They climbed down the embankment and headed toward a group of fishermen busy with their nets. Shuffling her feet, Tanya made her valenki glide on the lake surface for a while, then paused to look down. She was standing on a smooth spot where the wind had blown the snow away, leaving clear blue ice. Deeply frozen, it was nevertheless fully transparent, and as she looked, mesmerized, there was movement below. She peered closely. In the cold, unfrozen waters beneath the many feet of ice, a school of fish scampered back and forth, secure in its undine empire.

"Isn't this a beautiful sight, Tanya?"

Holding Tanya's arm, Paul bent low, his warm breath brushing her cheek and sending little shivers of delight down her spine.

"Good morning, my good men!" he called to the fishermen.

"And a good day to you, Excellency," echoed the men good-naturedly.

"Will it disturb the fish if we watch?"

"No, Excellency. Omul is too deep to care. Come closer."

Paul and Tanya approached. The men were lowering the net into a deep hole in front of them. Leaning over to peer into the hole, Tanya slipped and narrowly missed falling down. Paul caught her around the waist, and the force of his sweep propelled her against his chest. She felt her heart beat wildly like the wings of a trapped bird. The fishermen guffawed and warned, "It's fun to watch the fish, but it's wiser to look at your feet!"

They tugged at the net and, satisfied that it was loaded, began to pull it up. Tanya glanced at Paul. His face was eager with anticipation, and he reminded her of a young schoolboy on his first fishing trip. He moved closer to the men and, placing his arm around the shoulders of the nearest moujik, leaned far over to look into the hole.

"Careful, Excellency—the fish may fly up and hit you in the face as we bring it up."

Paul moved back. "I guess it won't do to be kissed by a wet fish," he laughed.

"And a cold one at that!" added the men, winking at Paul.

Tanya was enchanted. She had never seen Paul so relaxed. It was a new man she was seeing, and she liked what she saw. He had warmth, he had humor, and he wasn't too class-conscious to engage in a friendly banter with the common man.

"Here they come—look!" Paul tugged at her sleeve.

The fishermen lifted the net full of omul onto the glistening ice, and the fish, jumping into the air in search of

water, gave out a sharp cry before flipping prone onto the
ice. The men moved fast, lifting the net to prevent the fish
from freezing to the surface.

Paul waved to the men. "A good catch, men! Good luck
to you!"

The men took off their hats and bowed slightly. "And
God be with you, Excellency. Take care of *barinya*!"

Tanya felt suspended in space. For the first time since
meeting Paul, she sensed total affinity between them, and
all her hurt and anger had at last disappeared. She looked
beneath her feet again, wondering if a dream had trans-
ported her into the land of enchanted castles, diamond-
studded pillars, and crystal floors. This was not the same
menacing giant they had crossed. This was a fairyland
lake, and it was a graceful host, sharing its wealth with
man, twinkling and sparkling in a rainbow of light.

From that moment, when she had recognized its compassion, she looked at Baikal without reluctance, memorizing
its panorama with pride and regret, knowing that she was
going to leave it soon, perhaps forever.

Three days later there was room for them in a boxcar.
They bid a warm good-bye to their quiet but generous hosts
in the izba and boarded the train for Chita.

CHAPTER 22

This time, riding the boxcar was a luxury to Tanya. No more sleighs, no more fighting the elements of the Siberian winter. The heat from a small stove in the center of the car eased the pain from freezing temperatures, and there was no wind to whip the face. Best of all, the resident fear was replaced by an undercurrent of excitement, a delicious anticipation of better things to come.

A little over a hundred miles from Mysovaya, they stopped for refueling in Verkhne-Udinsk, a town of twenty thousand inhabitants. Stiffened from the cramped boxcar, the eager refugees spilled out to exercise. Many went in search of food. At the station buffet, Tanya and Marfa bought cheese and cold cuts, and with the leftover dried bread from Mysovaya, which they soaked with carbonated water from a syphon, they made themselves a sandwich.

While she ate, Tanya noticed that Paul's hands were empty. Up until now, he had provided all the food that could be had along the way. Today, however, it was she who had paid for the purchases, and because she was thrilled to be able to choose from the assortment of goods she was seeing for the first time in many months, she hadn't been aware that Paul had bought nothing. Why? Was it possible he had run out of money?

Slipping back to the station buffet, she bought more cheese and cold meat, piled it all on the leftover piece of bread, and carried the sandwich to Paul.

"Here," she said casually, "please help me out, Paul. I overestimated my appetite, and with all the hunger around us, it would be sinful to waste this."

With a simple "thank you," Paul took the sandwich and ate it, while Tanya watched, wondering how she was going to manage the delicate matter of paying for his food from now on.

She turned to look at the busy street. Verkhne-Udinsk, with its log houses and snow-covered planked sidewalks, looked little different from Mysovaya, only larger and noisier. What impressed Tanya the most, however, was the variety of goods in the stores. The everyday things she couldn't find in Omsk, such as pens and pencils, and even cologne and face powder, were here in abundance.

In spite of subzero temperatures, vendors were busily cooking pancakes over an open hearth and selling them with sour cream, attracting customers not only by their food but by the heat from the glowing embers. Asian workmen were hauling water in barrel carts, the same barrels she had seen in Omsk. The town was teaming with Asiatic faces, and to Tanya's mute question, Paul shrugged. "Ataman Semenov's Buryat-Mongol brigade must be positioned nearby. We're not far from the Mongolian border. Besides, this is Buryat country, and their blood is thoroughly mixed with the Mongols."

They continued their journey, reaching Chita, three hundred miles away, in a couple of days. There, for the first time since their flight began, they were greeted by the cossacks in fur-lined capes and White Army forces in fresh uniforms. At the station they caught a glimpse of Ataman Semenov's armored train parked on a separate siding—its smoke stacks puffing lazily in the crisp afternoon air, its shining metal sparkling in the pale sun. Several cossacks stood at attention guarding the train, as if to remind those who might forget, that their leader had his headquarters inside.

In spite of the dazzling array of varied uniforms and the happy shouts of reunited comrades who surrounded Paul, Tanya was weary and anxious to find a place to sleep. Her concern over Sophie's delicate health grew daily, and she wanted to make her friend rest in reasonable comfort.

"Your Excellency! Prince Veragin!"

The four travelers turned around simultaneously. A tall officer, gaunt but clean shaven, shoved his way through the crowd. Dressed in a fresh greatcoat, he could have passed for a rear-guard member of the general staff were it not for his face—the bloodless skin taut over hollow cheeks and the skeletal protrusions of the frontal bones betraying his share of privations. A vessel pulsated on his temple, straining to burst, and as he smiled, the folds gathered laboriously around the sunken eyes, pulling and blanching the nostrils.

Paul frowned, recognition dawning slowly.

"Konev!"

The men embraced and patted each other on the shoulder. Paul turned to Tanya and Sophie. "Captain Konev was with me at the western front. We fought in several battles together." He smiled at Konev. "How many summers, how many winters have gone by? How long have you been here, friend?"

Paul looked at the captain's new uniform, his leather-trimmed *burki* boots, then back at his face. "Bring us up on the latest, Konev!"

"The place is rampant with rumors, Prince. I've been here with my regiment for a few weeks, and the information that filters through with each new contingent of refugees changes every day. The official dispatches are patriotic, if not always optimistic."

Konev hesitated, then continued. "Since Admiral Kolchak's death, Ataman Semenov has assumed the title of the Supreme Ruler under the sponsorship of the Japanese forces here. His cossacks and Mongolian troops are firmly behind him."

Paul studied him reflectively. "What about the Whites in Manchuria—are they giving him support?"

Konev shrugged. "We receive a lot of lip service from there, but no action. Once safely abroad, they swear allegiance to the cause, yet no one seems eager to return to fight for it. General Horvath is the administrator in Harbin, but he's not a military leader now and does not inspire a fighting spirit. The truth is, Ataman Semenov is the only one who's active."

"What sort of a leader is he?"

Konev stole a glance at Tanya and quickly looked away, but not before she caught its significance, wondering what this hesitation implied.

"Ataman Semenov is the only commander we have

who's willing to lead us," Konev replied evasively. "His methods are harsh on occasion, but we have little choice in the matter."

A rhythmic clip-clop of horses' hoofs, the sound muted by the packed snow on the road, made them skittle to the sidewalk, with scattering pedestrians following suit. A detachment of cossacks trotted leisurely up the street. Side by side they rode, in two rows, four abreast, horses snorting, steam rising above their bridles. With an inscrutable look the cossacks scanned the crowds below them, their dark and slanted eyes all but hidden beneath the tall furry *papakhi*.

Somber and fearsome, with spurred leather boots glinting beneath their flared and belted ankle-length coats, the pockets of ammunition sewn into their uniforms across their chests creating an illusion of muscular, broad-shouldered men, heavy daggers secured diagonally at the waists below their stomachs, the cossacks dwarfed the street with their exotic presence.

Tanya felt a stirring of pride in her breast and wondered what regiment they belonged to, for they were not wearing Ataman Semenov's blue and green uniform. But what did it matter? All cossacks had a legendary reputation for their courage and prowess, for their endurance and cunning in battle. Fearless and feared, they were known to have demoralized the enemy by a mere rumor of their approach.

A shrill scream startled her.

"Tikhon! *Tiiiiikhon!*"

Tanya turned around just in time to see Marfa, her face wild with joy, tears streaming down her cheeks, dash past her with the speed and agility of a filly. Oblivious of crowding horses, she flew among them blindly, slapping their flanks to make way for herself. She circled the leg of a young cossack in the rear row with both arms, buried her face in the folds of his coat, and burst into loud sobs.

"Oh, son—*synok, synochek!* I found you, found you!"

The cossack reined in his horse sharply, and the animal reared, raking the air with its front hoofs. He calmed the horse with a few words, then dismounted, and clasped Marfa in a tight embrace, his *papakha* pushed far back on his head, revealing the dusky complexion of a face that was a smiling extension of the weeping woman in his arms.

After a few curious glances at the reunited mother and son, the cossacks rode on, leaving Tikhon with Marfa.

What is Tikhon doing among the cossacks? thought Tanya, studying the young man curiously. She looked for Paul, but he and Konev lagged behind, deep in animated conversation. Sophie tugged at her sleeve.

"Isn't Tikhon supposed to be in the taiga with the Red partisans?" she whispered.

Tanya nodded. "I wonder what made him desert the Bolsheviks and come over to the Whites."

Life was ever thus. His mother's pleadings had no effect on him, but could it be that the Bolshevik savagery had roused his conscience? Tanya sighed and watched the dark-eyed youth with a smile. If only other young men were like him and saw the Reds for what they were, then the Bolsheviks would not have gained so much power.

"Tanya, it's getting dark. We must look for lodging."

Paul had joined them, and Tanya, taking Sophie by the arm, watched in the gathering darkness as Tikhon kissed his mother, mounted his horse, and galloped away to catch up with his comrades.

Sniffling, Marfa wiped her nose with the sleeve of her tulup, rubbed her eyes with the butts of her palms, and said proudly: "He's with the cossacks now," as if the obvious had to be underscored. "They are free for the night and are off for some fun. We'll see him tomorrow."

Tanya hugged Marfa, her pallor accentuated by the older woman's robust face. "Dear Marfa! I'm so happy for you."

Pushing her slightly back, Marfa studied her face. "Thank you, *kasatka*. And now it's time to rest. You and Sophie must be tired, and we should stop at the nearest izba."

The four of them started down the street, passing up the large stone buildings and heading for the outskirts of town, where the more modest izba owners would be willing to share their crowded space with the homeless wanderers. Elaborately carved eaves and window frames, one fancier than the next and painted in cheerful blue, green, or white, greeted them along the way.

Paul was pensive, and Tanya wondered what Konev had told him to upset him.

It was dark when they knocked on the first door. No luck. Time and again they were turned away, sometimes sullenly, sometimes kindly, but always with a suggestion to try the next izba. Near the edge of town, an old moujik, holding a candle high above his head, answered their knock and squinted at them under the unsteady flame. Studying them, his gaze lingered sympathetically on Sophie's wan face.

"As you see," he shrugged, pointing to the tiny porch stuffed with storage barrels, hay, and a crowd of people, "even the *syeni* is filled. There just isn't enough room for the four of you." He paused, sighing, and then added: "But I can make room for two."

Paul hesitated, but before he could say a word, Tanya pushed Sophie and Marfa forward. Later she was to wonder what had impelled her to act impulsively, to perform the seemingly minor act of charity that precipitated the far-reaching dramatic events that followed. But at that moment, without thinking, she prodded the two women inside, talking quickly.

"Thank you, *dyedushka*, for your kindness. God will reward you for your friendship. We'll come after them in the morning."

Before anyone could speak, Tanya pulled Paul by the sleeve and rushed out into the street. There was no moon, and in total darkness they stumbled forward, holding on to each other. Paul was unusually quiet, and Tanya, alarmed, had to know why.

"Paul, what did Konev tell you? Is there some bad news?"

Paul did not answer at once. When he spoke, Tanya thought she detected a trace of anxiety and repugnance in his voice.

"What Konev told me is so monstrous, Tanya, that were it not for the honesty of the man, I would have accused him of fabrication."

"What did he tell you? Please, Paul, I have to know!"

She surprised herself by the unchecked authority in her voice and fell silent. Paul responded immediately, as if he had been waiting to share with her the burden of his knowledge.

"I have heard rumors and hints that Ataman Semenov is not always scrupulous in how and to whom he metes out punishment and justice. One hears of harsh treatment even of his own men. But what Konev told me creates an image of a man who condones sadism in his men. There was some mystery about that sleekly polished, well-cared-for armored train of his. Well, a gruesome tale it is. Whenever the Red partisans or the Bolshevik regulars are caught, they are brought into the *bronevik* and occasionally forced at gunpoint to place their heads into the open furnace. Those unfortunates are used as human fuel for the locomotive! And what's so appalling is that those wretches are terrorized so out of their minds that none refuses to place his head into the firebox by himself. This kind of execution is the product of a warped mind."

Tanya shook her head in horror. "I can't believe such atrocities exist among the Whites, Paul. But if it is true, then Ataman Semenov must be unaware of what goes on. He's too busy fighting the Reds. Why, your friend Konev is condemning his own leader! Ataman Semenov is on our side. We must trust him."

Paul made no reply, and soon they came to a low, narrow building. A weak candlelight winked at them through a window. Paul held Tanya by the arm. "Wait! This must be an army barracks. Let's try it. We may have luck here. An izba or a barracks—what difference does it make as long as we're protected from the cold?"

When no one answered their knock, Paul pushed the door. It gave in easily. Inside, a scene of indescribable misery presented itself. Fully clothed soldiers, three to a cot, were slumped over one another like breathing rag dolls, snoring thunderously with each intake of breath. Sighs and moans rose and fell rhythmically from wounded men, their bandages soaked with blood and pus. A few women, pale and exhausted, slept fitfully on the floor, or sat against the wall, their children whining in the crooks of their arms. The mixed stench of festering wounds, foul breath, and stifled

air choked Tanya with nausea. She clutched Paul's forearm with trembling fingers.

"Paul, what about the hospitals? Where are they?"

"They'll get there in due time—if they don't die here
first."

Paul covered his nose with his glove. "Let's get out of
here. We can come back for the night if we don't find
something else. But first we have to find a place to eat."

Tanya ran out into the street, gulping deeply of the pure,
sweet air. Together, they headed back toward town, trying
new streets in the hope of finding a place to buy food.

Tanya began to shiver. "Are you chilled, Tanya?" Paul
asked, concern thinly veiled in his voice.

"No, but my skirt is soaked from brushing against the
snowdrifts." In spite of the cold, Tanya felt a flush rise to
her face.

With all the indignities and deprivations they had gone
through together, she still couldn't tell him that the slush
snow on her skirt bounced against her thighs, moistening her
underwear and causing her to tremble.

"Then we must stop at the next izba and ask to dry it."

Paul steered her into a side alley, where a lighted izba
beckoned them.

A huge cossack opened the door to their knock and
stepped aside to let them enter. The light was dim, but
Tanya was able to discern that the inside of the izba was
little more than a converted barn. Hay was stacked in the
corners, and a pitchfork and scythe hung on the wall. A
group of cossacks sat around a wooden table in the center
of the room, their Mongol faces distorted by the wavering
glow from a single candle stuck in an empty bottle.

The sight of black bread and sausage made Tanya's
empty stomach lurch painfully.

"Greetings to you, cossacks," Paul said. "We're strangers
in Chita and are hungry. Could you share some bread with
us?"

Silently, the cossacks slid on the benches, crowding one
another to make room for Paul and Tanya on both sides of
the table.

Squeezed between the powerful arms of two men, Tanya
ignored the strong whiff of vodka coming at her and ate

the salted chunk of bread, scalding her throat with hot tea.
Her lips trembled over the edge of the tin cup from the
almost forgotten feeling of relief—the safety, the buoyancy,
of having been freed from the pressure of fear. The enemy
territory was far behind them, and for the first time in
many months she and Paul were surrounded by the
warmth of fellow Whites, who exuded strength and inspired confidence.

How wonderful it was to be in a friendly camp! As she
tipped her cup for the last sip of the tea, her eyes fell on
the cossack sitting at the far end of the table from her.
With a gasp she cried, "Tikhon, it's you! I'm so glad to see
you again! Oh, how I wish Marfa were here!" Tanya smiled
and shook her head. "She'll be so sorry she didn't come
with us."

Tikhon did not smile, only nodded, and avoided looking
into her eyes. The significance of his strangely sullen response did not register with Tanya until much later. She
wanted to talk to him, to ask why he hadn't contacted his
mother all these months, but she sensed that her questions
would embarrass him and refrained from questioning him.
Right now she was intoxicated by her emotions, more so,
perhaps, than the cossacks, who were gulping vodka and
staring at her from all sides.

Paul finished his bread, took a swallow of vodka from a
bottle offered him, and then rose abruptly from his seat.

"Tanya, we must thank these men and go now to look
for a place to stay the night." He turned to the cossack who
let them in. "Thank you, good man, for your hospitality.
We won't forget it."

The cossack shrugged. "Don't thank me, Excellency.
You walked in on us; we didn't invite you."

The gruff sound of the man's voice startled Tanya. She
realized these were the first words spoken in the izba by a
cossack since they had entered. Why, she thought, these
poor men, tired and hungry themselves, must feel ill at
ease in the presence of an army colonel and his lady—it
was a pleasant thought to be mistaken for Paul's lady. But
Paul, she suspected, equally aware of the awkward situation, wanted to leave right away.

When she rose, the men rose, too, some of them drunk

enough to sway on their feet. Tanya suppressed a smile.
They probably couldn't wait for them to leave so they could
finish their vodka and collapse in the hay, soft and inviting
behind her.

She smiled, nodded to the cossacks, then started toward
the door. She had almost reached it when there was a sudden gasp and a swishing sound behind her. Before she
could turn around, a rough burlap sack came down over
her head to her waist, pinning her arms to her sides. One
strong arm clamped over her mouth through the musty
cloth and another circled her waist, roughly squeezing her
breast. She heard a silent scuffle near her, struggled to
unlock the strong arm, kicked, heard a muffled oath of
"Fighting bitch," smelled a hot breath stagnant with vodka,
then felt other arms grab her ankles and her thighs, poking,
shoving, lifting her in the air and carrying her, rigid, somewhere into hell.

She writhed and choked under the pressing hand on her
mouth, one frantic thought stabbing at her: Oh, God, there
are so many of them! How many? How can this be happening? Our own Whites! The cossacks! And Tikhon! Holy
Mother of God! Not in front of Marfa's son!

Nothing mattered—not the dreadful experience awaiting
her, not the fate that had befallen Paul—but the number of
her assailants. A few she could survive, but how many?

Her head spun, and with a moan she went limp.

CHAPTER 23

When Paul regained consciousness, the sack was still over his head. His wrists and ankles were securely tied and a gag was in his mouth. He remembered thinking, just before he was knocked out, that he had sensed the men's restiveness and feared a drunken brawl; but he had never expected the violence from the cossacks to be directed against him. Not from the decent, highly principled cossacks he knew. No. These were some wild Mongols playing a dangerous game.

Words and sounds began to reach him. As he listened, it became clear it was more than a game. Where was Tanya? What happened to her? A strong smell of vodka confirmed his fears that the men were still drunk. Through the rough weave of the sack, a faint light filtered through, shadows moving back and forth. The men were not idle, for he heard scuffling and grunts and a thud. For a few seconds there was no sound, and then a voice said:

"Naah! Delicate feelings these gentlewomen have. You can't touch them but they faint. She should come around soon. Let's wait. No challenge otherwise."

She. Paul's heart lurched. Tanya? He strained his muscles against the tight ropes as the voice continued. "Take the sack off his head. Let's have some fun with His Excellency before she wakes up, and then he can watch. More spice this way."

Another voice said uncertainly, "We should have gotten rid of him first."

The first voice cut him off sharply. "*Durak!* Fool! We don't want any questions or investigation. It'll be a long time before they find them. This izba has been deserted since last year, and no one will think of looking here."

The sack came off Paul's head, and he blinked, taking in the scene all at once.

Tanya lay unconscious on top of a small haystack. She was not tied. The men idled around her, gurgling long swigs of vodka from a bottle. Rivulets of liquid dribbled down their beards, and lust smoldered in their bloodshot, slanted eyes. With their yellow skin and unruly black hair, Paul had recognized them as Buryat-Mongol cossacks of Eastern Siberia the moment he stepped inside the izba. What a fool he had been to trust them! They bore little resemblance to the crack Don Cossack regiments of European Russia. Some of these were little more than unreined bandits, descendants of the Mongol hordes, and they were running wild in Siberia, beyond the reach of progress and civilized behavior. To fall victim to these savages was to destroy the dignity of death. Their cunning was primitive, Paul realized too late. How easily he had walked into their trap. They would never miss a ready-made opportunity for debauchery, and he, driven by hunger, had lowered his guard.

And Tanya? Oh, God! Paul counted the men. There were eight of them. The same eight who had trotted past them earlier on the street of Chita, for Tikhon was among them. The two men's eyes met and held. The younger man paled, and his eyes shifted from Paul to Tanya and, one by one, to the other seven men. As Paul stared at him, he became aware that the young cossack was moving stealthily backward toward the door of the izba.

"Well, well, Your Excellency—not very comfortable for you, is it?" chuckled a burly cossack, his beard so bushy that only the tip of his flat nose and the slant Buryat eyes peered at him beneath his karakul *papakha*. He pulled out his saber and with feline accuracy sliced a sheaf of hay by Paul's ear. It was so close that Paul felt the air current as the weapon whistled by.

"*Nu, nu,* Excellency," taunted the cossack, "did you shove your courage in the pocket? Or are your nerves too delicate for our cossack games?"

Paul's mind raced. This was no time for heroics. Immobilized, his only hope of surviving and saving Tanya was by outwitting the cossacks. A slim hope, but that was all he

had. But how to go about it? If only Tanya remained unconscious, maybe they'd get so drunk they'd pass out. Time
was his only weapon. Perhaps he could work through Tikhon. Where was he? Paul looked beyond the burly Buryat
to where he had seen Tikhon last, but the young cossack
had disappeared. Where? He had no time to think of an
answer, for his tormentor coiled a whip in his hand and
said very quietly: "What's the matter—you've lost your
tongue? Or don't you talk to a cossack?"

Unsteady on his feet, he staggered slightly, then swept
Paul a mocking bow. "Pardon me, Excellency, I forgot
you've lost your voice."

He threw back his head and guffawed. Then with lightning speed he lashed at Paul. The whip seared him across
the ear and cheek, setting the flesh on fire. Unable to re-
strain himself, Paul groaned through the gag.

"Aha! We're alive after all, huh?" The cossack took another gulp of vodka, handed the bottle to the man next to
him, and leered at Paul. "Want another one? My aim im-
proves each time." He coiled the whip again. Paul winced,
drops of blood from the broken skin crawling down his
neck.

The second lash landed across the first as Paul flinched
and turned his head to protect the healthy side of his face.

A piercing scream made the cossack wheel around.
Tanya had come around and saw the whip land on Paul.

The cossack's face turned purple with rage. "Where are
you idiots looking? Plug her up and tie her before she
brings the roof down. We don't want any strangers running
in!"

His attention was now diverted from Paul, and, coiling
his whip, he walked slowly toward Tanya.

Gagged now, she was spread-eagled, her wrists being
tied to two posts behind her and her legs held by two cossacks who couldn't find anything to tie them to and held
them down with both hands as she struggled to kick. Her
eyes, wide with terror, had left Paul's bloody face and were
staring at the cossack who was towering above her with the
whip.

"Well, well, well," grinned the huge man, playing with
his whip and throwing off his fur-lined cape, which had

made him look more like a bear than a cossack. "Let's see what we've got here!"

He moved closer, his black boots between her legs.

"Stenka!"

Without taking his eyes off Tanya, he waved to a young cossack hovering near him. "Keep the fire burning nicely—we don't want our delicate wench to freeze before we're through with her."

The young cossack dashed to check the small iron stove, which emitted just enough heat to keep the numbing chill out of the air. He added a few pieces of wood and came back.

"It'll burn for a while, Antip."

Antip nodded and threw the whip away. "Hey, pass the vodka over here!"

He grabbed the neck of the bottle and, tilting his head far back, gurgled the fiery liquid. His narrow eyes were almost closed, but, in the unsteady light thrashing inside the tiny stove, a slivered glint shone from below his thatched brows.

Handing the bottle to Stenka, Antip wiped his glistening moustache with the back of his hand and pulled the dagger out of its scabbard at his belt. Then he bent over Tanya and slit her dress from the neck to the waist. The dagger had cut through the underwear but didn't break the skin.

Antip lost his balance and began to rock back and forth to steady himself.

"Pull it off—let's see!" he ordered hoarsely, waving his hands in a fluttering gesture. Stenka obligingly pulled Tanya's clothing apart, sliding his grimy hands over her full breasts, the nipples rigid in the cold. Her white skin glowed in semidarkness, and Antip clucked his tongue appreciatively. "Not bad. I've seen some with puffier tits, but she'll do."

As Stenka's hand crawled over and pinched Tanya's nipple, Antip's grin turned into a scowl. "Hands off! I'm first, understand? You'll get your turn later."

Antip stepped back a little and, hooking his dagger under the hem of Tanya's skirt, flipped it up to her waist, exposing her woolen underwear.

"Stenka! Pull them off!" he ordered, and Stenka started

to drag the bloomers down eagerly, but they wouldn't come off Tanya's spread-eagled legs. With an oath, Antip stooped and slashed the waistband.

Horrified, Paul stared, unable to pull his eyes away. Stretched out in the hay, exposed, Tanya's body quivered like a tormented swan—her white thighs and the downy triangle of her pubis, vassal to her attackers' profanation. Watching, Paul was suddenly aroused, and, feeling his body tense, was mortified. Shame rose within him: shame for his physical reaction, for the primitive, unbidden urge. Hot tears filled his eyes as the thought of what the drunken cossack was about to do choked him. His hands shook convulsively, yearning to close around Antip's neck and squeeze the foul breath out of him forever.

Antip unbuckled his belt, pulled it off, and froze, his hand suspended in the air, his face, lusty and bloated, suddenly alert. He cocked his head and listened.

The sound of a galloping horse reverberated in the izba. Moments later it died down. Antip wheeled around, his face contorted with rage.

"Who's missing?"

Stenka stepped forward. "Tikhon is gone. It must be him. Lost his nerve, I reckon."

"Idiot! He must have gone for help!"

Comprehension dawned slowly across Stenka's face. Then he shrugged again. "So what! No one'll listen to him." He rubbed the front of his pants and grinned. "Come on, Antip, hurry up—I want my turn." He looked down at Tanya's opened thighs, her legs still pinned by two cossacks. The rest of the men shuffled impatiently from foot to foot, their flatulent faces absorbing the scene.

With his *papakha* firmly on his head, Antip walked over to stand over Tanya once more. He watched her squirm under his lustful glare and began to unbutton his pants.

"Come on, *rebyata*, we have time before Tikhon comes back. No use wasting her. At least there's time for me!"

"Oh yeah?" Stenka's voice rose a pitch. "You expect us to watch you shaft her and us go hurting? We all saddle her or none at all."

"To the devil with you! Ride into town and lasso yourself a kid—he'll do just as well."

Antip lowered himself to his knees between Tanya's legs. Stenka's agitation mounted as his eyes kept sliding toward Tanya's groin. "There's more fun with a wench and you know it! We all mount her. Shove off!"

With full force he ran his body into Antip. Taken by surprise, Antip lost his balance and crashed to the ground, his large bulk rolling over toward Paul. In a flash, he was on his feet and charging at Stenka, who wasted no time in dropping to his knees over Tanya.

Suddenly, a cossack who stood guard at the door yelled: "I hear horses! There are a lot of them. Listen!"

A distant rhythmic thud of hoofbeats was unmistakable. Antip was the first to react.

"It can't be Tikhon so soon. It's someone else. Whoever it is, we don't want them in here. Damn! Cover her up and let's get out of here. We'll come back later."

The two cossacks released Tanya's legs and flipped her skirt down. Freed, Tanya drew her legs up and slammed her feet against Antip's left leg. Her valenki glanced off his leather boot, barely touching it. An angry spark flashed in his eyes, and he pinned her ankles with one foot. "You bitch!" he roared, and with one vicious lash he landed his whip across Tanya's legs. An animal groan gurgled in her throat in spite of the gag.

Mumbling and swearing, the cossacks rushed out through the narrow door. Stenka held back, crouching behind Tanya's head. Stealthily, he reached down from behind, flipped her tulup open, and, grabbing both breasts, kneaded them with his huge palms. Tanya moaned with a high-pitched sound. Antip stuck his head back through the door.

"You strutting cock! We all need a bitch, but leave this one alone till later!"

Swearing, Stenka reached the door in two leaps and disappeared into the darkness.

Outside, the cossacks were halted by a large number of men who reached the izba before the seven men could get away.

From the sounds of the stomping hoofs on the snow-packed ground and the horses' snorting, Paul estimated there were at least twenty of them. Snatches of conversation filtered through the closed door. "Antip, where have you been? . . . We've been looking all over for you. . . . Up to your pranks again? . . . Ataman has been asking for you. . . . He's in an ugly mood. . . . Hurry if you know what's good for you. . . . "

Antip's answer was muffled, and soon all was quiet.

Ringing silence hung in the izba, broken only by Tanya's spasmodic whimpers. The fire had died down, and the embers glowed like the burning eyes of a troll. Elongated shadows from the hanging pitchfork and scythe ceased their dancing in the flame's reflection and settled quietly along the wall. A hidden presence rustled in the hayloft . . . scratched . . . ran away. The smell of seasoned leather, dirty fur, stale liquor, receded through the wooden cracks, and the winter air came howling in.

Still gagged and unable to move, his welts throbbing, Paul strained against the ropes to peer at Tanya through the fading light. He ached to take her in his arms, to comfort her, to see how badly she was bruised.

Oh, Tanya, Tanya, I love you! his brain screamed in anguish, muscles pushing against his bonds. What a time to discover this! After all these months he saw the truth only when faced with what he thought was certain death.

And what about her? What did she feel for him? In this impossible position, trussed up like animals, they couldn't even talk. He couldn't give her tenderness, or comfort her over the violated privacy of her womanhood. Oh, how he yearned to tell her that he loved her, to touch her, to wipe away with his caresses the desecrating touch of Stenka's filthy hands!

A faint thumping sounded outside. Paul tensed. The sound was steadily growing louder. There was no doubt. A large number of horses were galloping toward the izba. Tanya heard them, too, and, lifting her head, peered in Paul's direction through the darkness. Paul nodded several times, hoping she would understand his message of encouragement. His own doubt and anxiety, however, mounted. Was this Tikhon bringing help, or were the cossacks coming back to satisfy their thwarted lust?

The horses stopped outside the barn.

"Light the torches!" a voice ordered. Paul recognized Konev's voice and almost wept with relief.

He squinted and blinked at the bright light as several men pushed their way into the izba. Konev took in the scene at a glance and in an instant was beside Tanya, slashing the ropes and freeing her arms. Then he removed the gag gently. "Are you hurt? May I help you up?"

Tanya's first movement was to hug her tulup closely around her chest. "My clothes are . . . torn . . . and I'm not sure I can walk," she whispered hoarsely.

Konev nodded. "We have a sleigh outside."

Tanya tried to get up, holding on to her skirt and tulup, but several gentle arms wrapped her in a fur cape, picked her up, and carried her out to the sleigh. Paul couldn't look at her as she was lifted up, couldn't bear to speak to her in front of others, for he wasn't sure he could remain calm, and he was too proud to lose his self-control in the presence of his peers.

By the time Konev turned to him, Paul had already been freed and ungagged. Before the captain could ask him anything, Paul stopped him with a curt shake of his head. "I can manage on my own, thank you." He touched the welt on his face, felt the crusted blood.

"This will be reported, I assure you, Prince." Konev's voice shook with emotion. "Thank God you weren't hurt worse. There is room for you on the sleigh."

Paul shook his head and straightened his aching, stiff body. "Let me have a horse." He hadn't meant for his voice to sound so brusque, but Konev seemed to understand and nodded.

As Paul walked stiffly toward the door of the izba, Tikhon pushed his way past him, conspicuous in his cossack uniform. Paul grabbed him by the sleeve and turned to the captain. "Konev, I want to be sure that this young cossack is cited for his bravery and courage."

"It will be done, Excellency."

Paul was about to release him when something in Tikhon's face held him back. A look of desperation, of unconcealed anger so strong that it startled Paul. For a few seconds the two men studied each other, and then Paul said,

"Wait for me outside, Konev. I want to have a word with him."

Left alone, Paul waved Tikhon to follow him deeper into the izba.

"I want to thank you for what you've done, Tikhon. I promise you that if ever you need help, you have only to ask me. In the meantime, I'll see to it that you get a promotion."

The torch, stuck in the ground, threw restless shadows across the young cossack's face, effectively concealing his reaction.

"I don't need your promotion, Excellency." Tikhon's voice was sullen. "You need not trouble yourself. I won't be around to receive it."

"Where are you going, Tikhon?"

The young cossack took off his *papakha* and threw it vehemently on the floor. "I'm going back to the Reds."

"What?"

"I ran away from the Red partisans because they slaughter innocents, but at least they do it for a cause they believe in. I thought the Whites were different." Tikhon pursed his lips. "They're different, all right. They, too, torture and butcher, but not for a cause. For no other reason save for their own pleasure."

"Don't judge all Whites by these men, Tikhon. War does strange things to people, and you can't condemn the whole army for the actions of a few."

"I've seen enough. Tonight was only an extra drop that made the pot overflow. You needn't thank me for what I've done. I didn't do it because you are Whites and are fighting to restore the old regime. I would have done the same for the Reds. I did it because I hate brutality of any kind. At least the Reds have a dream—liberty for the oppressed and equality for all. The Whites have no goal at all."

"Of course the Whites have a goal, Tikhon. They—"

"No they don't!" Tikhon interrupted angrily. "The Whites want nothing but to keep things as they were—justice and freedom for the privileged few."

"Tikhon, you can't go back to the partisans. Don't you

know what they'll do to you? In their eyes you're a deserter."

Tikhon picked up his *papakha* and pushed it deep over
his brow. "And what do you think Antip will do to me if
he catches me before I get away? I'll take my chances with
the Reds. I can't stay here. It turns my stomach to see what
these cossacks are doing." He spat on the ground and
turned toward the door, then paused.

"I have one request of you, Excellency. Look after my
mother . . . and I'll leave it up to you whether to tell her
about me."

CHAPTER 24

One of Konev's officers, Lieutenant Protasov, offered his parents' home in Chita as a temporary refuge for Tanya and Paul. An escort went ahead with Tanya's sleigh, and by the time Paul came out of the izba Tanya was already gone.

They were received warmly by the middle-aged couple. The senior Protasov had done some favors for the current government, and because he served on the city council, he was allowed to keep his spacious mansion in spite of the influx of refugees.

Tall and solemn, with gold-rimmed pince-nez, Protasov spoke little, allowing his short, fluffy wife to do the talking and the fussing. She clucked her tongue and shook her head while she cleaned the lacerations on Paul's face with water and peroxide. He winced, but endured the discomfort without protest.

"Madame Bolganova's welt is not broken like yours," she volunteered calmly, looking at Paul searchingly. "She's lucky she wasn't violated. And aside from that one bruise on her hip, she wasn't even beaten. I can't understand why she's crying so much. There must be something else that's upsetting her. You'll have to talk to her. She wouldn't tell me. Your room is next to hers, so maybe you can help."

Madame Protasova led him across a wide entrance hall, whose painted plank floor was covered with small Oriental rugs. At the foot of the stairs she paused, picked up the ruffled hem of her long striped skirt, and climbed the stairs with surprising agility for a woman of her bulk. Paul, still shaken from the ordeal, followed her stiffly, conscious of the long-forgotten fragrance of freshly soaped skin and cheap cologne.

Upstairs, she led him down a narrow corridor, and, opening one of the doors, showed him in.

"I hope you'll be comfortable here, Prince Veragin. Madame Bolganova is next door on the right. Our cook, Fyokla, is preparing a tray for you. She'll be up shortly."

Paul looked around the room. Its heavy oak bed with a canopy and deep red eiderdown comforter were inviting, but he knew he could never fall asleep until he had seen Tanya. There was a large inset mirror in the tall armoire at the far corner of the room, and cautiously he approached it. A colorless face with an angry red welt slashed across it stared back at him, as if someone had taken a thick red crayon and tried to smudge the image. His blond hair had lost its luster, but his pale eyes still burned with zeal.

While he waited for his food, he checked the adjoining bathroom and found it thoughtfully equipped with necessary toiletries. A long luffa and a bar of soap lay on top of a wooden stool; on a shelf over the basin, a razor was placed near a leather strop hanging from a hook in the wall. Paul bathed and shaved, and when he came back into the room refreshed, the dinner tray was waiting for him.

After he had eaten sparingly—in spite of a long fast he was not very hungry—Paul turned the kerosene lamp out and left the room. He knocked on Tanya's door, and when her muffled voice said "Enter," he let himself in and closed the door behind him.

She was standing in the middle of the room, dressed in a loose-fitting robe that Madame Protasova must have loaned her, its bulk caught at the waist by a cord. Paul had never seen Tanya's chestnut hair undressed and cascading around her shoulders in wavy strands. Lost in the folds of the oversized dressing gown, she looked bruised and vulnerable.

When she saw him, she turned away and buried her face in her hands. Gently, Paul turned her around. Pressed against his chest, she shook with dry sobs, and Paul, sinking his lips into her silky hair, rocked her from side to side, whispering, "Shsh, Tanyusha, it's over! It's all over!"

She wrenched herself free and stepped back. Her chin trembled. "Oh, Paul! This terrible, degrading experience! To think that those dregs were the Whites—our own Whites!"

"Tanya, I'd have given anything to have spared you this dreadful incident, but think how lucky you are to have escaped a worse fate."

"I know, I know. But oh, Paul—it was such a shock to know who they were! I think I hate all my people!"

"Don't say that, Tanya. You can't mean it."

"Don't you see? I trusted the Whites. I thought they were so noble, so chivalrous. My faith in them carried me through the whole ordeal of the past few months. . . . Now it all seems such a mockery. The Reds . . . the Whites . . . they are all the same. They deserve one another!"

"Things can't be so simply dismissed, nor everyone equated, Tanyusha," Paul said reflectively. "While there's good and bad in all of us, these particular men are little more than savages. In their unbridled freedom, they've turned into beasts, and you shouldn't, you mustn't, judge all cossacks by these ruffians."

"But what's the matter with Ataman Semenov? Why aren't these cossacks disciplined? I don't think I'll ever be able to trust anyone again. Thank God for Tikhon!"

"I talked to him, Tanya. I tried to thank him for what he had done for us, but he rejected my gratitude. He told me that he left the Red partisans because he abhorred their violence. Yet tonight he decided to return to them. So you see how it is in life—we must choose between two evils and settle for what offends us the least. In our troubled times we shouldn't set our ideals too high—then the disappointments are less painful."

Tanya began to cry. "I want to get out of Russia! I want to go home, to Harbin. All my life I've heard what great heroes the cossacks were, how brave and honorable, and tonight . . . tonight . . ." Choking up, she shook her head.

Paul took her in his arms. "Tanyusha, don't! Please, look at me!"

For a few minutes, Tanya continued to cry against Paul's chest, and he let her weep, sensing that her outraged emotions could no longer be contained within, that the flow of tears had become a catharsis of all the trials of the past.

He held her close, stroking her hair with one hand, his cheek against the side of her head. She trembled, and her soft and yielding body clung to Paul, igniting him with a flame that began to grow and burn and envelop him.

After a while she raised her head. For the first time, her eyes focused on his laceration. With a sharp intake of breath, she reached up and touched his chin with the tips of her fingers. "Oh, Paul, forgive me for not seeing this before! What a painful thing it must be!"

"No more painful than yours, Tanyusha," Paul said. Instinctively, she touched her thigh where the whip had landed, and he placed his hand over hers. Thus touching, they looked at each other and fell silent.

Later, Paul could not remember who made the first move, but suddenly he was crushing her against him, this precious woman whom he had loved, unknown to himself, all these many months . . . had cared for and ached for, and had never once admitted that he loved. And fate had almost snatched her from him! But the miracle was there, tonight, for she was in his arms—a living testimony of her love.

Discovering the joy of loving, his mind swam, all conscious thinking, all reason, drowned in one consuming thought—he loved her! His body tense with passion, he found her lips with a deep and crushing kiss and drank of her mouth with exquisite thirst.

There was no subtlety in their lovemaking. So many months of smoldering emotion now erupted with volcanic force. Tanya responded greedily, with hunger and impatience, as though her very soul were starved for him. Her hands tugged at his clothing, searched for his naked chest, his shoulders, her mouth on his neck in deep and drawing kisses.

And he—he could not get enough of her. His face deep in the softness of her skin, he tasted it—her moist and tender skin—and searched the curves and hollows of her flesh, and felt her restless arms and legs entwine him.

But all of that was not enough. He had to see her, all of her, to know that it was truly she, unblemished, undefiled, and eager for his love. So, breathless, he tore the covers off, not to abuse, but to enjoy the intimacy of their bodies, to see her closeness, her desire. And when at last she cried his name, it drove him madly into a frenzied push for union.

His senses soared, remained suspended, unwilling to let go of this acute experience, this blinding moment, and as his force exploded, draining him, his mind whirled, floated blissfully, and then dissolved in endless pleasure.

They slept in each other's arms, loath to part, afraid to break the dreamlike quality of peace. Sometime during the night they woke each other gently and, with the urgency appeased, made love again—this time with tenderness and care. Paul reveled in the words "I love you," saying them with wonder and delight, and, in turn, heard them whispered in his ear.

But morning came, as morning must, and the realities of their lives took precedence over the night's enchantment. They thanked their hosts and went out to collect Sophie and Marfa.

Reluctantly, Paul thought of what they had to do. Sophie and Marfa. It seemed that aeons had passed since they had parted. So much had happened in one night: the terror of near death, the dreadful scene in the izba, his own awakening to love, and love itself. Oh, Tanya, Tanya—he ached for her all over. He felt a stranger to himself to have been blind for so long.

Today, the world looked bright to Paul, and he felt detached from the misery of which he and other refugees had been a part. Even the starkness of having run out of money appeared too mundane to be of importance to him this morning. Now that they had discovered their love for each other, he no longer felt uncomfortable to have Tanya cover for him. They both realized that it would be a temporary arrangement. As soon as he established himself in Harbin, they would marry.

Since the exodus began, he had trained himself not to project his planning any further than the following day, and he refused to ponder how he, a military officer, could earn a decent living in Harbin—a commercial city with a nonexistent Russian army. As it was, by virtue of his birth,

he never had had to worry about money, and the thought
vaguely disturbed him. But, then, Harbin was far away,
and Paul dismissed the meddlesome thought with annoyance. More pressing action was required of him right now.

Marfa! What, if anything, were they going to tell Tikhon's mother about her son? That he had performed a heroic deed only to rejoin the Red partisans? Marfa had been
stoic and calm in the past; but the sight of her son had torn
apart her guarded restraint. Was it better for her to think
her son disloyal for not having sought her out again, and
thus live with a mother's hurt, or to wrestle with the pride
in Tikhon's heroism on the one hand and the heartbreak
over his misguided idealism on the other?

How could he divine a tough Siberian woman's heart?

Deep in thought, Paul was about to steer Tanya, who
had been walking quietly beside him, across the street and
away from the railway station they were passing, when
something caught Tanya's attention and she grabbed Paul
by the arm. Startled, Paul looked toward the station platform.

A group of cossacks were leading a prisoner along the
siding. It was Tikhon. Pulling Tanya roughly behind him,
Paul hugged the wall of the station building, well out of
sight of the men. Tikhon had shed his cossack uniform and
was dressed in tulup, padded trousers, and valenki. Conspicuous on his head was a flat, fur-lined cap with a Bolshevik red star on the front.

He had been beaten, for one of his eyes was swollen shut
and his lip was cut and bleeding. The cossacks were taking
him to the front of the armored train, where the black be-
hemoth puffed ponderously on the siding. Its swivel-gun
platform cars were turreted; the chain-drive trucks were
lined up on the flatcars; machine-gun muzzles poked
through traverse ports; and this whole floating fortress was
encased in steel plate, including the cossack barrack and
stable cars. Whenever the *bronevik*—this armored mon-
ster—rumbled into the station, with all its machinery swiv-
eling into action, the terrified populace ran.

Now, with the rifles and machine guns hidden behind
the slits, the train looked innocuous enough—but for the
scene taking place on the platform. The cossacks reached

the massive locomotive and tried to shove their prisoner inside, but Tikhon balked. At that moment, Ataman Semenov came down the steps of the next car. Although Paul had never seen the notorious leader, he had no doubts as to the man's identity. Dressed in his blue and green uniform, wearing a sable cape and highly polished leather boots, and festooned with a dagger and a sword, he had a commanding presence, and the guards jumped to attention as he ambled toward the small group at the locomotive. His broad, beardless face and high cheekbones betrayed his mother's Buryat-Mongol origin, and his immaculately groomed handlebar moustache made Paul wonder how much of this flashy appearance was designed to cow his subordinates and how much was prompted by the man's vanity.

The ataman's shifty green eyes sized up Tikhon instantly, and he said something to the young partisan. In reply, Tikhon spat at Semenov's feet and received a staggering blow from the cossack who flanked him on one side. It was the bravado gesture of a doomed man, and Paul recognized it for what it was. So did Tanya, for Paul could feel her hand tighten on his arm.

A menacing glint flickered in the ataman's eyes as he issued a curt order to the cossacks, and then, turning sharply on his heel, his cape scything the air, he ambled off in the opposite direction.

The cossacks waited until their leader was out of sight, then spun Tikhon around and, lifting him bodily, threw him into the cab of the locomotive. Then they followed him in, shutting the door behind them.

Life on the station platform returned to its early-morning bustle. A square, heavily bundled charwoman was sweeping the snow in front of the station-house door with a besom of birch twigs. She paused briefly, shot a furtive glance at the *bronevik*, and returned to her chores with diligent attention. Several guards stood at ease, watching the activity at the station house, where a truck with food supplies was being unloaded. This seemed to interest them far more than the fate of the current prisoner who had been taken inside the locomotive.

Instinctively, Paul put his arm around Tanya and held her close, watching the *bronevik* and knowing with a sick-

ening certainty what was about to happen, and hoping, ir-
rationally, that somehow it wouldn't happen. As they stood
waiting, the dormant locomotive came to life. Its chimney
regurgitated a dense belch of smoke that shot its tendrils
upward into the gray sky, polluting the crisp air, filling
Paul's nostrils with the stench of burning flesh.

Tanya choked a pitiful cry and thrust her head against
Paul's chest. He held her tight, himself stunned and nau-
seous from the imagery of what was causing the firebox
inside to smoke, conscious of his own impotence to save the
man who had rescued them.

Tanya sobbed without a sound, shaking inside Paul's embrace, and the two clutched at each other, unable to speak,
for no spoken word could have defined the outraged
thoughts of the two people watching the atrocity.

Taking Tanya by the arm, Paul pulled her off the platform and away from the station.

They didn't tell Marfa about Tikhon. After the horror
they had witnessed, the decision was taken away from
Paul. They couldn't tell her anything, and to explain their
bruises, they improvised a story of assault by street hood-
lums.

When the first available train took them out of Chita,
they greeted the boxcar's discomforts almost with gratitude,
thankful for their own obscurity. Marfa fussed at first,
asking them to go on without her and saying that she
wanted to wait for Tikhon. Tanya reasoned with casual
tenderness that Tikhon was probably detained and would
not contact her again for a long time and would want her
to remain with her friends. Paul marveled at Tanya's newly
discovered ability to adapt the truth to satisfy a friend's
aching, suspicious heart. Urged by her friends, disappointed in her short-lived happiness, Marfa gave in to their
arguments and went with them.

One day they crossed into Manchuria and stopped at the
border hamlet, called Manchuria. Slant-eyed coolies, with
thin, dangling braids bouncing on their quilted cotton jackets of faded-ink hue, greeted them with easy warmth. Their
staccato chatter fractured the words in pidgin Russian, and
their yellow skin readily crinkled into clusters of happy

wrinkles. Paul was astounded by the contrast between this scene of agile humanity and the lethargic menace of the Chita station.

He brooded in sudden anxiety. A new country. An alien land where women wore pants and men had braids. Friendly, hospitable land, largely populated by his compatriots. Friendly, but foreign nonetheless. He no longer had the status of a prince or the authority of a colonel, for his title and his rank were now obsolete. He would have to shed his uniform, give up his citizenship, and find a new identity. His worry mounted. He didn't know what he could do in Harbin. What could he offer Tanya, the woman he loved and wanted for his own? He was now a penniless refugee standing on foreign soil.

Tanya, on the other hand, seemed transformed by radiance, by her happy anticipation of homecoming, and she stood out alone among the anxious faces of her friends.

As if sensing Paul's doubts, she touched his arm.

"Paul, how wonderful to be safe again! To be home. We're together, and that's all that matters."

CHAPTER 25

Kurt Hochmeyer's office was in the downtown section of Harbin called Pristan. As Tanya walked down the main street on her way to see him, she was apprehensive. She hadn't called him to let him know she was in Harbin, and now she wondered how he would react to her surprise visit. She knew she had the advantage of catching him off guard, and she realized it was selfish of her not to have prepared him for their meeting. But here she was, a few blocks from 75 Kitaiskaya Street, and having come this far, she couldn't allow herself to lose courage.

Intent upon watching the street numbers, she missed a curb and nearly fell. As she regained her balance, she became aware of an aroma of freshly baked bread. She was standing near a bakery whose window was packed with baked goods. There were loaves of black and white bread; plain loaves, braided loaves; some sprinkled with sesame seeds and poppy seeds; custard-filled Napoleon pastry; curd tarts, jam tarts. Having starved for so long, it made her head spin. Turning away from the window, she looked around her, hardly believing she was back in her own home town.

Everything looked the same after three years, yet there was a subtle difference. She herself had changed. The things she had once taken for granted, or hadn't noticed at all as an eighteen-year-old girl, now took on a special kind of importance. Shiny, fragrant bagels side by side with crusted, unleavened Chinese pancakes; the smell of fried piroshki wafting from a café; the abundance of warm, well-fitting clothes in the stores; houses with central heating and hot running water. Although these things were all available to her again, would she ever look at them without wonder and awe?

Two days earlier, when she had finally arrived in Harbin and they were all allowed to stay in the train for a few days while they looked for lodging, Tanya had been anxious to find out about her house and how much money Kurt had been able to save for her. But first she wanted to contact her friends the Korchagovs, learn what Lydia and Oleg were now doing, and hear what they had to tell her about Kurt. After she had eaten her first meal in Harbin, she located a telephone and called 46-75, amazed that she remembered the number. When Madame Korchagova answered the phone, Tanya felt as if the last three years had never happened. After talking to her, however, the illusion was quickly dispelled: Lydia had died from tuberculosis the previous year, and Oleg was in America, studying civil engineering at the University of California. Then Tanya asked about her house. There was a slight pause, and when Madame Korchagova answered, her voice had changed perceptibly.

"Mr. Hochmeyer is still taking care of it for you, my dear."

Mr. Hochmeyer, Tanya noted mentally. He had become Mr. Hochmeyer to Madame Korchagova, and her voice was frosty. Tanya distinctly remembered Madame Korchagova referring to him with a patronymic in the past. Now he was Mr. Hochmeyer. She wondered why.

"Is he married now?"

Again that slight hesitation; then Madame Korchagova said rather sharply: "No. But you should know, there are rumors. Evidently, he has a . . . he has been seen around town with lady friends."

Tanya shrugged to herself. Kurt was not married. He was entitled to have women friends. Idly, she wondered who they were. She didn't take time to dwell on it, for other thoughts were crowding her mind.

Kurt had been taking care of her house all this time. With his keen business acumen, he must have saved a sizeable amount of money for her. She owed him a great debt of gratitude. Kurt would have no idea of how much it meant to her now to have some funds, for she was the only one among her friends who had something to fall back on—not only money in the bank, but also a house she could share with others. To see Kurt—to talk to him, to find out all that had happened in her absence, and to re-establish a link with her past—had now become a pressing matter.

Reason, however, held her back. First she wanted to tell Paul about her relationship with Kurt and ask his advice. Somehow she didn't want to get too deeply indebted to Kurt and secretly hoped that Paul would take the initiative and find work for all of them and save her the embarrassment of asking Kurt for a job.

She had hoped for the impossible, and she hadn't taken the time to see the futility of such a hope. When she saw Paul, he was scanning the want ads of the *Zarya*. This was a newspaper new to Tanya, for the only one she remembered from pre-Revolution days was the *Harbin Herald*. Curious, she looked over his shoulder, and when he lowered the paper, she told him about Kurt. Paul listened attentively.

"I'm not surprised, Tanyusha, that Kurt was in love with you," he said after she had finished. "You may find that he still is. You must tell him about us, for we have to be honest with him from the beginning. Since he was a family friend, I'm sure it won't keep him from helping you. If he's as successful in business as you say, he must have many contacts in town. You know what this means to all of us, don't you?"

Tanya bit her lip. He had hit on a raw nerve. She was the only one with an influential contact in town, and she mustn't forget she had a place to live and money in the bank. She also had a moral obligation to Sophie, who now depended on her, and to Marfa. Especially to Marfa! Ever since she had witnessed Tikhon's terrible death and stood by helplessly while it was happening, she felt a responsibility toward Marfa, for keeping his death a secret and for not having been able to repay Tikhon for saving her life.

Her obligations to Paul were too numerous to count, and the greatest of all was her love for him. The memory of the cossacks' abuse of her during the assault was possible to deal with only because of Paul's presence in the izba. They had shared the horror, and it was in the sharing that their emotions had been fused and their love realized. A flush rose to her face when she thought of their first night together in the Protasovs' house in Chita. She had enjoyed sex with Yuri, but never with such abandon, such mindless hunger, as that night with Paul. Yes, she would do anything for him. It was her turn now to take care of all of them, even if it meant asking Kurt for more favors.

"What does Kurt look like?" Paul's voice was a bit too casual, his face too impassive, for her not to suspect a touch of jealousy in his question.

"He has always looked old to me and rather pedantic," she replied with a shrug and changed the subject.

The next day, she exchanged her remaining gold rubles for dayans and received three and a half to one in Chinese currency, glad that in the last days in Siberia she had traded her jewelry and saved the rubles.

Whatever urgency there was in getting her friends settled, Tanya's feminine pride took over, and she had to make herself look presentable. Marfa waved away Tanya's offer to go shopping. "These are the clothes I've worn all my life, and I'm not going to waste money to make myself look like a city *barinya*," she said, and Tanya and Sophie went to town without her.

Tanya paused in front of Churin's only for a moment. It was one of the oldest department stores in Harbin, having become over the years the largest and most elegant in the city. Tanya's mother had been one of its best-known customers, and now, Tanya's pride wouldn't let her enter the store dressed in tulup and valenki, the soles of which were almost worn through. Besides, no lady of consequence would be seen on the street wearing a peasant's felt boots. They were conscious of their shabby outfits when elegant women, wrapped in sheared beaver or karakul coats, their faces hidden beneath opossum collars, hands tucked snugly inside matching muffs, looked at them with unabashed curiosity. It was an unpleasant feeling for both of them, but Tanya in particular chafed at the looks, for at one time she was one of these women, well dressed, warm, belonging to the privileged class of Harbin. Now she was a part of another world, an intruder in her own city, and she was determined to regain her former status.

She pulled Sophie resolutely behind her across the street from Churin's to the corner of Pekarnaya Street where the more modest Japanese Matzuura department store offered them a variety of ladies' boots and conservative cloth coats. Tanya picked out a brown coat with a fur collar to match, while Sophie chose a black fitted coat with a gray collar, which flattered her blue eyes and pale blond hair. Chilblains reddened her fingers, and Tanya selected a pair of wool-lined leather gloves for her friend, adding a fur muff to match the collar of her coat. Sophie protested.

"Tanya, I haven't learned the value of the dayan yet, but this must cost you a fortune. How long will it take me to pay you back?"

"We've shared everything for a long time, Sophie. You've given me your food and I never counted how much I owed you. Someday you'll do a favor for someone else, and that way you'll repay me."

Sophie's eyes filled with tears, and she hugged Tanya impulsively.

When the two women walked out of the store wearing their new leather boots lined with lamb's wool, they were giddy with pleasure from the almost forgotten comfort of walking on warm, protected feet.

The rest of the day was spent making rounds of offices looking for jobs, and by the time they returned to the station they were tired and dispirited. There were no openings, and Tanya knew now that there was no alternative for her but to appeal to Kurt for help.

The following morning she dressed carefully for her meeting with Kurt. The day was clear, and the brilliant sun sparkled on the city as she hailed one of the sledges parked at the railroad station. As she took her seat, she enjoyed the luxury of being its sole passenger, in spite of the biting wind that chilled her face. She didn't mind it, for as they climbed the viaduct over the railroad tracks, she thrilled to the sight of familiar streets and buildings.

After passing Novogorodnaya Street, with its bustling commerce of open markets and vegetable carts, she told the *izvoshchik* to let her off at the top of Kitaiskaya Street.

She wanted to walk, to recognize old landmarks, to feel the permanence and stability of her native city.

Everywhere around her there were signs of growth. The town had burgeoned during her absence, for it had become the far eastern refuge of the White Russians, who poured from Siberia by the thousands, and the Russian population had grown to 125,000. Some, like the Korchagovs, were fortunate enough to have left the country before the revolution started. Lured by the virgin land of Manchuria and the opportunities it had to offer—with its wealth of available fur in the taiga, its mountains and lush valleys abundant in wild game and birds, its fast rivers plentiful with fish—they prospered and all but forgot that this was not their native country. Others, like her father, had been sent to staff the Chinese Eastern Railroad and help maintain it. The businessmen, seeing a land of plenty, borrowed money and turned it to profit, so that trade blossomed. The newly arrived intelligentsia staffed the universities, schools, conservatory. Opera and ballet flourished.

The Chinese lived in an all-Chinese sector of the city called Foudziadzian, leaving the major part of Harbin largely in Russian hands under the leadership of General Horvath. A retired officer of the Tsarist army, he had been courageous enough to risk independent action by returning the railway to the Chinese government, thus losing the right of way to Russia, but preventing the territory from falling into Bolshevik hands.

Nevertheless, it remained an unusual Russian city on Chinese soil. Even the streets bore Russian names: Kitaiskaya, Tyuremnaya, Diagonalnaya, Politseiskaya. The Russians brought prosperity to Chinese commerce and tradesmen. The native artisans and servants learned to speak pidgin Russian, and Harbin, a provincial town in pre-Revolution days, had now become a cosmopolitan Russian city, with cultural events and higher education of international stature.

But what of the military men, Tanya thought, who had been trained in Russian military tactics and very little else? Facing the civilian world without the security of their government salary, they would have to rely largely on their wits in adapting their individual skills to eking out a living.

What would Paul be able to do? She had never asked him
what, if any, additional training he had had.

The city noises pressed in upon her, forcing her attention
back to Kitaiskaya Street. It seemed the whole of Russia
had shrunk into Harbin, for the illusion of a Russian city
was preserved in detail. Even the shop signs over the T-
framed windows were printed in Russian, and Orthodox
Church bells peeled in the distance. "Café Moderne," proclaimed one sign over a door, and the Japanese Matzuura
sign was spelled out in Cyrillic alphabet.

There were few Chinese on the streets, and most of them
were rickshaw coolies trying to drum up some trade. They
followed her for a while, and again she heard pidgin Russian: "Ricksha, madama, good ricksha!" They wore thick
padded cotton pants with jackets of faded blue and pointed
cloth shoes, and when they trotted past her with a customer
inside, their thin braids, dangling from beneath their black
skullcaps, whipped their backs in jaunty rhythm.

The streets were crowded. In spite of the March sun, the
snow-packed road was still frozen, and Russian coachmen
rode past her, their snorting horses pulling sleighs filled
with passengers whose legs were snugly hidden under the
fur throws. Coolies pulled loaded carts along the street and
scurrying pedestrians, their fur collars lifted to protect their
ears, maneuvered their way through the crowds on the
sidewalks.

It had been a long time since Tanya felt so confident
about her appearance. She knew her brown outfit was becoming; the crisp air nipped at her cheeks; and she enjoyed
the admiring looks she collected from passersby.

Yet at 75 Kitaiskaya Street doubts crept in. Kurt's offices, housed in a large stone building, occupied a square
block, and now Tanya stood before it.

Straightening her shoulders, she opened the door and
went inside.

CHAPTER 26

There was no entry hall or corridor, and Tanya found herself standing in a large, noisy room cluttered with small desks. The firm's employees, mostly women, were working over papers, typing, or counting on the abacus in an arrhythmic concert of clicking beads. A narrow center aisle led to two cubicles whose doors were closed. Tanya wondered if one of them was Kurt's office.

It took a few seconds for her to adjust to the stuffy air filled with the smell of ink, treated wood, and cigarette smoke.

Unsure of her next step, she waited for someone to notice her, but everyone seemed intent upon their work and ignored her. Intimidated, she was about to speak to the young woman nearest her when a plump middle-aged man approached her. His pale eyes, deep set below a high, shiny forehead, looked at her appraisingly.

"Good-day, madame. May I help you?" His voice was thin and slightly nasal.

Too warm in her inner-lined coat, dizzy from hunger and lack of fresh air, Tanya felt more and more uncomfortable.

"I'd like to see Mr. Hochmeyer," she said, her voice barely above a whisper.

The man nodded and swept his arm toward the two cubicles. "Please follow me, madame. I'll see if he's free."

He led her to an empty cubicle with a sign that said "Manager" on the door and offered her a wooden armchair near a large desk cluttered with papers, chewed pencils, an ashtray full of cigarette butts, and a half-empty coffee glass in a silver holder. As she sat down, the warm air and the smell of steaming coffee from an aluminum coffepot on a side table overwhelmed Tanya, and the room began to spin.

When she opened her eyes again, the manager was bending over her, rubbing her hands and gently slapping her face. Blushing, still dizzy, Tanya sat up in her chair and groped for words.

"Please don't apologize. Am I correct in assuming you're one of the recent refugees?"

When Tanya nodded, he continued: "I was once a refugee myself, and I know how you feel." He went over to the side table. "I'll pour you a cup of coffee. Would you like a *bublik* with it?" Without waiting for a reply, he passed her a cup of coffee and a bagel, then went on: "Allow me to introduce myself. I'm Ivan Efimovich Kozlov, manager of the firm."

The taste of the fresh *bublik* and hot coffee absorbed Tanya so completely she forgot to introduce herself. Mr. Kozlov sat down behind his desk and unbuttoned the jacket of his double-breasted striped suit. He studied Tanya for a few moments and then, clearing his throat, said:

"Mr. Hochmeyer is usually quite busy this time of the day. Could I perhaps help you in any way?"

Tanya hesitated for only a moment. "I was going to ask Mr. Hochmeyer if he knew of a vacancy anywhere for a bookkeeper."

Kozlov looked her over from head to foot and then began asking about her qualifications. Shivering slightly from his appraising look, she told him of her schooling in Omsk. He tapped a pencil on the writing pad before him.

"It so happens that we're looking for a bookkeeper right now. The salary is sixty dayans a month—an adequate sum."

Tanya leaned forward. She wanted to tell him that she knew all about dayans, that she was a native of Harbin, and not exactly a refugee in the full sense of the word, but somehow the words stuck in her throat. In spite of her new outfit, she knew she looked undernourished and hungry, and she wasn't ready to tell a stranger that she was Countess Merkulina's daughter.

"Unfortunately," Kozlov went on, "there are already so many applicants for the position that I hesitate to make the decision without Mr. Hochmeyer's approval." He paused and looked at her again with an appreciative look. "Of course, there are always extenuating circumstances."

The implication was clear, but she swallowed her indignation and tried to keep her voice calm. "I'd like to see Mr. Hochmeyer, please."

Kozlov rose from his chair. "You were fortunate to have come today, madame, before the position has been filled. With the influx of qualified refugees it has become increasingly difficult to find work to fit individual professions, and many have to settle for menial jobs. I'll see now if Mr. Hochmeyer is free."

At the door, the manager hesitated, stopped, and turned around. "Excuse me, but who shall I say is calling?"

"My name is Tatiana Bolganova—I mean Levitina— that is, I . . . " Tanya stumbled over words and felt herself blush.

Kozlov raised his eyebrows and looked at her suspiciously.

"I beg your pardon?"

Tanya spread her arms helplessly. "What I mean is, my name is Bolganova, but Mr. Hochmeyer knows me only by my maiden name, Levitina. Please tell him that Tatiana Andreyevna Levitina is here to see him."

As soon as Tanya mentioned that Kurt knew her, Kozlov's attitude changed perceptibly. He nodded politely and walked out.

Left alone, Tanya realized that if Kurt gave her the job, she would be dependent upon him for her livelihood, since she would be working for his firm. In a few moments, Kozlov returned. "Mr. Hochmeyer is waiting for you in his office. Please follow me."

When she entered his office, larger and more comfortable than Kozlov's, the manager quietly closed the door behind her, and she was left facing the man she had come to see.

Kurt was very pale as he came around his large oak desk, his eyes fixed on Tanya's face. He had grown a shade thinner, and there was a new, finely etched furrow between his brows. Taking her hands in his, he whispered, "Tanya, Tanya, it's you! It's really you. I'd almost given up hope of ever seeing you again."

He raised her hands to his lips, his eyes never leaving her face. He kissed her hands reverently one at a time and then looked down at them. His smile froze, and for a few seconds he blinked fast before he looked at her again. "You're married." It was a flat statement, not a question, and his voice was well controlled. Tanya shook her head slowly.

"No, I'm a widow."

Closing her eyes, she thought: If you show relief in your face, I'll hate you forever. But when she looked at him, there was only tenderness and compassion in his eyes.

"Dear Tanya! When?"

Tanya felt her throat choke up. "Four months ago," she whispered, "in Omsk. I've been—I wanted to—I've been here only two days."

She didn't want to cry, for she was afraid to break down and be comforted by him. Kurt led her to a leather sofa and sat down next to her, still holding her hands in his.

"You're here now. Home. Safe. And that's all that counts, Tanya!"

Looking at him, she was terribly disturbed by what she saw. The sight of him brought a flood of happy memories, a warmth of feeling for the man who'd been almost a part of her family, who had known her in her happier days. Yet this was a different Kurt from the one she remembered. She would have been more comfortable in the presence of the man she had known before—reserved, distant, cool. The Kurt who sat next to her now was unsettling. His happiness at seeing her was so ingenuous and so complete, she was distressed by the obvious intensity of his emotion.

She tried to tell him about the last three years, about Grandmaman, and Yuri, and the subsequent ordeal, but her words were jumbled, incoherent. Kurt patted her hand and told her softly that there was plenty of time to talk later, that first things had to come first. In spite of her confusion, Tanya smiled inwardly. This was the Kurt she remembered—rational, methodical, pragmatic—and as he talked, telescoping the last three years, she felt at ease with him again, enjoying the illusion of being Tanya Levitina once more.

"There's a bank account in your name, Tanya," he said, "but unfortunately, it's very small. I had to use the funds for major repairs in your house. I'm happy to say it remained rented ever since you left for Russia, but a lot of things had gone wrong. The furnace, for instance, had to be replaced, and then a few months later the water pipes broke and flooded the floor in the kitchen and the hallway. The current lease, however, is not due to expire for another month, and you can either give notice to the tenants or offer to rent them the part of the house you won't need."

Kurt rose, went over to his desk, and wrote something on a piece of paper. Then he came back and sat down beside her again. "Here's the address of the Hotel Imperial on Tyuremnaya Street, where several of my employees live. It's only a few blocks from here, and you might consider renting a room there for the time being."

It was a blow to discover that she had practically no money left, and although she realized how indebted she was to him already, she knew that now more than ever she needed that job. Kurt saved her the embarrassment of having to ask him for it by telling her how happy he was that she could work in his firm. And when at last they parted, she left his office without telling him about Paul and herself. Although she'd asked him to find jobs for her three friends and told him who they were, she couldn't bring herself to shatter his almost childlike delight at seeing her again. There was plenty of time to tell him at an appropriate moment, she decided lamely as she headed toward Tyuremnaya Street.

She was anxious to rent a room right away, because it would be foolish, she reasoned, to pay for a return trip to the railroad station only to turn around and come back to the hotel—especially now, when every kopek had to count. She had warned Paul that she might not return the same day, so he wouldn't worry about her. She'd go back in the morning, collect her bundle, and tell her friends what had taken place. In the meantime, she would decide on what to tell Paul, and she'd think of a good reason why she hadn't told Kurt about their relationship. At the moment, she was so confused that she didn't know herself why she hadn't done it.

It would be good to be alone, to sort out her feelings and reactions, and to assimilate all of the impressions that she had experienced in one day.

At the Hotel Imperial, the first thing that hit her nostrils was the long-forgotten smell of fried piroshki. It was the second time she had smelled them that day, and her stomach was gnawing from hunger. The mixed fragrance of onions and beef and dough boiling in fat was the same as she remembered from home.

She rented a small room on the third floor; it had a bed, a table with two wooden chairs, and a painted white dressing table. With the key in hand, she ran down the steps, holding on to the black iron railing, bought two meat piroshki and a pot of hot tea, and returned to her room. It was a heady experience to have a whole room to herself after those recent months of deprivation.

As she ate the piroshki at the small table, she glanced out the window. The blue Byzantine cupolas of a Russian church with its three crosses shimmered in the setting sun. Her grandmother's words rang in her ears: "We run to the church to beg, to complain, to ask favors. But how often do we remember God when happiness comes our way?" Instinctively, Tanya looked to the right corner of the room, where the icon should have been. It was empty. She gulped the last of her tea, snatched her coat, and ran downstairs.

The church was a block away. The sun had disappeared behind the rooftops, and the damp evening chill was settling to the ground. Small wisps of vapor escaped her mouth with each breath, and by the time she reached the church steps, her face was very cold.

Inside, the evening vigil had begun. The jeweled icons sparkled in the reflection of flickering candles. Tanya prayed before the image of St. Serafim Sarovsky, whose face seemed animated in the semidarkness.

Her anxiety for the future was fading. Whatever problems were still facing her, they appeared insignificant now that the struggle for survival had been won. She prayed on her knees for a long time, and a feeling of euphoria enveloped her. Kurt had promised to do his best for Sophie and

Marfa and Paul. Tonight she could rest peacefully. She
needed to be by herself, for she wasn't sure she was prepared to share all her impressions with Paul.

On her way back to the hotel, she walked slowly. The
twilight had deepened, and in the hush of the evening, lazy
snowflakes settled gently on her brown coat. There
wouldn't be much snow anymore. She knew her city's climate well. Fragrant, flower-filled spring would step in
soon, intoxicate the unwary, and then surrender quickly to
the scorching summer, with the hot winds blowing sporadi-
cally from the Gobi desert. Spring was around the corner
now, and with it, better things to come.

Once inside her room, weariness permeated her body,
and the reaction from the day's excitement set in. She
glanced toward the bed. It was large, with an iron frame,
and on it were huge feather pillows and a quilted comforter
encased in a white sheet envelope that buttoned on top, just
exactly like the ones she had had at home. They looked
inviting beyond imagining. Her hands began to shake. How
many nights had it been since she had slept in a real bed,
with a mattress and soft pillows at the Protasovs? She
couldn't remember.

After she undressed and slipped under the covers, she
felt cradled in the folds of total bliss. Feeling a little selfish
for being the first one among her friends to enjoy these
luxuries, she rationalized that they would insist she take
advantage of any privileges that came her way.

She stretched sensuously between the smooth sheets, her
body tingling with pleasure. Turning the light out, she
stretched again, purposely reaching to the corners of the
bed with her toes, reassuring herself that the wide, comfortable bed was all hers. Cautiously, she ventured to think
of Paul and of being a woman again. The memory of the
night in Chita returned, and she was overcome by a physical need of him, a longing to feel his arms around her, to
respond to his eager and impatient body.

Soon. It will all be possible soon. I'll tell Kurt about my
love for Paul, and practical, reasonable Kurt will understand.

CHAPTER 27

May in Harbin was Tanya's favorite month. The city was like a debutante perfumed and adorned with flowers. On a busy commercial corner of Novotorgovaya Street and Bolshoi Avenue in the Novy Gorod section of town, Chinese vendors peddled violets, lilacs, and lilies of the valley out of large buckets placed at the curb.

Tanya sat on one of the benches that lined the wide sidewalk in front of Churin's branch store in Novy Gorod and waited for Paul. She had written him to meet her there at noon. It was now one o'clock. She had come early to buy a package of aspirin and camomile tea and had gone to the corner pharmacy across Bolshoi Avenue, skirting droshkies parked in the median and dodging milling pedestrians. Lately, she had been bothered by abdominal pains, alternately sharp and diffused, and since the medicines gave her symptomatic relief, she didn't want to alarm Paul and spoil their rendezvous this Saturday afternoon.

After the pharmacy, she stopped at Zazunov's bakery and bought three Napoleon pastries and a loaf of poppyseed sweet bread. An hour of waiting stretched into eternity, and she walked around the corner to the Bolshoi Avenue side of Churin's to make sure Paul hadn't misunderstood her.

It had been her idea to meet Paul near Churin's rather than ask him to come to her house, where they would have no privacy. She hadn't seen him ever since he had left Harbin for his job almost two months ago, and she could hardly suppress her excitement.

Cradling the pastry in her arms, she sat there people-watching and smiling at passersby. This was an ideal spot to indulge in such a pastime, for the benches were separated from the noisy cobblestone streets by a hedge of privet shrubbery, giving the corner an illusion of a garden lane.

The sidewalks were crowded with promenaders, and Tanya admired the women's fashionable clothes as they strolled by. She studied their elegant styles without envy, for she felt herself a part of this world again. Although all her savings were now gone, she was still a native of this prosperous and vibrant city and felt that sooner or later things would improve for her and she'd be able to buy new clothes for herself. Gratified to be living again in her childhood home, she wondered how others, less fortunate than herself, had adjusted to living in a less affluent area.

But while at home she had no time to indulge in sentimental memories. The house was full. She had rented her father's study, the parlor, and the dining room to a Russian couple with a teen-aged son, and kept the two bedrooms for herself and Sophie. The bathroom and the lavatory were in separate rooms, which aided in accommodating five adults.

The servants' wing of the house contained two small rooms for the Chinese cook and the Russian maid, a pantry with an icebox and storage loft, and a large kitchen with a wood stove. The servants had been hired by the renters, and Tanya and Sophie paid a small amount to have their rooms cleaned.

Soon after she had started working for Kurt, she had told him about Paul. One evening after work, having walked through the city streets, they were sitting in the Café Moderne in downtown Pristan. The weather was still chilly, and they stopped in for tea to warm up. Tanya took advantage of the quiet moments while they waited to be served and said, "Kurt, I want to tell you how much I appreciate all you're doing for my friends. Especially for Prince Veragin." She paused, waiting for Kurt's reaction. When none came, she went on: "Paul and I love each other, Kurt . . . have loved each other for some time now."

Kurt remained silent. Tanya looked at him searchingly, but he seemed preoccupied with stirring sugar in his glass of tea and wasn't looking at her. "We're going to be married as soon as he's established financially. I wanted you to know that, Kurt."

"Getting the jobs for your friends presents no problem. I'm glad to do it, Tanya. All it takes is a few telephone calls and letters of recommendation." He reached over the table and patted her hand. "That's the least I can do for you."

He completely ignored her confession. Surprised by his lack of response to her enormously important statement, Tanya was baffled. She knew he still cared for her; then why the silence? Did he think she wasn't serious about Paul? Well, she wasn't going to press the point. She had made it clear she was going to marry Paul, had been honest with Kurt; and if he chose to ignore it, he must have had his reasons.

True to his word, Kurt found jobs for all her friends. After days of fruitless search in Harbin, Kurt had secured work for Paul and Marfa in Handaohedzi, a settlement about two hundred miles from the city on the eastern branch of the railway and populated mostly by Russian railroad workers and farmers.

Paul became a policeman on the force protecting the railway from the marauding Chinese *hunhuzi* bandits. Inexperienced in living within the limits of a monthly salary, unaccustomed to counting his expenses, he was forced, Tanya guessed, to exist on a frugal budget, unable to permit himself the slightest luxury, and adjusting to his economic restrictions by trial and error. Always correct in his manners, he had called on Kurt to thank him and later told Tanya that Kurt was courteous but aloof.

Marfa worked as the pharmacist's assistant at the hospital clinic in Handaohedzi and occasionally helped the local doctor deliver babies. The salary she made was barely enough to subsist on, and she rented a converted pantry room in a farmer's home. Her plight bothered Tanya, who felt responsible for Marfa's welfare, and this worry nagged her like a toothache. She herself barely eked an existence, totally dependent on her paycheck, and even the tenants' rent did little to help her budget.

Sophie was finally hired as a salesgirl at Churin's branch store in Novy Gorod. Since Churin's was only a few blocks from Tanya's house on Pochtovaya Street, Sophie, always one to sleep late, was able to stay in bed an hour longer than Tanya, who had to get up earlier in order to catch the droshky three blocks away for the half-hour ride to her downtown office. Sophie said that the Lord knew the extra rest she needed and therefore had provided her with a nearby job—just a ten-minute walk through the employees' entrance on Azhikheiskaya Street.

Lately she was humming and smiling to herself continually, for she was dating a young man, Nikolai Urugaev, whom she had met one day when he accompanied his mother on a shopping spree at Churin's. Nikolai was a mathematics instructor at the YMCA, and since it was only two blocks away on Sadovaya Street, he frequently met Sophie on her lunch break, when they would buy pastry at Zazunov's and spend the time on the sidewalk bench in front of Churin's.

Tanya had to listen to every detail of their conversations, and she knew Sophie was falling in love. For her part, Tanya did not share her complex feelings with Sophie. Kurt continued to court her, taking her out to restaurants and to the theater, unfailingly correct in his behavior. Flattered to be seen at the best places in town, she was certain Kurt was courting her with marriage in mind. Several times she had attempted to steer the conversation to Paul, but each time Kurt had skillfully changed the subject.

Somewhere deep inside her a warning hovered. If she continued to see Kurt, wouldn't she be leading him on? Yet she couldn't bring herself to turn his invitations down. She had to admit that she felt more and more comfortable with him. Although she was an aristocrat and he the son of poor missionary parents, she found on their outings together that they had much in common.

They were linked by more than a family friendship. She realized that the bond had grown stronger with each crisis in her life—when Kurt had eased her plight after her parents' death, and then again upon her return to Harbin. How could she explain all this to Paul, make him understand that she felt it would be ungracious to refuse to go out with Kurt?

Alarmed by her growing affection for Kurt, she longed to see Paul and be with him. This longing was more than psychological. It was physical as well. The memory of those rapturous hours in Chita had never dimmed, and Tanya was too acutely aware of her own passionate nature not to be conscious of what might happen when she saw Paul again.

This weekend was the first time that he was able to get away to see her since he'd started his new job. Tanya suspected that he might have had to take an advance on his salary in order to afford a hotel room in Harbin. His letters were tender and loving and full of the kind of intellectual intimacy that is shared by those who have known each other for a long time. Yet he never mentioned marriage in his letters, only plans and hopes for a better future. A note of desperation occasionally slipped through, impassioned under a thin veil of reserve, reaching out to her, asking her to understand and be patient.

Deep in thought, she didn't see Paul until he was standing before her. Her heart beat violently as she rose. Dressed in a dark blue suit, he looked different from the dashing Prince Veragin in the officer's uniform, the valiant hero of the Siberian exodus. Clean shaven and smiling, he appeared younger than his thirty-one years. Yet there was something about the commanding stature of his body that still elicited respect toward this aristocrat, who probably wasn't even aware of his own natural grace and patrician bearing. How different he looked from Kurt's ramrod figure, which betrayed the guarded stiffness of a self-made man!

Paul's large clear eyes held her hypnotized. "The Adonis of the North" they had nicknamed Tsar Alexander the First, and Tanya, struck anew by the resemblance between the two men, thought that Paul could be that Adonis of the twentieth century.

"Are you sure you're not one of the bastard descendants of Alexander the First?" she asked, her laughter strained in an attempt to break the awkwardness of the moment.

Paul smiled and kissed her hand. "Tanya dear, it's a whim of nature, and I suffer these questions everywhere I go. First of all, I want to apologize for being late—the train was delayed. But to answer you—no, I'm only a Veragin."

Tanya trembled at the sound of his voice, fighting a wild desire to throw her arms around his neck and press her mouth to his.

"Paul, it's so good to see you!"

"Let me look at you, Tanyusha—feast my eyes on your dear face." He pushed her a little away from him, studying her with a smile. "You look well—I'm glad."

Passersby were turning around to look at them, and Tanya blushed. "Paul, let's go to the *pitomnik*—our beautiful arboretum—it's only two blocks away below Sadovaya Street. And on the way I'll show you where Sophie's boyfriend teaches. Or would you rather see my house first?"

Paul, holding her by the elbow, listened to her chatter with an indulgent smile. "Tanyusha, whatever you say. Let's go to the *pitomnik* first, though. I'm not in any hurry to see your house." Noticing Tanya's surprise, he added hastily, "I can always see it later. There are people there. This is my first visit to Harbin in almost two months, remember? I'm going to be selfish today. There's so little time before I have to return to Handaohedzi, and I want to have you all to myself. Alone."

He bent over to look into her eyes, and Tanya's heart, as if hiding from itself, seemed to stop beating.

They walked through the arboretum and sat on the benches, admiring the profusion of lilies of the valley, forget-me-nots, and violets, inhaling the delicate fragrance of the Manchurian spring.

It was a heady experience for Tanya to be alone with Paul without the stress of daily survival, without having to steal time from life as they had done during their flight in Siberia. She stopped on a sandy path and turned to look at him in wonder. His face, well etched in memory by now, appeared so new to her on this translucent day.

Without the stress of war, there was now time to share another kind of food between them—the nourishment of intellect—and Tanya listened with rapt attention.

"Am I boring you with my ideas?" Paul said, and when Tanya shook her head, he smiled, his eyes warm, and pulled her toward a bench set deeply in a niche of lilac bushes. "Let's sit here, darling, and talk some more."

Thrilling to his touch, deliciously aware of her need of him, Tanya sat down close to him. "I want to hear all about you, Pavlik," she said, and thrilled to the sound of his diminutive name which escaped her lips like a caress.

His face suddenly intense, Paul took her hands in his. "Oh, darling, I'm trying to share a lifetime of private thoughts with you in one short afternoon. How selfish of me! I yearn to hold you in my arms, and I resent this arboretum and the strangers who walk by, witnessing our reunion. Let's go away from here."

Tanya put her arm through his. "Do you want to see my house now and visit with Sophie?" She swung the carton of pastries in the air. "I've told her I'd pick up some cakes for tea."

Paul shook his head. "No, Tanya. I know from your letters that Sophie is doing well. You can stop worrying about your friends, angel. Even Marfa is managing on her small salary. She's never had much and is content with her present arrangement. We can think of ourselves now, Tanyusha. Come with me." He leaned over and slowly kissed her hand. "We can indulge our love. We deserve the happiness of being alone together."

Aware of her growing physical tension, Tanya made a feeble attempt to resist.

"Paul, I shouldn't go to your hotel."

"Why not, Tanya? It was meant for us to be together."

"Like this?"

"Life is cruel, Tanya. Why shouldn't we take our happiness when we can? We have waited long enough."

"Someone might see us go in."

"You're not accountable to anyone, Tanyusha. Besides, you're not an unmarried innocent girl whose reputation would be ruined."

They walked from the arboretum through the quiet Azhikheiskaya Street to the Oriant Hotel four blocks away, where Paul had taken a room.

Paul looked around the quiet street. "Where are we, Tanyusha? I'm constantly getting lost in your city. I guess I don't understand why it is divided in sections, as though there are different towns within a city."

"We're in the residential part of Harbin, Paul, and it's called Novy Gorod because it was a new part of town after the downtown Pristan was built from the harbor. You see, Harbin wasn't built all at once. Each settlement expanded and blended with the next, and each took on its own name and individuality. I guess the original builders hadn't expected the city to grow so fast."

"Then how many settlements are there in Harbin?"

"I'm not sure," Tanya said, "but probably around a dozen. I'm familiar with only a few. Downtown Pristan, of course; then the two residential areas, Novy Gorod and Modyagow; and"—Tanya chuckled—"Nakhalovka, adjacent to Pristan."

Paul stopped and burst out laughing. "What a name! How did they ever come up with the word *impudence* for a section of town?"

Tanya smiled. "There's a good reason for it. Harbin is overrun by refugees, and the need for housing is so acute that Nakhalovka was built without the city authorities' approval of the chosen site. Hence the name."

"How ingenious!" Paul marveled, slipping his arm through Tanya's.

She didn't answer him. The warmth of his touch, his closeness, the Oriant Hotel which was now just around the corner—all combined to fill her mind with one consuming thought: her hunger for him.

In his room, conscious of the mutual passion that was about to engulf them, Tanya made no attempt to stem the onrush. She put down the carton of pastries and dropped her arms helplessly.

"Oh, Paul! What are we doing?"

"Don't talk, Tanya."

His lips were on her mouth, teasing, whispering endearments. She couldn't resist him, and she knew that in his arms her willpower would vanish every time he touched her. She'd never felt that way before, had never yielded to a human being so completely with trust and gladness.

Paul undressed her slowly. This was not the frantic hunger for each other of Chita. As each part of her was freed into his sight, she felt the tingling movement of his breath upon her skin and longed for more.

Paul's eyes darkened, his face suffused with passion. He knelt beside the bed, his hands cradling her face.

"My Tanya. My love. I worship at your body."

He kissed her neck, sliding his hands over her shoulders and arms, his touch light and tender. Half-conscious of what he was doing, her body coaxed into submission, she did not move, aware of him beside her, intoxicated by the musky odor of his skin, which tantalized her senses. He was slow in his caresses, deliberately languid, and as her tension mounted, her belly and her limbs responded with impatience to his searching mouth. Her nerves grew taut, anticipating pleasure that her brain refused to voice—a state of trance perhaps so great that it transcended everything she had felt before. Then, suddenly, her mind screamed in shock and protest at the pressure of his lips and of her desire—a strange desire, unthinkable, compelling, undefined—until she felt his mouth entrap the hidden peak of that desire and she let out a cry of mingled ecstasy and shame. Her mind floated in weightless bliss somewhere into a different dimension where all the barriers were removed to let her savor this abandon, and she writhed and gasped and wept from the impact of this new experience.

Did time stand still? These stunning moments, the exquisite delicacy of his lovemaking—did she imagine them? What whispers rustled in the air? The dusk had darkened and the night had come. In the quiet of the room, he held her in his arms and stroked her hair. She tried to talk, but could not phrase the things she felt.

"Oh, Paul! What have you done to me? I mean—I thought—".

Paul pressed her hard against his body. "Don't talk, my angel. Why explain anything when words fall short of what we feel? Your thoughts—I know them; you needn't voice them. Remember, you're mine, and so precious to me I think of you as an extension of myself. Not just your face, your lips, your heart, but all of you, all equal and deserving of my love. Without you I'm only half a person now."

Tanya reached for him and felt him tense against the pressure of her hand and thrilled at his response to her caressing touch. They made love again, with her this time an active partner. When at length they lay still, satiated, hearing in the quiet of the room the muffled sounds of droshky wheels on cobblestones, Paul cradled Tanya's head against his chest and talked.

He reminisced about his past in St. Petersburg, where he was born, and told her of his days in the cadet corps, the glamor of life at court, where he was a page, regretting that she hadn't been a part of it with him. Tanya sighed at his daydreams and, suddenly aware of the stark and impersonal hotel room, freed herself from his embrace.

"Paul, when are we going to get married?"

He raised himself on his elbow and pulled her back down on the pillow. "We'll talk about it later."

But Tanya got out of bed and started to dress. "Paul, please, I want to know."

For a few seconds Paul looked at her, then got up and dressed. Pulling her down on the small love seat beside him, he held her hands and said: "Tanyusha, we've gone through much together, and now that we're safe and near each other, there's no reason we can't wait for a little while longer until I'm better situated and can offer you a comfortable life."

Tanya wrenched her hands free and jumped up, moving about the room in agitation. "Paul, what nonsense! Do you think I'm 'comfortable,' as you call it, living alone in one of the rooms in my house, with only Sophie to share my daily meals? Besides, she will probably get married soon and leave me. What are you talking about? I want to be with you all the time, and that's the only thing that counts."

Paul rose and paced the floor, his hands clasped behind his back; he didn't turn to look at her.

"Tanyusha, I wish I could make you understand. Do you have any idea what it means for a Veragin to be plunged into an existence of servility? I'm not complaining—I know I should be grateful to have a job and be spared the degradation of not having one at all. But can you imagine Prince Veragin marrying the daughter of a countess in my situation?"

"What's servile about being a policeman?"

"In itself—nothing, Tanya. But besides other officers

like myself, there are former soldiers and peasants among my associates, and some of them seem to delight in rubbing it in. Their grammar is so atrocious they can't tie two words together correctly. This accursed revolution has turned us all into minions." Paul laughed mirthlessly. "What do I have to offer you? A sterile shack of a room, about which the best that can be said is that you'll be protected from the cold and the wind? No, my lovely Tanya. No! I'll marry you only when I can offer you something better."

Tanya threw her hands up. "Have you forgotten that I'm the one who has never been to Petrograd, or seen the court you speak of"—she pointed at herself with an index finger—"or enjoyed the luxury and the glitter of the palace life? I've been brought up among the working people, the bourgeois professionals, and I have great respect for them. No honest work is demeaning to me, and I'd rather live with you in one room than be alone in a mansion."

Paul spread his hands and shook his head apologetically. "I know, I know, Tanyusha. Come to think of it, it is rather pompous of me to talk like this, and possibly ludicrous to cling to a vanished past—but while you feel at home here, it's a whole new world to me." His expression hardened. "I can't change my thinking overnight, Tanyusha. Even the simple comforts of life as I see them are beyond my ability to provide for you right now. I have to adjust to my own position in life first, before I can subject my wife to it. I couldn't live with that now. Can't you understand that?"

Grabbing her suddenly by the arms, he looked into her eyes. "Darling, please try to see my side of it!"

There was desperation in his voice, and Tanya nodded slowly. "I do see. I understand only too well, Paul. I guess I'm impatient, that's all. I want the happiness that's within my reach. Is that so wrong?"

Paul folded her in his arms, pressing her to his chest and running his fingers through her hair. "It won't be long, Tanyusha, before I get a promotion or something better will come my way. After all, I'm experienced in leadership, and I could easily be a manager somewhere. In the meantime, we'll see each other as much as possible."

Later, Tanya couldn't remember on which side of Poch-tovaya Street she walked home, or whether she felt the evening chill. She wouldn't let Paul take her home, for she couldn't bear the thought of witnessing his warm reunion with Sophie when all she wanted to do was to retire to her room and be alone with her disappointment.

They would have to wait, Paul had said. But competition was keen, and he had no profession that was now in demand. Somehow, someway, she would have to break down his pride, convince him that they couldn't wait indefinitely, that time was running out on them. Kurt wouldn't wait too long. She was sure he would ask her to marry him soon. It would be easier for him if she forestalled his proposal by announcing that she was marrying Paul. She hated to think of hurting Kurt again. But how could she tell all this to Paul?

She stopped on the sidewalk. Was it possible to love two men at the same time? She dismissed the thought immediately. How could she even think of such a thing! She was hurt and angry with Paul for refusing to marry her right away, but that in no way diminished her love for him. Warmth washed over her as she remembered the hours she had spent with him, and she unbuttoned the collar of her sweater. It could never be the same with Kurt. What she felt for him was affection based on gratitude and habit, not romantic love.

She put the key into the lock of her front door, but before she could turn it, the door swung open and Sophie, laughing with excitement, grabbed her by the hand and pulled her inside.

"Oh, Tanya, do I have a surprise for you! I can't wait to see your face! We've been waiting hours for you. Hurry, come into my room." Sophie could hardly contain herself, and as Tanya pulled her sweater off and hung it on the hall coat hanger, she felt a cautious stirring of hope. *We.* Sophie said "we." Was it possible that Marfa had found a better job in Harbin and was moving back to be with them? Immediately, she thought of vacating the dining room, and the relief she'd feel in having Marfa close by, under her protection.

She wasn't really listening to Sophie's incessant chatter.

When they reached her room, Sophie threw the doors open and, without a word, pushed Tanya inside.

Crossing the threshold, Tanya stopped, grasped the door frame to steady herself, and stared in shock as Countess Paulina Arkadyevna Merkulina, arms outstretched, rushed forward to embrace her.

A stabbing pain pierced Tanya's abdominal wall—the worst she had yet experienced—and gasping, clutching at her grandmother's shoulders, she slid down in a faint.

CHAPTER 28

Kurt Hochmeyer stood by the window of his third-storey apartment, holding an open letter in his hand and looking thoughtfully at the dark clouds in the evening sky. Erect and slender, he looked taller than his six feet. Dressed in a brown suit, a high-collar starched shirt with a pearl stick-pin in his brown-and-white striped tie, he could have passed for a young executive were it not for a deep worry wrinkle between his brows that betrayed his thirty-seven years. His chin, tucked squarely against his neck, made him look at the world from under his brows, creating an air of suspicion and sternness. His dark hair, parted just past the center of his head, was neatly combed to the sides. No gray dulled its gloss.

He glanced back at the letter. Elena was subtle and clever; there was no doubt about that, he thought. She had written him regularly every week since he had last visited Vladivostok a year ago, and from the hints she had planted in this letter he knew she had someone spying on him.

Who was it? His manager, Kozlov? He should never have hired Kozlov, who had fled from Vladivostok and had come to him looking for a job on Elena's recommendation. But then hindsight was always wiser, wasn't it? he thought.

Could it be someone else—one of the old maid secretaries in the office, perhaps—who had spied on him? Whoever it was had done a good job of reporting his moves.

Kurt crushed the letter in his hand. He resented Elena now; and to think he had once been attracted by her taunting green eyes, and by those teasing half-sentences that had kept him at her flat one evening last year when, in a moment of weakness, overcome by loneliness, he had stayed through the night.

After Tanya's departure for Russia, his longing for her had been so strong that it had threatened to reflect in his work, and the women he had taken out only intensified his loneliness. Seeking diversion, he had gone to Vladivostok, less than six hundred miles to the southeast, to visit Elena, the only young woman with whom he had anything in common.

He had met her a few years before he came to Harbin. Elena's uncle, Pyotr Polakov, had taken him into his sewing machine business when Kurt had returned to Russia after finishing his postgraduate work in business administration in Bern. He had come to visit his mother, who had moved to Vladivostok from their home in Smolensk after his father died. His father, a Lutheran missionary, had been a proud Swiss who took his job of trying to convert the Russians to the Lutheran faith seriously, and taught his son that the virtue of success in any endeavor was single-minded perseverance.

Soon after Kurt's arrival, his mother died of a heart disease, and Polakov, who had been his parents' friend in Smolensk, offered him a position with his firm, with the understanding that he would earn his promotion and become a junior partner within a year.

Everything went well, and Kurt became so indispensable to Polakov that the older man soon turned all the bookkeeping over to him. As the rumors of war reached Vladivostok in 1914, Kurt had concluded, with the pragmatic reasoning that later earned him success, that the best way to safeguard their invested capital and come out ahead was to sell the business while the bargaining power was still on their side, move out of the country to Harbin, and start anew. Polakov, plagued by gout, couldn't face the idea of uprooting himself, and procrastinated until the war started and the fear of doom had settled over the city.

In the meantime, Kurt had noticed Polakov's niece, Elena, who had been helping with secretarial work in the office. Blond and voluptuous, with dancing green eyes and a ready smile, she was provocative and always cheerful, in contrast to Kurt's serious nature, and he was drawn to her in spite of her shallow mind and her flashy taste in clothes, which embarrassed him.

Unexpectedly, Polakov died of a heart attack and Elena, an orphan and his only relative, inherited the estate. Kurt, who had the power of attorney to sell the business, rationalized that the old man's stubbornness had cost him a sizable profit, for now, threatened by the uncertainty of war, no one was eager to buy. When, finally, Kurt found a buyer, he signed over to himself more than his share.

Aware of what he had done, Elena said nothing, and continued to treat him with the usual friendliness. Kurt knew that in a court of law his act would be labeled embezzlement—a word with nasty connotations, no matter how he minimized it in his own mind with justifiable excuses. He was also uncomfortably conscious of Elena's silence on the matter, but although he suspected that she was hoping to marry him, he was not ready to commit himself, for he knew he did not love her. The incriminating papers had disappeared from his desk, and he deduced that Elena had taken them as future insurance. Well established in the city, she wanted to remain in Vladivostok until her aging and infirm nanny died.

"I'll expect to see you soon," she said to him with a smile when he came to say good-bye, her eyes watchful. Kurt promised to keep in close touch.

Once in Harbin, he bought a clothing business and within a year started to prosper beyond his own expectations. He worked hard and made few friends. The Levitin family was one exception. He spent long, enjoyable evenings talking to Tanya's father about world affairs, railway politics, and the burgeoning business in Harbin. Aside from that, his recreation was hunting. It was a sport not without danger, for the dense taiga, along the eastern line of the railway in particular, was overrun by bands of Chinese *hunhuzi.*

Kurt was fascinated by their origin, which dated back to the seventeenth century, when the followers of the fallen Ming rulers, unwilling to surrender to the victorious Tai-Ching dynasty, escaped into the Manchurian taiga, from which they raided government posts, settlements, and towns. Kurt chose to ignore the fact that with time, the political faction disappeared and the ranks of *hunhuzi* were replenished with adventurers, malcontents, and ordinary criminals. On the contrary, he kept reminding himself that in Manchuria, *hunhuzi* played an important role, sometimes politically, for occasionally the local population required protection from the arbitrary rule of the Chinese bureaucrats. The government forces, unable to control these functionaries, frequently hired whole gangs of *hunhuzi* into their service and bestowed the rank of general on the head of the group. Thus Marshal Chang Tso-Lin, originally the leader of a large gang of *hunhuzi*, became one of the prominent government generals.

At the same time, Kurt chuckled at the audacity of some of the feuding bands in rural areas who made raids on peaceful villagers, often kidnapping rich merchants for ransom. To defend themselves from their attacks, the local residents paid regular bribes to the bandits in whose area the village was located, thus buying their protection from the neighboring rival bands.

Kurt had his own arrangement with the *hunhuzi*. Through his Chinese guides, who acted as intermediaries, he kept an uneasy truce by offering hard-to-get flour and salt in return for the privilege of hunting unmolested on their territory. It was imperative to know the location where he hunted, however, for if he trespassed into a hostile area, he ran the risk of being kidnapped for ransom, or even killed.

There was another, less tractable danger: the Manchurian tiger, the king of the taiga. Kurt remembered the time when the guides had panicked and run upon hearing that a tiger had killed a railway guard and ten Chinese workmen in the small station of Lukashevo. The man-killer was tracked down, shot, and dragged into the neighboring village of Imyanpo for display, and Kurt studied in fascination the magnificent animal, with its stripes on the silken fur narrowing over the forehead into what the superstitious Chinese workmen swore was an hieroglyphic depicting the word *wang*, or king.

The incident had forced the hunters to move in groups

of ten or twelve, armed with two kinds of firearms—one for the animals and one for the *hunhuzi*. And in spite of all the precautions, they couldn't always trust their guides, who occasionally betrayed them to the hostile bandits. To safeguard themselves against this treachery, they drew lots to decide on their destination at the last minute, allowing no time for the guide to inform the unfriendly bands. Still, Kurt loved these expeditions, and the element of danger added spice and excitement to his otherwise sterile and scheduled life.

He had written to Elena infrequently from Harbin, adhering rigidly to an impersonal tone, and after Tanya had left for Russia, he thought there would be no harm in a friendly visit to Vladivostok. The interlude had given him only a temporary respite from his growing apprehension. During the clumsy, inept lovemaking, he had fantasized that it was Tanya he held in his arms, but the illusion was fleeting, and it only intensified his loneliness.

Yes, it had been a mistake, he mused now, and one he still regretted, for at the time it had increased his anxiety about Tanya's whereabouts and deepened his concern over her safety. He smoothed the crumpled letter and read it again.

"I need not tell you of my affection for you," Elena wrote, "and I'm living for the day when I shall be moving to Harbin. The Bolsheviks are on our doorstep and it's only a matter of time before they take Vladivostok. I don't want to be here when that happens and am so happy at the thought of being near you again. I've heard of the new bookkeeper you've recently employed. Had I arrived sooner, I could have taken her place, but perhaps you'll find another use for me."

The hidden implication was clear. Who had told her about Tanya?

Sweet, lovely Tanya.

His anger melted. He pulled his chin in a stretching motion; ever since he had started wearing the high-collared shirts, it had become a habit. He sighed. Tanya, Tanya. She had become an obsession with him. He had watched her blossom and develop into a beautiful young girl, assuming he had plenty of time to court her. Then, suddenly, she was gone. She had slipped away from him once, but he wasn't going to let this happen again. Fate had given him a second chance. This time, no one was going to come between them. Those three years without her had been difficult for him. The uncertainty, the worry—he wouldn't want to go through it again.

During her absence, many scheming mothers, hoping for a brilliant match, tried to entrap him for their eligible daughters. One of them was Madame Korchagova, who pursued him with hints and invitations until Lydia became ill and died before Kurt was forced into the awkward position of having to turn her down.

He had had a series of fleeting affairs, mostly to fill the lonely hours at night, yet he was always careful to break off the relationship at the first sign of the woman's emotional involvement.

Tanya's confession returned to haunt him. She had had her fling with romantic love at the time of her youthful marriage. Now she told him she had fallen in love again, this time with her husband's glamorous commander, Paul Veragin. She was very young. Kurt counted the years. Why, she was not yet twenty-two, a mere child. No wonder she had become infatuated with the romantic image of a White Army hero who had protected her, saved her from death on their flight through Siberia. Kurt closed his eyes and shuddered. It must have been dreadful: the suffering, the privations. No wonder she thought she was in love with the prince. She would get over it, here in Harbin.

Still, he had deemed it prudent to send Veragin out of town, and had recommended him for a job in Handaohedzi. He wanted to woo Tanya without competition, to let her see in many subtle ways how much more he could offer her than her penniless prince.

But then, one day, when Veragin had come to his office to thank him, Kurt had been shaken by the encounter.

It had been one of those rare days for him when everything had gone wrong. A long-awaited shipment of woolens from abroad had been delayed at the border through misunderstanding, and he'd been forced to dictate indignant protests to the officials. Two of his accountants were ill, and their ledgers were not turned in to him on time—a fact that automatically put him in a bad mood, because he was fanatical about punctuality, and any delays annoyed him. So when Kozlov announced that a Paul Veragin was asking to see him, Kurt's irritation deepened, and only a fleeting thought skimmed over the surface of his brain, without registering deeply: Paul Veragin has dropped his title. Good.

"Show him in," Kurt ordered, without raising his head from the papers strewn over his desk.

When the door opened to admit Paul, Kurt looked up and slowly rose to greet his visitor. He hadn't stopped to think what he had expected Paul to look like, but he was totally unprepared for the magnetism of the blond giant who stood before him.

After shaking hands and offering him a seat, Kurt returned to his chair behind his oak desk.

"Please forgive this intrusion upon your business hours," Paul said warmly with a smile, "but I'm on my way to Handaohedzi, and I couldn't leave without expressing my gratitude to you for your efforts on my behalf."

In Paul's voice, the stilted words sounded natural and sincere. Reluctantly, Kurt realized that Paul Veragin was the first genuine prince he had ever met, and the knowledge made him shift in his chair uncomfortably.

"I was glad to do what I could," Kurt replied, surprised at his own detached tone of voice.

"It is my good fortune that you're Tanya's friend," Paul continued easily, "for I doubt that otherwise you would have recommended me sight unseen. I appreciate your help."

Kurt noticed the familiar use of Tanya's name. He stiffened. Although reluctant to admit it, he recognized in Paul a more formidable rival than he had imagined. Yet, incredibly, he found himself charmed by the handsome aristocrat, who, in spite of his reduced circumstances, was able to retain his dignity. Unexpected jealousy assailed Kurt, and since he didn't intend to share Tanya with Veragin, he referred to her with a patronymic. "I am indeed Tatiana Andreyevna's friend, and whatever I do for her will always be in her best interests. She is home now and deserves to regain what she lost."

Kurt watched with satisfaction as Paul stiffened and his face suffused with color.

"I'm pleased that you have a secure position in Handaohedzi," Kurt went on. "I don't know if you're aware of it yet, but a position with the railway company, no matter how modest, is an enviable one. The company takes good care of its employees. You'll get free medical care and lodging with it."

Paul nodded. "It's a good start, Mr. Hochmeyer. It'll give me a firm foothold to look for better things in the future."

Kurt studied him speculatively. How long would it take before this aristocrat, accustomed to instant respect, learned that it took training and luck to exchange poverty for prosperity in this country?

Leaning forward, Kurt cleared his throat. "I'm sure you're aware that experience and lots of time are necessary for advancement here. I wish you luck."

When the interview was over and the two men rose to shake hands, it was obvious that Prince Veragin understood that he was not being treated as an equal and was chafing underneath his well-mannered exterior.

In the weeks that followed, Kurt saw Tanya every weekend, restraining himself from asking to see her more often, afraid to rush her and frighten her away. It soon became an unspoken understanding between them that they spend the weekends together, and he was misled into believing that he had succeeded in winning her over. Then, one day, she told him candidly that she couldn't see him the following weekend, because Paul was coming to Harbin and she was going to spend it with him. It was a stunning blow, made worse by Tanya's casual tone of voice, as if she took his understanding for granted.

The thought of them together at that very moment stung him painfully. What a fool he'd been to think he could woo her slowly, make her see the hopelessness of her involvement with Veragin. He had overestimated her maturity. He'd have to act fast if he was to keep her from slipping away from him again.

He crumpled the letter in his fist and aimed it at the wastebasket near him. He had to get out of his flat, away from the oppressive thoughts, from his active imagination which threatened to run away with him. He checked the house key in his pocket, opened the door, and froze.

On the other side of the door, dressed in a worn coat, her hand raised to knock, stood a smiling Elena.

Surprised and annoyed, Kurt bowed slightly and, stepping back into the apartment, said the first thing that came to his mind: "Why didn't you let me know you were coming? I would have prepared for your arrival and have found you a place to stay."

Elena laughed. Her laughter had a cheerful, bell-like quality that used to amuse him. Now it irritated him.

"I already have a place to stay, Kurt dear. I thought I'd surprise you, and so here I am!" She spread her arms playfully and swung around the center of the room. "Aren't you going to take my coat and invite me to sit down?" she asked, throwing him a coy glance.

Remembering his manners, Kurt said stiffly, "Of course. Forgive my lack of hospitality, but you did take me by surprise. Here, let me have your coat."

He came around her and held his arms above her shoulders, waiting for her to take it off. As she removed it and turned around toward him, her body brushed against him. It was a deliberate gesture, and Kurt wondered if she had come to seduce him and woo him away from Tanya.

He hung her coat on a wooden hanger stand at the door and poured a glass of cognac from a red and white crystal decanter on the sideboard.

She took a sip and looked around the room. "What a roomy flat. But such austerity! One can certainly tell it needs a woman's touch. Not a flower anywhere."

Kurt winced at the transparent hint and watched her move from one piece of furniture to the next. She touched every ornament, stroked the sofa pillows, ran her fingers along the rough surface of a carved dragon on the Chinese sideboard he had purchased a month before, and played with the silk tassels of the lamp shade. She even glanced through the open door into the bedroom, where his desk was neatly tidied by his Chinese maid and his wide bed was covered with a tapestry spread. Then Elena turned to him.

Taking another sip of the cognac, she looked at him over the rim of the glass.

"I like your taste, Kurt. It's so like you, masculine and restrained."

Her clumsy attempt at flattery was too obvious to please him.

"It's cold, is that what you mean, Elena? I remember your flat in Vladivostok as cozy and warm. It must have been difficult for you to leave it. Tell me about it."

He pulled up a chair near the sofa and sat down, hoping to steer her thoughts away from his apartment. "What is going on in Vladivostok now?" he asked.

Elena shrugged. "You can't imagine the confusion in the city, Kurt. No one seems to know what to do. You should hear the tales they tell in the streets! Rumors are repeated on every street corner, and the stories are distorted with every retelling. You know how we Russians love horror tales—the gorier the better. It stands to reason, of course, that sooner or later Vladivostok will fall to the Reds. How can it hope to stand up to the Bolsheviks?"

Kurt's nod was pensive. "I agree. It's too late to fight them. From now on we have to learn to get along with them. After all, they're going to be our neighbors, and it's unrealistic to think that small, scattered bands of Whites can organize a full-scale uprising at this point."

Elena shook her head. "I wish they would stop the carnage. Whole villages are burned down if there's even a rumor that they might have helped the Whites in any way. No consideration for women and children, who starve or freeze to death. I heard brutal accounts of lawlessness in rural areas. An enraged, illiterate mob gets a taste of power for the first time in their lives, and then what happens? They go berserk at the sight of blood, and take revenge on the landowners by pillaging their homes and raping their women. They tell revolting stories of moujiks queueing up for their turn at the bloodied thighs of some ravaged daughter for as long as she's still alive."

Elena paused, gave a shudder, then went on. "I'm so grateful I'm safely out of Russia. It's no longer my country—not the one I loved and cherished in the past."

"What about the economic climate of the city? We read in the papers that there is chaos in Vladivostok."

"The city is gradually becoming paralyzed. No one seems to be carrying on the business of living. The afternoon promenaders on Svetlanskaya Street have disappeared, and one sees clusters of gossipmongers who loiter on street corners waiting for news. When the Allies left Vladivostok, I knew the city was doomed. The tension in the atmosphere was actually palpable. I'm sorry I didn't leave sooner."

Elena raised her glass of cognac to her lips and took a sip. Choking on the fiery liquid, she began to cough. Kurt leaned over and lightly struck her on the back. Red in the face from coughing, tears glistening in her eyes, she looked at him. "Oh, Kurt, if you only knew how happy I am to see you!"

Avoiding her eyes, Kurt rose and went over to the sideboard to put down his glass of cognac. Elena followed him, put her hand on his. "Kurt, do you have any idea what it was like for me these last few years, alone in Vladivostok?"

"I thought you had many friends in the city."

"Friends are helpful only to a point. They have their own lives to lead. Tell me, how is Kozlov doing?"

"Fine. Do you know him well?" Kurt looked at her and watched with amusement as a flush spread over her face.

"Not exactly. He's kept in touch with me, but he's never been a close friend."

So, thought Kurt, it *is* Kozlov who has been spying on me. He felt no animosity toward Kozlov, however, for his petty interference.

"I'm glad you know Kozlov," he said smoothly. "You'll have at least one acquaintance in the city."

"It's not the same as having your own family. I've missed you, Kurt. More than you know." Still flushed, Elena took off her suit jacket, revealing the seductive curve of her breasts under a clinging silk blouse.

It had been a long time since she had stirred him, and he was surprised at his reaction now. All at once, his self-control disintegrated and his frustration turned into anger: anger at Tanya, who was with Veragin at that very moment, possibly succumbing to his embraces, anger against

Elena, who was hinting at marriage and was shamelessly throwing herself at him. Well, why not take what was offered? It would help him forget Tanya and Veragin, wipe the images of the two of them out of his mind.

He reached for Elena.

Later, he was to think about that night with shame. He had always prided himself on his restraint, and he couldn't understand what had made him lose his head and behave as he did. All he could remember clearly was an overwhelming urge to inflict pain, to vent his anger in physical force.

Without a word, he pulled Elena into the bedroom. Roughly, he threw her on the bed and tore off her clothes. In the fury of his passion, there was no room for gentleness or for caresses. He pinched and squeezed and sucked her flesh, and knew it hurt her, and couldn't stop. But still, he couldn't escape, for Tanya's face was there before him, mocking him, and his mad, mad jealousy of the other man crazed him into frenzy.

Wild for release, he pushed against Elena, bruising her with savage thrusts and drowning himself at last in a carnal deluge.

Reason returned to him slowly. The discovery of an ugly side of his nature was more shocking than the sight of Elena's red-blotched skin. His self-disgust was greater than his scorn for the woman who had meekly submitted to his abuse. He struggled to regain his composure. What could he say to her? How could he justify his unforgivable behavior?

He listened. There was no sound, no movement from Elena. He rose and dressed, unable to find the words to explain his actions. He went into the sitting room, poured a glass of cognac, sat down. What had he done? How could he face Elena now? His hand shook, threatening to spill the cognac, and he turned to put it down on the table. A shrill sound of the telephone jarred him. Annoyed, he reached for the receiver.

Sophie Pavlova's shaking voice spluttered fragmentary sentences into his ear: Tanya in the City Hospital with acute appendicitis . . . to be operated on immediately . . . doctors suspect a ruptured appendix . . . .

Slamming down the receiver, Kurt jumped up. City Hospital; that wasn't good enough. She couldn't be moved now, but as soon as possible he would transfer her to Dr. Mindlin's private clinc, where she'd get the best possible care he could provide for her. He had chosen to be her guardian and he loved her. Oh, God, nothing must happen to Tanya, he thought. His Tanya! She belonged to him. He wouldn't let anyone take her away from him. Not Paul Veragin, not illness, not the devil himself.

As he headed toward the door, Elena's sharp, high-pitched voice stopped him. "Kurt! Haven't you forgotten something?"

My God. She must have come to Harbin without much money, if any. Of course. That's why she'd come tonight, to ask for help, and he had taken advantage of her instead. Ashamed, he fumbled in his pocket, pulled his wallet out, and placed a fifty-dayan bill on the table. But before he could say anything, Elena, disheveled, half-dressed, her face flushed, gave him a resounding slap across his face.

The slap sobered him, restored his composure. He studied Elena with sudden pity. How could he have desired this woman only an hour ago? He must have been out of his mind. As he looked at her, Elena's lips quivered, and tears spilled over her cheeks.

"Oh, Kurt, how could you? Do you think I'm—" She stopped, unable to go on.

Avoiding her eyes, Kurt gave her a stiff, formal bow and, without a word, left the apartment.

CHAPTER 29

On a busy afternoon in July, Kurt did something he had never done before. He left his office, took a droshky to Churin's in Novy Gorod, and walked the four blocks to the Protestant church on the corner of Mukdenskaya and Bolshoi Avenue.

Not a religious man, he hadn't been inside a church since his mother's death. Some malevolent force, however, was now threatening to consume him, and had driven him toward the church, and prayer.

Brown and dark, it stood in a garden that was barren but for some tall oaks and stunted evergreens. The park occupied the length of the block between Mukdenskaya and Telinskaya streets and was surrounded by a tall wooden fence, the gate of which was padlocked. Kurt peered through the slats for a better look. Hidden deeply inside, the church seemed to cower from the onlooker. Only its spindly Gothic steeple rose above the trees in a bold thrust to impale the sky. He knew there were no services during the weekdays, but to find the church locked was disconcerting. He released his hold on the gate slats. He didn't need the church; he could pray anywhere. He checked himself. Pray for what? What was he doing there in broad daylight, during office hours? Disciplined Lutherans were attending to their business of working, reserving Sundays for worship. *He* was acting foolishly. He turned on his heel and headed back across Mukdenskaya Street.

On either side of the block, two more churches vied for his attention. A large Catholic cathedral stood on one side. It had no fence, and its many steps widened at the sidewalk in an open embrace. On the opposite side, the gray stone Pokrovskaya Orthodox Church, its onion domes sparkling in the sun, squatted firmly at the edge of an old cemetery. The low stone fence hugged the block-long multitude of graves and crypts. Around these monuments to human residue, lilac bushes proliferated; iron gates and sandy pathways led the living to the granite sculptures of the dead.

As he neared the entrance, a timid breeze reached out from the graveyard and tugged at him. He hesitated for only a second and then, as if pulled by an undefined force, stepped inside.

What had gotten into him? He'd never visited cemeteries, and he disapproved of the Russian custom of using them as parks, where parents walked their children through the shady lanes and read the brooding epithets engraved on the tombstones. Now *he* was succumbing to this morbid Russian habit. He walked to the nearest bench and sat down. Strangely, he discovered that no gloom pervaded the memorial park, and an atmosphere of serenity and peace wrapped around him. He could think.

Everything had gone well for him, until that fateful night over a month ago when Elena came to his apartment. His unpardonable treatment of her still filled him with shame. To make up for his callous behavior in some small measure, he had found her a teller's job at the Russo-Asiatic Bank. Since then, he had tried to forget that part of the night; most of the time he succeeded. But he could never erase the memory of his subsequent long vigil at the hospital, which remained vivid in his mind.

Tanya's appendix, although inflamed, had not ruptured, and she came through the operation without complications. Concerned over her weakened physical condition, however, he insisted she remain in the hospital beyond the customary ten days. Finally, she was released into her grandmother's care.

Grandmother! Kurt shook his head. Countess Paulina Arkadyevna needed more care than Tanya. It would have been amusing were it not so tragic to watch the countess preside over a one-room court with the aplomb of a dowager empress. Totally inept in household chores—how was it possible for a woman to reach maturity and not have

learned to cook the simplest of meals?—she was more a
hindrance than a help during Tanya's recuperation. Sophie
did what she could at night, after work. She reported to
Kurt that the countess was not only helpless, but spent her
days living in the past, grieving over the loss of her servants Oksana and Matvei.

It had been Matvei, now an important commissar in the
local soviet in Samara, who had obtained an exit visa for
the countess. She was able to leave the country unmolested
and went through Paris to London, and from there by boat
to China. It had been a long, tiring journey for her.

Kurt had listened patiently to her complaints. Enchanted
by the elegance and charm of the older woman, witty when
she wanted to be, literary when the mood shifted, he was
completely disarmed by her thorough knowledge not only
of the French classics but of Goethe and Schiller as well.
In small doses, she was a delight—so different from Tanya's mother—and in spite of her frequent journeys into the
past, he found himself spending his evenings with her
while Tanya was still in the hospital.

Accustomed to servants and luxury even in her reduced
circumstances in Russia, the countess often fussed about
her inability to adapt to caring for herself and living in a
house without help. With eyes clouded by tears, she made
light of her efforts to make an omelet in the communal
kitchen and the indignity she endured from the Chinese
cook's reprimand: "Madama forgot to wash the dishes."

True, her grandmother was Tanya's responsibility, yet
Kurt was often tempted to tell the countess how easy it
would be for him to provide the accustomed comfort in her
declining years and make her life pleasant again. But he
knew it would be blackmail pure and simple, and he
wanted so much for Tanya to come to him of her own free
will.

As soon as she was allowed to be moved, he had trans-
ferred her to Dr. Mindlin's clinic by ambulance, provided
her with a private nurse, and dressed her room with flowers. The day before she was released from the hospital, he
held her hand and, without undue emotion, as though the
fact had long been established between them, said:

"Tanya dear, I've loved you for many years. . . ." In spite of his effort to keep his voice even, it broke, and he coughed to hide it. "I've waited a long time and perhaps could have waited longer, but your operation has changed everything. I realize now that life itself doesn't wait." He paused for a moment and squeezed her hand. "Tanya, I want to marry you."

When she tried to answer, he raised his hand and shook his head. He knew what it was she wanted to say, and he didn't want to hear it. "Please don't talk now, Tanya. I'm not pressing for an answer. After waiting this long, I can wait a while longer." He smiled. "I wanted you to know my intentions. Think it over. Take your time. When you're well, we'll talk about it again."

He kissed her hand and hurried out of the room without giving her a chance to say anything.

That had been three weeks ago. Since then, she'd recuperated at home. He suspected it must have been difficult for her to watch her grandmother's clumsy efforts at nursing, yet he didn't want to offend her by offering her a loan so she could hire temporary help. She returned to work ghastly pale and very thin, with eyes that burned like black onyx.

On the afternoon of the second day she fainted, and this time Kurt insisted over her protests that she accept a loan from him, take a recuperative leave of absence, and go to Barim, a small village where her parents had taken her in the past for summer vacations. It was about three hundred miles west of Harbin, and safely distant from Handaohedzi and Paul Veragin. Kurt wanted to make reservations for her at the resort hotel, but Tanya insisted she was well enough to stay in the same cottage her parents had often rented. It was owned by a farmer's family that consisted of a grandfather, his son, his daughter-in-law, and a small grandson. Tanya assured Kurt that they would take good care of her if the need arose.

She'd been there over a week now, and he was pleased she was away from the emotional stress of seeing the countess struggling to manage without servants. Then, too, the added excitement of Sophie's engagement and approaching marriage to Nikolai had kept her from getting a much-needed rest.

Kurt pulled out his gold watch from his waistcoat. It was four o'clock, and he was invited for tea with the countess.

He rose. In spite of her maladjustment, Kurt had to admit he thoroughly enjoyed her company. Tanya's grandmother was refreshing. He replaced his watch and started down the sandy path toward the gate.

A tall, cadaverous beggar, his hand out for alms, hobbled toward him, favoring a leg wrapped in dirty rags. Kurt glanced at the man. The taut skin over his cheekbones was waxy, his stare glazed. Although opium and heroin were easily obtainable from the Chinese population, addiction among the Russians was rare.

Filled with sudden pity, Kurt pulled some coins from his pocket and placed them in the beggar's palm, then watched the man shuffle away. He wondered how many more army officers—forthright, cultured men with an abysmal lack of skills—would succumb to drugs and worse in the next few years. He couldn't understand why the Russian gentry were so inept in adapting themselves to the practical world of honest labor. Having himself worked hard all his life, he couldn't understand such rapid deterioration of character. And what kind of moral fiber did Prince Paul Veragin possess? Evidently Tanya was willing to take a chance on him. She had gambled once before, and he had stood aside and let her disappear into the bowels of Russia. By God, he wouldn't let her do it twice. He couldn't.

Turning abruptly, he headed toward Pochtovaya Street, and Tanya's house.

"You can't imagine how delighted I am to see you, Kurt Albertovich."

The countess was fluttering over the pot of tea she had just placed on the table with much accompanied fanfare. You'd think she had just created an epicurean delight, Kurt thought. After four weeks of almost daily contact, she still addressed him by his patronymic, although he had asked her twice to call him by his first name. "Why, Kurt Albertovich!" she had said, genuinely shocked. "You'll al-

ways be Kurt Albertovich to me." And Kurt sighed, feeling
the formality underscore his thirty-seven years.

"I can never get water into this pot without spilling it.
Oh, how I wish I'd watched Oksana do it. But then
. . . " The countess shrugged and let her voice trail off with
an apologetic smile. "There I go again. How foolish of me."
She patted the table with a towel, poured tea into a glass in
a silver holder, and, handing it to Kurt, sat down opposite
him. Her pale eyes looked at him with childlike curiosity.
"Now tell me, what's the news from home?"

Kurt hesitated. She'd refused to read the papers, brand-
ing them biased, and had fallen into the habit of asking
him for the news, as if she expected his interpretation of
events to make them more palatable.

"The Bolsheviks are well entrenched in Russia, Paulina
Arkadyevna, and their power is spreading."

"But I thought General Wrangel had taken Kiev just a
month ago."

Kurt sighed. "Not General Wrangel, Paulina Arkadyevna," he explained patiently, "but the Polish Army, who
came to his assistance. He made a bad mistake. The national feelings were outraged by the Polish invasion, and
now even General Wrangel's loyal supporters are going
over to the Reds. But then General Denikin made a stra-
tegic error, too, by not listening to General Wrangel's advice. He should have kept his White army together instead
of splitting it into three fronts when he advanced on Moscow." Kurt shook his head. "The course of history is
changed through the errors of a few men."

For a few moments the countess sat still, the fragile
china cup in her hand clicking delicately against the saucer. Her eyes, awash with tears, stared at Kurt. Blinking
hard, she brushed a curl from her forehead and smiled
brightly.

"Nonsense! Our Baron Wrangel is a patriot and a great
strategist. I'm sure he will rally the people to his side and
drive the Bolsheviks out. You'll see!"

You really believe that, don't you, dear countess?
thought Kurt with compassion. One coped with anguish by
playing games with facts or building fences around the bat-
tered mind, and the countess was no exception.

Paulina Arkadyevna smiled at him over the rim of her cup. "I don't expect to live like this the rest of my life, you know. Harbin is a nice city, but it's not my home."

"It could have been worse, Paulina Arkadyevna," Kurt said evenly.

The countess shrugged and changed the subject. "Prince Veragin left just before you arrived. He's a charmer, isn't he? Small wonder Tanya is in love with him."

The words fell lightly as the countess glanced at him briefly and poured him another glass of tea. Rigid, Kurt sat holding his glass, pulse hammering in his temples painfully. Veragin is in Harbin. . . .

Conscious of an awkward silence, he nodded. "I've met him only once."

Paulina Arkadyevna sliced a piece of lemon and offered it to him. "He didn't know Tanya was in Barim. He doesn't look like a village policeman." The countess chuckled, waiting for a comment. When none came, she went on. "What a comedown for an aristocrat! Wasn't there anything else more—more appropriate for a prince?"

Kurt measured his words carefully. "Paulina Arkadyevna, we have a different set of values here. There's nothing dishonorable in being a policeman. One's profession or trade is respected more than parental ancestry here."

The countess pursed her lips. Leaning back in her chair, she crossed her arms in front of her. "I see." Her voice was flat and her eyes narrowed as she digested his words. Kurt waited, sipping his tea.

"Am I to understand that unless Prince Veragin acquires a skill of some sort, he has no future in his present work?"

Kurt shrugged his shoulders. "I can't foretell the future, Paulina Arkadyevna, but it doesn't look promising."

"How tragic for them—for Tanya."

The countess busied herself with the dishes. Kurt watched for a while. He had always been a loner. Even in school he had remained aloof from his classmates, never confiding his thoughts or feelings to anyone. He had been accustomed to solving his problems alone, and it had never occurred to him to ask for advice. But now he suddenly felt a need to share his feelings with the countess.

"Paulina Arkadyevna, I've asked Tanya to marry me. I

know she's in love with Prince Veragin, but I hope it's a passing infatuation. We've known each other for a long time, and I've loved her for many years. I can offer her so much. . . ."

He let the last words sink in for a few seconds and then added, "I can provide her with comforts and even luxury. I don't mean to imply that love is not important in marriage, but I feel Tanya has a genuine affection for me, and I do want to emphasize that she deserves the best in life. It would be my pleasure to see to it that she doesn't want for anything."

Paulina Arkadyevna stopped collecting the dishes and sat down again.

"What has Tanya said to you about it?"

"I haven't pressed for an answer. Before she left for Barim, I told her to take her time thinking about it."

The countess laughed. "Clever man, Kurt Albertovich! You know my granddaughter well." Her eyes twinkled. "She's impulsive and headstrong, and usually goes after what she wants. The Siberian ordeal matured her, however, thank God, and it's good she has time to think things over."

"She should be coming home in a few days. I'll ask her then."

"I've had a letter from her this morning, and she talks about a minor accident that will keep her there a little longer. I hope she doesn't extend her stay in Barim for too long. I miss her."

"What happened to her?"

"I don't know. She said only that it's nothing to worry about. She seems strangely secretive about it. It's not like her at all. She's usually quite open with me. Perhaps she didn't want to upset me. I don't know."

Kurt stiffened. He would write tonight, tell her she was missed at work, hint gently that she couldn't stay away too long.

He was sure Veragin had neither the time nor the money to join her in Barim. Then what was delaying her? He had to find out.

CHAPTER 30

Tanya walked slowly along the dirt road that led from the Kursaal Hotel which stood apart from the village, toward the cluster of houses where she was staying with the Fedikins. She had been so pleased with her decision to live with them and be a part of their family that after her daily walks she could hardly wait to get back to her cottage and join them for the evening meal.

Today, however, halfway between the Kursaal and the village, she turned abruptly off the road and took a foot-path through the willow thicket toward the river. She was not ready to face Agrafena's friendly curiosity about the day's events, the ten-year-old Grisha's hungry questions about everything, and the gregarious collective mood of the Fedikins. She had to be by herself. The shock had been too great and unexpected for her to hide it effectively from the solicitous eyes of the well-meaning family, and she could not answer the questions that were sure to follow. She had to think, to absorb the enormity of her problem.

Threading her way through the willows, she went down to the rushing waters of the Yal and sat down on a boulder, wrapping her arms around her legs.

She had always loved Barim, this remote Manchurian village settled by the Russians and little different from the Siberian hamlets across the border. Far behind her, the village with its whitewashed houses and planked roofs nestled in the valley, its distant sounds of squeaking cartwheels, sluggish cowbells, and barking dogs comforting to Tanya.

Wild berry trees fringed the edge of the river below her, and above, hazelnut bushes fluffed the hills, which narrowed to a dark gorge. To her right a steep mountain rose above the trees. Catherine the Great, the villagers had named it, for nature had carved a majestic figure of a woman with a crown on her head, sitting on a granite throne and playing a piano. Deep crevices were scratched below her, as if a mammoth cat, trying to reach the empress, had pawed its way above the timberline.

The sun-bathed air was full of ringing sounds, both imaginary and real, and as Tanya studied the moving pebbles on the bottom of the river, she could feel the icy water trickle through her body. The pink, cherubic face of the country doctor floated before her eyes, all smiles and goodwill. "Madame Bolganova, I have good news for you—you're in an interesting condition." What was so interesting about it? she wondered. Did other languages have such an inane term for pregnancy? In her case, *disastrous* would be a more appropriate term.

Impulsively, she had asked the doctor if he could perform a discreet abortion while she was in Barim. Understanding dawned slowly on him, and when it did, he spread his arms regretfully. Sorry, Madame Bolganova. There were no facilities for that in Barim. But he could highly recommend Dr. Mindlin's clinic in Harbin. They had a high reputation for their excellent skill, and these procedures were routine with them. Thank you, Doctor. Thank you very much. Where would the money come from this time without Kurt finding out about it?

It was hard enough to make ends meet. There was no way she could pay for an abortion herself, or buy the new clothes that would be needed during her pregnancy. She thought of the seamstress who came to their house when she was a little girl and worked on her mother's sewing machine for days at a time, taking her meals with the family. But even that expense was beyond Tanya's resources now, and she was already deeply in debt to Kurt.

Dear, sweet Kurt. He had paid for all the hospital expenses during her illness and advanced her salary for this trip. But even his capacity to forgive surely had its limits. He loved her and wanted to marry her. But with Paul's child?

She didn't want an abortion. She wanted the child, an extension of the man she loved. Yet she dared not tell him about it, for she knew what Paul's reaction would be. With his impeccable sense of honor, he would marry her right away, to save her the disgrace of giving birth to an illegitimate child. But to marry him now seemed a practical impossibility. Between them they could hardly provide for the newborn child. She would have to repay Kurt the money he advanced her.

The sensible thing to do would be to marry Kurt and write Paul afterward. With the marriage a fait accompli, there would be nothing Paul could do but accept the fact that he had lost her.

But in matters of love she was not a sensible woman. Oh, God, how could she give Paul up? she cried quietly to herself. The man she loved was near, and happiness within her grasp. They were both young. Perhaps they could manage somehow to rear a child in the unity of their love. Maybe there was a way out she hadn't thought about, and Paul would find a solution, as he had done so often on their flight across Siberia. But a small voice kept whispering in her ear that this was no longer Siberia, and there was no way out but to marry Kurt, for what tangible evidence was there for economic improvement in Paul's life? None. He hadn't accepted it yet; but she had been reared in Harbin, had lived there too long not to be aware of the pragmatic aspects of her city's life.

And there was Grandmaman. Poor Grandmaman, so brave and increasingly unhappy. She had difficulty digesting her own poorly prepared food, and the medicines for her stomach disorder were stretching their already thin budget. There was also Marfa. Tanya had been sending a few dayans to her every month, more because of her own sense of obligation than out of any real need Marfa might have had. And now she had the added responsibility of yet another human being, who hadn't asked to be brought into the world.

With so many lives dependent upon her, to marry Paul would be an act of supreme selfishness—a betrayal of trust.

She buried her face in her arms. Maybe she could wait. But she was as practical as Kurt, and her impulsive daydreams crumbled one by one against the pressure of logic. The innocent child would carry the stigma of illegitimacy for the rest of his life. What right did she have to impose this on her baby? Every mother wants the best for her child, and what could she offer that budding life inside her?

Suddenly she began to nod, remembering. In wishing the best for her child, she was using the same arguments her mother had used in wanting her to marry Kurt. It was now her turn to protect her child. She didn't want her baby to suffer poverty and privations. She had had enough of it herself. The irony was almost too much to bear.

Still, a seed of blind optimism refused to be smothered, and she knew she would write Paul now, and tell him she had decided to marry Kurt. She'd give him the chance to take the initiative without telling him she was carrying his child. That was her secret, and hers alone.

As for this moment, the shock of her pregnancy was too recent for her to think things through clearly. She still had a little time before she would have to return to Harbin and face her problems.

She rose reluctantly, slow to leave the water's lulling rush. Looking for little comforts now, she thought how nice it would be if she could return to the cottage without having to talk to the family.

She need not have worried. The entrance to the cottage was in the inner courtyard, across from the barn and the outhouse. As she crossed the yard, she was relieved that no one was in sight. In the heat of the day, the only sounds she heard were the barking of a dog and the cackling of chickens in the pen.

Inside the cottage, she checked the pot on the wood stove in the kitchen. Agrafena always brought some leftovers for her midday meal: and, opening the lid of the large tin pot, she smelled the fragrance of her favorite, dill-spiced carp in sour cream, which they had had the night before. Although she wasn't hungry, she made herself eat a little, and then, tired, went into the inner room. Cushioned benches along the wall circled the room, leaving a niche for her bed, over which an icon's lighted lamp spread a warm, rosy glow. She stretched out on the bed, trying to sleep, but sleep would not come.

She postponed writing to Paul for several days, wishing the temptation to go away. But finally, one evening, she sat down and wrote him.

In the stillness of the night, under her down comforter, she was restless, haunted by vague, shapeless dreams that refused to go away. In the morning she rushed to the railroad station to mail the letter, afraid she would change her mind and destroy it.

She walked back slowly, forcing her mind to respond to the pulse of the village: the soothing sounds of cowbells, the grinding of cartwheels on the dirt road, the rushing sound of the milking stream against the pail, the gentle lowing of the cow.

"Tanya!"

The familiar voice behind her disrupted the pastoral sounds of the morning. Tanya wheeled around. Kurt, waving from a distance, hurried toward her.

For a few mindless seconds Tanya stood rooted to the ground. Then the enormous relief at seeing him blocked everything else from her mind.

Stumbling over the ruts in the dirt road, weeping and laughing, she ran straight into his open arms and clung to him fiercely.

CHAPTER 31

Sophie was hurriedly putting perfume bottles away and tidying the display counters. Churin's doors had just been closed. It had been a busy day, but Sophie wouldn't have minded had it not been for an incident that occurred during her lunch break, one she was anxious to share with Nikolai. All that mattered these days was Nikolai, her new husband. He was waiting outside, to walk with her to his parents' home on Diagonalnaya Street, where they were now living. She had been fortunate to get a transfer to the Churin's store in Pristan, and she cherished these long walks, for this was the only time when they were alone in the long day.

Set deeply behind a stone fence with an iron gate, the two-storey brick house had been Nikolai's parental home for many years. They rented out the downstairs, but kept the second floor for themselves. From their large living room, Sophie and Nikolai had an unobstructed view of the courtyard and the street beyond, where tall oaks lined the avenue and dwarfed the small brick homes that looked like toy houses behind their picket fences.

The last bottle put away, Sophie dashed out from behind the counter. She had a mystery to solve, and she was anxious to see her husband.

These days, Nikolai filled most of her thoughts, and there was no room in her mind for idle speculation. She'd share the problem with Nikolai and let him solve it for her. She marveled at her happiness. The past had been blurred in her memory like a bad dream, vague and incapable of scarring her anew. Nikolai adored her, and she worshiped him in return. His parents, the Urugaevs, couldn't do enough for her. Never having had a daughter, Madame

Urugaeva took Sophie under her wing, fussed over her, and treated her like a pampered child. There was always a hot dinner on the table waiting for them at night, and her mother-in-law, a thickset smiling blonde with streaks of gray in her braided hair, fed the newlyweds steaming *pelmeni*, or meat pies, or borscht with buckwheat groats, while her father-in-law surveyed the scene indulgently over his rimless spectacles. Sophie began to feel that along with a husband she had acquired adoptive parents. Orphaned in early childhood in Orenburg, south of the Ural Mountains, she was raised by a maiden schoolteacher aunt, who was more interested in disciplining the child than in giving her affection, and Sophie grew up without paternal love.

She didn't think there were any endearments left in the Russian language that she and Nikolai hadn't used for each other. She called him *Zolotko*, my golden one, and he settled on *Moosik*, which had no meaning at all.

Walking arm in arm along Novogorodnaya Street toward an open market where she had to buy a chicken, Sophie nestled against Nikolai. He bent down to look at her.

"Why so pensive today, Moosik? A hard day at the store?"

"No," Sophie replied, shivering more from habit than from cold, for it was a warm evening.

"Then what's bothering you?"

"I'm not sure myself, Zolotko. I don't know whether I'm being nosy and interfering, or whether my conscience is telling me to do something."

"Stop talking in riddles. What happened today?"

They had reached the open market on Mostovaya Street, and Sophie's attention was distracted. "Do you think one chicken is enough? They're so expensive. I'd just as soon buy pheasant instead. Last time I paid twenty kopeks for two birds, and I know chickens cost more. Besides, I like pheasant better, especially with sour cream sauce like your mother makes."

Nikolai laughed. "Confess, Moosik, you'll do anything to avoid watching a chicken killed. I'm sorry, but Maman particularly wanted a chicken for tomorrow, and I think we'd better get one."

Sighing, Sophie selected a fat chicken. The butcher severed its head with one stroke and threw it on the ground in front of his stall, where the headless bird, its stump bleeding, ran round and round in frantic circles, stumbling and finally collapsing at Nikolai's feet. Sophie looked away and let her husband carry the chicken home.

After leaving the marketplace, they walked one block and turned right on Shkolnaya Street. From there it was only two blocks to the house.

"You started telling me what happened to you today, Moosik," Nikolai said.

"I saw Paul Veragin cross the street a block from where I stood."

Sophie waited for Nikolai's reaction, but he continued to look at her expectantly. "And?"

Herself confused, Sophie tried to explain. "He saw me. I'm sure of it. Yet he deliberately turned his head the other way and hurried in the opposite direction."

"Are you sure it was Paul Veragin?"

Sophie nodded emphatically. "No mistake. I'd recognize that head of hair and posture anywhere."

Unimpressed, Nikolai shrugged. "Then what's the mystery?"

"Don't you see? Why wouldn't he want me to see him? And what is he doing in Harbin now? With Tanya's wedding only a week away . . ." Sophie shook her head. "I don't like it."

Her heart ached for Paul. She admired Tanya's strength of character, but at the same time she condemned her for giving up her love. How well she remembered her surprise when Tanya told her that she was going to marry Kurt Hochmeyer. None of the reasons Tanya had given her for marrying him seemed valid. The Countess. Marfa. Future children. Illness. Debts. Paul's salary. Dim future. Sophie listened to Tanya's heated justifications, and as she listened she became incensed.

"Shame on you!" she blurted out. "You're selling yourself for the sake of security!"

Tanya, who was pacing the floor, wheeled to face her.

"And what if I am?" she cried angrily. "I'm tired of poverty, tired of hunger, of denying myself the basic comforts of life!"

Shocked by Tanya's outburst, Sophie fell silent. We all react differently, she thought, and Tanya is strong and practical; but I want no part of that kind of wisdom. She wanted to laugh and giggle and act silly and hold hands with Nikolai in public and cling to him whenever she could, and it really made no difference whether she did it in their own modest room or in the large, luxuriously appointed house that Tanya had started remodeling.

Sophie sighed. It was true that she and Nikolai were better off financially and had no dependents to worry about, but— She shrugged off the unpleasant thoughts. She had no right to judge Tanya. She mustn't forget the saying that the human heart is a mystery.

Near their home, they passed a group of laughing school girls, giddy with the freedom of their summer vacations, their large bows at the napes of their necks bobbing up and down with each outburst of mirth. Entering the gate Nikolai held open for her, she looked back at the girls and sighed again. Too bad the responsibilities of adulthood so often dampened the uncomplicated joy of the young.

After dinner, Nikolai's father lit his pipe and settled into his favorite leather chair with the paper. Nikolai fidgeted. "Papa, I've heard rumors today about Ataman Semenov."

Dmitri Alexeyevich put down the paper. "What rumors?"

Nikolai shook his head. "They're vague but worrisome. It seems Ataman Semenov is having troubles in Chita. He's losing his authority, and insubordination is rife among his cossacks."

Dmitri Alexeyevich puffed on his pipe thoughtfully. "I wouldn't be surprised if he abandoned his people to the burgeoning chaos. He's the kind of predator that causes trouble and then skips town when things get too hot."

Nikolai nodded. "As it stands now, the Red partisans are growing bolder and the threatened cossacks more savage. I almost wish the Red Army regulars would step in and end the whole mess once and for all."

"Don't let your colleagues hear this or you'll be branded a Bolshevik. Personally, I tend to agree with you. I'm not sure who is worse—the Bolsheviks or Ataman Semenov's little kingdom in Chita. Let's hope that when he flees to Manchuria—as assuredly he will, with the help of his Japanese sponsors—his viper's sting will have been largely neutralized. It's too bad that a few unscrupulous men are sullying the honorable record of our cossacks."

"Surely the historians will be able to recognize the criminal element among Semenov's cossacks as isolated cases."

"I doubt it. All the courage and valor of those men over the years can be destroyed by a single act of atrocity."

Sophie listened absentmindedly. Political discussions always bored her. She continued to fret over having seen Paul in what seemed a clandestine appearance in town, and whether she should do something about it.

Galina Ignatyevna looked at Sophie and stopped clearing the table. Always candid, she came straight to the point. "What's bothering you tonight, child?"

Sophie smiled apologetically. "Daydreaming, I guess."

Galina Ignatyevna pursed her lips and shook her head. "You're not fooling me. Out with it!"

A dear, kind woman, thought Sophie, looking at her mother-in-law with affection. "Maman, something happened today that I don't understand, and I hate mysteries I can't solve."

With the dishes pushed aside, the older woman sat down and listened as Sophie described the noonday incident: how she had seen Paul walking toward her a block away; how, upon seeing her from a distance, he had turned abruptly on his heel and hurried in the opposite direction; and how she, surprised by this maneuver, pursued him for a while to make sure it was Paul.

Her mother-in-law narrowed her eyes. "And you're wondering whether to tell this to Tanya, aren't you?"

Sophie blinked, then nodded miserably. Galina Ignatyevna shook her head.

"Most assuredly—no. First of all, there are two things you don't know: one, what he was doing in Harbin, and two, why he avoided you. The only thing you can be sure of is that he didn't want you to know about his presence in the city. If he knew that you had seen him, he would count on your discretion."

"But I'm also Tanya's friend!" protested Sophie.

"So? And what good would it do to tell Tanya that Paul is in town? If she already knows about it, you'll only embarrass her, and if she doesn't, you'll cause her further heartache."

Unable to solve the problem, Sophie shrugged it off.

"Thank you, Maman. You're always so wise." Then, with an apologetic smile, she added: "I could have been mistaken. Maybe it wasn't Paul after all."

Her mother-in-law gave her a knowing smile. "It's not your problem anyway. Let's get these dishes done."

CHAPTER 32

Paul received Tanya's letter while on duty. He hurried from work to the privacy of his tiny room to read it beneath the twenty-five-watt electric bulb near his bed. The neatly written words cavorted before his eyes, mocking him, as if he had failed to see some monstrous joke. Too stunned to move, he stared at the piece of paper in his hands, a beehive of questions assailing him.

The possibility of losing Tanya to another man had never entered his mind. He had thought that time was on their side. They were out of danger, beyond the grasp of the Bolshevik bands. Why couldn't she wait? Even the countess seemed to be adjusting to her new environment and, thank God, there was no child involved.

Suddenly his room crowded upon him. He had to get out. He needed to talk to someone, to sort out his thoughts, place them in proper perspective. If he could voice his thoughts, perhaps understanding would come, and then he could take action.

Rushing from his room, he ran to the railroad station and on the platform nearly collided with a husky peasant, Ivan Kurenko. Round faced and squatty, Ivan was one of the other policemen who lived alone, spoke a dialect common to the Ukrainian region, using an *h* in place of the hard *g*, and never talked of his past. He treated Paul in a deprecating manner, calling him by his last name only, and although Paul no longer wanted to be addressed by his title or rank, he did appreciate other men using the polite *gospodin* before his surname or his first name and patronymic. But it was not so much Kurenko's attitude that repulsed Paul, as a streak of cruelty he had noticed in the man.

Whether intentionally or not, the man had become Paul's irritant, and now he was the last person Paul wanted to see.

"Veragin! I've been looking for you all over. We've caught a valuable bird in the taiga—Fu-Chao-Lin himself. He ventured too close to the railway and we captured him. The chief is off this afternoon and I need your help in interrogating him."

With an effort, Paul focused his attention on Kurenko. "Who is he?"

"He's the leader of one of the *hunhuzi* bands that are hostile to our area."

"How can you be sure you've got the right man?"

"He was recognized by one of our men."

Paul wanted to get away from Kurenko. "I don't see how I can help you question him. I don't speak Chinese."

Kurenko's vacant face creased in a crafty grin. "Who said anything about Chinese? I speak it well enough myself. I need you to help me with my special brand of questioning, so"—he waved abruptly for Paul to follow him—"come with me."

In a small shack off the main building, stuffy from summer heat and the odor of garlic emanating from the sullen prisoner, Paul found himself face to face with the largest Manchu he had yet encountered. He was as tall as Paul, but his massive frame made him seem even larger and more menacing. His drab blue coolie pants and high-buttoned shirt were in direct contrast to the glint of arrogance and malice in his slanted eyes. Although his hands were tied behind his back, he did not cower but stood erect and defiant. It occurred to Paul that perhaps he had more in common with this man of an alien culture than with the unprincipled Russian peasant with a mouthful of tobacco-stained teeth.

"Here, Veragin—I want you to help me with these."

Paul looked down at the handful of bamboo sticks Kurenko placed in his hands. Their ends, sharpened to needle points, were discolored with dark stains.

The cossack giggled, his breath quickening. "Thin and sharp, aren't they? I've seen them go a good centimeter or more under the nails."

Instinctively, Paul glanced at the *hunhuz*. Although he

was undoubtedly familiar with this method of torture, the bandit's face remained impassive.

Paul turned to Kurenko and studied him with disgust.

"What is it you want to find out from this man?"

Kurenko hedged. "Something about their number in the taiga."

"And if he refuses to talk?"

"That's not important. The main thing is to teach him a lesson and make sure he doesn't come too close to us again."

"Is this the official policy of the railway company?"

Kurenko pursed his lips. "How do I know? I've never asked them, and they haven't questioned my methods of interrogation. Anyway, who's being questioned here, Fu-Chao-Lin or me? Here, help me with these!" Impatiently, Kurenko reached for the bamboo sticks in Paul's hand.

Paul shook his head and moved his hand out of Kurenko's reach. "I'm not going to be a party to this. You better let him go, and fast! You know very well the railway company has an agreement with these *hunhuzi*, and so far they've kept their part of the bargain. You're playing with fire holding one of their leaders without cause."

"He's been trespassing. That's reason enough."

"Not as long as I'm standing here. Release him!"

"If I let him go without teaching him a lesson, he'll think we're weaklings. They go to great lengths to save face, and he'll think we've lost ours. You don't know this man. Fu-Chao-Lin is notorious. He's kidnapped sons of rich Chinese merchants, cut off their ears, and sent them in a package to the parents when the ransom was delayed. And you're telling me to release this criminal?"

Paul's patience was wearing thin. "Yes, I am. The man hasn't committed any crime against us. Now cut his ropes!"

Kurenko's face turned a dark red. "Do you know, Veragin, how he got rid of the leader of a rival band? He challenged him to a duel, then threw a rope over a branch of an oak and looped nooses around both their necks. After that, the two bandits fought. When Fu-Chao-Lin beat the other *hunhuz*, he pulled the rope and strung him up. When his rival was dead, he cut his head off and impaled it on a stake by the roadside for all to see."

Paul shrugged. "They all do it with their enemies, I hear. At least Fu-Chao-Lin shows he has a sense of fair play. He could have had his rival killed by his men. Even more reason to let him go."

"Who do you think you are, ordering me around?" Kurenko spat on the floor. "You swell-headed *bolvan*, you're nothing but another policeman like me. A stinking aristocrat! The Bolsheviks didn't nail enough of the likes of you."

Paul felt the blood drain from his face. "Impertinent bastard! If we were alone, I'd teach you a lesson! I'm telling you, let him go, or I'll report you to our superiors."

"Our superiors won't like your meddling. You may lose your job."

"That's the chance I'll take. Now untie his hands."

Paul's voice was firm, hard; Kurenko's eyes wavered. He grumbled something about "you'll be sorry if you set this dog free," but went over to cut the rope around Fu-Chao-Lin's wrists. Stepping aside, he barked a short order in Chinese.

Still silent, Fu-Chao-Lin looked at Paul. His saffron-colored face showed no emotion as he studied Paul for a brief moment. Then, with a panther's agility surprising in such a large man, he bolted out the door. Paul watched him disappear, pleased with his minor victory. (Years later, however, he was to remember this incident with mixed emotions, and tried to recollect the bandit's reactions, without success.) Revolted by Kurenko's lust for violence, Paul turned his back on him and left the room.

He crossed the village square, hurrying toward the yellow clinic buildings scattered over the hill. The hot sun had wrapped the landscape in a golden haze, blurring the contours with an intense heat. Somewhere close, a rooster's "*coo-ka-re-koo*" rose in the air, hung timorously in the afternoon lull, and then dissolved behind the hill. A few women, chattering excitedly on the corner, fell silent as Paul strode by, then resumed their gossip.

Halfway up the hill Paul saw Marfa coming toward him. A strange relationship had developed between them. In spite of the difference in their backgrounds, they were linked by a common bond—loneliness. Marfa seldom mentioned her son these days, but Paul knew she still nurtured the hope of seeing Tikhon again, and he tried to cheer this simple, grieving woman with his friendship. But there was another reason why Paul was drawn to this earthy, stoic woman of humble origins. Treating him with the natural deference of a peasant whose lodging had been honored by a visit from a prince, she kept the memory of his past alive. In his dreary life now, it was the only respite he had from the constant insults to his ego.

He chuckled wryly. We play games with each other, and I'm allowing her to make me forget that my title is no longer an asset but a veritable albatross around my neck. But she provided the link, however fragile, between his tenuous present and the vanished past.

As usual upon seeing him, Marfa bowed from the waist. "Your Excellency, will you honor me and have a glass of tea?"

Something in Paul's face must have alerted her, for she glanced at him several times as they walked across the square to the corner house where she was renting a room. Instead of entering through the courtyard that led past the cow shed and a noisy flock of chickens, she took him through a shallow front garden to the screened porch, which served as the front room for the farmer's family, and from there through a succession of dark corners and hallways to her room at the opposite end of the house. There she prepared tea and served him a glass with a cube of the small table with her own cup of tea.
sugar and a slice of lemon. Only then did she sit down at

Waiting for him to speak, Marfa placed a cube of sugar on her tongue and took a sip of tea. Still scalding, she poured a little on the saucer, held it up on the spread fingertips of one hand, and, blowing on the hot liquid, studied Paul.

Paul placed his glass on the table and looked at her. "Tanya is going to marry Kurt Hochmeyer."

Marfa gasped. "Why?"

Paul shook his head. "I wish I knew. It would help if I could understand it. Perhaps then it would be easier to accept."

Marfa raised her eyebrows. "Accept? Forgive me, Prince, for what I'm about to say, but I've never been one to mince words. Are you trying to tell me that you're going to take this like a serf, without fighting for what is rightfully yours?"

Paul flushed. "I don't know what I'm fighting against, Marfa. I can't understand her reasons, the motives for her decision. It's so precipitous."

"Doesn't she give you any explanation at all?"

"None that is valid, in my opinion. She talks about her obligation to her grandmother and her pessimism about our future together."

"She knew these things before. Something must have happened recently to change her mind."

Paul shook his head. "I don't know what to think. As it is, I've been going crazy trying to make sense out of her letter."

"Then you should go to her and find out for yourself."

Marfa's words cut through his befuddled thinking. "Yes, I must see her . . . even at the risk of losing my job. I've already taken off work more than I should."

"You can get another leave of absence. They won't fire you; they need policemen." Marfa stood up resolutely and nodded. "Go to her. Fight for her! She loves you, and—who knows?—maybe she has written you this letter hoping you would take the decision out of her hands and keep her from marrying this other man."

The hot July wind from the Gobi desert blew sand over Harbin, blanketing sidewalks, benches, fences, and even bushes with a dull monochromatic hue. Even the tiny stone squares set in the sidewalks' diamond-shaped slabs were gritty with dry earth. In the evening heat the dust swirled in front of Paul's feet, covering his shoes with a gray film. Walking against the hot wind, he felt the sand on his lips and squinted to keep the sharp particles from lodging inside his eyelids.

By the time he passed Azhikheiskaya Street, he was tired and weary. It was a long walk up the hill from the railroad station and through the quiet blocks of Pochtovaya

Street, where palatial homes, sprawling behind stone walls, seemed to accuse him of trespassing. Now, having reached Tanya's house, he moved into the shadows across the street.

It had been a trying day for him. He arrived from Handaohedzi in mid-morning and went directly to Tanya's office, hoping to catch her outside during lunch break. Instead, he almost ran into Sophie, walking toward him on Kitaiskaya Street. It was fortunate he had seen her a block away and hastened in the opposite direction. He didn't want anyone to see him and tell Kurt he was in Harbin.

Tanya hadn't come out for lunch, and in the afternoon, when the offices closed, he caught a glimpse of her getting into the waiting droshky with Kurt. He returned to the railroad station and called her house. The cook answered the telephone and told him that the young madama was out to dinner and would not be home until later.

Footsore and discouraged, he allowed himself a spartan meal of two piroshki and a bowl of cabbage soup, then headed toward her house. Once there, he waited. The vigil tested him, for the minutes dragged with mounting tension. Accustomed to the green hills of Handaohedzi, the sandy grayness of the city streets depressed him and intensified his growing despair.

He had time to think and try to find a solution. Tanya's letter inside his breast pocket burned against his chest like a stinging nettle. No matter how much he longed for her, wanted her, it still seemed impossible for them to marry. He couldn't give up his job in Handaohedzi, and what could he offer Tanya and the countess if they moved to the village? Tanya would not find work in Handaohedzi, and even without the countess, the two of them, on his salary alone, would have an existence that would be a far cry from what he'd like to provide for her. If Tanya rented all of her house, the money would help to make ends meet, but that was all.

No. There was only one thing he could—he *would* do: persuade Tanya to wait. He thought of Kurt. Had he no pride, wanting to marry a woman who loved another?

A vague, desperate idea surfaced. If his pleas proved ineffective and Tanya refused to wait, he would marry her then, and they'd live apart until he found a better job in

Harbin. In spite of the summer heat, a little shiver ran
through him as he tried to think of what could he do in
Harbin. He had no contacts, and he certainly couldn't ask
Kurt for any help. For the hundredth time the same question confronted him: What was there for him in the future?

An unfamiliar sound of a motor was moving up the
street. He stepped deeper into the shadow behind a privet
bush and watched through the thicket of leaves. An automobile rolled down the street, coming to a stop in front of
Tanya's house. Its wheel spokes and shiny black fenders
glittered under the street lamp, and when the headlights
were turned off, Paul recognized Kurt behind the wheel of
the glamorous vehicle. Tanya sat beside him. As Kurt
helped her down from the high seat, Paul realized that
she'd had time to change since leaving her office. Wrapped
in satin, with an ostrich-feather trim that framed her face,
she looked radiant. Paul knew she did not have enough
money of her own to afford these luxurious clothes. It was
obvious that her elegance and glowing happiness were provided by Kurt. Another man was supplying what he was
yearning to give her. The realization was painful, and suddenly, resentment against her welled within him. She had
an aura of assurance about her, a degree of relaxed contentment he had never seen in her before. What right did
she have to look so elegant, so much a part of a world he
could not share? The large, solid house behind her, the
shimmering satin, the luxury of a private car, and a gentleman in tuxedo kissing her hand . . . not bending over it,
but raising it high to his lips with both hands in a clearly
possessive gesture.

Every muscle taut, fists clenched, Paul shut his eyes,
fearful of making a sound. When at length he trusted himself to look again, Tanya had gone into the house and Kurt
was climbing back into his automobile. His foot, elegantly
clad in a patent-leather shoe, gleamed under the street-
light. Paul thought of his own shoes, scuffed over the toes
and covered with dust. They were the only pair he owned.
A few moments later, Kurt's car rolled past him and
turned at the corner into Girinskaya Street.

Silence settled on the street. Only the sand, dislodged by

the wind from its collected mounds, rolled down the side-walk, scraping the cement with tiny sounds of protest. Paul watched the house. A light appeared in a window, throwing a yellow shaft across the sidewalk. The aspen tree before it quivered in the wind, its shadow prancing, jumping—its leafy fingers reaching toward Paul.

The moon was hazy, the heat oppressive. He stood in the shadow of the bush, a trespasser in someone else's garden, an intruder in the night. He could not move, he could not think of anything but the deadly certainty of failure. And through that failure, pride dictated a course of action. Leave Harbin, wipe out the past, and, for the first time, look the future squarely in the face. He knew he could not deprive Tanya of the kind of life that Kurt could provide. How long would the euphoria of happiness last before real-ity took over? He loved her too much to deprive her of her newly found security; loved her enough to entrust her into the care of a luckier man.

He would leave. Yet moving away from Tanya's lighted window was not an easy task. The urge was great to knock, to see her, touch her, love her one more time. He clutched the stiff, sharp leaves of the privet bush, feeling them cut into his palm and fingers, grateful for the distraction of physical pain.

The light in Tanya's window went out. She was still awake. There was still time. He had a few more minutes to make up his mind. As he fought his urge, the memory of their rendezvous at the Oriant Hotel last May returned to taunt him. No part of her had he not loved or kissed; no curves or hollows of her body were a secret to his eyes and lips.

He stood without moving, restraining himself with all the power of his will from dashing out across the street. An alley cat ran noiselessly over cobblestones toward him and disappeared on the other side of the privet bush. Moments later a high-pitched screech rose from the base of the bush, sending shivers down Paul's spine. He looked down to see a rat scamper out of the tangled branches and skitter across the garden into the darkness.

A block away an owl hooted. The moon had disappeared behind a cloud, and the darkness thickened, touching Paul with its torpid July breath. His mouth was dry, his throat constricted.

Slowly picking his way along the sidewalk to minimize the scraping sound of sand beneath his feet, he headed back toward the railroad station. There was no hurry. He had all night to walk the length of Pochtovaya Street and Voksalny Avenue.

CHAPTER 33

The day before her wedding, Tanya found it impossible to relax. Although by now she had accepted Paul's choice, not to stop her from marrying Kurt, the hurt remained. She had received his letter only two days before, a terse note wishing her happiness—the kind any stranger could have written. It was its coolness, its detachment, that hurt the most. As if his wounded pride were more important to him than his love for her. He wasn't going to fight for her or ask her to wait for him. Well, she was glad she had made this decision. Glad Kurt had come to Barim to collect her at a time when she needed him the most. Glad to be marrying him—turning all her worries over to him.

Keeping busy, filling her hours with preparations for the wedding, left her little time for brooding. One source of happiness was her beloved Grandmaman, who seemed transformed by the anticipation of moving into the other rooms in the house and not having to share the kitchen with strangers.

Tanya's jealously guarded secret remained intact. Her morning sickness was minimal, and so far she had managed to hide it from her grandmother. Today's excitement, however, caused her stomach to be queasy, and she paled at the sight of the chicken à la Kiev the cook had prepared for their dinner. It had been a bad day all around. That morning her nausea had been so strong she had to excuse herself from the table after the countess had placed a cup of hot cocoa and freshly baked cottage cheese turnovers in front of her. She was able to make it to the bathroom in time, and when Paulina Arkadyevna made no comment upon her return, Tanya was sure her secret had not been discovered.

But this evening, the smell of the deep-fried cutlets precipitated a wave of sickness so powerful, she felt the blood drain from her face. Her hands clammy and shaking, she pushed the chair away and ran to the bathroom.

She was sick a long time, retching, and wishing for a loving hand to support her forehead, as her mother had done when she was a child; but she dared not call her grandmother, who, in spite of the ingenuous look in her eyes, was clever and worldly.

When she finally rejoined the countess, Paulina Arkadyevna had removed the offensive cutlets from the table, and in their place Tanya found a bowl of raspberry *kissel*, her favorite homemade custard. She sat down, wondering what plausible excuse she could give for her sickness.

When she raised her head, she met her grandmother's speculative look. Their eyes locked and Tanya found herself unable to avert her gaze. The longer the impasse continued, the deeper became Tanya's conviction that there were times when silence was more eloquent than any spoken words.

At length, the countess rose from her chair.

"Come over to the sofa, Tanyusha, and sit beside me. Bring your *kissel* if you wish."

Meekly, Tanya picked up the bowl and followed her grandmother to the love seat. Paulina Arkadyevna took the dish of *kissel* out of Tanya's hands, placed it on the table, and then took her in her arms, pressing her head to her shoulder as Tanya, no longer able to hold back her tears, began to cry.

When her weeping subsided, the countess patted her shoulder, then took Tanya's face between her hands and looked at her with such depth of understanding and love that the tears returned, this time from relief.

The countess pushed a damp curl off Tanya's forehead.

"Tears are purifying, Tanyusha. They wash out pain that tires the soul. Too bad you've carried this around so long. It's not good for the budding life within you. It's been about two months now, hasn't it?"

Tanya nodded, and her face crumpled with a new spasm of tears. "Oh, Grandmaman, I'm so ashamed!"

Paulina Arkadyevna raised her eyebrows in surprise.

"Ashamed? You're a grown woman now, Tanya, not a child anymore. Be grateful you carry the seed of your love within you, and think how Providence has favored you by giving you Kurt."

The countess took Tanya by her shoulders and looked deeply into her eyes. Speaking slowly, she said: "How fortunate you are that you're so fond of Kurt. He's going to be delighted to have a child born so soon in his marriage."

Grandmother and granddaughter looked at each other for a long moment. Then the countess said, "It won't be difficult to convince Kurt of a premature birth. Be good to him, Tanyusha——he's an exceptional man."

"I know, Grandmaman. I know! But what about——"

"Paul must never know, Tanya." The countess raised her hand, cutting Tanya short. "The child will belong to you and Kurt. It is your child's welfare that should be uppermost in your mind. I'm sure you've come to that conclusion yourself, or you'd have told Paul by now."

Tanya nodded. "You're very perceptive, Grandmaman. I've never been able to keep anything from you for long. I realize there would be no advantage in telling Paul once I'm married. But still, the temptation is there."

"Then why dwell on it?"

"I keep thinking I'm being unfair in denying him the knowledge that the child is his."

The countess picked up the bowl of custard that Tanya had set aside earlier and pushed it resolutely into her granddaughter's hands. "Here, eat this, and stop giving me this nonsense about being unfair to Paul. You're not pulling any wool over my eyes. Unfair, indeed! You're suffering because you're sacrificing your love for the sake of your child, and you want him to suffer, too. Admit it!"

Tanya bit her lip and averted her eyes.

"Don't forget," the countess went on, "he's already suffering enough——he has lost you to another man! Now eat your *kissel*——you haven't had anything in your stomach this evening, and you need nourishment!"

Tanya spooned the custard and ate it obediently. Her grandmother was right, and she knew it, but it helped to voice her thoughts and hear what she knew all along. Paul must never know.

For the first time in many weeks, Tanya slept soundly through the night. How comforting it was to have Grand-maman's support and to be told that she had made the right choice, the only choice.

On her wedding day, busy with preparations and attention to details, she filled her mind with immediate plans and tender thoughts of Kurt, successfully forcing all memories of Paul to remain on the periphery of her conscience. Yet she found it impossible to banish Paul's image from her mind entirely.

For her wedding outfit, Tanya chose a short pink dress of delicate georgette fabric imported from Paris, its scalloped hem complimenting her slender ankles and feet in silk stockings and matching pink shoes. She insisted that the countess discard her old green bombazine dress which she had been wearing on special occasions and have a new dress made. How delighted she was to be able to spend money on her beloved grandmother without worrying if her remaining dayans would last until the next paycheck!

Yet, in spite of it all, she shunned the memories of another time, another wedding, and had insisted on a private ceremony in Kurt's church. He had invited a handful of associates to the wedding, and Tanya had asked only Sophie and Nikolai. Kurt wore a dark suit and vest and glowed with such happiness that he seemed ten years younger.

The simple Lutheran ceremony took only a few minutes. Kurt had arranged to have the small reception and banquet in the Zhelsob-Railway Club—where obliging waiters continually refilled their glasses with vintage French champagne.

Reserved in the beginning, Sophie and Nikolai grew more expansive as the evening progressed and toasted Tanya and Kurt, wishing them many years of happiness.

Paulina Arkadyevna sipped her champagne slowly, saying little, and watching Tanya through half-closed eyes. The groom, acting the hospitable host, completely captivated Sophie, whose rapt attention amused Tanya. You'll soon come to my way of thinking, dear Sophie, she thought ruefully. Uncompromising idealism doesn't fit into our life in exile, and the sooner you learn it the better for you.

"Gorko!"

The countess had raised her glass and was toasting the newlyweds with the traditional wedding call for a kiss. Kurt turned to Tanya and, bending over her slightly, touched her mouth with his lips. Tanya flushed, realizing in dismay that this was the first time Kurt had kissed her, and was chagrined it had to be in public. Kurt's eyes lingered on her face. He had never pressed her for intimacy, had waited patiently for this day, and now that she was legally his, he was obviously expecting her to respond with some warmth. He had been in love with her for many years, had disciplined himself for her sake, and she should have been more responsive to him before this.

She looked at him with a shy smile and watched his face color with pleasure. Impulsively, he took her hand and raised it to his lips.

Nikolai guffawed. "Not the hand! The lips—*gorko, gorko!*"

This time Kurt's kiss was bolder and longer. She returned it and then brushed a kiss on his cheek.

Over the clapping and the laughter in the room, she barely heard Kurt's whispered words: "I love you, my Tanyusha."

She squeezed his hand and thought: I'll make up to you, dear Kurt . . . for all the hurts I've caused you in the past.

When the reception was over, Nikolai and Sophie took the countess home. Kurt had reserved a room for their wedding night in the elegant Hotel Moderne downtown, ostensibly to be closer to his dacha, the summer cottage he had rented on the other side of the Sungari, where they were to start their brief honeymoon the next day.

Inside a luxuriously appointed bridal suite a bottle of chilled champagne awaited them. The canopied double bed was recessed in an alcove, but the main room, with its twelve-foot ceilings and intricately carved frieze border, brocaded draperies, and lace curtains, awed Tanya with its opulence. Kurt stood watching her with a bemused look on his face, as she studied the thick Chinese rug, the embroidered silk panels on the walls, the dark green velvet chairs.

"A glass of champagne?"

Tanya turned around to see Kurt holding the bottle of champagne in his hand. She shook her head and smiled. "Not right now, thank you. I think I'll change first."

There were heavy velvet draperies separating the bedroom alcove from the main room, and Tanya drew them together gratefully. How different was this demure gesture from her unrestrained passion with Paul at the Oriant Hotel!

As she slipped into her satin and lace peignoir, she kept her mind blank, forcing her attention on the minutiae of her physical moves. When she rejoined Kurt, she heard his intake of breath, saw him close his eyes for a brief moment, and knew his restraint was wearing thin. Unexpectedly, she felt a rising titillation within her and, knowing that she was the object of his desire, felt a feminine urge to tease.

After a few sips of champagne, Tanya put her glass down on a sideboard. Kurt caught her hand in midair, picked up the other, and raised them both to his lips. Then, turning them over, he kissed her palms in a deep, lingering kiss. It was his first sensuous gesture and it was not unpleasant. Slowly, he pulled her to him. Enfolded in his arms, Tanya felt secure, protected. He had always been there when she needed him, stepping in and taking over each time the world seemed ready to crush her. I really care for him she thought, nestling into the crook of his arm. His embrace tightened and she felt his body harden. Lifting her chin, he covered her mouth with his. There was nothing gentle in his kiss this time. When he forced her lips open, she closed her eyes and yielded to this man who was so good to her, who loved her; and surely she would come to love him . . . .

In the darkness of the alcove, Tanya lay awake in the canopied bed beside her sleeping husband. Confused and surprised by her own reaction to Kurt's lovemaking, she couldn't sleep. She was ashamed and incredulous over what Kurt had been able to do to her.

When his timid, slow caresses grew bolder and she felt him tremble with desire, he still held back, waiting for her

to react, to show some sign of her own arousal. Tenderness
and gratitude for his long and selfless patience welled up
within her, and she wanted to please him, to give herself to
him without restraint. She put her arms around his neck
and pressed herself against him.

When it was over, she was filled with affection, a tender
satisfaction at having pleased the man who loved her.
Physically, however, her body had remained unaroused.
She had not remained passive, had returned his caresses,
his kisses; but, in the end, he knew.

For a few moments he lay quietly beside her and then,
without a word, reached for her again. His hands, more
aggressive this time, caressed her again, deliberately reaching for greater intimacy, moving with a purpose, invading
the warm, drowsy hollows of her flesh. She didn't want to
be aroused and struggled to be free, but Kurt wouldn't release her.

Aware of his intent, she arched her body against him in
panic. That kind of experience was too intense, too close in
memory to Paul's lovemaking, and she didn't want to share
it with Kurt.

But Kurt persisted. Found her. Caressed her gently,
tenderly, sending shivers through her body, driving her
senses to a pitch of such intensity she heard herself begging
him to go on, and waited breathlessly for him to coax into
explosion that indescribably acute epicenter of her being.
And when at last it came, leaving her shuddering and
weeping, Kurt held her in his arms and said not a word.

Now, lying next to him quietly, she tried to sort out her
feelings. Why be ashamed of her own sensuality? What was
wrong in allowing her husband to give her pleasure? Since
she had given to him willingly, why was she a poor receiver
of what he wanted so much to give? Was it because in
those final seconds of reaching out toward the last shattering moment the image of Paul's impassioned face had escaped her tightly shuttered memory, and she had imagined
it was Paul who was making love to her?

Reproving words whispered in her ear, floated in the
alcove's inky darkness. She was a traitor. But to whom? To
Paul? To herself, for being capable of experiencing a sensual peak of ecstasy with Kurt? Or to her husband of one

day, whose efforts to satisfy her had succeeded only with the help of the unbidden fantasy of another man? She hadn't expected this to happen. Hadn't thought beyond her wedding day. She *had* done the right thing in marrying Kurt: the only sensible avenue open to her. Fortunately, she was not accountable to anyone for her mixed emotions, and she would not allow them to affect those whom she loved. It would have to be her own private struggle, a struggle to clear her conscience and glean what personal happiness she could from her marriage. And she *would overcome* it. She didn't intend to live a life of self-recrimination in the years to come.

Right now she would live one day at a time, adored by a kind, generous man, comforted by the thought that she had provided security for her grandmother and her unborn child.

Snuggling under the down comforter, she finally slept.

CHAPTER 34

In the early morning of January 19, 1921, across from 312 Pochtovaya Street, a red-faced coachman clapped his mittened hands and shifted from foot to foot, looking expectantly at the gray stone house. In spite of the earflaps of his fur-lined cap tied securely under his chin, and a sheepskin coat held snugly by a cord at the waist, he had to stomp his valenki to keep warm. In the snowy hush of the morning nothing else moved, not even the sleepy rooks nestled on the ledge of the high wooden fence. Great clumps of snow occasionally slipped from the heavily weighted branches and ruffled the silence with a muffled sound.

The horse snorted, exhaling clouds of vapor into the frosty air. The coachman patted its neck a few times and then went up to the house, the snow crunching beneath his valenki. The rooks, huddling together to husband what warmth they could muster, followed him with their beady eyes.

A lean Chinese cook, his hands white with flour, opened the door. "Ho! You're early today, Timofei. Madama is not ready yet."

"Father Frost is mighty powerful today. I thought I might warm up a bit by the stove." The coachman wiped off a tiny icicle from the tip of his nose and, throwing a sidelong glance at the freshly baked bread on the table, took off his hat. The cook waved him in briskly. "Come in, come in, before the winter freezes the kitchen." The cook then broke off a chunk of black bread and pushed it toward the Russian. *"Ho*—good—eat some bread. Salt on the table."

* * *

While the coachman ate bread in the kitchen, at the other end of the house Tanya was getting dressed for the ride to the Sungari, where she and her grandmother were going to watch the yearly celebration of the Feast of the Epiphany. She had just closed the casement window above the crossbar of the double-paned glass. That was the only small opening to let the fresh air in; the rest of the window was sealed with caulking for the winter, and Tanya firmly believed in airing the rooms every day. Two glass cups of alcohol imbedded in a thick layer of cotton wool between the panes kept the inside glass from fogging. On the outside, however, multistarred designs frosted the window, hiding the street from view.

Tanya moved slowly these days. Her swollen figure caused her no serious problems, and her pregnancy, aside from the initial morning sickness, had gone without complications. The countess was convinced Tanya was going to have a girl. "From time immemorial," she said, "it's been a well-established belief among the country women that if the expecting mother's weight is more evenly distributed over her body, she'll have a girl, and if she remains slender and most of her weight is concentrated in the forward protuberance, then it's going to be a boy."

Since she secretly wished to have a little girl, Tanya chuckled at the superstition and hoped her grandmother would be proven right.

Her life had become serene and content. Indulged by an adoring husband, coddled by her grandmother, waited on by servants, Tanya reached her eighth month of pregnancy without difficulty. Kurt had been delighted when she told him she was expecting a child, but the more pleasure he manifested, the stronger grew Tanya's uneasiness.

In the beginning, she did much soul-searching. More and more, she wanted to clear her conscience, to confess the truth to her husband and beg his forgiveness. Kurt had treated her like a fragile china doll, and many a night, after gentle lovemaking, she lay beside him staring at the dark ceiling and pondering the consequences of such a confession. The urge to share her secret and lighten the burden was at times so strong she had to bite the sheets to keep herself from waking Kurt. The temptation was great to purge herself of the lie and make things right. Yet every time she was about to tell him, some instinct warned her against it. Wouldn't it be an act of selfishness to place the weight of knowledge on her husband?

Whenever Kurt talked about the baby, Tanya's discomfort had not gone unnoticed by the countess. One day, as they sipped their afternoon tea, Paulina Arkadyevna spoke up.

"Tanya, I've indulged you in many ways, approved of your life and growing maturity. But now I suspect your misplaced sense of honor is threatening to get the best of you. Tell me if I'm wrong in assuming you're thinking of telling Kurt the truth."

Under the countess's scrutinizing look, Tanya averted her eyes.

"I thought so," the countess went on. "What you're contemplating is a cowardly act, for sometimes it's easier to confess the truth than to have the courage to conceal it. You see, if you tell Kurt about the child, you'll be trading one problem for another. Do you think for one moment that you'll not regret your confession? And once the damage is done, you won't be able to remedy it. Ever. Remember the proverb: 'A word is not a bird—once out of the cage, it can't be recaptured.' So, my dear child, take yourself in hand. It's not too great a price to pay for the love he's given you."

The countess rose; walking around the table, she lifted Tanya's chin, forcing her to meet her eyes. "Men are like the oak trees. They do not bend, and in a storm are apt to be torn out by the roots. But we women can bend like willow reeds without breaking. And we come up again. We do come up! Learn to live with your guilt. It's not too great a sacrifice for what you get in return."

Tanya put her arms around the countess. "Grandmaman, I knew this all along, but I couldn't let go of the idea. I'm so lucky to have you share your wisdom with me. You've been a real comfort."

The two women looked at each other with tenderness. The countess laughed softly. "You're the one who's been my joy for a long time, Tanyusha, but it's nice to know that my advice and my old creaky bones don't annoy you."

Her grandmother was right.

No. She wouldn't do it. She'd live a lie—for the rest of her life, if necessary—in order to protect Kurt's peace of mind, his pride. She'd pay for her dishonesty, justifiable as it may have been, by coping with it alone.

Thus the true number of months of her pregnancy was successfully concealed, and as her time drew nearer to term, Tanya's apprehension turned in a different direction. How was she going to convince Kurt that the baby was going to be born prematurely? The answer came gradually. Under some pretext, she determined, she must go to Handaohedzi and have Marfa deliver her child. In Kurt's absence, it would be easier to find a reason for a premature birth.

After that, she promised herself, there'd be no more lies.

She hadn't seen Paul, but Marfa had written that he was still at the same job. While in Handaohedzi, she wouldn't seek him out. In fact, she hoped she could avoid running into him entirely, for she was afraid her heart would betray her. That much she owed Kurt and her own conscience.

But, until the time came, she put off dwelling on it. And on this crisp, wintry day, she took pains to dress warmly. Following her mother's early example, she pulled on wool knit underpants imported from Germany, which protected her thighs and reached below her knees. "No one's going to look under our skirts, *mon enfant*," her mother used to say, "but while my friends shiver with the cold, I'll have my kidneys and abdomen protected."

The winter of 1921 was cold even by Harbin standards. The temperature consistently dropped to $-30°C$, but it proved no deterrent to the adventurous Russian youths on this brilliant January the nineteenth, the day of the Epiphany.

Earlier in the morning, feverish activity had taken place on the frozen Sungari in preparation for the pageant. A rectangular hole had been cut through the frozen surface to the water below to simulate a baptismal font, and the day before, an eight-foot-high Orthodox cross had been carved out of ice and placed near the pool. Its sparkling prism dazzled the eye, animating the cross with a multicolored aura. The Russians believed that after the ritual blessing of the water had taken place, anyone plunging into the pool would be protected from catching a cold by the now holy water. Every year several young men volunteered to take part in the ceremony, and to Tanya's knowledge none of these men had ever become ill.

She hadn't seen the pageant since she was a child and was looking forward to this day. Paulina Arkadyevna, anxious to compare the event with the ones she had attended in Russia, had decided to join Tanya for the ride. By now well into her element as the old grandame, the countess enjoyed the luxury of a personal maid and the comforts of a generous budget provided her by Kurt. A touching rapport had evolved between her and Kurt, and Tanya was pleased to see her husband's affectionate deference to her grandmother.

Before going to his office that morning, Kurt had admonished them both to bundle up well. Now, dressed in seal coats and hats and fur-trimmed boots, the two women sat closely together on the sleigh while the ever-solicitous Timofei fussed over them, placing the rabbit-fur throw around their knees and carefully tucking it in. Tanya inhaled the air with childish delight. She loved the gliding ride, the tinkling rhythm of the sleigh bells, and the horse's steaming odor that wafted toward them through the frosty air.

She felt cold from the wind whipping her face in the speeding sleigh and buried her hands deeper into her muff.

"Why so pensive, Tanya? Are you cold?"

The countess sounded concerned. She had been more solicitous of Tanya's condition lately. Tanya hastened to reassure her. "I'm fine, Grandmaman. I'm enjoying the ride, but I'm afraid to talk in the cold air."

Satisfied, the countess nodded, and the two women did not talk for the rest of the ride, which took them over the windblown viaduct and down Kitaiskaya Street to the Sungari.

At the river, Tanya carefully negotiated the very same steps she had climbed on the night of her graduation ball. She smiled inwardly. She'd managed to see a lot of living in the short four years since then. Her once willowy figure was now heavy with child. Afraid to slip on the icy steps, she grasped her grandmother's arm for support. At the bottom, they were surrounded by Chinese coolies and their singsong Russian: "Madama, *tolkai-tolkai!* Good *tolkai-tolkai.*" Paulina Arkadyevna chuckled. "They'll do good business today taking people across to the hunting lodge after the ceremonies are over. Look how they've cleaned up their sleds for the occasion."

Tanya nodded. "Yes, and we'll be among them. Kurt promised to meet us there for lunch—and I must say, a bowl of steaming *pelmeni* and a glass of vodka will taste good after this cold."

Paulina Arkadyevna winced. "Tanyusha! Well-bred ladies don't drink vodka!"

Some months earlier Tanya would have bristled at the gentle reprimand and would have defended the more liberal mores of Harbin, where the lines of class distinction were not so marked. But she had learned to recognize her grandmother's occasional lapses into prissiness in spite of her genuine attempt to keep up with the times. She smiled and winked at the countess. "Shsh, Grandmaman! You won't tell on me, will you?"

Paulina Arkadyevna shook her head and looked back at the *tolkai-tolkai.* "We'll have to take one to the edge of the pool."

"But it's only a few steps from here. I'll feel foolish riding in a *tolkai-tolkai* such a short distance."

"You'll feel even more foolish if you slip on ice and precipitate premature labor," the countess said significantly.

Tanya relented. Turning toward the first coolie, she climbed the high sled and waited for the countess to follow. The man covered their legs with a fur throw and positioned himself on a ledge behind, straddling a spike and pushing it into the ice to propel them forward. (This maneuver had prompted the coolies to adapt the Russian word *tolkai*—push—as the name of their winter taxis on the frozen river, and the name stuck.) The Chinaman pushed the sled onto an icy road which connected the two shores, and a few minutes later he was helping them out.

A large number of people had already assembled near

the pool when Tanya and the countess, gliding their boots over the slippery ice and holding on to each other, worked their way into the crowd.

The clergy was moving slowly toward the pool. Deacons and acolytes carrying censers, jeweled icons, and religious gonfalons headed the procession, followed by priests robed in white chasubles, richly embroidered in gold and red. Several young volunteers, wrapped in woolen blankets and fur coats, stood at the edge of the pool, waiting for the priests to perform the ritual of the blessing. With prayers and chants in ancient Slavonic, they dipped a large golden cross into the pool three times while the deacons faced the crowd and swung the censers in three directions. The faithful crossed themselves and bowed in response, mindful of the symbolism of the moment—the Orthodox could now reenact Christ's baptism safely in the holy water.

Around the solemnity of the service, the daily activity on the river continued uninterrupted. The *tolkai-tolkai* coolies pushed their sleds rhythmically across the river, while the ice-boat runners scraped the frozen surface around them. Sails taut in the wind, these triangular skiffs frolicked on the ice with graceful irreverence to the adjacent ceremony.

At the nod from a priest, one of the waiting young men threw his blanket off and jumped into the water. Moments later he was climbing out of the pool with the help of his friends who stood at the edge. They pulled him out of the water and placed him, shivering, on a towel to keep his feet from freezing to the ice surface. Three or four men immediately patted him dry with large towels, then wrapped him in a blanket and a fur coat. The young man bowed to the priest, who held the cross high above him. Seeing the young man's face glow with a sense of accomplishment, Tanya was convinced no harm would come to him. As she watched him leave, she thought of her baby soon to be born and baptized, and knew that Kurt would not object if she raised her child in the Orthodox faith. As she thought about it, she realized that her time was running out, for she had only a little over a month left, and as she stood by her grandmother she decided she must talk to Kurt soon.

After the pageant was over, however, and she went home, Tanya found excuses to put off the conversation. In the next few weeks she planned her words carefully, but when she finally confronted Kurt, it wasn't easy to convince him that she was bored with the monotony of the Manchurian winter and for a change of scenery wanted to visit Marfa in Handaohedzi. Kurt argued that it was risky for her to be traveling so late in her pregnancy, especially since the plague was on a rampage again among the Chinese in Foudziadzian. Although the city authorities had strengthened rodent-control measures to keep the disease from spreading to the Russian population, there was always an element of danger. So far, the dreaded killer had not spread to Harbin proper, but, as Kurt pointed out, the train had to go through the outskirts of the city, where they were burying the dead, and Tanya would be exposing herself to unnecessary risks.

"But the plague isn't widespread yet, is it?" Tanya asked.

"I'm afraid it is, Tanyusha. It's reaching epidemic proportions, and all we can hope for now is that it won't decimate the Foudziadzian population, as it did ten years ago."

Tanya waved the problem away. "Kurt dear, all the train windows are sealed. This is winter, remember? There's no way anything can get inside the train, and certainly I'm not going to get out. The train won't stop on the outskirts of town, and the first stop after that is far to the east. Please, let me go to Handaohedzi! I feel so restless. I need a change—I haven't seen Marfa for almost a year. Once the baby comes, I won't want to go away for a long time. Please, dear, let me go!"

She found it difficult to act a lie, but in a way she *was* restless, *did* want to see Marfa, and that part at least was the truth.

Kurt averted his eyes and went over to the window. Tanya knew he wasn't really looking outside, for the window was frosted and he couldn't see out. For a few moments he remained silent. Then, in a voice that sounded a little too casual, he said, "Are you going to see Paul Veragin in Handaohedzi?"

So that's it, thought Tanya. It wasn't her pregnancy that concerned him as much as the possibility of her seeing Paul. Dear, sweet Kurt! Why, she could handle that! "Oh,

Kurt," she said, "have more faith in me! Certainly I'm not going to seek him out. But the village is small, and should I run into him, it won't make any difference to me. It's all over with and forgotten."

But, she asked herself, was it really all over with and forgotten? In recent months she had trained her mind not to think about Paul, yet whenever his name was mentioned, her heart would turn over.

Kurt walked over and took her in his arms. "Tanyusha dearest, I shouldn't have said that. Of course you may go, but please, for my sake, be careful and take no chances. How about asking Sophie to accompany you?"

Tanya chuckled. "My dear Kurt, when Sophie was pregnant, she survived untold hardships in Siberia, and she won't understand now why I'd need her to go along with me on a comfortable first-class train. Besides, you know she has a job and can't leave it at will."

Kurt made no more objections, and Tanya packed the next day. The countess must have guessed why she was going away, although nothing was said between them. As Tanya said good-bye to her grandmother, the countess blessed her with a sign of the cross and embraced her.

Riding the train out of Harbin station, Tanya sat by the window, relaxed and at peace. How many train rides was she destined to have in her lifetime? This one, by far, was the most comfortable she had ever had. The whole compartment was hers, and, stretching her legs over the plush seats, she looked forward to the spectacular scenery ahead. She had never been to this part of the country, for her parents had always taken her west of Harbin for summer vacations, and now she looked forward to seeing the mountains and the dense taiga of eastern Manchuria.

The train puffed along the stockyards and out into the plains on the outskirts of Harbin. It moved slowly, clearing the suburbs and its scattered *fanzi*. As Tanya looked at the snow-covered running ground, the scenery suddenly changed, and she sat up, staring at the frenetic activity outside the train windows.

Several open lorries were parked near the railroad tracks, and beyond them, three groups of Chinese men dressed in white sanitary gowns and wearing masks were working around deep holes dug in the ground. Fire and smoke was rising from one pit; in the other two, dozens of bodies were piled up like so many logs of wood. She shuddered, remembering the stacked, frozen bodies she had seen from the first train out of Omsk. One group of men was throwing lime into the mass grave, covering the bodies with the milky-white powder, while others, using long, two-pronged pitchforks, were scooping the dead into a common grave, careful to keep their distance from the contaminated corpses.

Watching the long pitchforks hook over the bodies and roll them down from the lorries, then shove them into the pit, Tanya could almost feel the sharp prongs puncture her own skin. Those had been human beings once—identified by name, alive and loved; now they were obliterated by a common pestilence. Her stomach churning, she leaned back on the plush seat. Control yourself, Tatiana, she thought. One more ordeal ahead; one more lie and then it will all be over.

The landscape had changed. Mountains and taiga, somber and statuesque in winter clothing, moved past her as the train rolled on, bringing her closer and closer to Handaohedzi and Marfa. And Paul.

Her baby's father. How ironic that she was going to give birth to Paul's child in the same town where he lived. And he will never know. He *must* not know, she resolved.

CHAPTER 35

The pains began in the middle of the night. By five in the morning they were coming at regular intervals, and Tanya knew her labor had started. She awakened Marfa, who, having given up her bed to Tanya, was sleeping on a mattress on the floor.

Although a week had passed since Tanya's arrival in Handaohedzi, Marfa was still ignorant of the real reason for Tanya's visit. In her mind, Tanya had rehearsed a plausible story to account for the premature birth when the time came; but while she waited, nothing had been said about her unexpected arrival, and whatever Marfa thought she kept to herself.

As the days passed, Tanya enjoyed this respite from her responsibilities in Harbin. The farmer's family from whom Marfa rented her room supplied her with dairy products at a fraction of the store prices, and Tanya took advantage of everything they had to offer. She particularly loved the steaming milk, lukewarm and foamy fresh from the cow's udder, enhancing the taste of heavily salted dark rye bread. Following a childhood habit of eating yogurt before breakfast, she enjoyed it with sugar and cinnamon at the kitchen table.

Marfa didn't come home from work until after dark, and Tanya was left alone for most of the winter days. It was inevitable that her thoughts often drifted to Paul. She discovered that in thinking about him her earlier ache was now replaced by a gentle sadness. Although she knew Paul would never be happy until he found work that would restore his self-esteem, she wondered if in the meantime he had come to terms with himself and his pride. She thought of the possibility of meeting him, either on the street or at

Marfa's; she knew he visited her regularly. While the desire to see him was strong, her common sense kept her
from seeking him out on her own. During the day, while
Marfa was at work, she took long walks around the village,
enjoying the fresh country air and staring at the hills that
crowded on the settlement from all sides.

Handaohedzi seemed to have been the settlers' afterthought, wedged in as it was between the railway station on
one side and a steep, towering mountain on the other. On
the opposite sides of a small square, one-storey wooden
houses with glassed-in porches and picket fences stretched
along a single street that curved into the mountain at the
other end of the village. There, a public bathhouse, steaming hot and none too clean, offered villagers wooden stalls
and wet besoms to expurgate the grime from their pores
and stimulate circulation. A small grocery store opposite
the bathhouse did brisk business, but after her daily shopping for fresh produce, Tanya preferred to walk around the
square at the other end of the village.

The confined area of Handaohedzi's pastoral landscape
appealed to Tanya. She had never liked the wide expanse
of the Siberian steppes, which dwarfed and frightened her
with their limitless horizon. This village, on the other hand,
nestled in a cradle of steep mountains so close that she
wanted to reach out and touch their walls. On this particular morning, she stopped at the foot of the hill where the
hospital buildings clung to the sloping ground.

Aware of the slippery, snow-packed road, she turned
around slowly, eager to encompass the fairyland beauty behind her. All of it: mounds of shoveled snow glittering in
the sun; stately firs and pines dressed in winter ermine;
saplings wrapped in white frost; smoking chimneys peeking
through plump snow on the roofs; sparkling icicles that
looked like crystal carrots hanging over the burdened
eaves. Tanya took a few steps, and the sound of her
crunching boots fractured the winter hush, causing a few
sluggish rooks to cark in surprise at the human figure brav-
ing the cold.

For a while there was no one in sight. Then, from
around the corner, a horse-drawn sled, heavily laden with
wood, slid quietly by, disappearing into a side street, and

once again Tanya was alone in the square, smiling at the mountain and the snow and the birds, her rapture elfin.

A short distance away several children, bundled in wool-like balls of yarn, appeared on the slope, pulling sleds behind them. They skidded down a sled run, their squeals of delight animating the frozen tableau. Tanya watched with envy, yearning to join in their fun and chuckling at the silliness of her wish.

Reluctantly, she turned into the side street and picked her way carefully along the snow-packed road. A muscle cramp streaked across her abdomen. She came to a halt, waiting. It disappeared as suddenly as it had come. Was this the beginning? Best she get back to the house. She'd been out too long as it was, loath to leave the enchanted serenity of the village morning.

That afternoon, however, a much stronger flash of pain convulsed her, but that, too, vanished as quickly as the first one. She undressed and lay down on the bed. Might as well be comfortable before the pains start in earnest; and if this was going to be a false alarm—well, then at least she would have a good rest. She lay quietly, waiting for the next pain, listening for some secret sounds, as if the onset of labor could actually be heard. Nothing happened the rest of the afternoon, and when Marfa came home from work, Tanya had the tea ready on a small table, which she dressed up with the white cutwork linen she had brought Marfa for a present. Until she was sure of her pains, she couldn't tell Marfa about them, for she would have to explain why she suspected the onset of labor so prematurely. When the real labor did start, she could then tell her the prepared story of having precipitated premature birth by slipping and falling during the previous day.

Her hand shook as she picked up her tea. Marfa, preoccupied with her own thoughts, lowered herself heavily into the chair. She looked at Tanya without really seeing her and sighed.

"Tough day today, *kasatka*. These old bones are beginning to hurt. It's been a long year for me without a word from Tikhon. My name and address are listed with the Red Cross in Harbin, but so far I've heard nothing. I'm beginning to wonder if I'll ever see my joy again."

There was no bitterness in Marfa's voice. Her acceptance of fate had come from her strength of character, and
Tanya wished for one tenth of Marfa's patience in enduring pain as an integral part of living. Her Tikhon: Here
was another lie Tanya had to live with. But in this case she
was motivated by compassion, for surely a mother's heart
would break from the impact of such a truth.

The evening came and went with only a vague discomfort in her stomach. During the night she awoke several
times, twinges of pain washing over her, but at last there
was no doubt that the baby was coming. She stumbled out
of bed and turned the light on. The round clock with two
alarm bells ticked loudly on the table. The hands pointed to
ten minutes to five.

Blinking, Marfa took a few seconds to understand what
Tanya was saying. Then she was off her makeshift bed on
the floor and urging Tanya back to bed. The first really
violent cramp shot through Tanya's lower abdomen. Taken
by surprise, she gasped a shuddering "oooh" and clutched
her belly. Marfa leaned over, concern plainly written on
her face.

"What happened today, *kasatka*? Did something scare
you? You're not due for some time yet, are you?"

Tanya looked into Marfa's affectionate eyes, so open
and full of worry, and suddenly she was tired of lying,
tired of covering up. Her vision blurred; she blinked the
tears away, unable to avert her eyes from Marfa's probing
look; and as she waited, the concern in the older woman's
eyes gave way to comprehension.

Straightening slowly, Marfa nodded a few times. The
truth must have come to her all at once, for she leaned
over and patted Tanya on the cheek. Then the midwife in
Marfa took over.

"Lie down, *kasatka*, while I get things ready."

Tanya felt her thighs and buttocks deluged with wetness.
"Marfa, I must be bleeding—I'm all wet."

Marfa grabbed some towels and, after drying Tanya,
spread several layers of them under her. "Take it easy, *kasatka*. Your water broke. Let's hope it won't be long now."

But Marfa was wrong. Reluctant to leave its sanctuary,
Tanya's baby took its time arriving in the world; and

Tanya, helped by a generous dose of laudanum Marfa had given her, drifted in and out of awareness on the crest of each tidal pain. Minutes stretched into hours as the contractions assaulted her body with burgeoning intensity. During the peak of each cramping pain she obeyed Marfa and bore down, sure that all her organs would turn inside out, and the nightmarish vision of her ovaries and bowels slithering out behind the baby made her cry out in mingled pain and terror. And then, as Marfa's hands kneaded her abdomen, came another pain, a jackhammer stomping into her lower back, a force so intense she screamed, "*Aaah!* How much longer?"

"It's coming," came Marfa's soothing voice. "A few more pushes and it'll be over."

Sure that her insides must already be ripped, nothing else mattered but to get rid of the clawing cramps. She pushed and pushed and pushed, her mind twisting, drowning in the whirlpool of agony.

She must have fainted. Why else would the pain be gone so abruptly? She was aware of the smiling, tired faces floating above her: Marfa . . . and Matrona, the farmer's wife, who had come to help; and aware of the gentle stroking of her forehead by some angel's knowing hand. And then came the wail, the lusty, healthy wail of an outraged newborn. Tears choked her throat, but she smiled when she heard Marfa's words.

"It's a girl, *kasatka*. A healthy, dimpled little girl." Marfa turned to the farmer's wife. "Go find me an extra blanket, Matrona. We need more blankets for the baby."

As soon as Matrona left the room, Marfa placed the towel-wrapped infant on the scale that sat on the table.

"*Ish-ty*, hold still, you little froggy," chuckled Marfa, bending over to read the scale. Then, picking up the baby, she walked over to Tanya. "It's hard to read the weight when the newborn squirms, but we'll say it's under six pounds, give or take a smidgin."

Tanya began to cry. Bless you—bless you, dear heart, she thought, for minimizing the truth, for turning the lie into a believable fact.

Marfa placed the baby beside Tanya, making sure her

arm fenced the child securely. Then she busied herself with the afterbirth and the cleaning-up.

Tanya looked into the baby's face. All babies look alike at birth, they said. Not so. Tanya studied her daughter's tiny features and was sure she could see Paul in them. Marfa's voice sounded above her.

"You've had a long labor, *kasatka*. It's almost seven o'clock now. Do you want some supper?" And when Tanya shook her head, she nodded and went on: "Then go to sleep. One good thing came out of your labor. You dilated fully and there is no tearing. We don't have to call the doctor to sew you up. You're lucky the baby is small."

Tanya slept soundly, through the night and most of the next day and in the afternoon, Marfa awakened her. "*Kasatka,* I have to go now to get some food for us. Take the baby. It's nursing time. I shouldn't be gone too long, but if you need anything, Matrona is home and she'll help you." Marfa placed the child in Tanya's arms and smiled down at her. "What name are you going to christen her with?"

Tanya looked at the baby. "Lyubov. Her name will be Lyubov—my little Lyubochka." Tanya avoided looking at Marfa. She knew what the older woman was thinking. Lyubov meant love. Her daughter was the fruit of love. She'll be called Lyuba for short, or Lyubochka.

After Marfa left, Tanya cuddled the baby for a while, and then, freeing a full breast, placed her nipple into the baby's tiny mouth. The child suckled hungrily, making liquid noises and trapping Tanya's finger in her minuscule fist.

There was a knock on the door.

"Come in, Matrona." Tanya raised her head as the door swung open, and gasped.

Paul walked into the room.

A kaleidoscope of emotions flashed over his face, suffusing it with color as he watched Tanya hastily cover her breast.

She looked at him, at his handsome face, and knew at once that all the months of self-delusion had been in vain. One look at Paul had told her that her love for him had not diminished, was as strong as ever.

Paul closed his eyes, as if it were too painful for him to see her in the happy role of motherhood. When he looked at her again, his expression had taken on a mask of formality.

"Why are you in Handaohedzi, Tanya?"

She noticed immediately that he had reverted from the intimate *thou* to the formal *you*. So he had burned the bridges behind him. Aloud she said:

"I came to visit Marfa, since the baby wasn't due for sometime yet. But yesterday I slipped on the snow and the fall started the labor."

She was amazed how easily the lie had come out.

Paul cleared his throat. "Have you had any difficulty with the birth?"

"No. Thanks to Marfa, everything went well."

He was still standing, and Tanya waved toward a chair. "Please sit down. Marfa should be home soon and will fix us some tea."

Paul turned the chair around and sat down facing her.

"What is the baby?"

"It's a girl. I've named her Lyubov."

Tanya was careful to avoid Paul's eyes. Although she was proud of her calm voice, she was afraid her eyes would betray her.

"Congratulations. My best wishes to you." Paul's voice was cool, polite.

"Thank you. And how have you been, Paul?"

"Very well, considering the circumstances."

What exactly did he mean? She hoped he would go on, but his laconic answer cut off her easy flow of words.

Paul shifted in the chair. "How is the countess?"

"She is very well, thank you."

"Please give her my regards."

As in some second-rate melodrama, they carried on a hollow conversation, full of inane, ambiguous clichés.

Her physical strength was sapped, and the buffer for self-control was now thin. She didn't trust her voice, and the ensuing seconds of awkward silence were mercifully ended by Marfa's timely return. Momentarily taken aback by Paul's presence, Marfa recovered quickly and broke the impasse with a steady chatter.

Paul refused tea and soon rose to leave. Tanya offered her hand for him to kiss, but he turned toward Marfa. Positive that he had seen her hand before turning away, Tanya wondered if he was afraid to come near her. At the door he paused and bowed to the two women stiffly.

"My sincere wishes for your speedy recovery, Tanya. Marfa, I'll see you again in a few days."

When the door closed behind him, Tanya turned her head toward the wall and began to cry. Marfa took the baby and let her weep for a while, sensing, perhaps, that she needed the comfort of tears. The sting of his aloof manner was far more painful than any emotion he might have shown. She loved him tragically, hopelessly, and because the hurt was so deep, an irrational hatred stirred beneath her pain.

Marfa sat down on the edge of the bed.

"That's enough, *kasatka*. A little crying is good. It prevents the pressure from hurting your nervous system. But too much of it will weaken you. Dry your tears, and let's talk about practical things. What have you told the prince? I have to know."

When Tanya told her, Marfa nodded approval. "And that's the way it's going to be. As for the prince, I know he still loves you. I sense it. Whenever I talk about you, he changes the subject. Don't you see? His pain must be still too great, too deep for him to talk about. Tell yourself the past is gone and there's no place for him in your future. You're now blessed with the child. That's more than he has. Think of it and stop being sorry for yourself."

Marfa's words sobered Tanya. Yes, she had Lyubochka now, her precious little baby—a real, live part of Paul. She could touch her and caress her and transfer all the unfulfilled love for Paul upon her. No one was going to deny her that right. Not Paul, not Kurt, not life itself.

CHAPTER 36

The railroad tracks, their polished steel shimmering in the undulating air of the July morning, snaked forever through the flat fields of poppies and forget-me-nots. Three-year-old Lyuba, her arms extended in a graceful butterfly flutter, white socks clinging neatly to her plump calves, balanced herself on the rails, carefully moving forward heel to toe, swinging her body like a miniature ballerina.

For the third consecutive summer, Tanya and Sophie were spending their vacations together in Fulaerdi, a popular resort some one hundred sixty miles west of Harbin. Located on the west side of the River Nonni, it neighbored both the railway depot settlement of Tsitsikar on the eastern shore of the river, and the larger town of Tsitsikar twelve miles from the railroad. Fulaerdi was a sleepy village, with the placid waters of Nonni lapping the low beaches north of the railroad bridge. Above the station's wooden platform, a large sign announced in Russian: Entrance to the Beach; below it, a wide staircase led down to open fields and, beyond to the right, to the River Nonni. Here and there, a clump of willow reeds concealed a growth of treacherous nettle, and many a child playing hide-and-seek among its prickly leaves cried out in anguish from its burning sting.

Farther out into the field, near the edge of a grove of trees, a roofless wooden structure stood alone, at a discreet distance from the beach. This was the solarium, built for health-minded Russian women who wished to sun-bathe in the nude.

But the center of activity revolved around the Kursaal and its surrounding dormitories, hidden cleverly in a lush park of maples, oaks, and lindens. There, white and pink

and lavender tobacco plants, artistically arranged on hillock
flower beds, displayed their flamboyant cascade of color.
Their fragrance permeated the park, making the labyrin-
thine pathways the favorite sanctuary of young lovers. Dra-
gonflies darted from flower to flower, searching out an
unwary insect, while vacationing entomologists, with nets
ready to trap varied species of butterflies, waited stealthily
in the shadows.

In the large dormitory, Tanya and Sophie rented a room
with a sunny screened porch. The room was large enough
to have a youth bed with rails for Lyuba, and although
Tanya could easily afford a separate room, she tactfully
suggested to Sophie that they would enjoy each other's
company more if they stayed together. Sophie, whose paid
vacation lasted only two weeks, pleaded delicate health and
obtained permission to take additional yearly leaves of absence. When Tanya offered to share a room, she was grateful for the chance to accommodate her budget.

The resort was largely populated by women and children
spending their summers away from the heat and periodic
dusty winds of Harbin; the more affluent husbands joined
their families on weekends.

The two friends took their meals at the Kursaal dining
hall; and, freed from all responsibilities of running a household, Tanya enjoyed these leisurely months away from
home, for they afforded her the rare opportunity to care
for her adored Lyuba alone, without the doting interference
of the countess and the ever-present nanny. Tanya was secretly relieved when, that first year three summers ago, the
countess had declined her invitation to accompany her to
Fulaerdi. Although Tanya argued politely that it would be
good for the countess's health to go away from the city, she
could not convince the determined older woman, who
scoffed at the suggestion.

"I have a lovely circle of friends now, Tanyusha, dear,
and while I appreciate your concern, I'm happy to stay
here and enjoy my Thursday-night soirées and my games
of whist. You go ahead and have a rest, while I keep company to dear Kurt. Besides," she added with a smile, "I'm
spoiled, and don't enjoy the spartan living conditions you
describe in Fulaerdi. To think I'd have to share a hallway

bathroom with strangers! God forbid! I'm used to creature comforts in my old age."

"Grandmaman, remember, we no longer have the luxury of our country estates, and it's good to go away and have a change in our routine. You can't live on the periphery of life and pretend nothing has changed since 1917."

"And why not, dear child? It's easy for you to say this. You were born here and you're a *Harbinka*. It's your home. But for me . . . why should I do what is supposed to be best for me and not what makes me happy?"

Tanya conceded that, in the face of her grandmother's logic, she should be allowed to do what made her the happiest. Besides, the countess's constant presence made it difficult for Tanya to shower her attention on her love child, or to display under grandmother's watchful eye her special attachment to Lyuba.

It was gratifying to see the metamorphosis in her grandmother, the happy reversal of her personality to the carefree and loving woman she had known in Russia. The countess's excessive affection for Kurt, however, the source of her total happiness, vaguely annoyed Tanya. Her grandmother, ordinarily so objective in judging people, was blindly protective of Kurt, and came to his defense at the slightest disagreement between husband and wife.

Not that there was that much friction between them; on the contrary, they were slowly drifting apart. Their physical love had been stunted in its growth, and Tanya had become aware of Kurt's gradual withdrawal within himself, his silent resignation to their relationship.

Although their sexual life was far from satisfactory, Tanya no longer dwelt on it. She had made an honest effort to please him and had failed. The frequency of their lovemaking had dwindled to an occasional interlude where both of them seemed duty bound to keep up pretenses with each other. She knew he wanted nothing less than to see her respond to his sexuality with total fulfillment, but that was something she could not do. His failure to satisfy her must have hurt his ego terribly, although he had never mentioned it to her, choosing instead to make fewer and fewer demands upon her. Yet a complacency of habit, the genuine friendship of two people who had known each other far too long to strain the ties, had remained intact, and an unexpected bond between them had surfaced early in their marriage, growing stronger through the months and making it possible in time to soften the failure of romance.

Tanya had displayed a serious interest in Kurt's firm, convincing him that her zeal to learn and share in his business life was genuine. She found the social life idle and shallow and—extraordinary for a woman of her milieu—preferred the stimulating environment of the commercial world. It challenged her intellect, and with an inborn perception she began to identify his business transactions, approving the sound ones, questioning the risky ones, arguing her points with an insight surprising in one so inexperienced.

Fascinated by this development, Kurt was eager to teach her the intricate dealings of his firm. He instructed Kozlov to show her the financial statements of the fiscal year, but when Tanya perused the books with their profits and losses, depreciation, and the renewals of contracts with import companies, she realized that her bookkeeping training was inadequate to cope with the complicated finances of the rapidly expanding firm. With Kurt's approval, she returned to school and embarked on a three-year accountant's curriculum.

This summer vacation had given her special satisfaction, for she had earned her degree and could now hold her own in managing the Hochmeyer firm in Kurt's absences, which had become more frequent and prolonged. With Tanya's ability to take over, he felt relieved of the constant responsibility to his office, and more and more he indulged his passion for hunting.

With the exception of their lovemaking, Kurt seemed happy with their marriage. He adored little Lyuba, calling her his little princess and showering her with expensive toys. Lyuba was a Swiss citizen with a country to protect her. This security was of vital importance to Tanya who, having become a refugee from her own country, appreciated its value.

The Hochmeyer name, which the child bore, had not, however, kept Tanya from smiling wryly at the endearing title of "Princess" that Kurt had lovingly bestowed upon Lyuba. The blood of Prince Veragin and Count Merkulin blended well in the little girl, who walked with the natural grace of a born aristocrat, spoke politely in sentences well constructed for her age, and obeyed her elders in almost everything. More than once, Tanya had thanked Providence for allowing her own genes to be the dominant factor in her daughter's coloring. The child's hazel eyes and brown curls with a touch of bronze occasioned their friends' references to Lyuba's resemblance to Kurt. Lyuba loved to dance and prance around the house and the garden, light on her feet as a butterfly. In this respect she defied her mother's and great-grandmother's warnings to be careful, when she balanced her tiny feet on the edge of the sidewalk or climbed the arm of a chair in the living room.

In Fulaerdi she took immediately to the railroad tracks, fascinated by trains and seeing the limitless challenge in the length of the narrow rails. Here, Tanya indulged the child in this harmless pastime as long as she remained within easy reach, for they had been warned time and again not to venture too far into the countryside. There the ever-present *hunhuzi* bands remained a constant threat, for their informers prowled the towns and resorts, on the lookout for an affluent victim to be kidnapped for ransom, and Tanya, well aware that Kurt's wealth made him a prominent figure in Manchuria, took precautions not to wander out of populated areas.

She could not admit to herself that her overprotectiveness of Lyuba was partially due to her constant awareness that Paul was not far away. She wondered how this year of 1924 had affected him, for it had brought a drastic change in the lives of the railway company's employees. The Soviet Union had signed an agreement with the Chinese government to administer the railway line and its territory in a joint commercial venture. Outwardly, nothing seemed changed, but the Soviets presented the Russian employees of the company with an ultimatum: Either accept Soviet citizenship or be fired. Tanya had learned that upon hearing of this abuse of human rights, the Chinese government had come to the White Russians' rescue, offering them the alternative of becoming Chinese subjects and remaining on the job. Faced with a loss of livelihood, the Russian employees had little choice but to select one or the other.

There was no doubt in Tanya's mind which citizenship Paul must have chosen. She had not seen him since that day in Handaohedzi when Lyuba was born, but the quiet ache remained. She held on to the memory of her love with sorrow and regret, yet grateful for having experienced it and mindful of the full life she now enjoyed. There was so much to be thankful for: her beautiful child, the security of a good marriage, financial independence, her grandmother's happiness, and her new professional interest and participation in her husband's business, which consumed her free time and rewarded her with a sense of personal achievement.

Sophie had remained a loyal and delightful friend. Her round eyes perpetually looked at the world in wonder, her figure a tangle of perfect circles. Herself a child in a childless but happy marriage, she taught Lyuba to call her auntie, *tyotya* Sophie, and threatened to spoil the little girl with her constant attention.

"Mamochka, look!" Lyuba called to her mother in her tinkling voice, breaking into Tanya's reverie. "I can balance without holding on to *tyotya* Sophie!"

"Fine, and now I'll race you both to the solarium."

Tanya turned and pretended to run while trotting on the same spot. When Sophie and Lyuba caught up with her, she smiled, and, taking her daughter by the hand, strolled toward the wooden solarium in the field.

As always in the late morning, the place was crowded. By now Tanya had gotten over the prudishness of her adolescent years and thoroughly enjoyed the sun's warm touch on her bare skin. Lying on a terry cloth towel spread over a wooden bench, she pulled the sun visor over her face to protect her skin from the sun's parching rays. Lyuba's busy chatter with other little girls, and the low murmur among the women around her, gradually lulled her into a state of delicious languor. In a sensual abandon to the sun's caresses, she stretched her nude body and let her mind drift.

In this somnolent air, somewhere at the edge of slumber, the quality of sounds changed. The laughter and the murmurs ceased, and in the hush that followed, gasps of surprise and indignation rose around her.

Opening her eyes, Tanya squinted to adjust to the brilliance of the unshaded light. Sophie was sound asleep beside her on another bench, and Lyuba, wide-eyed with curiosity, stood near her, chewing on the corner of her towel and looking to the other side of the solarium. There, peeking over the wooden walls, silhouetted against the sky, were yellow-skinned faces with slanted eyes.

Shock and anger at the violated boundaries were her first reactions. She rolled off the bench, and, grabbing her towel, threw it over the front of her body. It was unheard of among the Chinese, especially in groups, to trespass the white women's sanctuary. As her apprehension mounted, Tanya stood riveted to the ground, refusing to believe her eyes as a couple of men with feline grace catapulted to the ground inside the solarium. Shrieking in panic, the women scampered for cover. In one leap the two men reached the entrance and opened the door to admit a large group of men. They could have passed for ordinary coolies, with their loose, high-collar cotton shirts and baggy black pants, were it not for the rifles they held pointed at the hapless women.

Hunhuzi! flashed through Tanya's mind, and she instinctively crushed Lyuba to her side, throwing the large towel over them both. Sophie, awakened by the commotion, cowered behind them. "Oh, God, Tanya, what do they want with us?"

"Don't be naive, Sophie," Tanya said quietly. "Whether *hunhuzi* or not, they are men and we are women. I don't understand how they dared to come here."

"Haven't we been warned against them?"

"Yes, but not for a raid like this, in broad daylight."

A memory surfaced. She had escaped rape in Chita and had been rewarded by a love experience that had changed her life. This time, however, she was sure there was not going to be an escape, and the experience threatened to be ugly. Lyubochka! What about Lyubochka? She'd do anything . . . *anything* to spare the child the trauma of wit-

nessing the assault. But what possible chance did she have
to protect her child? With the men blocking the only exit,
escape was impossible. To scream for help would be futile,
since the solarium had been purposely built far enough
from the beach to give the sunbathers total seclusion.

As she stood there clutching Lyuba to her side, her mind
raced, wondering how best to get through this ordeal. In
spite of her fear she noticed that the *hunhuzi* stood in a
corner of the solarium chuckling at some of the fatter
women but making no move to attack them.

Sophie whispered behind her: "Tanya, I'm so scared.
Are they going to kill us afterward?"

"I don't think they're going to rape us, Sophie," Tanya
said slowly. "They would have started by now. I've heard
the *hunhuzi* almost never attack women. No. They're after
something else."

Suddenly, Tanya felt chilled, in spite of the midday heat.
Kidnappers! These were *hunhuzi* kidnappers. They've
come to kidnap some wealthy woman and hold her for ransom. My God, I never thought they'd raid the solarium. So
close to Fulaerdi. Quietly, she turned her head to Sophie.
"Stand still and don't talk. We don't want to attract attention to ourselves."

In spite of Tanya's warning to be quiet, Lyuba began to
whimper, frightened by the strange men and the commotion they had caused.

In the meantime, the *hunhuzi* were scanning the faces of
the cowering women, searching for someone. At last, the
front bandit, holding a carbine in his hand, detached himself from the group and sauntered to the side of the solarium where Tanya and Sophie clung to each other. Abruptly, he stopped in front of Tanya.

"You. Madama Hochmeyer. You come with us."

Although his voice was surly, he spoke in good Russian.
They singled me out, Tanya thought in panic. They raided
the solarium to kidnap me. She pushed Lyuba behind her
and spoke to Sophie in French. "Pretend she is yours.
Quickly!"

"No!" barked the *hunhuz*. "The child comes with us."

Although she knew it could be suicidal to anger the man,
it was not in her character to submit without protest.

"What do you want with us? Why are you—"

Instead of replying, the *hunhuz* grabbed Lyuba roughly by the arm and pulled her toward him. Lyuba screamed, flailing at him with her small fists. The bandit held her easily with one hand. His slanted eyes flashed a warning at Tanya.

"Get dressed. And hurry!" he ordered menacingly.

Frozen to the spot a moment ago, Tanya was now galvanized into action. She threw her clothes on and then grabbed the child away from the *hunhuz*, slipping Lyuba's dress over her head and lifting her into her arms. "Shsh, Lyubochka, stop crying—Mama is with you."

The *hunhuzi* led them out of the solarium, the naked women huddling in the corners, terror and relief written on their faces. At the door, Tanya looked back and called, "Sophie! Telegraph Kurt immediately!"

Outside, they were lifted roughly onto a horse-drawn cart, and, surrounded by horsemen, they headed into the countryside. At some point, she and Lyuba were blindfolded, but her hands were left untied and she continued to hug and comfort her trembling child.

Her thoughts were desultory. The first tenuous hopes vanished as fast as they crossed her mind. Escape or even rescue seemed impossible, for she'd had time to notice that the *hunhuzi* had cleverly hidden the cart and the waiting horses on the north side of the solarium; no one glancing in their direction from the railway station or the beach would have noticed anything amiss. Hate for the *hunhuzi* grew out of her fear for Lyuba; and anger against government authorities, whose inadequate protection allowed the bandits to execute daring raids with impunity, threatened to choke her.

But even stronger than her hatred and anger was her fear. As the cart carried them deeper into *hunhuzi* territory, she could only pray that the kidnappers' negotiations with Kurt would go without misunderstandings, for she knew that any delays could result in the vicious mutilations for which the *hunhuzi* were notorious.

CHAPTER 37

Blindfolded, Tanya couldn't tell how long they had traveled on the rough dirt road. Exhausted from crying, Lyuba had finally quieted and now slept in her mother's arms, sniffling occasionally in her fretful dreams. It wasn't until Tanya heard a distant barking of dogs and the snorting of pigs that she knew they were close to their destination. At last the cart came to a creaking halt and her blindfold was removed. She squinted.

They were on the outskirts of a small hamlet in the middle of a Chinese burial ground, where various-sized tumuli crowded around them like watchful sentries.

At the edge of the village a stake was driven into the hardened dirt near a paling fence. Three severed *hunhuzi* heads, their braided hair tied together in a knot, dangled from the top like a cluster of oversized gourds. As Tanya pushed Lyuba's face in the opposite direction, the *hunhuz* who had spoken to her in the solarium motioned her to follow him. Climbing off the cart, she lifted Lyuba into her arms and stumbled after the bandit.

They walked along a single dirt road between clay *fanzi* with thatched roofs, debris piled high against their walls. Children stood by the roadside staring at them curiously, one of them squatting, his white bottom peeping through the slit in the crotch of his baggy black pants, which had been provided for just such a call of nature. Scrawny dogs foraged for scraps of food in a garbage heap; its stench was sour and acrid.

At the other end of the road, the *hunhuz* leader entered a *fanza* and waited at the door for Tanya. It took her a few seconds to adjust her eyes to the darkness inside before she saw anything, but the rancid air assaulted her nostrils and insulted her stomach.

The dwelling was empty except for a large clump of straw piled in one corner of the dirt floor. A dim ray of daylight filtered through a piece of cracked yellow oil paper that covered a two-by-two square hole in the wall. The *hunhuz* pointed to the pile of straw. "That's for toilet."

He lifted a shovel off the ground and leaned it against the wall. "There's extra straw at the back of the *fanza*. Every time you use the pile, shovel more straw on top. Helps to keep the flies away. Your food will be brought to you. Over there is a tin of drinking water." When Tanya looked at it suspiciously, he added: "It's boiled—you can drink it. Stay here till I come back."

Tanya swallowed her fear and pride. "My daughter needs fresh air. It'll be impossible to keep her inside all the time. She'll cry."

The *hunhuz* hesitated for a moment, then nodded abruptly. "You may take her out to the back of the *fanza*, but stay off the road. A piece of advice to you: Don't try anything foolish. You wouldn't get very far from here, and then, when we caught you, it'd be much worse for you. As long as you obey, you won't be harmed."

The warning was delivered calmly, but Tanya's imagination raced unchecked. No tortures that her mind would conjure up could be worse than starvation for Lyuba; no suffering greater than to see her child abused. She had heard of the contaminated food given to the hostages, the fatal cholera that followed. No, she'd behave. She'd survive the agony of waiting, as long as her precious Lyubochka remained unharmed.

The bandit walked out and they were left alone. Tanya looked around the hut. She had never been inside a Chinese *fanza* before. The dirt floor occupied only half of the small space. The other half was elevated about two feet off the ground to form a clay flooring the whole length of the *fanza* and was covered by straw mats. This was the *kan*, the ingenious Chinese stove that served as a heating element of the dwelling as well as the sleeping area for the whole family. Outside the door of the *fanza*, a small pantry housed a huge cooking caldron with two pipes leading from it. One pipe exited through the roof and the other curved through the *fanza* underneath the *kan*, conducting the heat and making the elevated space warm. In the summer, the vent into the *fanza* was shut off, and all the cooking heat was routed through the chimney in the pantry.

Lyuba had stopped crying but now was hiccuping with loud, frightened gasps and clutching the two large beach towels that Tanya had grabbed before leaving the solarium. Taking them from the child, she spread one over the straw mats and rolled the other up as a pillow. Lyuba tugged at her mother's skirt.

"Mamochka! That bad man scared me. I want to go home! Where is *tyotya* Sophie? I want *tyotya* Sophie!"

"Shsh, Lyubochka. *Tyotya* Sophie is going to tell our papa to get us out of here. We can't leave here ourselves. You must be a good girl now and not cry."

"I want to drink something! I'm hungry!"

"I'll give you some water, but we'll have to wait until they bring us something to eat. Didn't you hear the man say that someone is going to come with the food? Now you be a good kitten and help Mamochka."

Tanya picked up the tin cup that stood beside the pail, wiped it with the edge of the towel, then poured a little water into it and gave it to Lyuba.

Although no one came, Tanya was afraid to venture outside. After more than two hours, she finally managed to lull Lyuba to sleep. Then she examined the *fanza* closely. It had been recently swept clean, and she saw with relief that the pile of straw at the other end of the hut was fresh. This would keep not only the flies away, but also the rats, for there seemed to be no rotting food anywhere around. Yet a putrid stench hung in the air. It was true that the ventilation was almost nonexistent, for the wooden door to the narrow entrance was closed, and the oil paper over the window allowed practically no air to come in. Although she felt stifled, she was glad it was summer; it was surely better than shivering in the freezing cold.

It was quiet in the *fanza*, and because there was nothing to distract her, Tanya's stomach knotted in rising panic.

Would her captors' ransom demands be manageable? Were these particular *hunhuzi* patient enough to wait for the money before hurting her and Lyuba?

No answers came; instead, silence rang in her ears until Lyuba awoke. The child rubbed the sleep from her eyes, then wrapped her warm arms around Tanya.

"Mamochka," she fussed, "I'm hungry! My tummy hurts."

To divert the child's attention, Tanya picked up several strong pieces of straw, broke them in half, and arranged them in large squares on the ground. Lyuba watched. "What is it, Mamochka?"

"We're going to play house, Lyubochka. This is your room, and this is Mamochka's bedroom, and here is our dining room."

Lyuba crouched. "Where is the door to the outside?"

Tanya broke a piece of straw into smaller pieces and formed an entry hall with an opening. "Here it is. Now let's play."

Lyuba moved from room to room, ordering imaginary children around, and soon the hunger was forgotten. Tanya was drawn into her daughter's fantasy world, and it was with a start that she lifted her head at the sound of the door's grinding hinges. A slender young woman carrying pots of steaming food entered the *fanza*. She was dressed in a loose shirt and baggy black pants that narrowed at her ankles. She must be a Manchu; only Manchu women of her age would have unbound feet, thought Tanya, looking at the woman's V-shaped black cloth shoes as she knelt before Tanya and pointed at the food. She placed two tin plates with bamboo chopsticks by the pots, and as she rose to leave, her slanted eyes narrowed almost shut in a smile. She nodded several times in rapid succession, patting Lyuba on her shoulder and pushing her toward the food: *"Ho chi-fan!"*

"We need more water," Tanya said slowly, but the woman shook her head.

"Putunda!"

Tanya had heard that word a long time ago from her father when he told her the story about the first Russian engineers in Manchuria, who tried to survey the land around Harbin at the turn of the century. They asked the villagers, in Russian, for the names of their hamlets. The reply was a repeated *"putunda."* In the end, the exasperated Russians had marked the villages on their map as Putunda One, Putunda Two, and so on in increasing numbers, without realizing that what the villagers were saying to them was a simple "don't understand."

At any other time Tanya would have chuckled at the memory, but now she repeated the word *water* and pointed to the nearly empty pail on the ground. The woman nodded, picked it up, and walked out of the *fanza*, leaving the door slightly ajar.

Tanya ladled the food onto the plates. One pot contained steaming millet, the other had a generous portion of soybean mash. To her surprise, the combination was palatable. Either they were too hungry to be discriminating or the food was fresh and well prepared. In a few minutes the woman returned, bringing the water and some vegetables— squash and sour cabbage. Tanya fed Lyuba for a while, but when the plates were half-empty, she showed the little girl how to handle the chopsticks. Lyuba's little hand was too small to master the intricate implement, and after a few futile tries she went into a tantrum and threw the chopsticks on the ground. Ordinarily, Tanya would have spanked her for such a display of temper, but now she let Lyuba cry awhile, then took her in her arms and held her tightly.

In the evening, when it was dark, Tanya placed the empty food tins outside the door, then shoveled some straw onto the refuse pile, keeping the door closed and praying that no rats would slip in.

She slept lightly that night, her subconscious on guard, her hand constantly reaching to touch Lyuba even though she could hear the sleeping child's even breathing. At one point in the night, she awoke to a sound that made her shudder, not so much from fear as from an overwhelming sense of loneliness. Close to the village, a chorus of plaintive, dolorous howling filled the night air as a pack of jackals set out on their nocturnal prowl. A little later, Tanya thought she heard a laughing hyena mocking the darkness, but surely the sounds couldn't be real, for she knew there were no hyenas in Manchuria.

At last she sank into an exhausted sleep, and she didn't awaken until Lyuba began to squirm beside her. It was morning, and in the dim light from the window, Tanya looked at her watch, only to discover that it had stopped some time during the night. She remembered then that she'd forgotten to wind it the day before. She poured a few drops of water onto the end of the towel and wiped Lyuba's sleepy face, then shared a few sips of tepid liquid with the child. A short while later the same woman brought them tin canisters of kefir and udder-warm goat's milk and, with them, a bowl of sorghum and unleavened, hard-crusted pancakes, still hot and smelling of cinders. Lyuba spat out the strong-smelling goat's milk, but drank the acidulous kefir, which she had always liked. Tanya washed down the pancakes with the milk, although she, too, disliked its pungent flavor.

After breakfast, mother and daughter ventured outdoors and, mindful of the *hunhuz*'s warning, went to the back of the hut. The air outside was only slightly less foul, because the pigsty was close to the hut. But Tanya was glad to stretch her legs walking Lyuba up and down the length of the dirt path between the *fanzi*.

In the open field beyond, a single, cone-shaped tumulus rose to the right of them, and to the left, several youngsters were skittering around like ants engaged in some frenetic activity. A neighboring hut concealed their playground, but Tanya dared not leave the confined area of her freedom to look. She leaned against the clay wall, stroking Lyuba's head absentmindedly. There were no men around, and the women were busy with their chores inside, for she could hear their high-pitched voices and see the steam from the cooking caldrons. She was grateful for the smell of ginger and garlic that thinly disguised the offensive odors around her.

Aside from the children's chatter, the morning atmosphere of the village was placid, disturbed only by the cackling chickens, the snorting pigs, and the occasional feisty bark of a dog.

On each of the ensuing days, Tanya used one of the
chopsticks to scrape a line in the hard earth. They saw no
one and no one came to see them. After the initial curious
stares from the onlookers as they were led into the village,
nobody was in sight when Tanya took Lyuba out. She wondered if the villagers had been given orders to avoid them
completely. Twice a day the same woman brought them
food, and once she gave them a candle and some matches
to use at night. After the first fussy day, Lyuba became
quiet, and, with the instinct of the very young, she kissed
and hugged and patted her mother with her tiny chubby
hands. Tanya could hardly keep her tears in check when
the child's large eyes looked at her with trust and hope.
Once she said, "When is Papa coming to take us home?"
and when Tanya groped for words, Lyuba nodded and supplied the answer: "Soon, very soon, Papa will come."

But then Lyuba developed a heat rash, and although
Tanya tried to apportion a little water for washing, it
wasn't enough to keep the perspiration from irritating the
girl's tender skin. As if that weren't enough, the insect bites
on her body had turned into pustules from nightly scratching, and Tanya, herself bitten and itching, had used most
of her drinking water in an attempt to relieve their feverish
burning. When the child began to fuss again, alternately
crying and whining, Tanya used sign language to ask the
woman who was bringing them food for some kind of med-
icament. The woman pretended not to understand, shaking
her head and mumbling "*putunda.*" Discouraged, Tanya
was forced to use the sour beach towels over and over,
grateful that she at least had those.

Toward the evening of the fifth day the *hunhuz* entered
their *fanza* without knocking. Tanya jumped up and
clutched Lyuba to her.

The bandit carried a large candle in one hand, paper and
pencil in the other. His eyes blazed, and Tanya could tell
he was very angry. He came straight to the point.

"Your master refuses to pay unless he gets a letter from
you. He wants proof that you are alive. Here, write and tell
him no one has touched you or the child."

Tanya began to shake. This must be some trick on their

part, she thought, a way to get the money from Kurt and then get rid of them afterward. But if she didn't write the note, they would probably cut off her ear or do something to Lyuba. She looked at the *hunhuz* and said, "How do I know it's not a trap? Why do I have to write this note? I'm sure my husband wouldn't wait for it to pay you."

"Your master wants the note in exchange for the payment. Write!"

Suddenly Tanya was convinced that the *hunhuz* was bluffing, that once she had written the note he would kill them. "I won't write anything until you bring me a letter from my husband. Then I'll write."

With lightning speed, the *hunhuz* leaped at her and slapped her across her face, sending her sprawling over the straw.

"You stubborn *cholera*!" he shouted, air hissing through his teeth. Lyuba shrieked, and the bandit clamped his hand over her mouth. "Write, or you won't see the child again."

Tanya picked up the paper, and with a shaking hand she began to scribble, barely able to see her own writing in the flickering light of the candle. The bandit pushed Lyuba aside and walked over to stand before Tanya.

"Tell him to pay, and pay fast," he ordered. "Tell him also that if he doesn't pay, we'll kidnap his other madama."

Tanya looked up into the *hunhuz*'s face, tears blurring her vision.

"My grandmother wouldn't survive a kidnapping. Surely you don't want to murder her!"

The *hunhuz* sneered. "Not the old one. The young one. His other madama, on Pekinskaya Street."

The air was cut off in Tanya's throat. Suddenly she guessed who lived on Pekinskaya Street, but the implication in the *hunhuz*'s words came as a total surprise. The *hunhuz* was not bluffing, for he had evidently done his spying well.

She wrote a terse note, begging Kurt not to delay any further, telling him they were still unharmed, and then, signing her name, handed the note to the *hunhuz*. He narrowed his eyes. "Did you tell him about the other madama?"

Afraid to lie, Tanya took back the paper and added a

postscript. "They are threatening with another kidnapping on Pekinskaya Street." She couldn't bring herself to say anything else.

For a long time after the *hunhuz* had left, she hugged Lyuba closely in her arms, unable to stop shaking, in spite of the hot air that blew through the half-closed doors.

Finally, the little girl squirmed out of her embrace and, with a child's easy forgetfulness, began to arrange the straw pieces on the ground for another game of house.

CHAPTER 38

That night, after Lyuba was fast asleep, Tanya lay curled up on the straw mat, staring at the moon blurred by the oil paper on the window, and listening to the nightly wail of the jackals. In her overwrought imagination, she heard the laughing hyena again, and it seemed to her its mockery was intended for her. It came from the hostile expanses of uninhabited plains, echoing through the tumuli and past the humans asleep in the hamlet, through the walls of the *fanza*, to bounce derisively against the *kan*. Over and over the phantom hyena laughed, haunting the *fanza* with its maniacal cries.

What right did she have to presume she deserved all the blessings of life? Kurt was unfaithful to her, but hadn't she been guilty of a subtler kind of infidelity? Marrying Kurt under false pretenses, she had sought to make it up to him by being a good and loyal wife. Having chosen to become Kurt's wife, she had given the vow of fidelity and had been proud she'd never broken it. God help her! Lying in bed beside a sleeping Kurt, she had thought about Paul often enough, had yearned for his lovemaking and the sublime experience of that last unforgettable night. Yet never had she succumbed to the nagging temptation to see him.

The hyena laughed again. The irony of it all: She had remained faithful while Kurt had returned to Elena. Soon after their marriage, she had playfully repeated what Madame Korchagova had said about his lady friends, and Kurt had readily admitted seeing other women while she was in Russia, telling her about Elena in particular. Because his confession was so offhanded, she thought no more about it. To learn now of his clandestine affair was painful enough, but to hear it from such an unlikely source as a kidnapper was especially humiliating. Thinking about it, though, she could hardly condemn him for straying. He was, after all, a disappointed man. And while her hurt remained, it was somewhat mitigated by the realization that it was at least partially her own fault.

She moved on the straw uncomfortably, releasing a fussing Lyuba from her arms. Yes, she, too, was unfaithful, for she fantasized about Paul while making love with Kurt, pretended it was Paul's hands caressing her when in fact they were Kurt's; and it was Paul's face that haunted her dreams.

She shook her skirt to force some air under the dress. She was overreacting. Perhaps it would be better not to think ahead, not to anticipate Kurt's response. She reached for Lyuba and began to shake her skirt to ease the child's discomfort. But the worry refused to go away. How grave a danger to her marriage did Elena pose? Had Kurt's affair become serious enough for him to want a divorce? Bile rose to her throat, and she clutched her stomach. Every major decision she had made in her life had gone sour. Young and defiant, she had fled from Kurt to Russia; married Yuri only to lose him within a year; fell in love with Paul and sacrificed her love for the sake of their child. And now, was Kurt going to abandon her?

The uncertainty of waiting in ignorance was the worst of all. Why had Kurt bargained with the *hunhuzi*? By antagonizing them he had taken a terrible risk. She couldn't believe she meant so little to him now that he would jeopardize her safety without valid reason. Whatever his motives, he must have acted in their best interest—if not for her sake, then surely for Lyuba's. His daughter was his joy, and he adored her. No; it was unfair to accuse him of doing anything that would endanger their lives.

An owl hooted near the window. The hyena had gone, but the jackals howled and wailed all night.

In the morning, hot, itching, her nerves on edge, Tanya examined Lyuba and prayed that the child's sores would not worsen and start to bleed. Several times during that day she took her outside to get what fresh air there was. A little breeze picked up in the shade behind the *fanza*, and Tanya pulled the child's damp, clinging dress away from her body to let the air touch her skin. Lyuba whined constantly now, in vocal rebellion against her discomfort.

Another three days went by slowly, torturously; and on the ninth day of their captivity, the *hunhuz* returned, followed by the woman, with a bundle of clothes in her arms. He barked an order, and she obediently spread out two pairs of ink-blue cotton pants and two loose white shirts. Tanya smelled a faint odor of carbolic soap and could hardly wait to get out of her sour-smelling dress. She looked at the *hunhuz*, controlling her anger with difficulty.

"I see you have given us a fresh change of clothes after all. I've asked this woman repeatedly for something clean to help my child's sores, but she pretended not to understand. Why haven't you helped us before?"

"Shut your mouth and be silent. Your master has paid up and you will be released tonight. Put on these clothes before I change my mind!"

Afraid to antagonize him any further, Tanya bent over to pick up the clothes. The bandit turned to leave and then paused at the door. "Stay inside today until I come for you."

The woman remained in the *fanza* and motioned for Tanya to undress. Reluctant to change in her presence, Tanya nevertheless dressed Lyuba and then herself in the Chinese loose cottons. The woman stared at the discarded dresses with unconcealed greed, and as soon as Tanya dropped them, she swept them off the floor and reached for the two towels. Tanya grabbed the other end of one towel and tugged against the woman's pull. Pointing to the straw and to her wristwatch, Tanya tried to convey the message that they needed the towel until they were released, but the woman shook her head, spouting a stream of high-pitched, angry words. Still holding on to the towel, Tanya was determined to keep at least one of them, but the woman jerked hard and pulled it out of her hand. Aware of the woman's strength, Tanya clutched her arm and pinched her, hoping to release her hold on the towel, but the woman shoved her aside, then jumped up close and, hawking noisily, spat into Tanya's face.

Wiping her cheek with the sleeve of her shirt, Tanya slumped onto the straw. There she scraped the phlegm off her sleeve with some straw, and for the first time in nine days she burst into tears.

Time seemed to have come to a standstill. Minutes crept sluggishly, like the centipedes on the wall. Every loud noise outside brought a fledgling hope of approaching release, only to be dashed again. Lyuba's incessant whine had taken on the purpose of "When are we going to see Papa?" without so much as a pause for reply. Surprisingly, she looked adorable in the dark pantaloons and loose, long-sleeved shirt—a Chinese urchin with hazel eyes. It hurt to think how much better protected against dirt and insects they could have been if clean clothes had been given to them earlier.

She forced herself to dwell on the freedom that was within grasp and tried not to think about Kurt. Although she knew the excuses, apologies, and accusations to come were unavoidable, she dreaded them. The reference to the other woman in her note, dictated as it was by the *hunhuz*, certainly called for some kind of explanation.

When at last the door opened and several men walked in, her heart lurched wildly. The leader stepped forward. "It is time to go. You'll be blindfolded, and if you keep quiet there won't be any trouble."

This time Tanya knew better than to disobey the bandit's orders. If they had indeed received the money, there was nothing to stop them from killing their hostages at the slightest provocation. Meekly, she picked Lyuba up in her arms and followed the men out.

It was dusk. The door of the neighboring *fanza* was open, and smoke from the burning stove rose from the chimney, the motley of fragrances making Tanya's empty stomach growl with hunger. Sunset's carmine reflection on the horizon suggested a stormy day to come; the dimming light silhouetted the darkened tumuli, forever guarding their spectral charges. The cart with two mules waited for them on the road, and after they climbed in, they were blindfolded again.

The return ride held a different quality of fear for Tanya. Were they being released, or was this a cruel trick to take them to the open plains and leave them as feed for the jackals?

Lyuba squirmed in her arms. With tender words Tanya tried to calm her, but the child began to cry.

At last the cart came to a stop, and their blindfolds were removed. Blinking, Tanya looked around and realized that they were back at the north wall of the solarium. The *hunhuz* pressed his finger against his lips in warning.

"Lyubochka, the man is telling us not to talk," Tanya whispered. "You must be a good girl and keep quiet. We're almost home. *Tyotya* Sophie will be waiting for us, and soon we shall see Papa again."

After they climbed down, the *hunhuz* pointed toward the railroad station. "You are free to go now, but don't turn around. Your master is waiting for you at the station."

Kurt had cared enough to come to Fulaerdi to meet them. She felt a great relief, realizing that the threat of losing him had been magnified not only by the night creatures of the plains but by the stress of abduction.

Mother and daughter hurried along the path. It had never seemed such a long walk before. Tanya carried the heavy child as long as she could. When she was finally forced to put her down, Lyuba stumbled along beside her, crying, holding tightly to her hand.

At last they reached the railroad station, but no one came to meet them. The part of the platform that Tanya could see through the opening atop the stairs was empty, and there were no voices. Had the *hunhuz* tricked her into believing someone was there to meet her? A few more steps and she'd be on the platform. Lyuba stumbled, scraping her knee on the wooden step. She sat down and refused to go any further. As Tanya tried to coax her to go on, several shots rang out behind the solarium. Terrified, Tanya lifted Lyuba in her arms and struggled up the last few steps. When she reached the top, she was suddenly swept into strong arms, and in the thickening twilight Kurt's ashen face floated above her. Police, railway officials, and Sophie crowded around them, their faces swimming before Tanya's eyes. Kurt spoke, but his words made only a partial impression: "Are you hurt? . . . Is Lyuba all right? . . . We had to be quiet and hide . . . it was part of the bargain. . . . Heard shots . . . God!"

His arm around her waist, Kurt led her to a waiting litter with two coolies ready to carry her to Kursaal. Tanya protested that she could walk the short distance, but Kurt insisted, and she and Lyuba were carried to the Kursaal dispensary, where a *feldsher*—medic—examined them.

Cleaned, fed, their worst bites treated with zinc oxide ointment, they were finally released into the welcome privacy of the room that Kurt had reserved, across the hall from the one she and Sophie had shared. When Lyuba, who had been clinging to her papa the whole time, was finally lulled to sleep, Tanya sat down wearily on a wicker chair by the window and looked at Kurt.

It had been a shock to see what nine days of stress had done to him. His face, haggard and deeply lined, evoked sympathy, but then she wondered how she herself must look, and was in no hurry to seek out a mirror.

Kurt took her hands in his and groped for words. "Tanyusha. My Tanyusha. I nearly went out of my mind conjuring up horrors, not knowing what they were doing to you and Lyuba."

"It was dreadful." Tanya's voice shook. "Especially the waiting. Not knowing anything for sure."

"Yes, that was the worst part of all, Tanyusha. I panicked and wanted to pay immediately, but Paulina Arkadyevna insisted I consult the police, and when I did they told me I ran a grave risk of losing you altogether. You see, when the payment is delivered to them without a bargain, the *hunhuzi* often act upon a whim and kill the hostages. When I demanded a note as proof that you were still alive and unharmed, the *hunhuzi* guessed I had notified the police and that if any harm came to you there would be trouble for them. Believe me, it was the hardest thing I've ever had to do in my life!"

Kurt's voice broke, and he buried his face in Tanya's hands.

"The *hunhuz* dictated the note," Tanya said, then added quietly, "all of it."

Kurt raised his head slowly, his eyes clouding with embarrassment. He rose and walked over to the other end of the room, his back to Tanya, his hands behind him, one fist hitting the palm of the other.

"I can't tell you how sorry I am that you found out in such a way."

Tanya was stunned. She hadn't expected him to admit it so readily, wanted him to deny it, to reject it as a false accusation.

"The *hunhuz* probably thought you knew, Tanya. After all, the Chinese custom of having a concubine is so commonplace that his threat, more than anything else, was directed against me, demanding a double ransom."

This easy admission—this casual reference to a breach of the marital contract—didn't his conscience bother him? Did he expect her to condone his behavior?

"And that's all you have to say?"

Tanya hadn't intended to accuse, hadn't meant for the question to slip out.

Kurt wheeled around but made no move to touch her. "Of course not. I love you, Tanyusha, and always will. That hasn't changed. And you know I adore Lyuba and wouldn't want to hurt either of you. But . . . I'm also a man, Tanya." He hesitated for a second and then added softly, "A disappointed man."

He had placed the blame on her. From now on she would never trust him implicitly, would never accept his assurances without doubt.

He walked over and, picking up her limp hand, kissed it tenderly. "Tanyusha, I'd give anything to take this added hurt away from you. I can only say that the place you have in my heart has not changed, and the unity and security of my family life is inviolate."

He was telling her that his involvement with Elena was not threatening their marriage. He was sorry she knew, but he made it clear that he was making no promise to be faithful in the future or to end his affair with Elena. But, knowing about Elena, could she ever be sure that things wouldn't change in the future?

She couldn't even demand that he end the affair, for she was unable to give what he wanted from her. That part of her belonged to Paul, and he suspected it. She was mature enough now to know that she shouldn't push her luck. Her carefully laid plans, her own lies, had boomeranged. The cornerstone of her marriage had been undermined. She must be thankful that it had not crumbled entirely.

Very well, she thought grimly, she would swallow her pride and accept the flaws in her marriage, trying to be grateful for its positive aspects. The trick, perhaps, was to remember that life was not all black and white, that many shades of gray lay in between.

The secret, then, was to find comfort within them.

CHAPTER 39

The kidnapping experience had made Tanya appreciate the mundane things of life. She no longer sought to develop a closer relationship with Kurt. Outwardly, they were still friends, and courteous to one another, both involved in mutual business interests and family life. But Elena's shadow had erected a wall between them that neither wished to scale, and she resigned herself to the established pattern of their bourgeois marriage. She began to catch herself asking when his next hunting trip was coming up, eager for him to leave town so that in his absence she could run the business alone. She enjoyed the responsibility of making her own decisions, the heady feeling of independence. During one of his trips she had negotiated a profitable contract with a large textile firm in Germany. Far from being annoyed, Kurt was highly pleased by the transaction.

"Tanyusha, I'm so proud of you! What a relief to have someone you can trust implicitly in the office!"

Tanya flushed with pleasure at having pleased him, and doubled her efforts in seeking new ways to expand their business. Studying the latest trends in Parisian styles, she examined fabric samples sent to her by the leading firms in France, and with shrewd foresight she selected the popular cheviot and bombazine and taffeta fabrics for the winter months, silk and cotton batiste and the new French georgette for the summer—textures that would please a wide variety of Harbin society.

With their business flourishing, Tanya felt less threatened by Elena. Her name was never mentioned between them, and Tanya wasn't sure Kurt was still seeing her. He always made it a point to be home for supper, to play with Lyuba and enjoy a leisurely game of whist with Paulina

Arkadyevna and her friends. If he ever absented himself in the evening, it was in connection with some business meeting with visiting merchants, which could have been easily checked if Tanya wished to do so. She chose to look through her fingers at his absences, and since they were infrequent, she appreciated his tact and discretion.

She continued to send Marfa a monthly check, increasing it gradually over the months. Once or twice, Marfa chided her for not visiting her anymore. Tanya avoided going to Handaohedzi again, but she had sent the train ticket for Marfa to come to Harbin instead. Her friend's visit was poignant, for it was the first time she had seen Sophie since their arrival from Siberia, and their reunion was tearful and happy. Tanya's grandmother received Marfa with open arms and thoroughly enjoyed the latter's natural deference to her rank.

The next time Marfa came, she looked thinner and paler and complained of pains in her chest. Tanya urged her to have a thorough checkup while she was in Harbin, but Marfa brushed it off. "I'm not about to sit around a doctor's office and waste my time while I'm with you. I promise to have Dr. Leikin go over me when I get back to work."

After spending a couple of weeks with them, however, she looked rested and her pallor disappeared. The day she was leaving, Tanya hugged her with assurances of another reunion in the near future.

Over a year had passed since the kidnapping; and with the first snowfall in November, Kurt announced he wanted to take off for a two-week hunting trip in the taiga near Handaohedzi. It was a dangerous area, a challenging one, a place where the king of the taiga, the Manchurian tiger, fearless and awesome, stalked his victims. It was also the territory of large feuding bands of *hunhuzi*. Kurt assured Tanya that his guides knew exactly where they were going, and he was taking along plenty of salt, *gaolyan*—millet— and flour as a bribe for hunting on their territory. Tanya was dubious.

"You've never been gone this long, and it seems to me you're taking unnecessary risks going this deep into the taiga. It isn't only the tiger or the bear but the human element that concerns me. Remember, I was kidnapped in broad daylight in a place where kidnappings were rare—so what's going to stop the *hunhuzi* from kidnapping you while you're at their mercy?"

Kurt shook his head. "I appreciate your concern, Tanya, but so far, I've had no trouble with them. They have their own code of honor, you know. If they make a deal with us, they keep it—and I'm taking along more than they asked for in the bargain. Besides, if they do kidnap me—" Kurt suddenly stopped in midsentence and burst out laughing.

Tanya was annoyed. "I don't see the humor in it at all, Kurt. I'm worried about your safety and you find it funny?"

Still chuckling, Kurt hugged her. "No, dear Tanyusha, your concern only reminded me of a story I heard yesterday."

"Let me in on the joke."

"It seems the *hunhuzi* are not without their own ideas of how a marriage should be run, or the wife's proper behavior. In one case of mistaken identity, they kidnapped a poor man, and when one of their couriers went to deliver a ransom note to the wife, he found her in the courtyard scrubbing clothes on a washboard. The *hunhuz* gave her the message, but instead of being upset, the woman calmly wiped her hands on her apron and waved at him. 'You can have him,' she said, 'he's no bargain to me. I'm not going to pay a single kopek for him.' Taken aback, the *hunhuz* returned to his camp. When the leader heard what the wife had said, he became so indignant, he released the kidnapped man with the following admonition: 'Your madama is no good. Go home and beat her up!' "

Tanya laughed, but quickly grew serious again. "It's all fine to joke, but I want you to promise not to take chances. These *hunhuzi* are mercurial and are not to be trusted. How many of you in the group this time?"

"Three others, Tanyusha. It is a small group because it is easier for us to stay together in the taiga."

Despite his assurances, Tanya was still uneasy when Kurt left a week later. She tried to shrug off her anxiety, blaming it on her vivid imagination. In Kurt's absence she decided to keep so busy she wouldn't have time for worry.

She participated in the countess's Thursday-night soirées, where young writers and poets recited their works, and took part in the lively discussions that followed. She admired her grandmother for keeping up with the current literature and encouraging the budding talent that flourished in Harbin. Invitations to Countess Merkulina's weekly soirées—her "Thursdays," as they had become known—were greatly sought after, for they were frequented not only by aspiring writers but by well-established authors as well.

In the mornings, Tanya spent several hours at the office, listening to Kozlov's reports, checking outstanding accounts, and going over the books, but the afternoons were reserved for little Lyuba, who had grown into a precocious, beautiful child. She loved dancing, and she was now asking her mother how long it would be before she could begin ballet lessons.

Through these days, Tanya waited anxiously for Kurt's return. Toward the end of his two-week absence, she realized that although she'd enjoyed her independence for shorter periods of time, in the long run she missed him and needed him to share the burden of running the firm.

She still dreamed of Paul. It had become a habit and, like all habits, a comfortable crutch. Self-accusation had long since disappeared, and her fantasies became a welcome departure from the monotony of living. Her physical longing for Paul was no longer tainted by any sense of disloyalty to Kurt. In fact, she deliberately fantasized about her lovemaking with Paul as a small measure of revenge for Kurt's infidelity. A few times she thought of writing Paul, but she dismissed the idea as too dangerous. Kurt still loved her, and, despite his involvement with Elena, his attitude toward her had not changed; but she knew that in her own relationship with Paul she could never keep that kind of detachment. She loved Paul, and that made the difference. As long as she didn't see him she could cope with herself and her dreams. And that is the way it had to remain.

The winter dances at the Zhelsob were soon to begin again, and she decided to ask Kurt to take her there more often. They both enjoyed dancing, and she wanted to develop their common interests. In the meantime, there were only two days left before Kurt's scheduled return, and the uneasiness she had felt earlier had now disappeared. After the renewed contracts with foreign firms were drawn up and ready for Kurt's signature, she instructed Kozlov at the office to start working on existing accounts.

Kurt would be pleased with her efficiency, and she looked forward to his approval.

CHAPTER 40

One part of the hunting expedition Kurt enjoyed was the train ride. There was a special kind of pleasure in the self-imposed inactivity, of which he was a willing captive. Sitting in the plush compartment, he watched the wilderness rush past his window. This ride was longer than his customary jaunts, and he looked forward to an extended hunt in the taiga beyond Handaohedzi. The train rolled through a mountainous terrain dotted with villages built by Russian settlers at the turn of the century. If it weren't for scattered *fanzi* and Chinese burial grounds with their tumuli, it would have been impossible to tell whether he was in Manchuria or Siberia: the same fast rivers, now frozen and covered with snow; the taiga, and an occasional clearing with felled timber; the hush of untrampled valleys, both peaceful and forbidding.

But it was the wealth that lay hidden within that attracted Kurt. Formidable predators roamed the forests—the princely tiger and the equally imperious bear, both rivals for the supremacy of the wilds. And there was also the boar, its five-hundred-pound bulk frequently a fatal weapon against the tiger's claws. Kurt remembered once seeing the awesome sight of these two giants lying side by side in death. Trapped in mortal combat, both had lost: The boar had succumbed to his enemy's fangs, but not before he had gored the tiger. Kurt had hunted boar in the past, but this time he was after elk. He knew of the ever-present hazards that lurked in the taiga, but he would never admit to Tanya, or perhaps even to himself, that he sought the perverse pleasure of taunting the dangers that faced him. He needed to see her concern, to be reminded that she cared. She was sentimental and warm. In the beginning, he was so enthralled with the thought of having finally possessed her that he acted like a lovesick schoolboy, trying to kindle a responsive flame in her. Although he knew she had been in love with Paul, he could not believe she would cling to her unattainable puppy love after their marriage. He would not, *could* not, admit the possibility that she might indeed be seriously in love with Prince Veragin. It was impossible for him to reconcile Tanya, the practical, sensible businesswoman, the product of Harbin's realistic climate, with the incurable romantic of the nineteenth century. The idea that love born of and nourished by tragic circumstances would endure once the shared experiences had ended was so alien to him that when he could find no sign of Tanya's continued infatuation with Paul, he dismissed it summarily. It took him several months of self-delusion before he finally faced the truth.

His continuing failure to satisfy her—indeed, even to arouse her—had become a humiliating treadmill of sexual frustration. One morning, after a particularly frustrating night during which he had made a special effort to please her with a totally reverse effect, he spent several restless hours at the office. In the afternoon, having dismissed his waiting droshky, he walked aimlessly on Kitaiskaya Street, nodding to acquaintances and stopping to talk to no one. He was a man who was the envy of his peers, a man who had everything: a beautiful wife who shared his business interest and was a valued partner; an adored daughter, the bright sparkle in his life; a titled grandmother-in-law whose social prestige had brought to his household the respect of the intellectuals; and the wealth and freedom to indulge in his favorite recreational activity. Seemingly, he had everything, and yet he felt cheated.

So absorbed was he in his thoughts that afternoon, he hadn't noticed the thinning crowds of the upper Kitaiskaya Street until he stopped at an intersection. He was passing Mostovaya Street, where the Russo-Asiatic Bank was located, and suddenly, on an impulse, he decided to look in on Elena, who worked there. He hadn't seen her since the night of Tanya's surgery, but Kozlov kept him informed of her life, and because the information came unsolicited, Kurt suspected that Kozlov was in love with her.

He reached the bank and looked through the windows. He spotted Elena sitting behind a desk just as she raised her head and recognized him. Her face flushed to the roots of her blond hair, and as he watched her reaction, an unexpected warmth permeated him. Elena pushed her chair back and hurried outside.

It had been a long time since he had had the satisfaction of seeing a woman show the kind of reaction he yearned to see in Tanya, and this time, hungry for a response, he greeted Elena with unconcealed admiration. "You look wonderful, Elena. Harbin's climate agrees with you."

Elena's flush turned a deeper crimson. "It's good to see you, Kurt. It's been a long time. I've missed you. Will you wait for me a few minutes? I'm almost through with my work for the day, and I'll be right out."

Kurt nodded. How pleasant: no games, no awkward explanations to clear the way for renewed friendship. The telegraphed message was received instantly, and accepted by an eager recipient. He waited. A few minutes later, Elena, dressed in a forest-green cheviot suit that flattered the now sparkling green of her eyes, joined Kurt. They walked past the marketplace into Shirokaya Street, where a narrow strip of city garden stretched for one block. They paused, then sat down on a slotted wooden bench. Kurt looked at her appreciatively.

"You must be enjoying your work. In the three years since I've seen you, you've grown more beautiful."

There was nothing demure about Elena, and she didn't lower her eyes in false modesty. She laughed softly with the same bell-like quality he remembered. "Thank you, Kurt. I do like my work and the exposure to different people during the day. And I have you to thank for getting me this job."

"I'm glad you're happy, Elena."

She smiled ruefully. "*Happy* is not exactly the right word, Kurt dear. I'd say *content* is more appropriate. But I hear you're happy and lead a full and rich life. You're a lucky man."

Uncertain of what she was leading up to, Kurt said cautiously, "Thank you."

"I understand your wife comes from an aristocratic family."

Kozlov again, thought Kurt, but this time he didn't mind—as a matter of fact, he was grateful to Kozlov for sparing him a reluctant recitation of his family's achievements. For once he didn't want to think about them.

Elena gave him a sidelong glance and then added: "I'm sure she's proud of your success and prominence in the business world."

Kurt wondered if this reference to Tanya was an oblique warning that she still held the trump card in her hands, biding her time for the propitious moment to strike and damage his prestige—his carefully built image of a scrupulously honest man. He knew he couldn't be legally prosecuted in Manchuria for whatever his indiscretions had been years ago in Tsarist Russia, yet a very real danger of ruining his reputation in the city still existed. Instinctively, however, he sensed she wouldn't do anything about it. He changed the subject.

"Do you live far from here?"

"No, I found a flat close enough for me to walk to work. Would you like to see it?"

"I would, very much."

They walked the three blocks to her apartment on Yamskaya Street, a two-storey stone house set deep behind a fenced yard. Inside her one-room flat, he watched Elena fuss over a *primus*, pumping kerosene into a bigger flame to reheat leftovers from the dinner she had bought the night before. The cabbage rolls and pickled *rassolnik* soup were still in her *sudki*, two enameled pots stacked snugly into a metal frame. She pulled them apart and heated each one separately. Her movements were deft and unhurried, and Kurt enjoyed this domestic scene of unprententious hominess, which he had missed since childhood, when his mother had done all the cooking in their home.

He looked around the room. Elena had made her home warm and provincially feminine. Needlepoint pillows were piled high on the sofa. A mixture of comfortable chairs, their brown plush arms and back protected by white crocheted doilies, and groups of family pictures created a cozy sanctuary from the outside world.

During the simple meal they talked of trivialities that Kurt doubted either of them would remember later, and even as he ate, his desire for Elena grew. How different it would be this time! He wanted her now, and the anticipation teased his imagination. The tension between them mounted, and when at last he reached for her, she came into his arms easily, as if she had waited for him to return to her all along. She was a passionate lover; her soft, voluptuous body trembled under his hands as she responded to his caresses with unabashed sexuality. Intoxicated by the long-denied joy of being the object of a woman's passion, Kurt found himself swept to the heights of such sexual ecstasy that their union climaxed in a pleasure exquisite beyond imagining, beyond comparison to anything he had experienced before.

He didn't love Elena and never would, but that encounter had been a tour de force that had enslaved him, lulled his conscience, and, in the days that followed, drove him back to her again and again to gratify his body's hunger.

In a few weeks, he moved her to a better apartment on Pekinskaya Street, more secluded, and far enough from his home to avoid awkward situations.

Soon after the beginning of their affair, Elena opened a drawer in her night table and removed a sealed envelope from under a sheaf of papers. She gave it to Kurt as he was preparing to leave her apartment.

"You may do with this what you wish, my dear. It is proof of my love and trust in you."

He knew immediately what it was when he saw the name of her uncle's firm in Vladivostok printed on the yellowed envelope. Later he read the incriminating paper and burned it in his office the next day. Clever Elena. By removing the threat to his security, she had placed herself under his protection, demanding nothing but his gratitude and devotion in return, and in so doing bound him to her more permanently than any danger to his reputation could have done.

He still loved Tanya and desired her, although it was no longer important for him to satisfy her. He had acknowledged the fact that she would never respond to him the way Elena did and, with tacit acceptance, refused to delve into its cause. He would always love her. After his many years of patient waiting had culminated in their union, he couldn't imagine life without her. She had given him a beautiful child, and for that alone he was grateful: his little princess, on whom he doted. Her premature birth had alarmed him, and he worried about her, but she was a healthy and normal child. Sometimes at night a recurrent dream haunted him. Nine months before his precious Lyuba was born, Tanya had her appendectomy, and it coincided with Paul's visit to Harbin. In his dream, Lyuba's eyes were blue, and she eluded his embrace by standing just out of reach of his arms. Each time he awoke from that dream, he'd reassure himself by hugging his daughter and looking deeply into the child's hazel eyes. Lyubochka was his, and he resented the dream.

There were other threads that attached him to Tanya. She was his partner in the full sense of the word, loyal and intelligent, and he was vastly pleased with her interest in his firm, her willingness to share the weight of its management.

Some chauvinistic part of him, however, had smarted with frustration when he realized he was not the object of Tanya's passion. When Elena had supplied that important deficit in his life, he turned the blame around, and with a unipolar reasoning he placed it squarely on Tanya's shoulders.

A greater inner contentment filled his life, and it lasted until the day of the kidnapping. The danger of losing them—either or both of them—was real. The thought was so traumatic that he acted completely out of character by rushing to obey the kidnappers' demands without thinking the matter through. It was only after he had listened to the police that he bowed to their reasoning and asked for a note from Tanya. When it arrived, with the reference to Pekinskaya Street, he destroyed it immediately to prevent the countess from reading it. Not only was it important for him to keep his own image intact in the eyes of his grandmother-in-law, but he also wished to protect Tanya's pride. Appalled as he was that she had been told about his affair, he decided not to lie to her now that the truth had surfaced. If Tanya demanded that he end his affair, he knew he would refuse. He had no intention of giving up Elena, and to lie and cover up now was to lose his self-respect.

Although he had a distaste for emotional scenes, he gambled on Tanya's breeding and restraint when he hinted to her at the reason for his duplicity. Intuitively, she must have guessed that she was at fault and chose to close the subject.

If he had failed to achieve complete happiness in his marriage—well, then he had found an outlet to satisfy that bothersome streak in his character.

The train was slowing down. Kurt had made this run so many times that he knew before it stopped that it would be Handaohedzi. He pulled his gear down from the top shelf and put it all together, checking his 8mm Mauser, his ammunition, and the sacks of salt, millet, and flour. When he stepped from the overheated train compartment onto the platform, a blast of piercing wind burned his face. He pulled the earflaps of his rabbit-lined cap over his ears and took a few steps toward the station building.

The smell of fried piroshki hit his nostrils, and he was surprised to discover how hungry he was. He looked around for the vendor and chuckled. Amazing how adaptable the Chinese were. Barely inside the station door one of them, his yellow skin smooth and glistening like a watermelon, popped crisp, fluffy piroshki out of a deep kettle of boiling fat, just as tasty as, if not better than, those of any Russian cook. He bought two, one filled with meat and the other with cabbage, and then walked to the edge of the platform to look at the settlement. He had always enjoyed coming to these quiet hamlets, away from the vicissitudes of his complicated life in Harbin. Even the thought that Paul Veragin was still employed in Handaohedzi no longer bothered him.

Enjoying the pure village air, he chewed the last bite of the proshki and listened to the Chinese vendor carry on in his singsong Russian, "*Ho* piroshki, good piroshki, *ho* piroshki." On an impulse, Kurt bought a few more to take to Marfa.

But halfway to her house, his three companions, two of whom were Russian, met him and urged him to start before dark toward their first night's stopover. Since it was too early for Marfa to be home from work, he left the piroshki with the farmer's wife, telling her he would come back to see Marfa in two weeks. After loading their sleigh, they headed toward the taiga, flanked by two huskies, and as they reached the forest, one of the hunters brought him up to date.

"We scouted the area carefully. Our friendly contact says Fu-Chao-Lin is stirring up trouble again in a dispute over the hunting grounds. We'll aim to keep well away from the borders to avoid any possible confrontation. Fu-Chao-Lin is a man to be reckoned with, and if he's in an ugly mood, well—" The guide let the sentence hang, dismissing it with a wave of his hand.

Kurt nodded. He had learned long ago not to shrug off their warnings. They were professional hunters, well acquainted with the roads and clearings in the taiga. Although each time they exaggerated the danger, he continued to listen to them with respect. They were well paid for their services, and without their guidance through the maze of taiga trails, no amateur would have dared to venture into its wilderness.

The silence in the forest enveloped them immediately. Kurt, elated by nature's virgin beauty, inhaled the pine fragrance and peered ahead. Giant ferns and burdocks covered with thick layers of snow fanned around them; and above, dense boughs of spruce and fir blocked any glimpse of the blue sky.

It wasn't long before the narrow road brought them to a clearing, where a bonfire blazed in front of a subterranean clay hut. The hill dwelling rose about six feet above the ground and was covered with bark and fir boughs. As the men approached, an old Chinese trapper emerged from the cabin and took the bargained-for sacks from the guide without a word. Kurt leaned on a cedar, smelling the pungency of its resinous trunk, and watched the transaction. The trapper checked the contents of the bags and, nodding in satisfaction, offered the men steaming bowls of maize mush.

Their faithful huskies nestled close to the bonfire, guarding the men, ever alert to the sounds of approaching intruders.

The heat from the fire felt good, and after they ate, the men crowded inside the hut. Kurt put on his squirrel-lined deerskin greatcoat, styled after the Siberian *dokha*. It reached to the ground and fitted loosely over his clothes. Settling down on a straw mat, he fell asleep and dreamed of a rich bounty the next day.

CHAPTER 41

Kurt was awakened by his guide at the first glimmer of dawn. Darkness had thinned slightly, enough to see the outlines of the other men. He slipped off his *dokha*, gathered his equipment, and groped for his gun. When he was ready, they filed out of the hut, called their dogs, and, leaving the horse and sleigh at the campsite, vanished silently into the wooded thicket.

The snow was crisp in the primeval forest, and the men's deerskin boots hardly made a sound. The night music of the taiga continued. The great-horned owl that hooted far in the distance during the night was now silent, but the large animals' stealthy movements still whispered through the fir boughs. Cautiously, the hunting party moved forward, the huskies nervous behind them, cocking their heads suspiciously at every sound. This was big-animal country, and danger lurked behind each bush, each felled tree, each stream, ravine, or clearing. Although the bear hibernated during the winter, the tiger was ever on the prowl for food—elk, deer, or man. Yet the immediate danger only sharpened Kurt's sense of excitement, while the human danger from Fu-Chao-Lin and his *hunhuzi* was pushed to the back of his mind.

It wasn't long before they spotted an elk, his head, with a magnificent rack of antlers, raised upward, listening. Kurt sighted his gun on the elk's head and tracked its movements, the alert nervousness of its body, the graceful curve of its neck, and then fired. He heard the explosive report of his gun and saw the elk shudder and fall, the snow around him turning crimson. The men dragged the elk to the center of the clearing and covered it with fir boughs and snow. Out of dead branches they fashioned a

trestle above it and attached a piece of cloth impregnated
with human smells to keep the ravens and animals away.
To make doubly sure neither the tiger nor the wolves
would touch someone else's kill, one of the guides circled
the elk, urinating around it.

In the next few days they killed three elk, leaving them
in a similar manner, to be collected later with the sled.
Camping in tents, they built bonfires and kept them burning all night to protect themselves from the freezing cold
and the prowling tiger. The huskies, sensing the danger of
being an easy target of the tiger's hunt, huddled so close to
the fire that their fur was singed, and the suffocating smell
spread throughout the campsite.

Toward the end of two weeks, though tired and cold,
Kurt was vastly pleased with the results of the hunt. They
had moved the horse and sleigh with their provisions to the
end of the road and then had gone deeper into the wilderness north of Handaohedzi, into the mountainous country
of the northern edge of the Liao-Yi-Ling range, with its
western and eastern ridges densely covered with taiga. The
local people called this area Shu-Hai—Forest Sea. It was
wild and uninhabited except for a few scattered trappers,
gold prospectors panhandling the mountain streams, and
marauding bands of *hunhuzi*. The only signs of human
habitation along the narrow trails were occasional miniature pagoda shrines erected in honor of the Great Mountain and Forest Spirit, where sacrifices, sometimes human,
were offered if some ancient law of the taiga had been
broken.

Pragmatic in his approach to life, Kurt dismissed these
stories as local fables and admired the shrines as colorful
landmarks of the Manchurian taiga. Skeptical over the
warnings about the *hunhuzi* menace, he considered himself
safe, in friendly territory where he had bought his safety
with a generous bribe, and was reluctant to leave the forest.

On the way back, the hunting party came to a split in
the trail beside a frozen valley stream. After a brief discus-
sion, the two Russian hunters took the west fork, while
Kurt and the Chinese guide, taking one husky with them,
went east in the hope of finding more elk. Knowing the

terrain quite well, they were to meet at the campsite at the end of the day.

The sky had been clear, and the untrampled snow reflected the sun, blinding Kurt and the Chinese hunter with its brilliant glare. As they left the valley floor and reentered the cedar forest, darkness enveloped them. The giant trees towered above, and they stumbled for a few seconds before their sight became adjusted to the dark.

They had walked single file for several hours without seeing any game when they came upon a huge felled cedar blocking their way. The trail disappeared beneath the log, and the two men circled it, stepping over branches, careful not to slip in the snow. The Chinaman's boots, the boat-shaped *u-li,* laced high above his ankles, were light on his feet. Made of felt and rawhide and inner-lined with thicknesses of grass, they kept his feet warm in the winter and cool in the summer. Now they served him yet another purpose, for his steps were noiseless and quick. Kurt, on the other hand, lagged behind him, stepping carefully between the scattered underbrush in his heavier high-laced leather boots. Intent upon the ground before him, he had not watched his partner's movements until he heard swooshing sounds through the trees, followed by a brief cry of dismay.

"Ai-yi!"

He looked up. A dozen Chinese men stepped from behind the trees and quickly disarmed the guide. Kurt's first reaction was to run, but he knew the folly of such a move. The husky began to bark frantically. One of the bandits walked over and with one swing of his carbine butt knocked the dog to the ground. The animal cowered, whining piteously at Kurt's feet. Moments later, the *hunhuzi* surrounded Kurt and disarmed him. Then, without saying a word, the bandits prodded the two men forward with their guns.

They walked only a few minutes before they came upon a clearing, where a large *fanza* stood by a frozen creek. Kurt and his companion were pushed inside the hut, where a few men lounged on the *kan.* One of the men was a huge Manchu who reclined with half-closed eyes, smoking a pipe, and made no move when the two hunters were brought before him. He seemed oblivious to the bandits, who chattered excitedly and pointed at the two men.

Without turning to look at his companion, Kurt whispered, "What are they saying?"

"That's Fu-Chao-Lin himself over there. We're in his camp. The men are saying they've captured the Russian who had once caught Fu-Chao-Lin and brought him to the Handaohedzi station for questioning."

So this was Fu-Chao-Lin, the dreaded warlord of the wilderness. Kurt studied the big man on the *kan* curiously, noting his weatherbeaten yellow skin, the enigmatic look in his squinting eyes, his enormous hands that looked like the paws of a bear, and the padded jacket belted around his thick body. It wasn't until a few moments later that the last words of his partner's sentence made sense to Kurt. A case of mistaken identity. It shouldn't be difficult to clarify.

Fu-Chao-Lin said something in a deep baritone, and a hush fell on the rest of the men.

The hunter interpreted quietly. "He says you don't look like either the policeman who once brought him to Handaohedzi station for questioning or the one who released him. He says his men are wrong and you're not one of those who had betrayed him earlier. But he—he says you cheated him once by bringing him less millet and salt than was agreed upon."

"That's ridiculous! I've never seen him before in my life!"

His partner translated Kurt's outburst and listened respectfully to Fu-Chao-Lin's reply. "He says not many hunters come this far into the taiga, but that you had."

"Tell him I can easily prove who I am. I always carry identification papers on me."

As Kurt reached inside his fur-lined jacket, Fu-Chao-Lin raised his hand. "That won't be necessary. Your papers could have easily been falsified."

Kurt stared at Fu-Chao-Lin in astonishment. His Russian was nearly perfect and his accent only slightly noticeable. Kurt shook his head. "With due respect to your opinion, you've made a mistake. I'm a businessman from Harbin and I hunt for recreation. I would never have ventured this far into the taiga. Today we took a wrong turn and have become lost. You can see by my clothes that I'm not poor and would have had no reason to cheat you."

"You lie! You've betrayed my trust in your bargain, and I've been waiting for my revenge for four years. As for your rich clothes, much could have changed in your life during this time, and your present position means nothing to me."

Kurt turned to his partner. "Tell him what you know about me."

The hunter burst out with an excited stream of words, and the exchange between him and the warlord was heated but short. The hunter fell silent and gave Kurt a sidelong glance. Then he spoke quietly, apologetically, to Kurt, as if his failure to convince Fu-Chao-Lin were his fault.

"Fu-Chao-Lin doesn't believe me. He says—he insists—the law of the wilderness be carried out and the Great Wang, the king tiger, be appeased."

"What tiger? What do you mean?"

The hunter shook his head, bowed, and didn't answer. Fu-Chao-Lin answered for him.

"The law of the taiga is strict, and we have to obey it. We could kill you outright, but we choose to give you a fair chance. You'll be taken some distance from here and left in the forest alone throughout the night. If the tiger finds you, then justice will be done, but if the Great Spirit favors you, then your life will be spared. Your partner will be set free to find his way out of here and report on our judgment."

Fu-Chao-Lin turned to the men standing by him and, giving them a short order, resumed smoking his pipe.

Kurt stared at Fu-Chao-Lin. "What kind of justice is it when you're using the wrong man?" he said.

Fu-Chao-Lin studied him through half-closed eyes. "You *are* the right man. Anyway, it doesn't matter."

Stunned, Kurt turned to the hunter. "I can't believe Fu-Chao-Lin will go through with this, but go back as fast as you can and bring help. Hurry!"

Avoiding Kurt's eyes, the guide slipped out of the *fanza* and disappeared into the forest.

Kurt tried to reason with Fu-Chao-Lin, but the *hunhuz*'s eyes glinted menacingly. "*Tsu-ba*—get out!"

Several bandits pushed him out of the *fanza*. Kurt struggled to get back in, but the men shoved him away. They tied his elbows behind him, circling the rope around his chest; then, lighting the way with a pitch torch, they pulled him up a steep grade toward a mountain crest. The husky, held down by one of the bandits outside the *fanza*, barked behind them for a long time. Kurt stumbled in the darkness, unwilling to believe the ease and speed with which his life had become forfeit at the whim of one man. Fu-Chao-Lin must be using him as a warning to others not to trespass into his territory.

Surely the bandits would not leave him tied all night.

A volley of shots sounded deep in the taiga. *Ra-ta-ta, ra-ta-ta*—they echoed through the treetops. Had they killed his guide? His survival depended on the man getting out alive. He stopped to listen, but the *hunhuzi* jerked at the rope. He moved on, finding the climb more difficult with each step. The trail seemed endless, but eventually they reached the crest of the hill. There, among large boulders and shrubbery, was a well-stomped path marked with animal prints. Kurt recognized it as a trail used by tigers in preference to ravines where the snow lay in deep drifts.

The bandits backed Kurt against a young cedar and bound his hands around the tree. Their job done, they moved away and started down the path, wishing Kurt a polite good night.

Alone, Kurt took stock of his situation.

All around him was the dense, dark taiga. Above, a few stars winked down from the velvet sky. The cold was cruel, but Kurt, straining to free himself from his bonds, hardly felt it. The ropes were tied securely, and he soon abandoned the effort in order to conserve his strength, judging that his adrenaline—that stimulant of life—might be needed later. He tried to control his growing apprehension.

Tense, he listened. Alive with night creatures, the forest hummed mysteriously. The ancient cedars creaked. The underbrush rustled. The owl hooted monotonously. Then, from far, far away, came a howl, and another, and yet another—the weeping, wailing cries of jackals, the scavenger heralds of an approaching tiger, following the king of the taiga at a respectful distance, to feast on what he might leave behind. Honed by fear, Kurt's hearing imagined the soft, stealthy padding of the beast's huge paws.

To die thus, as bait for the roaming predator, torn by his claws and fangs, crushed by his powerful jaws, was unthinkable. *"Mein Gott im Himmel, mein Gott, warum? Was habe ich gemacht?"* What have I done? Kurt reverted to his childhood German, praying out loud, mindless that the sound of his voice might attract the very beast he feared.

He was cold. A tremor shook his body from head to toe. His teeth chattered. He clamped his jaw tight to silence the noise in order to hear the moving sounds crowding upon him. He strained to see into the darkness. His feet ached from the cold, and he knew he should move to keep from freezing to death; but he was afraid to stomp, afraid to make a noise. Wiggling his toes, he tensed his calf muscles. An excruciating cramp shot up his leg, and he arched his body, biting his lip to choke down a scream. Carefully, he lifted his leg and moved it around to ease the cramp. When the pain subsided, he placed his foot on the ground slowly, listening, staring into the darkness. And as he stared, a pair of lights appeared through the forest branches, round and blinking, and then another pair of smaller ones on each side.

A tigress with her cubs—stalking, waiting. He stood perfectly still, afraid even to move his head. Mesmerized by the round eyes glaring at him, he watched as they grew big as moons, larger, closer, until he thought he could distinguish the sinuous striped body of the animal growing and growing into giant proportions, filling the forest to the tops of the trees, reaching toward the sky. It was then that he realized with a shudder that his numbing brain must be hallucinating. Blinking, he shook his head to block out the sight and looked again. The cedars moved and whispered and groaned, but the watching eyes had vanished.

Blackness hugged him in an icy grip. He lost awareness of the passage of time and couldn't tell whether an hour had passed or half the night. The waiting, the wondering, was torture in itself. Had his guide made it through? Was help on the way, or had those shots killed the Chinaman and he was doomed to be torn by a tiger?

The aching in his legs disappeared. The relief from pain was so great he was afraid to move and start hurting again. The stinging cold no longer bit at his face, and suddenly even the fear faded away. Dimly, he became aware that the howling of the jackals had also ceased. A good sign. The tiger must have been distracted by something else. Perhaps, if the guide had been killed, the beast, sensing fresh blood, had turned toward the ready prey. But then it meant that rescue would not be coming. The thought was confusing, and Kurt couldn't sort things out. When dawn came, he would work on freeing his hands. The ropes would then be easier to undo. In daylight everything would be easier. He would free himself and use his compass to find his way out of the taiga. *Gott sei dank,* he had his compass in his pocket. He'd find his way out and go back to Tanya and Lyuba. Lyuba, his little princess. She'd be waiting for him. He couldn't let her grow up without a father. She was young—young enough to forget him altogether. He mustn't allow that. *Gott im Himmel,* anything but that! His own little girl . . . and she was *his* little girl.

The night sounds faded, and everything was quiet around him. Dawn couldn't be far away. He dozed. Then the sounds began again. Good sounds. The ones he had been waiting for. Footsteps, voices. Human voices. And a woman's voice. It sounded like Tanya. Even a child's voice. What was Lyubochka doing in the taiga? He would hug her as soon as they untied him. Yes. He would hold her and promise he would never leave again.

But now, relieved, he felt tired and sleepy—so very, very sleepy. It wouldn't hurt to fall asleep for just a few minutes, until the rescuers reached him.

It would do no harm for such a short time. No harm at all.

CHAPTER 42

Tanya sat in the office, tapping her pencil on the desk and glancing at her watch. She had been discussing a new contract with Kozlov when he was called to the telephone. He was gone quite some time, and she was anxious to leave the office and get home.

Kurt was due to return today, and she was surprised how much she'd missed him this time. She had become accustomed to his stability, his kindness, his indulgence of her. She needed his quiet wisdom in business matters. This morning she had awakened early, and, filled with anticipation, dressed with care, checking the house to make sure everything was in order. One of the things she had learned about Kurt early in their marriage was his dislike of a disorderly house, and she had to be alert in seeing that the magazines and books the countess consistently left in odd places were picked up and put away. She had ordered Kurt's favorite—roast duck and baked apples—for dinner, and she was looking forward to hearing about his expedition.

Where *was* Kozlov? Obliging and prompt as a rule, he was now dallying somewhere, and her impatience turned to irritation.

She had been getting along well with the manager. Since their initial, unfortunate meeting, when Kozlov, not knowing who she was, had treated her in a rather grandiloquent manner, their relationship had improved, for he exerted a great effort to remedy his blunder. Tanya, well able to afford forgiveness, and realizing that his experience would be of great value to her, responded amicably to his offers of help. In the ensuing years she had ample proof of Kozlov's invaluable service in teaching her the firm's intricate administrative procedures. They worked well together, and she had come to appreciate his ability to produce data on short notice and spare her the tedious minutiae of daily routine. Although she knew Kozlov was Elena's friend from Vladivostok days, she could hardly hold that against him. He was, after all, an innocent party in the arrangement, and for all she knew, Kozlov might not have been aware of Kurt's affair.

Gradually, she had become so resigned to the idea of another woman that she was almost grateful to Elena for relieving her of some of her obligations to Kurt. Several times Tanya had thought of meeting Elena, the woman who had attracted her husband, but in spite of a mischievous gremlin within her tempting her to contact the other woman, she demurred. Admittedly, she would have preferred not to know about Kurt's infidelity at all.

Immersed in her thoughts, she hadn't noticed when the door to her office opened. Kozlov walked in very slowly, so out of character with his usual mincing gait.

"I'm rather in a hurry to get away, Ivan Efimovich, so let's—" She stopped in midsentence. One look at his face and she half-rose in her chair. His face was ashen, shocked. Although his eyes looked at her, she felt he wasn't seeing her.

"Ivan Efimovich, what is it? Are you ill?"

She came around the desk toward him as he lowered himself into a chair. Then he looked up at her as if he were seeing her for the first time. After a few seconds, he suddenly came alive, jumping up and motioning her to sit down in the armchair where he had been sitting a moment ago.

Frowning, Tanya sat down. "What's the matter?"

"Tatiana Andreyevna, that phone call . . . please be calm . . . it's about Kurt Albertovich. . . . There's been an accident . . . a tragic accident . . ."

Tanya grasped the wooden arms of her chair. "Accident? Who?—what?" She stared at him, a dull ache spreading through her chest. She pressed her hands against it. "Ivan Efimovich, please! Is he . . . is he alive?" She couldn't bring herself to say the other, terrible word.

Shaking his head, Kozlov averted his eyes. "I'm sorry!"

Tanya felt very cold, as if ice water now pulsed through her veins. *Dead. Kurt is dead.*

"What happened?" she asked, not recognizing her own voice.

Kozlov lowered himself heavily into the chair opposite. "He froze to death. He must have strayed into hostile *hunhuzi* territory. They tied him to a tree to be eaten by a tiger. His Chinese guide had been shot by the *hunhuzi* some distance away and . . . and the tiger found him first." Kozlov paused, mopping his forehead with a handkerchief, then added quietly, "Tatiana Andreyevna! Console yourself with the thought that he didn't suffer too much before he died. He fell asleep peacefully. Probably didn't even know that he was dying."

Tanya raised her head and looked at Kozlov. He suddenly seemed far away from her, a miniature of himself, and yet at the same time, every detail of his face was sharply focused, and she saw things she had not noticed before. *He has a mole on his forehead and one on his jowl. Funny, I've never noticed them before. And he's unnerved. Completely unnerved, while I feel nothing. Only ice in my body. Is that how Kurt felt . . . numb with cold . . . ?*

"Where is he now?" she asked, her voice flat.

Kozlov coughed, busying his hands with his pen.

"City morgue. You'll have to go there, Tatiana Andreyevna, yourself. I'll take you there. You mustn't be alone."

Tanya rose from her chair. "Thank you. Have the office contact the Lutheran minister and make arrangements for the services and the funeral. I'll check the details with you later."

Someone else was moving her body and using her voice. It couldn't be her. Kozlov helped her with her coat. "Will you be all right alone for a few moments while I leave instructions outside?"

Nodding, she sat down to wait. Kurt was dead. Once again she was a widow. The world took on a surrealistic quality, and she felt detached from it and oh, so calm. Life had dealt her a backhanded blow, convoluting upon itself, reenacting the past in a new set of circumstances.

She sat there remembering. She had been to the morgue

before. Only then Kurt had been with her. It was Kurt who identified her parents; Kurt who made sure she had only a fleeting glimpse of their bodies, enough to satisfy the authorities, and had whisked her out of there as fast as he could. Now it was her turn to take care of him. She would do her part, and she was grateful that Kozlov would be with her.

By the time the ordeal was over and she bade Kozlov good-bye at the door of her house, Tanya began to shake. She still had to tell her grandmother and Lyuba.

When she walked in, Paulina Arkadyevna sat on her favorite love seat, crocheting. "I'm glad you're home. Kurt should be coming home any minute now. Do you want some tea? I'll ring for it."

"Grandmaman, there's something I have to tell you."

"Yes? What is it?"

"It's Kurt. . . . There's been an accident. . . . He's—oh, Grandmaman, Kurt is dead!"

The countess looked at Tanya. "What? What did you say?"

"I said Kurt is dead. He's dead!"

Paulina Arkadyevna lowered her crocheting slowly.

"How?" she whispered.

Tanya sat down wearily into a chair. "*Hunhuzi* tied him to a tree and he froze to death. We're alone, Grandmaman. We women are alone again!"

She watched her grandmother's face shrivel and age in a matter of seconds. Pressing a handkerchief to her mouth, Paulina Arkadyevna stifled a sob and then began to weep quietly, hopelessly; and it was this quiet grief, so dolorous, so deep, that finally reached Tanya. Tears flooded her face, and with a thin, piteous wail, she knelt by her grandmother and the two women cried in each other's arms.

"Why not me? Why not me, an old woman?" the countess sobbed.

"God's ways are inscrutable, Grandmaman. . . . We mustn't question them. Our minds are not big enough to understand His wisdom. God, how I wish I could!"

"But why him? Why the young? I live on, with my useless existence, and they die. They all die! Your parents, Yuri, Kurt. In times like this I deplore my faith. It leaves so much unanswered. Oh, Tanya, Tanyusha—forgive an old woman! I should be consoling you!"

"We grieve together, Grandmaman, but we must seek our answers in our own way. Blaspheming against God is not going to bring Kurt back. Let's find solace in knowing that he died without suffering."

The countess swallowed hard. "Oh, Tanyusha, Tanyusha! There's a limit to how much an old heart can endure."

Tanya held her grandmother tightly in her arms and rocked her awhile like a child. Then she pushed her gently away.

"Where is Lyubochka? I have to tell her."

The little girl had been napping, and when she awoke, pink and warm, Tanya cuddled her and told her that Papa had gone to live in heaven. Lyuba listened quietly and then asked, "When is Papa coming back?"

Tanya stroked the child's downy hair. "Our papa is going to stay there, Lyubochka. He's not coming back."

Mercifully, the child did not understand the enormity of what her mother had told her, and, fitting the words comfortably into her mind, nodded. "Then we shall go to see him in heaven."

Pointing to the bed, she added, "Papa forgot his slippers. We'll take them up to him."

Tanya stood Lyuba on the floor and gently pushed her toward the nursery. Then, willing her voice not to falter, she said, "Run along to your room, Lyubochka. Mama is tired."

The week passed in a fog. Tanya went through the motions of making arrangements, attending Lutheran services, burying Kurt, as if she were capsuled in a shell of numbness that kept her from rummaging in her soul. But in the days that followed, she found herself plodding through a slough of treacherous, insidious emotions.

She had told her grandmother not to question God's ways, but she found that she herself could not accept her loss so meekly. She was afraid to query God and discover she had tempted a vengeful fate. She had given up Paul, had sacrificed personal happiness for the sake of her child

and her grandmother. True, she had provided them with
security, but what had she done to her own life? Was this
God's retribution for depriving herself of fulfillment? Better not dwell on it. Run from it, Tatiana, she mourned.
Run. There is plenty of time to face it later. Years of it.

The Orthodox liturgy had always been her comfort, its
ritual a calming influence on her mind. After listening to a
Lutheran service, she yearned to go to her own church.
The Lutheran God and the Orthodox God were one and
the same, but she wanted to talk to Him in her own way.
So it was that one Sunday after the funeral, she told her
grandmother she wanted to pray alone. Instead of the
neighborhood monastery church, where she was well
known, she went to St. Nicholas Cathedral on Bolshoi Avenue to pray unobserved in the spacious sanctuary of the
church.

At the entrance, while the attendant was counting out
her change for the candles she had bought, Tanya asked
that word be sent to the priest that she wanted a private
panikhida said after Mass. The twenty-minute requiem
service had already been held in the monastery church, according to tradition on the ninth day after death. But she
needed to pray alone now at this private *panikhida* for
Kurt.

The church was not full. Clusters of worshipers prayed
before the candle-lit icons. An enormously fat priest with a
thick auburn beard was hearing an old woman's confession
in the corner by the icon stand. With the front panel of his
chasuble he covered her head, making a sweeping sign of
the cross above it, and whispered absolution. Tanya
watched, praying for moral fortitude. She wished she could
confess her sorrow to the priest, but on this introspective
day Tanya shrank from human contact. She made a private bargain with her God: no questions, Lord, of Thy un-
fathomable ways, but give me faith to believe that what
Thou dost is always for the best. She *must* believe. She
would believe. After all, the intrinsic value of the Church
was to sustain the faith, the trust in God, and it had been
her reason for coming to pray today.

After the *panikhida* was over, she walked outside, where
a sunny winter midday greeted her with a blue and white

embrace, its invigorating air hushed by snow and cold. As she started to cross the large church square that fanned into five residential streets, she turned in the opposite direction from her house and walked on Bolshoi Avenue toward the ice skating rink and the Zhelsob where she had spent so many enjoyable evenings with Kurt.

Prayer had helped, and the trauma of the past week began to recede. She could now consider her present and ponder her future. In many ways she was fortunate: no financial problems; an established household; a child and a grandmother to love and be loved by. Indeed, she was infinitely luckier than the other woman who had shared her bed with Kurt. She knew virtually nothing about Elena except her address and that she was all alone in the world. Had she been provided for? Or was she, like Tanya herself had been not long ago, dependent entirely upon her salary, with no provisions for emergencies? And how was Elena coping with her grief? Elena loved Kurt, of that Tanya had no doubt. Was there anyone close enough to her to offer an understanding shoulder? Could she, the wronged wife, be generous enough to stretch a friendly hand?

Tanya paused in front of the skating rink, listening absentmindedly to the skaters' laughter and the loudspeaker's blaring waltzes. Her family was waiting for her at home. They could wait. Pekinskaya Street was only two blocks away.

Resolutely, she hurried toward it and Elena's apartment house.

CHAPTER 43

Tanya's first reaction on seeing Elena as she opened the door was one of unpleasant surprise. In spite of the woman's distraught state, Tanya found her more beautiful than she had imagined. She suppressed a twinge of jealousy, reminding herself of the Good Samaritan purpose of her visit.

Antagonism and defiance showed on Elena's face, and Tanya realized the other woman had the advantage of knowing who she was. After the first stilted phrases, Tanya was able to convey her goodwill, and Elena, disarmed, burst into tears. She recovered quickly and made an obvious effort to be gracious. Tanya accepted a cup of coffee and they talked quietly for a while.

"Thank you for coming to see me, Tatiana Andreyevna," Elena said, her eyes puffy and red from crying. "I'm touched by your largesse. There's no one in the world with whom I can share my grief."

"*I* share your grief, Elena Petrovna. I have no wish to delve into the past, and I feel no animosity toward you. Since Kurt's death was so premature and unexpected, I came to make sure you were not wanting in anything. I know he would have wished me to do this." Tanya hesitated and then added, "I also wanted to do this for myself. I've gone through privations in the past and know what it is to have your life shattered by the unexpected. Are your resources adequate for your future? I'd be glad to assist you in any way I can."

Elena flushed a deep scarlet. "I've been able to transfer most of my uncle's estate, which I inherited, from Vladivostok to Harbin. Kurt was kind enough to help me invest it, and I'm now independent."

"I'm glad you have at least that worry off your mind. It may be inappropriate for me to mention it at this time, but financial security is a major contributing factor to one's peace of mind. It is devastating enough to lose the man you love without having to fret over your next rent money. Do you have many friends in Harbin?"

Elena's chin quivered. "Hardly anyone. I knew Kozlov in Vladivostok, and he's the only one I've seen in recent months. I've—I've kept myself pretty isolated since Kurt and I—I mean—oh, God!" Tangled in her words, Elena burst into tears again. "Please forgive me! You must think me gauche for speaking out like this, but—but my whole life was centered around him, waiting for his visits, planning for them. I had become an extension of him, and now I feel like a worn-out shoe—useless, empty. . . ."

Tanya's jealousy turned to pity. *It is profane for a woman to give of herself in totality,* she mused. *Elena must have loved Kurt beyond reason—like I loved Paul, perhaps still do. And we've both paid for such a love.* Aloud she said, "Perhaps it would help to pray."

Elena looked at Tanya and suddenly began to wring her hands. "Pray! For what? Prayer won't bring him back. How could this happen? I thought he was protected by experienced guides. Did one of them sell him out?"

"We shall never know. The truth died with him. We can console ourselves with the thought that he wasn't torn by the tiger." Tanya closed her eyes. "At least he was spared the horror of that death."

"I envy you in many ways, Tatiana Andreyevna, but most of all your philosophical acceptance of his death. How can you be so calm? You must have loved him too!"

Unknown to her, Elena had touched a sensitive point. Tanya stiffened. "I've been widowed twice now," she said, looking at her levelly, "and while it's not any easier the second time, experience does help to control emotions. It serves no purpose to let yourself wallow in grief, Elena Petrovna. Sooner or later you have to pick up the pieces and carry on the burden of living."

Elena folded and unfolded her handkerchief. "You know, in different circumstances we could have been friends. I wish we could now. I'm so lonely! But I realize, of course, that in spite of your kind gesture today, it would be awkward for both of us."

"You say you've known Kozlov in Vladivostok. I think Ivan Efimovich could be of great help to you in the future. Don't discard the possibility of a closer friendship between you."

For days afterward, Tanya was haunted by the look of despair she'd seen in Elena's lucent green eyes. She knew Elena's sorrow was profound, knew her love for Kurt was greater than her own, and felt a hypocrite for acting a catalyst in assuaging her grief. Yet she was glad to have seen Elena, and felt in some small measure she had made up to Kurt in his death for what she had failed to give him in life.

Gradually, winter gave way to spring, and weeks and months ran into one another, busy and monotonous. The melting snow dampened the earth, and rivers of slush and mud covered the streets, sliding into the gutters. Under a gentle sun, the trees began to bud, the sidewalks dry out, and soon lilies of the valley, lilacs, and violets appeared once again at the peddlers' stands.

But at home the gloom persisted. Extending her mourning period beyond the customary forty days, the countess canceled her literary Thursdays. No amount of persuasion could change her mind. She drifted around the house, a shriveled, grieving shadow of herself, mouthing the question to Tanya and to herself: "Why do I keep living?"

It tested Tanya's patience and made it difficult for her to cope with her grandmother. Lyuba, on the other hand, after the first few weeks of nagging questions, returned to the business of childhood and stopped asking to visit her papa.

Tanya's days were occupied at the office, and while she was grateful for the flourishing business, the weight of responsibility began to pressure her. More and more she realized how much she needed a man to share the running of the firm—to make decisions, to relieve her of the lonely place at the top. Kozlov was of enormous help, but he was a subordinate, and as such, the final word still had to be hers.

If Elena had no one with whom to share her grief, then Tanya, too, had her own private sorrow that she could not disclose to anyone: Paul. Soon after Kurt's death she had entertained the idea of offering Paul a managerial position in her firm. She could well afford another manager besides Kozlov. With the added work Kozlov had begun to show signs of strain. With his administrative experience, Paul would fit in well. Although she heard from Marfa that he had been promoted to chief of police in Handaohedzi, she could offer him a much better salary. Clinging to a fickle hope, she began to dream. Together again, slowly, they could . . . But the thought never crystallized in her mind. With a woman's instinct, she knew Paul would never accept anything from her.

He had written her a formal note of condolence, and from what he omitted in the letter, she understood that he had never forgiven her, and quite possibly no longer loved her. Yet she had never ceased to love him, and now she was free to marry him.

It was summer again, and time to leave the city to escape the heat. She hated this time of the year in Harbin. Whenever the winds blew, everything from the roofs to the benches and the sidewalks was covered with a layer of grit. The sand swirled with the first gust of hot wind and prickled the body. At times, even talking on the street was hazardous, for the sand invaded the mouth, settling between the teeth. Tanya wore a hat or a kerchief over her head to keep her luxurious hair from trapping the sand, and on windy days she tried to stay off the streets as much as possible.

Sophie and Sergei had been solicitous and thoughtful throughout these months, but their total happiness only intensified Tanya's loneliness. She began to avoid them. This year she had decided to go to Handaohedzi to be with Marfa, whom she had not seen for over a year, and spend time in the village that she had enjoyed so much in the snow-covered months.

There was another reason for wanting to visit Handaohedzi, a reason she hugged close to herself. She wanted to see Paul, to find out if all was truly ended between them. Deep inside her a small hope that he might love her still lingered, and somehow she wanted to show him that her own love had never changed. It occurred to her that he might not even want to see her, but she had to try.

She was going to tell her grandmother of her plans to go to Handaohedzi, but when she came home that night, there was a letter waiting for her from Marfa. When she had read it, she wondered how many more mortal blows were to come her way.

"I'm dying, *kasatka*," Marfa wrote in her unsteady hand. "It won't be long now before the end comes. I've been hurting in my chest for a long time and have been putting off seeing Dr. Leikin. He is so busy. He told me I have a growth in my breast that has spread, and I know it is cancer. I'm in the hospital and am receiving good care. You must not worry about my needs anymore, for as you know, the railway company is paying for my medical expenses. But I want to see you and Lyubochka before I die. Come quickly. I've given up hope long ago of ever seeing my Tikhon again. I'm at peace with my memory of him, and I believe he's happy wherever he is. But Lyubochka is near, and when I took her from you at birth, she became a part of me. I want her to brighten my last days, and then maybe the pain I suffer will be easier to take."

Weeping over the letter, Tanya showed it to the countess. "How many more loved ones am I going to lose, Grandmaman?"

Paulina Arkadyevna read the letter and handed it back. "You still have to bury me, Tanyusha. But that will be the first overdue death you'll have to deal with."

Inappropriate as her remark was, Tanya was happy to see a first glimmer of spunk in her grandmother's eyes. Then she noticed that for the first time since Kurt's death Paulina Arkadyevna was dressed in a new gown and sat straight, without hunching. She seemed revitalized and alert.

"Will you manage without me, Grandmaman, or would you like to come along?"

"You know I don't like to travel anymore, Tanyusha, and while I feel sad over Marfa's illness, I think you'll do better without me. Don't worry about my being left alone. Old Count Udasov called on me earlier today and told me he tried to organize his own circle of writers on Thursdays, but they all admitted they needed me to moderate the meetings. I'm needed, Tanyusha, and I can't refuse to encourage young talent. While you're gone, I'll be busy reestablishing my soirées. You needn't think about me."

As Tanya leaned over her grandmother to kiss her, the old countess took her hand and asked quietly, "Are you going to see Paul in Handaohedzi, Tanyusha?"

Tanya flushed. "I don't know, Grandmaman. I have my pride too."

"Pride indeed! Don't be foolish, Tanyusha. You're the one who hurt him, and it's up to you to make the first move. Remember what I once told you: We women bend easier than they do. You can't be hurt any worse than you are already."

The next day, as Tanya was making final arrangements for her departure and leaving instructions to be carried out during her absence at the office, Kozlov greeted her ebulliently. She had never seen him so happy.

"Ivan Efimovich, share with me your good news!"

Kozlov kissed her hand. "Tatiana Andreyevna, my good friend Elena Petrovna and I are going to be married."

"I'm very happy for you, Ivan Efimovich. Congratulations." She hadn't meant for her voice to sound cool and formal, and when Kozlov looked at her in surprise, she busied herself with the papers on her desk. Kozlov cleared his throat. "I hope you will honor us with your presence at our wedding."

"When is it going to be?"

"In two weeks."

Tanya was ashamed at the relief she felt. "I'm sorry, Ivan Efimovich, but I shall still be in Handaohedzi at that time. I do wish you much happiness."

She had never felt such envy before. It was now her turn to envy Elena. Her world had turned inside out, and she couldn't even tell exactly what it was she was envious of. Surely she didn't covet Kozlov for a husband, and she was wealthier than both of them put together. Those were the obvious things. No; what she dreaded most of all was being a widow for the rest of her life, an existence she might have to contend with, and one she refused to face. She didn't want to be a witness to someone else's newly found happiness. Besides, Marfa needed her now. She had that sadness to face yet.

She resolved to remain in Handaohedzi throughout Marfa's illness.

CHAPTER 44

Marfa died two weeks later. During the last few days, when the pain was devouring the dying woman's body, Tanya spent whole days in the hospital, sitting by Marfa's bed and doing what she could to ease her suffering.

The agony of a spreading cancer was taking its toll, but Marfa accepted it with stoicism. When the malignant, crab-like entity crept upward, its claws reaching for her brain, the headaches became fierce and blinding in spite of heavy dosages of laudanum, and Marfa endured them like she did everything else, in silence and resignation.

Several days before she died, her pain abated for a few hours. Ignoring Tanya's pleas to lie still, Marfa raised herself on her pillows. She sat there, wan, cadaverous, and implacable, moving her eyes slowly, searching out Tanya's face. "Come close, *kasatka*," she said. "It feels so good to be free of pain for a while, I'm afraid to move my head. Bend over here so I can see you. That's better. Now I want to tell you something, and you listen until I finish."

Breathing cautiously, she held her head perfectly still, spacing her words between each intake of air. Tanya bent over to be in Marfa's direct line of vision.

"Yes, you listen to me, *kasatka*, and listen well. When Lyubochka, our angel, was born, I told you I thought the prince still loved you. At that time I believed it. I believe it now, because he has never again mentioned your name. Remember, he's not only a man but also a prince."

Marfa's lips stretched slowly in a timid smile. "The combination of the two is quite formidable, don't you know? His pride won't let him show humility, especially since he must think that you haven't loved him now for many years. Wait until he returns from the taiga. These patrols are never too long. Go see him. It won't be easy to break him down, but I know in my heart you're willing to try. I can see it in your face.

"But trying is not enough. You and I, I think, were made from the same mold, and our kind of woman has steel. . . . We don't break. He may reject you at first, freeze you with the ice of those blue eyes of his. You'll have to persist . . . you must . . . for your own sake, for Lyuba's, and for his. Beg . . . plead . . . and if need be, tell him Lyuba is his. That much, at least, you owe him. Promise me you'll swallow your pride—and a woman's pride is never as great—and tell him you've always loved him."

Exhausted by her long speech, Marfa fell back on the pillows, her eyes fastened steadfastly on Tanya's face.

"Marfa—dear, dear one—I promise to see him, but I won't tell him Lyubochka is his. I can't! If he has any feeling for me left, that will kill it. He might understand why I chose Kurt, but he would never forgive me for taking his child—his own flesh and blood—and giving her to another man." Tears welled in her eyes. "I'll have to make him love me again on my own. He has to love me for myself, not because I'm his child's mother. He must never, never know Lyuba is his."

Shaking her finger at Tanya feebly, Marfa frowned. "You have no right to dictate your rules. You'll have to accept him on any terms, whether through Lyuba or not, and take the consequences. You want him back, don't you?"

Tanya nodded dejectedly.

"Well, then, do anything it takes to get him back. You're destined for each other. Life has separated you for a few years . . . so what? You're both free now . . . don't let false pride hold you back. Beware of the wrath of God! He mows down those who stand too proud . . . blessed are the humble, remember? You're luckier than most of us— God is giving you a second chance. Don't throw it away."

"I plan to see Paul. I *want* to see him. I'll do anything to get him back. Anything, that is, except tell him about Lyubochka. Please, Marfa, don't ask that of me!"

"You shouldn't deny him the happiness of knowing he is Lyubochka's father. It's his right to know."

"If he can find it in his heart to love me again, we can have another child, and he'll know the joy of being a father."

"What about Lyubochka? Aren't you depriving her of paternal love? A stepchild is never the same. Blood talks, *kasatka*. Don't ever believe otherwise."

Tanya pursed her lips stubbornly. "I'll never tell him about Lyubochka, Marfa. Don't you understand? I can't tell him! I don't want to hurt him with the truth!"

Marfa sighed and looked at Tanya long and hard. "Very well. I won't ask you to promise me that. But one day you'll remember my words, and when you do, I pray it won't be in tragic circumstances."

Marfa's words sounded prophetic, as though there were something she sensed that could not be voiced. She closed her eyes and slumped in her bed. "The pain . . . it's coming back. . . . I'll rest awhile now, *kasatka*."

Tanya sat quietly by her bedside, listening to her labored breathing. It was torture to sit by her friend and watch helplessly as life trickled out of her shrunken body. Every day Tanya brought Lyuba to cheer Marfa for a few minutes, then took the child back to the farmhouse, where she left her in the care of the farmer's wife, and returned to the hospital. She didn't want Marfa's waking hours to be lonely, wanted to give her as much love and affection as her Tikhon would have done.

All this time Paul had not come to see Marfa. He was still in the taiga, on a routine check of smaller villages, and was due back in a few days. Tanya was glad he was away, for she hadn't bargained on her own devastation at seeing Marfa melt away before her eyes, and she wasn't sure she would have had enough restraint to face Paul. No, she didn't want to see him while Marfa's life was ebbing away. There would be time enough afterward.

Several days after their conversation about Paul, the end came. Tanya held Marfa's limp hand, stroking it to comfort her fading consciousness, wanting her to feel the love she was trying to project to her. Slowly, widely, Marfa's eyelids opened to reveal clear, luminous eyes looking at Tanya with full awareness.

"The pain is gone, *kasatka*, and this time I know it won't come back. . . . Remember what I told you, and don't weep over me." She smiled, and, incredibly, Tanya saw mischief in her eyes. "I go with joy, *kasatka*. . . . You know why? Because Tikhon is dead. . . . He has been waiting for me over there. . . . Take care of yourself."

Tanya was stunned. This was the first time Marfa had mentioned Tikhon in such a way. How long had she known he was dead? Could a mother's heart be ever deceived? Her hand, still lying in Tanya's, suddenly became heavy and lifeless. With tears clouding her vision, Tanya looked at Marfa's face. It was beautiful and smooth in its final repose, a suggestion of a smile gracing her lips. Tanya closed the sightless eyes, folded Marfa's hands around a small icon she had brought with her from Harbin.

That evening, after Lyubochka was put to bed, Tanya went for a walk in the village. The sun had just settled behind the highest peak, slanting pink and lavender shadows across the side of the mountain and over the village roofs.

One by one she had lost her loved ones. Her sorrow was so great that she decided to return to Harbin immediately after burying Marfa. Later on, when she regained her emotional strength, she would come back and see Paul; but now she had no stamina to face him. She wouldn't have found the right words to say. She'd go home and rest in familiar surroundings, safe in her house, comforted by her understanding grandmother. Having decided this, she felt a leaden weight slip from her shoulders.

The village, dressed in bright summer clothes, embraced her, its colors so vivid that she gave them scant credence— nothing so bright could be real. And the hills, the hills! Covered with daisies, forget-me-nots, lupine, they beckoned her to linger, to wait. But nothing could keep her. Grieving, distraught, she resented the kindness of the farmer's family, the children who played with Lyuba and made her laugh, the smiles of the villagers who, recognizing a stranger in their midst, bowed to her on the street. She wanted to run back to Harbin, to escape confrontation with Paul.

At the funeral, a cluster of villagers chanted requiem hymns, then placed a simple wooden cross inscribed with Marfa's name and the dates of her birth and death over her grave. The next morning, Tanya gathered her belongings and hurried with Lyuba to the station to catch the train to Harbin.

It was a hot day, and the sun beat on their backs as she pulled Lyuba across the road to the station steps. The farmer who carried her two suitcases climbed the stairs and placed the bags inside the station house hallway. Tanya thanked him and bid him good-bye, then walked into the stationmaster's office to purchase the tickets.

The overhang on the station platform shielded the office from the scorching sun, and the open doors and windows let in a slight draft that cooled the room. Tanya bought the tickets, placed the change in her purse, and, taking Lyuba by the hand, walked into the waiting room. The train was due in half an hour, but since it was the middle of the week, no passengers awaited to board it.

Lyuba tugged at Tanya's skirt. "Mamochka, I want to see the train. May I go out and watch it come in?"

"No, Lyubochka, you must wait here with me. There's plenty of time before the train comes, and then we shall go out together."

The little girl whimpered. "I'm hot. I want to go out-side!"

Sighing, Tanya shook her head wearily. "It's too hot out there now. You stay here, and I'll buy some lemonade for us from the siphon at the buffet."

She started to cross the room, looked toward the door, and stood still.

Framed in the doorway, tall and handsome in his police uniform, stood Paul.

CHAPTER 45

Rooted to the floor, Tanya stared at Paul, unable to take her eyes away from that wonderful face. Her heart thrashed, died, beat again. Time stopped moving, became an eternity. She had meant to run, but now that she saw him she couldn't move. It had taken five years of self-discipline to train her mind to think of him without pain. But her heart knew. It knew! And knowing, it wouldn't be convinced. Dimly, she wondered why he wasn't surprised to see her. And as she wondered, the answer came.

"Tanya, I found you! I'm so glad you haven't left yet. I've just been at the farmhouse to see Marfa. They told me she's gone. . . ." His voice faltered. "Matrona said you were at the station, waiting to leave."

He crossed the room in a few strides, kissed her hand, and looked at her anxiously. "Did she suffer much before . . . the end? I had no idea she would go so fast."

Tanya stood looking at him, fighting the tears that were filling her eyes. Incredibly, shamefully, she became jealous of the dead woman who had enjoyed his company during all the years she had longed to, and dared not, see him. Jealous of the affection Paul had for Marfa. Jealous of the attachment that must have grown between them, strong enough for him to have placed his love for Tanya in the second place . . . if there was any love left at all.

She became conscious of Paul's sad and bewildered face. "Tanya! Is something wrong? I asked you if Marfa had suffered terribly . . . was it that awful?"

He had misunderstood her silence.

"Yes. It was awful." Her voice was deliberately calm. "The cancer had literally eaten her away. She suffered unimaginable pain.

"The headaches were the worst," she went on mercilessly. "Marfa could only move her eyes. At the end she knew Tikhon was dead."

Paul gasped. "How could she know?"

"Through a woman's intuition. A mother's instinct, if you like. But she knew. She said so just before she died."

Paul winced. "All these years of protecting her, hiding the truth. We thought we were so clever, didn't we? Right from that first dreadful night." The pained blue eyes came around, fastened on her own, and held. Was he remembering, too? Not only the terrible part of that night—the cossack assault, Tikhon's heroism and subsequent death—but that other part, the beautiful part: the first awakening to their love, and the loving itself. Could he have forgotten even that? She searched his face and saw no trace of memories, only sadness. Something broke inside her, and with a sickening certainty she saw the truth staring back at her. He no longer loved her. She wanted to weep then for all the pain she had suffered because of him, for all the useless hope she had nurtured in the past few months.

"What about you, Tanya? How are you?"

There was concern in his eyes this time, but she recognized it as the same concern he'd shown a helpless widow at the railroad station in Omsk, and on the River Kan, and later on Lake Baikal. "I'm fine, thank you," she said. "These last few months have not been easy, but I'm managing. In fact, I was hoping to see you while I was here"—the lie came out easily, without hesitation—"because I need your help."

"I'll be glad to do what I can, Tanya. You know that."

Tanya took a deep breath. "I've been feeling the weight of running the business alone lately, and could use managerial help," she said. "Kozlov has been with the firm for a number of years and is a great asset to me, but his load is doubled, and I'm looking for another manager." Tanya paused, watching Paul's reaction. His face remained impassive, but she noticed that his mouth had tightened.

"I need not only a man with administrative experience, but one I can trust implicitly," Tanya went on. "I'm quite desperate at this point, and was wondering if you would consider taking the position. I can't think of anyone I'd rather ask, Paul. You're qualified for the job, and you'd be doing me a tremendous favor by accepting it."

She watched Paul's face suffuse with color. For a few seconds he didn't answer. Then he shook his head slowly.

"I see no reason why you'd want to insult me, Tanya." His voice wavered. "I could never accept your offer. I've been promoted on the police force, and while it may not seem as important to you, I'm well satisfied with what I have."

Tanya's anger flared. "What do you have against accepting a better position in my firm? Just because the head of that firm happens to be a woman shouldn't influence you adversely. It's time, Paul, to forget the past. I can assure you that what I'm offering is strictly a business proposition."

"I'm well aware of that, since it could be no other. Nevertheless, I could never be subordinate to a woman."

They stared at each other for a few moments, and then Paul's eyes softened, and his next words were almost a whisper: "Especially to you, Tanya."

Was it possible he still loved her? Looking at him, Tanya waited. Averting his eyes, Paul moved toward the window.

"Five years is a long time, Tanya. I've learned to live with my lot, if not entirely to accept it, and I've managed to achieve some small measure of success on my own. What you're suggesting is strictly a business proposition to you, but it's much more to me. You're asking me to swallow my pride again, and in a way that would be particularly grating."

Paul turned around and smiled at her. "But I am happy for you, Tanya. You seem to be well adjusted and content. God has blessed you, not only with material success, but also with a child."

Lyubochka! She hadn't thought of her daughter since the first moment she'd seen Paul, and she suddenly realized that Lyuba had remained very quiet during their conversation. She turned around to check on the little girl and found the room empty.

"Where's Lyubochka?"

Alarmed, Tanya ran to the door and looked down the corridor. Lyuba was not there. The hot morning sun beat down on the station, and even the lemonade vendor had left his post. The platform! The child must have taken advantage of their conversation and slipped out to watch the trains. Tanya rushed toward the exit, only to be thrust aside by Paul, who dashed past her and out the door. Regaining her balance, she ran out after him. Lyuba was standing on the very edge of the platform, bending over the tracks and looking into the distance from where the train was to come.

"Lyubochka!"

Tanya's shriek pierced the quiet in the station. Startled, Lyuba's body jerked, and before Paul could reach her, she tottered on the edge, lost her balance, and, without uttering a cry, toppled some six feet down onto the rails below.

My fault. My fault! I've killed my own child, Tanya screamed silently as her legs buckled and she clung to the door to keep herself from sinking to the ground. Dimly, she saw Paul jump down after Lyuba and disappear below the elevated platform. Men were running past her, crowding above the tracks, gesticulating, bending, pulling someone up. Strong arms led her back into the waiting room. She fought them like a tigress, frantic, wild, looking for Paul . . . and finding him behind her, with the limp body of their child in his arms. Hysterical, fighting the men who held her, she struggled to free herself, to go to Lyuba, who was hidden from her view by solicitous officials crowding around the little girl. She saw Paul talking to them, but the light had dimmed in her eyes, and the ringing in her ears blocked out the sound of his words.

Soon everyone left, and she was alone with Paul and the child. She had wanted security for her child and her grandmother, hadn't she? Well, she had received all the material benefits she could want, and jealously, selfishly, she had kept the child to herself, hadn't shared this joy with Paul. Her life had come full circle, and God had wielded a superb revenge. Her husband had been taken away from her, and now her child was dead.

Paul knelt beside her and tried to pull Lyuba out of her clutching arms. The two human beings she loved more than life itself were with her at that moment, yet both were lost to her forever. She let Paul take Lyuba out of her arms, and watching him cradle the child in his embrace, she began to cry with great heaving sobs.

"Oh, Paul, forgive me . . . forgive me! Find it in your heart to forgive me for what I have done. . . . Our child! This is our precious child whom you have never known, whose love I greedily enjoyed. . . . What have I done to you . . . to myself? . . . Is God so vindictive He would punish the innocent to get back at me, the real sinner? . . . Oh, Mother of God! How can she be dead when I am still alive?"

In her hysteria, she wasn't aware that Paul was shaking her shoulder until he gently slapped her face.

"Tanya, Tanya! Get hold of yourself! Nobody is dead— what are you talking about? Your daughter is only stunned. Look! She's coming around now. Look, Tanya!"

And Tanya looked, and saw a sight she had never thought she'd see: the child crying against her father's breast.

The relief was so enormous, Tanya began to cry again. "Not just *my* child, Paul. *Our* child. Yours and mine."

Paul stared at her. Comprehension came slowly, and when it did, his face paled, then suffused with color. There was a sigh, a long "oooh" from the depths of his throat, and then he gathered the child closer in his arms and rocked with her and shook with wracking sobs.

Tanya winced, tears rolling down her face unchecked. She had been widowed twice, had seen General Kappel's amputation, had stumbled past the freezing soldiers on Lake Baikal, had been trussed up for rape, had seen her beloved Marfa die a terrible death. But it all seemed more bearable than watching the man she loved weep.

"Paul . . . oh, Paul, I love you! I've never stopped loving you! Do you hear me, Paul? I love you . . . love you!"

Lyuba squirmed out of Paul's arms and hugged Tanya, sobbing, "M-m-mama, my knees h-hurt!"

Tanya hugged the little girl and examined her bloodied knees. Lyuba's forehead was bruised, and there were marks on her arms. Tanya kissed the child. "It'll soon go away, Lyubochka. We'll clean you up, put some iodine on, and after a while it will stop hurting."

Paul had risen and was pulling Tanya up beside him.

She placed Lyuba on the bench along the wall and turned to Paul. Pale and shaken, he was looking at her with tear-filled eyes.

"So much has become clear to me, Tanyusha. . . . I cannot blame you for your deceit, and though it hurts, I realize why you had to do it. Oh, darling, I've always loved you and always will! Can you understand now why I couldn't imagine working for you, being around you every day and believing you no longer loved me?"

"Paul, why didn't you come to Harbin to see me after I'd written you about my decision to marry Kurt? Maybe—maybe things would have turned out differently."

Paul held her chin between his thumb and forefinger. "No, they wouldn't have, Tanyusha, and you know it. I *did* come to Harbin. I hid like a fugitive in the bushes, waiting for you to come home, but when I saw you in that fancy automobile, dressed in elegant clothes and seemingly happy, I knew I could never provide for you as well. So I stepped aside and let a luckier man give you what you rightfully deserved and should have had."

"Oh, Paul darling, don't reject me now! I won't let you!"

"Everything has suddenly changed, Tanyusha. Lyubochka makes all the difference in the world. What a joy to know I am a father! Now it is not a question of my pride but of a father's duty."

He stepped back and smiled. "I'm afraid to touch you again, Tanyusha, and make a fool of myself. At least not here in broad daylight—in the station's waiting room."

Tanya lifted one eyebrow mischievously. "Not until I am Princess Veragina?"

Paul shook his head slowly. "I don't think I can wait that long."

He scooped Lyuba into his arms and lifted her up. "Lyubochka, how would you like to have a new papa?"

The little girl looked at him shyly, then smiled and circled her arms around his neck. "Will you let me take ballet lessons?"

Paul turned to Tanya. "Well, Tatiana Andreyevna, I won't let you slip through my fingers this time!"

* * *

Harbin had long fallen asleep around them, and the
house was very quiet. Tanya's head rested on Paul's naked
chest, his arm wrapped around her, caressing her bare
back. She savored this moment, the first gentle moment
after the mindless fusion of their bodies. There was a delicious sensation in the soft friction of their skins, the closeness saturated with love's abundance, minds drifting on
cushioned thoughts.

Tonight she had loved him the way she had dreamed of
loving him all those empty, restless nights, when she tossed
in bed reliving that interlude in May six years ago. Now it
was she who carried him to the same peak of ecstasy, for
she remembered his words when he said he loved her completely—not just her face, her heart, but all of her, all
equal and deserving of his love. And yearning to return
that love, she understood. She loved him totally—each
atom of his body, though a fraction of the whole, yet no
less beautiful and wondrous than the man. She longed to
know each tiny nerve, each secret part of him . . .
receptive, vulnerable to her touch. To her, in this unchang-
ing mystery of union, the private ways of joining were an
expression of her inner self.

Nothing less would do.

Thus she dazed him, with her tender search that would
not be denied its quest, and he succumbed in stunned anticipation, helpless, breathless, waiting. She watched him rise
into suspended rapture and knew such depth of intimate
communion that she herself tasted pleasure while giving
him the ultimate in pleasure.

At length, her senses satisfied, she lay content in Paul's
embrace, and soon her mind centered on their child. She
pulled away and looked at Paul.

"Darling, as soon as Lyubochka is old enough to understand, we shall tell her that her new papa is her real father.
Think how thrilled she'll be to become a true Princess Veragina!"

Paul raised himself on one elbow and leaned over Tanya,
studying her face. With one finger he traced her eyebrow,
her temple, the hollow of her cheek, the outline of her

parted lips. He slid his hand down the curve of her neck and over her breasts, glowing white in the semidarkness, touching them with feathery kisses, whispering above her, "*Moyi golubitsi*—my doves." Then, slowly, he shook his head.

"No, Tanyusha. Not quite. Lyubochka, of course, should know I am her real father. But there will be no adoption. I'm firm on that. I shall not adopt my daughter."

Puzzled, Tanya raised herself to face him. "But why not, Paul? She is your daughter! You can't deny her your noble name. She has a right to it—the right by blood. Think how hurt she'll be when she finds out you refused to adopt her!"

"I'll hurt her far more by giving her my name. You see, my love, the happiness I now feel has humbled me. It is more important to me to have security for my daughter in the future than to have my child carry on my name."

"What do you mean?"

"As Lyubov Hochmeyer, our child will remain a Swiss citizen, with all the privileges and protection of her country. As Princess Veragina, she will become yet another carrier of a useless title."

"Oh, Paul darling, don't be bitter about something that was beyond our control! Besides, you are no longer stateless, you are now a Chinese citizen!"

"I know, but it is a precarious position nevertheless. She will be far more secure the way she is." Paul kissed her lightly on the tip of her nose. "I'm wiser and can now face the reality of our future without false illusions. Russia is lost to us forever. Whatever changes take place in our country won't be for the better. At least not in our lifetime—of that I am convinced. Besides"—he smiled tenderly at her—"I have no ill feelings toward Kurt, Tanyusha." He scooped her in his arms and held her close. "How could I? We both owe him a great debt of gratitude. Having Lyubochka carry on his name and enjoy his citizenship is the least we can do to repay him."

They fell silent, listening to the first raindrops tapping on the window, washing down the restless sand, the windswept turbulence of the August heat.

Tanya looked at Paul, closed her eyes, and put her arms around him. He was the same Paul she had loved for years, yet he was closer to her heart than ever. They had walked their own thorny paths of schooling; now they could tread the road together.

ABOUT THE AUTHOR

Alla Crone was born in Harbin, Manchuria, of a Russian mother and a German father and grew up there among the White Russian émigrés. Her mother was one of the survivors of the epic Ice March across Siberia to Manchuria during the Russian Revolution in 1920. That historic event inspired Mrs. Crone to write *East Lies the Sun*.

Alla Crone married the Air Surgeon of the U.S. Army Air Force Staff in Shanghai after World War II. Since then she has also lived in Germany, Washington, D.C., San Francisco, and Seattle. She now resides in California with her husband, a retired Army general.

She embarked on her literary career in her youth and has published poetry in the Russian language. Trilingual in English, Russian, and French, she worked as a translator in Washington, D.C. Her articles have been published in national magazines, and she is now at work on a new novel set in Manchuria and Shanghai, China.

The controversial novel of the world's most fearsome secret!

GENESIS

by W.A. Harbinson

First came the sightings, sighted by nine million Americans. Then came the encounters. Then came the discovery of an awesome plot dedicated to dominate and change the world.

An explosive combination of indisputable fact woven into spellbinding fiction, *Genesis* will change the way you look at the world—and the universe—forever.

A Dell Book   **$3.50**   **(12832-3)**

The National Bestseller!

GOODBYE, DARKNESS

by WILLIAM MANCHESTER

author of *American Caesar*

The riveting, factual memoir of WW II battle in the Pacific—
and of an idealistic ex-marine's personal struggle to understand
its significance 35 years later.

"A strong and honest account, and it ends with a clash of
cymbals."—*The New York Times Book Review*

"The most moving memoir of combat in World War II that I
have read. A testimony to the fortitude of man. A gripping,
haunting book."—William L. Shirer

A Dell Book   **$3.95**   (13110-3)